Scarlet Wilson wrote her first story aged eight and has never stopped. She's worked in the health service for twenty years, having trained as a nurse and a health visitor. Scarlet now works in public health and lives on the West Coast of Scotland with her fiancé and their two sons. Writing medical romances and contemporary romances is a dream come true for her.

Traci Douglass is a *USA TODAY* bestselling romance author with Harlequin/Mills & Boon, Entangled Publishing and Tule Publishing, and has an MFA in Writing Popular Fiction from Seton Hill University. She writes sometimes funny, usually awkward, always emotional stories about strong, quirky, wounded characters overcoming past adversity to find their for ever person. Heartfelt, Healing Happily-Ever-Afters. Connect with her through her website: tracidouglassbooks.com.

4 4 0184

D0433090

Discover more at millsandboon.co.uk.

THE NIGHT THEY NEVER FORGOT

SCARLET WILSON

THEIR BARCELONA BABY BOMBSHELL

TRACI DOUGLASS

MILLS & BOON

All rights reserved including the right of reproduction
in whole or in part in any form. This edition is published
by arrangement with Harlequin Enterprises ULC.

This is a work of fiction. Names, characters, places, locations
and incidents are purely fictional and bear no relationship to
any real life individuals, living or dead, or to any actual places,
business establishments, locations, events or incidents.
Any resemblance is entirely coincidental.

This book is sold subject to the condition that it shall not,
by way of trade or otherwise, be lent, resold, hired out
or otherwise circulated without the prior consent of the publisher
in any form of binding or cover other than that in which it is published
and without a similar condition including this condition
being imposed on the subsequent purchaser.

® and TM are trademarks owned and used by the trademark owner
and/or its licensee. Trademarks marked with ® are registered with the
United Kingdom Patent Office and/or the Office for Harmonisation
in the Internal Market and in other countries.

First Published in Great Britain 2022
by Mills & Boon, an imprint of HarperCollins*Publishers* Ltd,
1 London Bridge Street, London, SE1 9GF

www.harpercollins.co.uk

HarperCollins*Publishers*
1st Floor, Watermarque Building,
Ringsend Road, Dublin 4, Ireland

The Night They Never Forgot © 2022 Harlequin Enterprises ULC

Special thanks and acknowledgement are given to Scarlet Wilson
for her contribution to the Night Shift in Barcelona miniseries.

Their Barcelona Baby Bombshell © 2022 Harlequin Enterprises ULC

Special thanks and acknowledgement are given to Traci Douglass
for her contribution to the Night Shift in Barcelona miniseries.

ISBN: 978-0-263-30128-1

06/22

MIX
Paper from
responsible sources
FSC® C007454

This book is produced from independently certified FSC™ paper
to ensure responsible forest management.
For more information visit www.harpercollins.co.uk/green.

Printed and Bound in Spain using 100% Renewable Electricity
at CPI Black Print, Barcelona

THE NIGHT THEY NEVER FORGOT

SCARLET WILSON

MILLS & BOON

To my fellow authors Tina Beckett, Louisa Heaton
and Traci Douglass.
Thanks for making this continuity an easy journey!

CHAPTER ONE

CAITLIN MCKENZIE'S HEART skipped more than a few beats as she ran up the last couple of stairs and threw open the doors to the helipad on the roof of St Aelina's. Against a too-dark night sky the glittering lights of Barcelona twinkled around her. The wind caught her hair instantly, her ponytail flapping around and several strands escaping against the warm breeze of the May night.

Usually, she loved this view. Few people knew that this was her escape. When things got too much in Theatre, when the stresses and strains of the job threatened to crack her strong veneer, Caitlin always escaped to the roof of the Santa Aelina University Hospital in Barcelona. From here she could gaze over the city, marvel at the outline of the Sagrada Família, raise her eyes towards Montjuïc Castle or turn and look out across the ocean and sometimes dream of back home in Scotland, where, doubtless, the temperature would be much colder.

No one would really believe her, but the similarities between Glasgow and Barcelona were not lost on her. Both were vibrant cities, full of colourful characters, multinational residents, fabulous restaurants and bars and a complete zest for life that she found hard to capture with words.

Barcelona had welcomed this Scottish girl like a warm hug and she'd be grateful for ever. It had taken her a few years to find her feet. She'd mastered the language, and her specialist role within the hospital as a cardiothoracic surgeon meant she could take referrals from all across Spain.

Just like this one.

She licked her dry lips and clenched her hands into fists as she watched the flashing lights of the approaching helicopter.

She couldn't believe she was about to set eyes on a link to Javier Torres again. It had been twelve long years. Her skin prickled, and it wasn't the stiff breeze from the incoming helicopter.

It was the memory of waking up next to those dark brown eyes and that warm-skinned too-handsome-for-words guy. Her stomach plummeted. They'd been rivals all through their time together at medical school in London, constantly pushing each other in the pursuit of one triumphing over the other. It had been relentless but strangely helpful. Caitlin had never stopped working hard. The thought of someone nipping at her heels for the best placements, the best opportunities had kept her at the top of her game. She'd spent her life at home keeping her head down and staying out of the firing line of her argumentative parents, who'd barely noticed she was there and never encouraged her. Attracting the attention of the good-looking, articulate Spanish young man had seemed odd to Caitlin. But he'd been straight with her right from the start. 'I'm keeping my eye on you. Apart from me, you're the brightest in the class. I need to make sure you stay beside me and not ahead of me,' he'd teased within a few days of meeting, and then for the next six years.

It was safe to say that at times Javier Torres had driven her completely crazy, challenging her, questioning her, teasing her and occasionally fighting with her. They'd even had a few stand-up rows, much to the amusement of the rest of their class. But he'd always respected her, and she him. At every exam time she'd checked her own marks first, then Javier's second. He was the only person who'd rivalled her.

The night they'd spent together when they'd graduated had been the result of years of pent-up attraction, relief, exhilaration and exhaustion, coupled with a few bottles of expensive champagne. It was a night that she would never, ever forget—the look in his eyes, the feel of his skin next to hers, the lack of inhibitions and the overwhelming sensations of finally connecting with her perfect rival. But as the sun emerged after hours of connection the glow she'd felt earlier had seemed to vanish. The confused emotions and awkwardness of the next morning had sat like a cold, heavy lump in her chest ever since. And if Caitlin could go back and do that morning over, she would. It might not change the eventual outcome of hurried goodbyes and the immediate loss of their momentary closeness, but at least she would have tried.

And at least then she might not still be nursing a broken heart.

How dramatic.

She shook her head at herself as the helicopter moved in to land. This wasn't about her. This wasn't about him. This was about the fact that the patient she'd agreed to see, assess and potentially operate on was Javier's sister, Natalia.

The request hadn't come from Javier. It had come from the Condesa de Maravilla, Javier and Natalia's mother. That might have stung a little—that Javier hadn't asked himself—but Caitlin didn't know how much Javier was involved in his sister's care.

There was an obvious conflict of interest. As a fellow cardiothoracic surgeon, Javier couldn't possibly operate on, or treat, his own sister. Part of her wondered if he'd recommended her to his mother…but that might be pushing things too far.

She'd always known that coming to live and work in his homeland, and both working in the same specialty field, it was likely their paths would cross at some point.

They'd had mutual patients. Their personal assistants often referred patients between them, on their behalf. But Spain was central to most of Europe so referrals also came from other sources. Caitlin's reputation for excellence, alongside a newly developed procedure within valve surgery, had meant that her surgical skills were greatly admired.

She was proud of herself. Growing up in a small flat in Glasgow, with a mum and dad who'd dropped in and out of her life, meant that Caitlin had worked hard, securing a scholarship to land her place at medical school at London. Most of her school friends had been surprised at her choice. University fees were paid in Scotland. She had easily achieved the grades to meet the requirements for any of the Scottish medical schools. But, instead, she'd chosen to study in England, where fees were higher and not completely covered for those from Scotland. But Caitlin had been determined. The medical school in London was linked with a prestigious hospital where cardiothoracic surgery excelled. She'd known from an early age where she wanted her career to go, and training in that medical school meant that Caitlin had met all the right people, learned from the best and made many contacts that would help her excel in her career.

She'd had to sign a contract to say she wouldn't take a part-time job during her studies. The university wanted their students to spend all their time studying. But her scholarship had only covered her fees, books and boarding. Caitlin had still needed to eat. So, when Javier had come into the bookshop and discovered her secret Caitlin had been distraught. Her biggest rival now had a chance to get her expelled from school.

She'd been worried sick as he'd pasted a smile on his face and walked across the bookstore towards her. 'Looks like you're working?' he'd said.

It was his casual stance. Those dark, knowing eyes. The teasing glare.

'I have to eat,' was all she could say as she'd grabbed the biggest stack of books she could and walked in the other direction.

He'd followed her around the quiet shop as she'd slotted them onto the shelves. 'Is this where you've been going after class? I thought you were taking extra lessons—or studying.'

'I study in the early hours of the morning,' she'd

snapped. 'There's not enough hours in the day to do everything I need to.' She narrowed her gaze and stared hard at him. 'Not all of us are dripping with gold.'

Javier had looked momentarily stunned. Then he'd leaned back and looked at her again.

'Are you going to report me?' she'd snapped.

His answer was instantaneous. 'Why would I do that?' Before she had a chance to say anything, he'd continued in an almost offhand way, 'If I get you kicked out, how will I prove that *I'm* the better surgeon?' He'd raised his eyebrows and turned and walked out of the door, while her stomach turned over and over.

And that was it. Javier had been as good as his word. He'd told no one about Caitlin's job, and even made a few excuses for her when she'd missed non-compulsory labs due to shifts. And his assistance meant that Caitlin was able to study and work in order to keep her place at the medical school of her dreams.

She would always feel as if she owed him for that. And that made it rankle even more.

Her hair was tossing in the wind like crazy; with each auburn strand she pulled away from her vision, another one instantly replaced it. Her ponytail band was no match for the fierce force from the helicopter rotor blades as the vehicle glided to a halt on the landing pad.

A few particles of dust hit her eyes and she averted her head as she rubbed them, still taking steps towards the body of the helicopter. The irony was she could do this with her eyes closed. She'd met many choppers, in countless emergency situations, and the only difference this evening was the patient.

A warm hand landed on her shoulder. 'Okay, doc?'

Marco, one of the cardiac technicians, was beside her. She nodded and blinked a few times, until the particles of dust finally freed themselves from her eyes. Her actions were automatic now and she reached the door of the helicopter in seconds, her arm thrusting the sliding door back with force.

A female voice started speaking instantly. It was the doctor doing the transfer—a serious-looking woman in her mid-forties, with her hair pulled back in a slick bun. This woman was used to helicopter travel. She kept talking, relaying medical details while pushing the end of the mobile stretcher towards Caitlin. The legs with wheels automatically extended to the ground as she pulled the stretcher closer, her on one side and Marco on the other. Another member of Caitlin's team appeared from the side, grabbing the portable monitor and oxygen cylinder attached to the patient and clipping them into place on the stretcher. The doctor kept talking, giving all transfer information for her patient, reporting heart rate, blood pressure, oxygen saturation and the results of her latest X-ray.

Amongst the noise, the wind and the dark, Caitlin's focus was unwavering, her eyes fixed on her patient—Natalia Torres. Her long dark hair, usually lustrous, was limp and damp and her Spanish skin was paler than usual. But her dark eyes were bright and interested and her hand clasped Caitlin's instantly. *'Hola, mi amiga,'* she said, a smile painted on her face.

Caitlin bent down and kissed Natalia's cheek, returning her greeting in Spanish. She'd known Natalia ever since she'd met Javier eighteen years earlier. She'd even spent a few holidays at the grand ancestral family estate in Spain and got to know Javier's sister a little better. They'd remained in touch, meeting for lunch or dinner a few times a year, if both were available to catch up. Their friendship had vexed Javier, Natalia respecting the woman who challenged her brother and Javier sighing that 'now he had to deal with his sister being best friends with his rival'. But the subject of Javier rarely came up between the two women. It was clear that Natalia realised something had once happened between them, but she was too classy to ask questions and for that Caitlin had always been grateful.

The doctor jumped down from the helicopter and Caitlin started to walk alongside the stretcher, just like she always did, to get her patient down to the fourth-floor cardiology unit as soon as possible, but something stopped her.

She couldn't even say what it was. It was like a charge. A lightning bolt in the sky that only she could see.

The helicopter blades had slowed but hadn't quite stopped yet. But she could sense someone else on the roof with her.

She was conscious of her thin, pale pink scrubs, hugging every curve of her body, and the continual unruly behaviour of her untamed hair. As she turned around, she tugged her ponytail band from her hair, and froze.

The black and gold scrunchie dropped from her hand.

Javier. Javier had emerged from the pilot's seat of the helicopter. Javier was the pilot? She hadn't even looked at the person in the pilot's seat—the dust had distracted her and she'd never for a second imagined it might be someone that she knew.

She couldn't move. His brown eyes were locked onto hers. So much recognition, so much depth—so much more. She drank in everything about him in an instant. White shirt, dark trousers, short dark jacket. For all intents and purposes, it could have looked like a regular pilot's uniform. But nothing about Javier Torres was regular. Not the way his broad shoulders filled out the jacket, nor the way the white shirt revealed the planes of his chest or how the dark trousers rippled against his muscular thighs in the wind.

At university they'd both been runners, pounding the paths and tracks at ridiculous times of the day and night—conscious of the fact a healthy body and mind contributed to cardiovascular health. It was clear that Javier, like her, was still a runner.

All of this taken in, in a blink of an eye.

And whilst Caitlin took in all of Javier's familiar form, her eyes were fixed on his face. She could see something else in his dark eyes—worry. Of course, he was here with his sister. Natalia's surgery would be complicated and had to be carefully planned. Caitlin had scheduled a full two weeks of preparation time to allow her to assess Natalia fully, and be sure about how to proceed. As a fellow surgeon he understood the risks in a way that most people didn't.

She should feel embarrassed. Last time she'd seen Javier he'd been naked, and so had she. In her head she'd always imagined she'd meet him again one day, probably at a conference with their cardiac contemporaries. In those daydreams of course she'd be in a sharp suit, with razor heels, perfect make-up and her auburn hair straightened and tamed. In every way she'd hoped she would look perfect—perfect enough that Javier might have paused to wonder what might have happened between them. She would have oozed confidence and sophistication. She would be polished and presenting at the conference, with everyone in awe at her expertise. Yes, those dreamlike imaginations generally occurred late at night, after a glass of wine, while she was curled up in her pyjamas. But a girl could dream—couldn't she?

Javier blinked. That single tiny action brought her back to the real world. One of the edges of his lips was turned upwards. Was he amused that she'd been frozen in space and time, staring at him with the whole of her life and regrets likely on display across her face?

A swift blast of cold air made her body react. She ran to catch up with the stretcher, catching more of the report from the staff doing the transfer.

Her brain was full. She needed to concentrate on her patient, not the man on the roof. It was ridiculous. Of course he would want to monitor his sister's condition.

But the shock of seeing him again meant her body was reacting in a way she hadn't expected. Her skin was tingling. Her whole skin. As if an army of centipedes were marching in formation over every single cell. It was affecting her focus and concentration, sparking off a million memories she normally kept locked tight inside.

One of his fingers tracing down the length of her spine as they'd lain tangled together. His mouth nuzzling at the base of her neck. The brush of his jaw with his overnight growth scratching the skin on her cheek.

All things that had been imprinted in her brain for the last twelve years and refused to move.

Part of her brain still couldn't really understand how it had all happened. Their fellow students had always called them the 'frenemies'. And they'd been right. She'd just never imagined that so much had bubbled beneath the surface between them, just waiting to erupt. And when it had…

It wasn't that she'd lived the life of a nun after her night with Javier. She'd dated, had a few short-term relationships, then a longer-term disaster. Trouble was, in the back of her mind, none of them had ever lived up to what she'd experienced and shared with Javier.

Sometimes she wondered if she'd romanticised that night. Remembered too much with affection that hadn't actually been there. But she hadn't mistaken the awkwardness between the two of them the next morning. That horrible feeling was also imprinted on her brain, in a way she'd always wanted to erase.

She'd instantly been defensive. Desperate to not lose face in front of her rival. She'd said the first words she'd thought of, turning their night of passion into something so much less. 'Well, at least we got that out of our system,' she'd tried to joke. 'Now we can go back to doing what we do best—fighting for the best roles and opportunities.'

His face had been unreadable. But he'd murmured something in agreement and she'd pretended that her heart hadn't plummeted straight down to her very bare feet as she'd scrabbled to find her clothes. That moment had stayed with her for far too long.

The way the edges of his lips had just turned up

flashed back into her mind. Why was Javier here? To toy with her? They'd had virtually no contact for twelve years. That didn't make sense. Or maybe, like herself, he'd just had a flashback to that night.

That would give her a bit more comfort. To know that the night she'd never forgotten was imprinted in his brain, just as much as it was in hers. But after twelve years, it was unlikely.

Javier had always liked to surprise her. She should have expected this. It used to be that she'd known this man like the back of her own hand. Twelve years couldn't have changed him that much, surely?

The elevator doors slid closed behind her, sealing her into an instantly quiet and wind-free space and leaving Javier behind for now. The ability to hear properly again made her ears pop. As the elevator started its smooth descent, she glanced at the monitor to watch Natalia's heart tracing. For someone like Caitlin, the PQRST wave of the heartrate told her just as much as a carefully written instruction manual.

The doors opened again to the bright white straight lines of the state-of-the-art cardiac unit. Caitlin knew how lucky she was to work here. In Spain, there were two cardiac units that everyone held in esteem. One was here, St Aelina's in the middle of Barcelona, the second was in Madrid, the unit that Javier worked in.

They'd always tried to impress each other before. He'd clearly heard about her heart valve research. But she was quite sure that Javier was doing cardiac research of his own. Him being here was unsettling. How much was he going to be around?

She gave a little shiver as the shock of seeing him

again caught up with her. She glanced down as she clamped her hands onto the rail of the stretcher and pushed it along the corridor to the already organised private room.

'Okay?' Marco was looking at her from the other side of the stretcher. The experienced older cardiac technician missed nothing.

Caitlin glanced down at her pale pink scrubs again, grimacing at her appearance as she gave Marco a quick nod. She tugged back her hair, feeling in her pockets for another scrunchie to no avail. At this rate she'd end up with an elastic band in her hair and it wouldn't be the first time. Her make-up had likely slipped from her face around six hours ago. She wouldn't know; she hadn't had a chance to consider her appearance since she'd got showered and dressed at six this morning. Even her multicoloured flat shoes that were her trademark at work didn't amuse her. It didn't matter that she had around ten different pairs, and they were as comfortable as slippers. Her whole appearance was about as far away from the message she'd wanted to convey to Javier Torres the next time she saw him as it could possibly be.

Too late now.

She put a wide smile on her face and touched Natalia's arm as the stretcher slid into the room. It was the largest on the fourth floor. All centralised monitoring was installed and a wide internal window gave a clear view of the nurses' station but could be shaded if required. There was an accompanying easily accessible bathroom and, whilst this was still a hospital, the

Condesa had already organised a private chef and a team of private nurses to assist with Natalia's care.

It had already been a bit of a battle. Caitlin had high standards for any staff that she worked with; she'd had to approve the nursing staff, to make sure they were suitably qualified for the tricky intensive care work they would have to undertake. She needed to trust the staff, and she'd made sure that the team of nurses had done all the training they required.

Caitlin gave out her standard list of instructions. New ECGs, a cardiac echo, another chest X-ray. A whole host of blood tests and a few other specialised tests that could only be performed within her unit, by her team. She liked to be thorough.

In the bright light, Natalia looked even paler. For a woman with a normally warm complexion, the effect was stark. Caitlin finished her instructions and gave a nod to the rest of the team as they moved Natalia seamlessly over to her more comfortable hospital bed and got her settled.

Caitlin concentrated on her patient. Natalia's condition was serious. She needed surgery—there was no doubt about that. The latest tests would put the final pieces into the jigsaw puzzle of exactly how delicate the surgery would need to be and, more importantly, the chance of success. Caitlin was nervous. She'd thought hard before accepting the referral. She knew Natalia and considered her a friend. But Natalia wasn't a member of her family, or Caitlin's best friend in the whole world. She knew she could treat her appropriately, and not let boundaries blur. She also knew she was the best doctor in Spain for this particular issue. It didn't make sense to send her anywhere else. So, even though they'd known each other for a number of years, she was certain she was the best person to treat Natalia.

'I'm glad you got here safely. How was the helicopter trip?' she asked.

Natalia smiled. 'With my brother as the pilot I wouldn't dare say anything other than it was very smooth.'

Caitlin tried to suppress all the questions she really wanted to ask about how and why Javier had landed on the roof of St Aelina's.

'What can I do to make you more comfortable?'

Natalia blinked her clearly tired eyes. 'Keep my brother busy. You know what he's like. He'll fret over every detail. I really appreciate you agreeing to be my surgeon. You're probably the only person who can keep him in check. Anyone else he would likely hound to death with questions.'

Caitlin wasn't quite sure how she was supposed to keep Javier busy. Her mind flew to a place it definitely shouldn't go and she could feel her face flush at the thought. There was no way she could let thoughts like that invade her brain. She had no idea what Javier's relationship status was. For all she knew he could be married. Whilst she knew he was a fellow surgeon who worked in Madrid, she'd made a point of never making any enquiries about his private life. She'd decided long ago it was better not to know. She didn't want a life full of regrets. But Natalia's words made her curious. Was there something else going on she didn't know about?

She spent some more time talking to Natalia, leaving the subject of Javier and getting a better overview of the condition that was beginning to affect Natalia's daily functioning. It was definitely time to intervene. She finally left when the personal chef appeared with a light supper for Natalia. She had other patients to review, and tests results to read.

Caitlin made her way to her office at the end of the cardiac floor. She was lucky; it was set on the corner, with two wide windows overlooking the city. Her own apartment didn't have the same views, but since she spent more time in her office than her apartment it didn't really matter. She had a comfortable fold-down sofa in her office, as well as a built-in cupboard where she stored some spare clothes and toiletries, and an ensuite bathroom with shower.

She opened the cupboard and glanced at the mixture of clothing in there. Some professional jackets, skirts and blouses. A few dresses. Some yoga pants, more scrubs, running gear, a pair of jeans and some casual tops.

Nothing wowsome. Nothing that might have the effect she might want.

For a few moments she stared out across the dark, twinkling city and cursed herself. Why was she even letting her brain go there? For all she knew, Javier had taken off in his helicopter again and was halfway back to wherever he'd come from. The chance of the big impact she'd wanted to have after all these years was gone. Instead of smart, sophisticated perfection, he'd got crumpled scrubs, unruly hair and multicoloured flats.

She sighed and sat down, flicking her computer on and starting on a new email. As soon as she started concentrating, all thoughts went to her patients. The part of her brain that focused on Javier would have to wait.

An hour later a smell drifted towards her room. Caitlin rubbed her nose, wondering if she was imagining things. A few moments later, a shadow appeared on the floor. She looked up. Javier was standing in her doorway, a plate in his hands.

It appeared that he hadn't left after all.

He'd known this would happen—the fact that his tongue would be tied just being in Caitlin's presence again.

One glance at her on the rooftop after twelve long years had literally taken his breath away.

'I bring gifts,' he said, a slight awkwardness to his words that made him want to cringe. Twelve years since he'd last seen her. The girl who'd been his best rival and, even though she didn't know it, his best friend. The girl who'd stolen his heart. The proud, independent, feisty Scottish girl who'd slipped into his life at medical school and he never should have let her slip back out.

Twenty-three-year-old Javier had been an absolute fool.

That first glance of her waiting on the hospital helipad with her auburn hair flapping madly in the wind had made his heart flap in a similar manner. Now she was here. In her office. The place she'd fought for, worked hard for and rightly won. He couldn't be prouder—though, of course, he'd never tell her. Then she might feel victorious, and Caitlin was *unbearable* when she was feeling victorious. He almost smiled at the thought.

She blinked and stood up. 'Hi,' was all that seemed to form on her lips.

Maybe her brain was as confused as his was right

now. It would be nice to think that, but did he really want her confused over a night from long ago when he needed her at the top of her game to operate on his sister?

He paused then took a few hesitant steps inside her office, hoping he would keep his normal confident disguise in place.

He held out the plate. 'I asked our chef to make your favourites, as a thank you.'

She crossed the room and looked down at the plate. He hoped the white chocolate and raspberry muffins were assaulting her senses in all the right ways. It was a poor attempt at bribery, but he'd try any measure.

'I'm surprised you remember,' she said softly.

He felt a pang in his heart. Had she honestly thought he would forget the little details of her that were embedded in him? His reply was soft too. 'Why would I forget?'

Her body gave the tiniest shiver. There was unintended weight to those words that she hadn't expected. And he knew immediately she wasn't ready for this. Not now. Not here. She had patients to concentrate on.

She lifted her eyes and stared at him for a moment. He had no idea what was going on behind those green eyes of hers as they looked up and down the length of his body in a way that made him feel as if she were undressing him. But her voice was light-hearted when she said, 'New job, Javier—flying private charters? Hope it pays well.'

She was joking with him. Something they'd used to do on a regular basis. He had the oddest sensation of coming home. He glanced down at his attire and held out his hands. 'Didn't realise it looked like a uniform. Wasn't thinking when I got ready. Guess I'm just trying to be a regular guy.' He tried to hide his smile.

'Does a Count get to be a regular guy?'

This was how it used to be. At medical school hardly anyone had known he was from a wealthy aristocratic family. But Caitlin had known. And had never once tried to use it to her advantage. In fact, it had the opposite effect on her and on the few occasions he'd offered to help her out financially when he'd known she was struggling she'd point blank refused. She had far too much pride to ever ask for help.

He rolled his eyes and nodded at the muffins. 'Sure, a regular guy with a private chef. When my sister's health is at stake, bribery is allowed, you know.'

She met his gaze. There was so much there. Twelve lost years between them. She lifted a muffin from the plate and walked around her desk, gesturing to the seat at the other side as she moved to flick some switches on her coffee machine.

He could sense she was trying to decide how to play this. He'd turned up unexpectedly. They'd had literally no contact since that last awkward morning after graduation. He'd replayed that day over and over in his head so many times. It had seemed clear that Caitlin had thought they'd made a mistake; she'd made a quick comment—'at least we got that out of our system'—and that they could get back to being rivals again. He hadn't said a word. Hadn't told her how much that cheapened what had happened between them and how, after one taste of Caitlin, she would *never* be out of his system. He'd let the hurt feelings go; he'd wanted to respect her wishes. The embarrassing retreat and hasty exit he'd had to make had been imprinted in his soul. He'd lost the person he'd been closest to for six years. It shouldn't have been worth it. Not for one night.

But, strangely, that night had meant everything. And he was still glad they had gone there. Even if the next morning had been a disaster.

He couldn't help it. His eyes went to her left hand. No ring. The sense of relief was unexpectedly overwhelming.

Ridiculous. And he knew that. He also knew he couldn't take a lack of ring to mean anything at all. Caitlin might well be married and just not want to wear a ring—she was a surgeon after all. She could also be in a long-term relationship. But he couldn't help but hope not...no matter how shallow that might make him.

He swept his arm around the room. 'Corner office? They must like you.'

'Of course they do. I'm their shining star.'

It was the way she said those words. The confidence in herself that had brought him here.

He glanced out at the dark view of the beautiful city of Barcelona, with all the familiar structures easy to pick out.

'You've done really well for yourself.' He said the words with a hint of pride. When any other physician mentioned Caitlin he always said that they'd trained together, and that she was a fine surgeon.

'I like to think so.' Her gaze narrowed slightly. She was getting suspicious of the small talk.

'We should catch up?'

Her eyebrows raised.

'I mean, twelve years is a long time. You could be married, divorced, a mother of ten.'

Her eyes widened. She clearly hadn't expected this line of questioning. 'None of the above,' she said quickly. She pointed to the small array of figures from a popular sci-fi movie. 'Can't you see, I have an empire to take care of.'

He laughed and leaned forward. 'You still collect these?' He couldn't believe it. Caitlin had always been a sci-fi fan. He used to laugh at her joy at finding the then thirty-year-old figures. It seemed her passion was still there.

He couldn't pretend there wasn't a wave of relief that she wasn't happily married. Maybe that was selfish. He was working on the assumption there wasn't a significant other, because surely that would have been her opportunity to mention it.

'What are you doing here, Javier?' Caitlin asked as she put some cups under the machine. It gurgled quietly, brewing coffee and steaming milk in small streams into the cups.

He gave a gentle laugh, trying to keep things simple. 'What do you think I'm doing here? I'm here to make sure my sister's treatment goes well.'

She raised one eyebrow and he realised how that had sounded and lifted one hand in acknowledgement.

He sighed. 'It was a last-minute plan. Natalia's condition has deteriorated quicker than expected. As you know, there aren't many cardiothoracic surgeons, so it made sense for me to assist in the transfer. I didn't want to hire an outside firm—we're trying to keep our presence here a secret to avoid any media interest. I want to be here during her surgery, and after, to make sure everything goes smoothly. But don't worry; I won't be idle. I've asked if I can work night shifts on a temporary basis at St Aelina's.'

She looked as if he'd stung her. 'Who did you ask?'

'Your director, Louisa Gerard. She was happy for the offer; apparently you have one colleague on maternity leave and another with long-term sick issues.' He gave her a worried smile. 'Don't worry. She's told me I have to defer to you as the Head of Department.'

She didn't seem to be taking this news well. Maybe, after twelve years, she still couldn't bear to have him around. This might be more awkward than he'd thought. He'd imagined if she'd accepted the referral to do Natalia's surgery, surely she must have realised he would want to be close by?

Caitlin carried the coffee cups over and glanced at her computer and her tense shoulders relaxed slightly. 'Louisa hasn't spoken to me this evening. But I can see she's sent me an email. I guess it must be the news about you.'

'Your mother—' she started, but Javier cut her off.

'I recommended you to do the surgery. You're the best. You know you're the best—well, apart from me.' He gave a short laugh as he picked up the coffee cup, trying to allay some of the awkwardness surrounding them.

Caitlin sat down opposite him, peeling the wrapper from her muffin. She stared him straight in the eye, her rich Scottish accent thicker than normal. 'I can see your ego hasn't changed much.'

He sat up straighter, knowing what might come next. Caitlin's accent got thicker when she was annoyed.

'Are you here to check up on me? Don't you trust me to operate on your sister?' He could see the indignant feelings breaking through her careful veneer.

Javier was surprised. 'I wouldn't have told my mother you were the best if I had any doubts about you.' He didn't doubt her skills or competence for a second. She was a rising star. She'd already had a number of papers published on the technique she'd developed around valve surgery. There wasn't a single other person on the planet he would trust with his sister's life.

'But I don't need your help,' she said firmly. 'I'll keep you informed of how Natalia does. You know you can't have anything to do with your sister's care. It's a direct conflict of interest.'

'I know that,' he insisted. 'But is this really so unusual? Most families want to be nearby if a loved one is having major surgery. Why would this be any different?' He was starting to get annoyed. This wasn't going exactly as planned. Then again, there really hadn't been much time to plan. 'I was also told that because of the sick leave and maternity leave you had a waiting list— one they wanted to help bring down by scheduling some night-time surgeries.'

Caitlin blinked. She knew him better than this, and she hated people trying to hoodwink her. It was an expression he'd learned from the many hours he'd spent in her company.

'So, should I expect the Condesa too?'

He shifted uncomfortably in his chair, knowing instantly it was a mistake. That was the problem of knowing someone so well. She knew him just as well as he knew her. She'd know he wasn't being entirely truthful. He gave another sigh. 'No.'

'Why not?'

'My mother is at home, looking after the estate. I'm here because Natalia asked me to come with her. She knew my mother couldn't come.'

Her gaze narrowed. 'This must have been a very short notice decision. Don't you have your own patients to see in Madrid?'

'Yes, of course I do. But I have a team who can cover in my absence. They know I need to be here with my sister.'

Caitlin tilted her head to the side and gave him a strange glance. 'Why is your mother looking after the estate?'

His heart squeezed in his chest and his skin chilled. She didn't know. He'd made an assumption that she might have seen something in the press. Or that Natalia would have told her. But he had no idea how much in touch she'd been with his sister.

He licked his lips and took a sip of his coffee. It didn't help with the dry feeling in his mouth. He raised his head again.

There was something cathartic about this. About seeing the woman he'd remembered in his head for the last twelve years. Her laugh. Her smile. Her accent. The little quirky things about her—how she hated anyone taking the last chocolate biscuit, or how she relentlessly pursued purchasing a certain brand of tea that was only made in Scotland, no matter how ridiculous the delivery costs. Or her insistence on only eating one brand of baked beans. The passion for her patients. The way her brain worked, never switching off, and her endlessly questioning how to improve procedures and care for patients.

He said the words that still hurt. 'My father died unexpectedly three years ago. Natalia has been running the estate since, and doing an excellent job. But I'm worried all the extra stress has exacerbated her condition.' He gave her a sad smile. 'I inherited the title as well as the estate. My parents, and now Natalia, have allowed me the dream of training to be a surgeon. But in the end I'm going to have to go back to take over. My mother is doing the job temporarily. But once Natalia recovers from her surgery I'll take her home and put plans in place to take charge.'

Caitlin sank back in her chair, clearly stunned by his words. Her brow furrowed and she shook her head. 'I am so sorry. I had no idea about your father. I was joking when I called you the Count—just like I always did.'

She was embarrassed by the blunder, and he gave a conciliatory nod. 'It's fine.'

She leaned forward instantly. 'But it's not fine. You can't give up what you do. It's too important. Too many people need your help. Our skills are unique, Javier. We're not instantly replaceable; it takes years to learn what we have.'

'I know that,' he agreed, his heart weighing heavy in his chest. 'And I've been through all this in my head a million times. But I have to put my family first. No one else will.'

She sat stock-still in her chair. He watched as she clearly processed what he'd just told her. He was surprised she hadn't known about his father. There was a pang deep down inside him. Maybe she didn't know the rest of his story either. The prolonged, and then broken, engagement to a family friend—an engagement his mother and father had approved of. But he'd never really loved Herzogin Elisabeth, nor she him. He'd tried his best to love her, to feel anything like the attachment he'd had to Caitlin. Their breakup had been a shock to his parents, and Javier was guilt-ridden in case that had in part impacted on his father's health.

Javier had never really been able to explain things properly. How could he tell his parents that the 'perfect' couple, the man who would be a Count and the woman who was already a Duchess in Germany, the darlings of the press, just didn't love each other? Elisabeth was intelligent, pretty and charming; his parents had adored her. Everywhere they'd gone, photographers had clamoured to take pictures, all asking about the date of the wedding that had never happened.

To the outside world they'd seemed like the fairy tale couple. But Javier knew better. Fairy tales weren't real. He'd tried twice. And failed miserably both times.

In a flash he could picture Caitlin lying next to him in bed, her auburn hair strewn across the pillow, her soft breathing at his neck as he'd stared at the tiny freckles on her nose.

The memory pricked sharply and he stood up just as Caitlin started to speak. 'You know that I'll take good care of your sister, Javier. You can trust me.'

But he'd already turned away. Maybe this hadn't been such a good idea after all. If he worked here for the next few weeks he would likely be flooded with memories of Caitlin. The friend who'd regretted their night together. The one who'd been imprinted on his brain for ever.

As he reached the door the phone started to ring. He heard Caitlin pick it up. Her voice was steady but he recognised staccato words and knew instantly something was wrong. She replaced the receiver. 'Louisa has cleared you? You can already work here?'

He nodded in response and pulled out the ID badge he'd collected in the last hour.

'Then don't go anywhere, Javier. I'm going to need some help.'

CHAPTER TWO

CAITLIN WENT ONTO automatic pilot. 'Major road traffic accident. Massive chest trauma to at least two patients.' She walked quickly to her wardrobe and pulled out spare blue scrubs, throwing them towards Javier as he stood in the doorway. Luckily his reflexes were as good as ever and he caught them easily. 'Just as well we have a visiting cardiothoracic surgeon. I can't be in two places at once, so come with me until we assess the damage.' She nodded to her bathroom. 'You can change in there.'

Whatever had been going on inside his head a few moments earlier had clearly been pushed away. He stripped off his jacket and cast it aside on her desk, the top two buttons were undone on his shirt and he pulled it off. She caught a glance of his Mediterranean skin tone and firm abs. He still had it. In spades. And she had to avert her eyes as he yanked the pale blue top over his head. Before she even had a chance to speak, the shoes were heeled aside, his trousers were off, flung onto her chair, and the scrubs pulled over his muscled thighs.

'Shoes?' he asked.

She opened the cupboard and dug around again, pulling out a pair of white Theatre-style clogs. Size was indiscriminate in these. Just about anyone could wear them. She flung them in his direction and if he objected to the generic shoes distinctly lacking in style he said nothing.

'Let's go,' she said, and he gave her a nod.

'What do you know?'

'Two mid-forties males, driver and passenger in a car that ran a set of red lights and impacted into the side of a building. Both have massive chest trauma. They were five minutes out from that phone call.'

They were walking along the corridor in long strides. Neither of them even contemplated waiting for an elevator, just pushed open the doors and ran down the four flights of stairs to the ER.

She probably should show him around properly. But Javier was bright enough. He'd figure out where everything was.

The place was in full swing. Caitlin headed straight to the resus room. Javier kept pace with her, glancing from side to side. 'This place is crazy busy,' he murmured.

Caitlin nodded in agreement. 'It is. It just never stops. Barcelona is one of the most visited cities in the world, and sometimes it feels like every traveller takes ill on holiday.' She slowed to read what was recorded on a whiteboard near the nurses' station. 'Here's where you'll find the summary of who is here right now. Four head injuries. Eleven fractures. Six infections. Four with chest pain/MI. Eight for surgical. Twenty-four minor injuries and sixteen paeds waiting to be seen.' She blew a strand of hair out of her eyes. 'We have the same staffing issues as everywhere else. Apparently we've just recruited a fabulous ER nurse from Cuba, don't know his name, just wish he was already here.'

She moved into Resus, where another dark-haired doctor met them. 'Can you meet your ambulances in the bay and assess if you need resus? We have another RTA heading in.' He looked completely stressed and glanced at Javier. Caitlin laid her hand on Javier's arm. 'David, this is Javier Torres, cardiothoracic surgeon from Madrid. Starting work with us for a few weeks, doing nights.'

'Perfect,' sighed David, 'because Julia, your extra on-call doc, is stuck in the traffic jam behind the RTA. At least you'll have an extra pair of hands if you need them.'

Caitlin looked down at her hand on Javier's skin. As David had been talking she'd used all her energy to concentrate on his words because right now the palm of her hand was doing backward flips of recognition of the skin it was touching.

Things like this weren't supposed to happen. A million sensations were shooting through her nerve-endings right now. The heat of his skin next to hers, the feel of the dark hairs of his arms under her palm. So familiar. They might only have had one night together, but they'd built up to that night for more than six years.

Six years of rivalry, teasing and familiarity. They'd regularly sat close together, skin brushing against each other while they'd shared their everyday life. There had been long nights of study, quizzing each other, before falling asleep with heads on the table. There had been multiple hugs for celebrations and tear-filled moments that factored into the job they were training to do. Javier had been the first person she'd told when she'd done her first minor procedure in Theatre as a trainee. They'd fallen asleep next to each other, on sofas, beds at parties, floors, on multiple occasions.

One of the things she'd missed most was being around someone she felt so in tune with, so comfortable with. She'd almost forgotten about the electricity, how somehow the air seemed to spark between them. Every part of that was flooding back with one touch. If she'd thought her skin had gone crazy on the roof, it was nothing to what was happening now.

Javier moved his arm and rubbed it with his other hand. What did that mean? She didn't have time to consider as the screaming alarms of the approaching ambulances echoed towards them. She thrust a package at him with a gown, mask and gloves. Years of practice meant it took them less than ten seconds to be ready.

Javier's long strides towards the ambulance bay meant she had to almost jog to keep up. It was odd. Caitlin was taller than most women but she was still five inches shorter than Javier.

The first ambulance had barely halted before he'd opened the back doors. One of the paramedics jumped out to join them and a nurse from the department appeared at their side.

Caitlin moved around the other side of the stretcher as it was pulled out, looking at the dark-skinned man lying limply, his breath rasping.

'Rian Caballero, forty-two—he was the driver. We think he might have had a MI behind the wheel. The report is he lost consciousness while driving. As he was slumped across the wheel, he's taken more impact on his chest than would normally be expected.'

Caitlin had her stethoscope out instantly, listening. Javier did the same; it was clear they reached the same conclusion. He pressed a button on the machine monitoring Rian's heart and read the strip that came out. 'Looks like an inferior MI, complicated by a suspected pneumothorax on this side.'

Caitlin was impressed by how calm he was. She shouldn't be, of course. She'd been by his side every step of the way in their training. But after spending the last twelve years working with a variety of different personnel it was nice to be alongside someone who never panicked, no matter what the situation.

'I think he has a haemothorax on this side.' She turned to the nurse. 'He needs to go to Resus. Trauma and Cardiology for the MI. We'll assess the next patient.'

The nurse gave a nod and, alongside the paramedic, pulled the trolley inside the department just as the next ambulance pulled up.

This time it was Caitlin who opened the door, and for a split-second paused. This patient had a long thin tube penetrating his chest. The paramedic in the back looked panic-stricken. Her gloves were covered in blood and there were multiple used wound pads lying on the floor of the ambulance.

'We cut and run,' she said bluntly. 'Injury was caused by impact of the car through a shop window that supplies plumbing equipment. He was losing blood so quickly I struggled to get a line in.'

Javier moved to take over, stepping inside the ambulance in a confident manner. 'But well done; you did get the line in.' He glanced at the bag of fluids running and looked down at the patient's chest. Even from her position, Caitlin knew the pipe had likely directly impacted the heart.

She turned to the staff who had appeared behind her and held up one hand. 'We're going to move this stretcher very, very carefully. Everyone in position.'

She knew she was holding her breath as she gestured for the slow, steady movement of the stretcher, first out of the ambulance and then onto the ground. A path was cleared to Resus, with Caitlin holding the pipe delicately between her fingers to ensure it didn't move and cause any more damage. She was standing on the runner of the stretcher so she didn't have to walk, but she also felt every tiny bump in the journey.

As soon as they were wheeled into Resus a wide-eyed David handed her the transducer for the ultrasound. 'I heard,' was all he said.

It was just what she needed. So, while others attached a blood pressure monitor, cardiac leads and oxygen mask, Javier's hand closed over hers to take over the delicate role of holding the pipe. This time they were both wearing gloves, but she was still conscious of his careful touch.

Her eyes fixed on the screen as the damage emerged quickly. 'Two chambers of the heart affected,' she said, knowing just how serious this was. Javier gave her a signal to go further down that she knew exactly. It was odd how they could communicate without words. She moved the transducer down and gave a nod. 'Also damage to the aorta.'

Their gazes met. This man had a very low chance of survival from injuries like this. His heart was likely to arrest any minute. But the damage to the main blood vessel also meant that he was likely to go into hypovolaemic shock.

Caitlin made the call, even though she knew some would find it controversial. 'Multiple chamber injury, plus major vessel injury. We take him to Theatre and put him on cardiopulmonary bypass to try and increase his chance of survival.'

'Agree.' It was a one-word answer.

She'd expected Javier to argue with her. She'd expected him to ask for more reasoning for this expensive and risky procedure.

If it were possible, her own heart swelled in her chest. 'What emergency theatre is open?' Caitlin shouted, looking around the room.

'Seven,' came the reply. 'Danielle Lunar is the anaesthetist.'

'Tell her we're on our way,' she replied as she started unplugging the machines around them and piling them onto the trolley.

The other member of the ambulance crew came in with a wallet in his hand. 'Roberto Puente forty-six. Shall I get the police to contact his family?'

Javier replied, 'Please tell them we're going into surgery and will update as soon as we can.'

Caitlin jumped onto the side of the trolley and they moved smoothly and carefully down the corridor to emergency surgery. A few of the theatre staff raised their eyebrows at the sight. Caitlin gave strict instructions and one of the staff took over from her position as Caitlin and Javier scrubbed for Theatre.

All theatres at St Aelina's were well-prepared. A bypass machine was made ready. The anaesthetist pulled up Roberto's details and, even though he was unconscious, she made sure he was anaesthetised and his vitals monitored. What was most surprising for everyone, his heart remained in a slow, galloping kind of sinus rhythm—the normal heart rhythm, even though there were more than a few ectopic beats. If she'd asked a group of students to describe the heartbeat of someone with this kind of penetrating injury she could guarantee not a single one would say sinus rhythm. But it was clear his heart was struggling as the ectopic beats increased.

Once they'd finished scrubbing, Caitlin went to her normal side of the operating table. Javier appeared next to her, then gave a nod and moved to the other side of the table. It was clear, as lead surgeons, they were both used to being on the same side.

'Okay?' she asked before starting.

She always did this. No matter how chaotic a situation, she always asked every member of staff in Theatre if they were okay before she started. It wasn't about being courteous; it was about making sure her team were in the right head space. This would likely be a long shift.

'Good,' Javier said, his dark brown eyes meeting hers. There was no wavering, no doubt, and still no questions about her decision-making. If she could, she would hug him right now.

Somehow, she knew that even though they hadn't been in each other's company for twelve years, Javier would have her back—the way he'd always done. That moved over her like a warm blanket of security. It had been a long time since she'd had that unquestionable comfort.

Her eyes went around all her staff, asking the same question, to answers of assurance.

She looked at her staff member holding the pipe. 'Someone get Lisa a stool, please,' she called.

A stool miraculously appeared and was wheeled in for Lisa to get comfortable on. They wouldn't be pulling the pipe out for a while, and it was important she didn't move.

Finally, when everything was done to her satisfaction, even though it had likely been less than two minutes, she was ready.

'Let's begin,' said Caitlin with confidence as she raised her scalpel.

Javier watched. She was cool, calm and collected. Nothing about Caitlin had changed. Her practice was meticulous. This was why he'd recommended her to his mother. This was why he had confidence that she was the right surgeon to operate on his sister.

Her green eyes were steady. He'd seen the question in them when they'd been in the resus room. She'd made a decision that other surgeons might not have had the balls to make. He would have, and he agreed entirely. But even back in Madrid another surgeon might have asked questions.

Right now, this man had around a twenty per cent survival rate with his catastrophic injuries. He'd just been in the wrong place at the wrong time. His friend had lost consciousness behind the wheel, and by misfortune had driven into a store where the items for sale had caused a penetrating injury to his chest.

The odds of something like this happening were slim. But this was life. And things did happen. And it was up to Caitlin and him to make the big decisions to try and increase Roberto's chance of survival. If he made it out of surgery alive, his survival rate would likely have gone up to around fifty-five per cent. Not great, but a fighting chance.

The surgery was slow and meticulous. The cannulas were put in place for bypass. Bypass commenced, removing the immediate circulating blood from the wound site. The whole theatre held their breath as the pipe was finally removed. Caitlin patched the right ventricle, and Javier patched the left.

The small tear in the aorta was repaired and Danielle kept a careful watch on intravenous fluids and coagulopathy, cardiac rhythm and blood pressure.

It was inevitable that Roberto's blood pressure would reduce at some point in the procedure, but everything else was kept carefully in check. There was always a tricky balance between making sure the blood wouldn't clot too easily and that the patient wouldn't bleed too much during surgery.

By the time Caitlin and Javier had finished their final stitches his muscles and back were starting to ache. He hadn't told Caitlin, but he'd already worked twelve hours before transferring his sister to her care. Now, he'd been awake for nearly twenty-four. No matter how much his senses were on alert around Caitlin, he really did need to get some sleep.

He was impressed by the staff around him. It gave
him reassurance for when his sister could be in one of
the theatres here. The equipment was all state-of-the-
art and the staff well trained and competent.

Roberto was wheeled into Recovery and Caitlin
pulled her surgical hat decorated with little hearts from
her head. She disposed of her gown, gloves and mask
before washing her hands again and walking out into
the corridor and finally giving her hair a shake.

'I really should cut this off,' she said.

'Don't you dare.' The answer came out automatically.

She lifted her head and looked at him in surprise.
'Why not?' There was an edge of challenge there. Caitlin had never liked someone else telling her what to do.

'Your hair is gorgeous,' he said without any hesitation. 'I've always loved it.'

She turned towards him. 'But what if I lost it?'

The words still had the same challenge in them. His
blood was instantly chilled. Was she telling him she
was ill? Because that made him feel sick to his stomach.

Her green eyes were fixed on his. He lifted his chin.
'I'd be sorry to see it go. But if you lose it, you lose it.
You're still Caitlin. That won't change.' He gave his
best half-hearted shrug. 'I was just commenting that
I like your hair.'

He stopped for a moment and put his hands on his
hips to stretch out his back. 'Why don't we get some
coffee? I need some sleep, but let's eat first.'

She was looking at him in the strangest way. He
wasn't quite sure what it meant. But finally she gave
a little nod. 'Let me change and grab a cardigan,' she
said, ducking into a locker room and emerging with

a light cardigan over her changed scrubs. 'I know the best place to go; follow me.'

They emerged out of the hospital main entrance into the early rising sun. Barcelona was framed in a stream of yellow, orange and red. From the dark Sagrada Família outlined beyond and the rest of the city, it was one of the most beautiful sights.

Caitlin sighed. Even though every bone and muscle in her body ached, she could still appreciate the beauty of the city she'd adopted as her own.

'I love this place,' she sighed.

He glanced at her. He'd wondered how she'd settled in his home country. 'You didn't consider the job that came up in London last year?'

'Of course I did.' She gave him a knowing glance. He didn't doubt she realised he'd considered it too. 'But there's something about Barcelona. I love this city. I've found it so welcoming, and the facilities at St Aelina's are second to none. It's my team. Why would I go to London, to be a much smaller cog in virtually the same wheel?'

He nodded, knowing that these were exactly the same thought processes he'd gone through when considering the job in London.

She pointed to a small café across the street. 'Let's go over there.'

'It's open at five a.m.?'

Caitlin nodded. 'It's open twenty-four hours. Let's just say that it learned to cater to the needs of the hospital staff. We do have a staff canteen, which is fine. But this local café has a real captive audience with us straight across the road. You'll love it,' she said with confidence.

She pushed open the door to the old-style diner and slid into one of the booths, giving a chef behind the counter a nod.

He appeared a few moments later with a latte in his hand for her. 'Usual?'

She nodded, and he turned to Javier. 'And what can I get you?'

Javier ordered coffee, an omelette and some toast. He seemed much more relaxed now. In the early-morning sun she could see a few little lines around his eyes. One tiny strand of grey hair at his temple. But there was no doubt about it; Javier was still too handsome for words.

It had always been like this. Anywhere they'd gone, Javier's tall muscular frame had always caused female heads to turn in admiration. Caitlin had never worried. At first she hadn't thought of Javier in a romantic manner. And when she finally did, she'd realised that Javier had always made her feel like the most important person in the room anyhow and she had nothing to worry about.

'The surgery went well. It was a good call.'

'You don't know how good it is to hear those words,' she said honestly. 'I half expected you to ask questions about it.'

He shook his head firmly. 'I would have made the same decision. It's risky. But the risks of not doing it outweighed taking a chance on the bypass. You've doubled his chance of survival.'

She reached over and touched his hand. '*We've* doubled his chance of survival.'

This time there were no other distractions. This time it was only them, and Javier looked down at her fingers on his hand and put his other hand over hers.

She held her breath. It seemed like such a big moment after twelve years. How was she supposed to interpret this?

Twelve years ago this would have been entirely normal behaviour between them. But that night together had changed everything.

As she looked at those dark eyes her stomach flipped. There was no getting away from it. She was every bit as attracted to Javier now as she had been then. And that broke her heart a little. Because he would never be hers. They didn't move in the same circles. This man was a Count. He had an estate. She came from a council flat in Glasgow—they were at entirely different ends of the spectrum. It didn't matter that he'd never treated her any differently. She knew what the big picture was here. He'd already told her the expectations placed on him now that his father had died. She'd always known this about him, but after they'd slept together and moved in separate directions it had felt as though she'd lost her best friend. That had made everything even sadder for her.

The chef appeared and set down their plates. She glanced down at the scrambled eggs and toast that she always swore by in this place, and knew that her appetite was virtually gone.

Javier looked as tired as she did. 'Do you have some place to stay while you're here?' she asked.

He nodded to his left. 'The hotel just a few doors down.'

Caitlin pressed her lips together. It was an exclusive

hotel, with bills to match. Even though it was close to the hospital, it was the kind of place that celebrities stayed when they came to Barcelona—partly because of the spectacular roof terrace and bar that faced over the city. Exactly the kind of place a Count could stay.

As Javier started to eat, Caitlin remembered the plate of muffins that must still be in her office. She hadn't even finished one.

He looked up at her. 'How do you find St Aelina's? I know it's relatively new. Tell me about it.'

She took a breath, wondering if he'd considered the job she'd got there. 'What can I say? It's state-of-the-art. Only a few years old. They've worked really hard to make the building and its surroundings environmentally sound. They also created the park next to the hospital at the same time, and patients and staff are encouraged to enjoy the outdoor space. Solar panels are blended into the design, there is eco-friendly staff accommodation built close to the hospital...' she gestured her head to the left in the direction of his hotel '...which I know won't be as fancy as your hotel but gets good reports. There's a cycle-to-work scheme where staff are given grants to buy bikes, a gym and swimming pool within the hospital, and counselling sessions for staff if required. You'll know that we're a teaching hospital, and I carried out the research for my heart valve work right here.'

'Impressive.' He gave a nod. Was he impressed, or was it just lip service?

She gestured to the right. 'The park is probably one of the best things. There are sculptures from El Poblenou's local artists, a play area for kids, cycle paths and a variety of trails and running paths throughout.'

'That's where you run now?'

She nodded. 'Mainly. I do sometimes pound the pavements of Barcelona, but I don't generally have a running partner, and you know we don't do regular hours. Barcelona, early morning or late night, is the same as every big city—you never know who you might meet. I feel safe running in the park. It's well lit and there are security staff patrolling it on a regular basis.'

He gave a nod and a half-smile and her heart melted a little. This was how she remembered things. The way they'd been so easy around each other.

'How's Madrid?'

He nodded and swallowed the last bit of his omelette. 'Good. I took over from my mentor and have a great team around me, all already trained. It gives me the time and space to do things like this.'

She swallowed, feeling a little envious already.

'It's nowhere near as modern as St Aelina's but I kind of like the traditional. Our theatre space has been re-done, and all our equipment is state-of-the-art. We've changed the layout of the unit recently to help with patient flow. But probably the best thing is the new research lab that's been built after acquiring an accompanying building. We have great plans.'

As she watched him, it brought back memories of all the time they'd spent together and how much joy he'd brought into her life. All of it marred by that last night, which had started so wonderfully and ended in a completely confused state.

It had taken her a long time to take a chance on love again. When she finally had, her ex had turned out to be a lying cheat. She'd learned her lesson. When it came to men, Caitlin now stayed well away and guarded her heart fiercely.

Just sitting here with Javier now made her want to let her defences down. She wanted to reach out and touch him. Feel his skin against hers again, lay her head on his shoulder and feel his arm around her. She wanted it so much it felt like an ache.

'You think your place in Madrid is better than St Aelina's?' She couldn't help asking the question. He'd had a chance to look at her place, but she hadn't seen his. She was curious to know what he thought.

He gave a careful shrug. 'Madrid is familiar. I know that team.' He met her gaze. 'Some trained alongside me, some I've trained myself. I have complete faith in them. Your place...clearly has some staffing issues right now.'

'That's unfair,' she said, automatically defensive. 'All hospitals have staffing issues. Just because I have a staff member who is sick and one on maternity leave doesn't mean we aren't as good.'

'I didn't say that.' But he had an almost smug look on his face. 'It's just that I know most of the staff I have trained will stay. My team are settled. Most of them have families in Madrid. It feels like my team are at the heart of the hospital in Madrid. Barcelona seems a more...' he searched for the word '...transient city.'

He said the words with pride and they rankled. Was this a dig at her, with her lack of family? Or at her because she was happy to leave the place she'd used to call home without many home ties?

She shook her head. The staffing issues were a problem for her. She was sure that was why Louisa had agreed to give him a temporary job. But there was no way she'd admit it to him.

'Our theatres and labs are all brand-new. I'm working alongside one of the medical providers around a surgical tool for vascular surgeries. The prototype is just completed.'

He pressed his lips together and paused before speaking. 'The layout of your unit and theatres is impressive,' he said slowly. 'Our older-style building doesn't lend itself to so much change. Not unless I want the walls to fall down. The work we've currently done is as much as we can do.' He gave a gentle laugh, and she realised he was actually admitting to a shortfall at his place of work, in the quietest of ways.

'I have all the equipment I need. But the idea of further expansion wouldn't work in the heart of Madrid. After acquiring the previous building next to the hospital, we have an embassy on one side and the building of a new motorway on the other.

She wrinkled her nose. 'Noisy?'

He nodded. 'Mainly, it causes more traffic problems right now. Eventually, it should make the traffic around the hospital much smoother.' He rolled his eyes. 'But I sometimes wonder if they'll finish it in my children's lifetime, let alone mine.'

It was like a spear to her heart. 'You have children? I didn't know that.'

He shook his head quickly. 'No. Sorry, just a turn of phrase. What do you call it?'

Her stomach was churning furiously. Why on earth would the thought of Javier having children cause such a visceral reaction in her? It was ridiculous.

He was looking at her with those dark brown eyes. Instantly, flashes of their night together were playing in her mind. Him, tracing his finger down her arm. Sliding his fingers in her hair and resting his hand at the back of her head as he'd pulled her mouth to his.

Caitlin pushed her plate away.

'Something wrong with your food?'

She shook her head. 'I think I'm just over-tired. It was a long day and night. I'm sure I'll feel better once I've slept for a few hours.' She couldn't think straight right now.

He put down his knife and fork. 'Is it just tiredness, or is it something else?'

She furrowed her brow in confusion. 'What do you mean?'

He leaned his head on one hand. 'We should talk.'

Words she would have died to hear twelve years ago.

Now, she was tired, emotional and it all seemed far, far too late.

He'd seen it. He'd seen her face when she'd thought he had children. Her reaction was ridiculous, and completely unjustified. And she didn't even want to explain it to herself, let alone to him. So many unresolved feelings. So many 'what-ifs'.

She shook her head. 'I can't do this.'

'But you know we should.'

That voice. That accent. Like honey on her skin. His deep voice had always sounded like a tune to her.

Her attraction to him was as strong as ever.

'We worked well together in Theatre,' he said. 'I heard one of the nurses refer to us as a dream team.'

He gave her a warm smile. 'Isn't that worth talking about too?'

He was right. They had worked today in perfect harmony. No one who'd seen them could deny it. She was trying to push all the current turmoil she was feeling aside. Maybe he hadn't realised what was happening in her head. He looked intense, but cool. When had it got so hard to read Javier Torres?

But a good operating partner wasn't worth the heartbreak she would endure if she started to let her walls be chipped down by the man she'd given her heart to years before.

She had a good life here. A good career. A perfect reputation. She was comfortable. She was happy. So why was she letting herself question that after a few hours in Javier's company?

She couldn't let him upend any of this for her. Already, she was thinking about those flashes of skin in her office as he'd stripped without a second thought. She wanted to see more. One glimpse had been enough for her to lose all her concentration.

She wasn't that person. She was a responsible surgeon.

'It's too late for us to talk, Javier. The time to talk was twelve years ago. And neither of us could manage it. The result was that we both lost our perfect rival. Our sparring partner. I've got no energy to rehash all that with you—and I have no wish to.'

Maybe it sounded blunt. It could be her tiredness was making her lose any sense of tact that she'd once had.

'You don't mean that.' His voice was quiet, with a hint of hurt. For a moment that made her pause.

He pulled a notepad from his pocket and scribbled something on it, pushing it towards her across the table.

'Here's my phone number and my room number. I want to talk, Caitlin. We should talk. Even if it's just to clear the air between us. We're going to have to work together for the next few weeks. I want you to trust me.'

She stared at him, long and hard. 'Trust was never the issue between us, Javier.' She pushed the paper back to him. 'And I'm not going to come to your hotel room.'

He looked at her, clearly hurt, and she realised he hadn't quite meant what she'd thought he had. But it was too late now.

'See you later,' she said as she stood up and walked over to the counter, leaving money to cover the bill. Then she was out of the door of the café before she changed her mind and risked having her heart broken again.

CHAPTER THREE

TOO MUCH HISTORY. That was what was wrong with them, Javier had decided. He'd only managed to sleep for a few hours, even though the bed was one of most comfortable he'd ever slept on. Thoughts about Caitlin spiralled around in his head, along with his underlying worries about his sister.

He'd realised the hotel room suggestion had come over in the wrong way, but she hadn't given him a chance to explain before walking out and leaving. His pride was a little offended by the fact she'd also paid the bill.

But everything that had happened between them had to be pushed aside. Natalia was the most important person here. He needed to have another conversation with Caitlin to make sure they were on the same page about that, at least.

What good would it do anyhow to pick apart what happened twelve years ago? He'd have to cast aside the fact it felt as if it had impacted on every other relationship in his life since. Having the person you felt destined to be with slip through your fingers would make any man feel like a fool. Maybe Javier was just a romantic at heart. But, no matter how hard he'd tried with Elisabeth, he couldn't force feelings that just weren't there. She was a nice woman, a good person, and he knew in the end he'd done them both a favour. She'd grown tired of the constant coverage of their relationship in the press; it had put her under intense pressure. So, he'd agreed there would be no announcement about their engagement being off, no declaration. They would both stay silent on the matter to stop any more press intrusion.

Elisabeth had gone on to meet a man she did truly love and had married him recently in secret. Javier was delighted for her, but it still left him nursing a sense of failure.

As he strolled back through the hospital, he was determined to keep all his focus on Natalia.

She was looking tired, but a bit brighter. She was wearing a bright pink nightshirt and her hair had been washed and was pulled back in a ponytail. His eyes went instantly to her monitor to check her readings. Everything seemed in order.

'Heard you were a hero last night, brother,' she said with a grin.

'Who told you?' he asked as he sat down in a large chair in her room.

She waved a hand. 'It's slow at nights up here. But the chat from the night shift staff is good. They were very interested to hear that you were my brother.'

He groaned. 'What on earth did you say to them?'

'Just that you were a cardiothoracic surgeon back in Madrid, and that you and Caitlin trained together.' She gave an amused smile. 'To be honest, I think it was more the old helicopter pilot thing that impressed them. The major surgery was just an add-on.'

'I just checked on that patient. He's doing well. I'm hoping we made the right decision.'

'You always make the right decision, Javier. You know that, and I know that.'

He knew she was getting at other parts of his life. But he didn't want to go down that route right now. Natalia had been key in encouraging him to pursue his career in surgery, while he knew his mother and father had merely tolerated it. Natalia had always wanted to work in the family business, and she'd done it better than he ever could. The conversation about taking his place back at the estate was likely to be met with resistance from her. He hadn't yet told Natalia that he'd had that conversation with his mother.

But he had to think about her health. Natalia's surgery would be risky. There was a chance she wouldn't make a full recovery and her life could remain impacted the way it currently was. She was pale. She was breathless. Her energy was depleted. She tried her best to hide how her malfunctioning heart valve affected her life, but he could see it in her every breath.

She'd accepted the fact she needed surgery. But he was quite sure that neither of them had truly accepted the fact it might not be successful. He hated that he couldn't do it himself.

He wasn't concerned about Caitlin's skills. She was an excellent surgeon. It was that element of lack of control that killed him. There were also the inevitable unknowns that could happen during surgery. They'd happened to him, and every surgeon he'd ever known. His sister could die on the theatre table.

He hated that deep down he knew that if something happened he would likely blame Caitlin. He'd said he was here to help assist her with the waiting list. But it had been twelve long years since they'd worked together. He'd never heard a bad word about her from anyone else, but he wanted to see her work for himself. He wanted to watch her in Theatre. Last night she'd been at the top of her game, but he'd seen that flash of worry in her eyes. And also the look of relief when he'd agreed with her decision-making. Was Caitlin really as confident a surgeon as he thought she was—or did she have doubts about herself? He had to find out. His sister's life depended on it.

'I heard some other news.'

'What kind of news?' he asked.

There was a glint in Natalia's eyes. 'I asked if Caitlin had met anyone lately. Apparently, she's happily single. I thought you might want to know.'

He shifted his feet, not wanting to admit he'd asked the question himself. His sister would jump all over him. 'Why would I want to know that?'

'Because I know you better than you know yourself, brother dear.' She waved a hand. 'I think she's still smarting over the "ratbag" from a few years ago. He cheated on her, and she wasn't so much hurt as livid that she hadn't caught on sooner.'

'How did you know that?'

'We meet, a couple of times a year. It's come up.'

'You never mentioned it.'

She waved a hand. 'We don't normally talk about

Caitlin.' She gave a smile. 'And, curiously, she doesn't like to talk about you either.'

She let those words hang there. But Javier didn't want to get into that kind of conversation with his sister. So he went for the most obvious words.

'Fool. He clearly didn't deserve her then.' It came out of his mouth without a second thought.

Natalia shook her head. 'You have no idea how hard it is to try and get information out of you two.'

It was clear she wasn't going to let this go. 'Why are you going on about this?'

Natalia stared hard. 'Because you're a no-go area with Caitlin when it comes to chatting. What happened between you two? You were friends, or maybe friendly rivals is a better description, and then everything just shut down dead. She never asks me a single question about you, and that strikes me as odd. Something must have happened. You trained together for six years. You brought her to the estate a few times so you could both have a break from your studies.'

He gave a shrug. 'You know how she is. You know her circumstances and where she came from. Holidays weren't really an option for Caitlin. It seemed ridiculous that we had all that space, and good weather that we could easily share.'

There was so much missing from that statement. Years ago, he had invited Caitlin to holiday at his estate, twice. She'd initially said no—of course. But once Javier had told her he was flying on a private jet, there would be no costs for Caitlin—because he would still be going home, whether she came or not, she'd finally come around to the idea of taking a week's break from studying. He'd known that part of the issue was not really wanting to go home to her parents in Scotland, but he hadn't pressed her on it.

He'd thought she'd love the huge grounds and vineyards around his ancestral home. But Caitlin had been strangely cold when she'd got there—particularly after he'd told her she could choose from over forty rooms.

It had taken him a long time to realise she must have been overwhelmed by the size, the people and the staff. What had been meant to be a kind offer had maybe looked as though he were pushing his wealth in her face—and that had never been his intention.

Natalia smiled and folded her arms. 'You two are so obvious. There's so much more going on here. But neither of you will spill.' He could see the look of pure amusement on her face.

He folded his arms too. It was a sibling stand-off. 'Well, if she isn't talking, neither am I,' he said, knowing that his sister would never let this go. She had too much time on her hands right now.

'I'll get it out of one of you,' she said, giving him a look of determination. 'I'll find out what happened.'

He shook his head and relaxed back into the chair, preparing himself for the onslaught from his sister.

She kept teasing him, asking about their mutual friends and telling him tales of the staff back home. This was when she was at her most enthusiastic—when she was talking about the job that she loved.

It pained him that there was a chance she might have to give it up. He definitely wasn't ready to have that conversation with his sister. And, knowing Natalia, it would be the hardest in the world. She would fight him tooth and nail for the job that she loved and could do with her eyes closed. But he couldn't let anything impact her health. If this surgery didn't work as he might hope and pray for, then he would have to face the inevitable. His life as a surgeon would be over.

He heard footsteps behind him and turned just in time to see Caitlin walk through the door. She was wearing dark blue scrubs today, and her hair was tied back from her face.

His heart gave an unexpected lurch. His two favourite women in one room. An unspeakable force. It was unlikely he would survive this.

Caitlin gave Javier a sideways glance, then pasted on a courteous smile. Didn't the guy ever sleep? She was hoping he wouldn't be around until the night shift tonight. 'Hi Natalia, hi Javier.' She moved quickly across the room, an electronic touchpad in her hand. 'I'm here to have a chat with you about some of your results.' She asked the question she always asked when family members were present. 'Would you like to discuss this alone?'

Natalia shook her head. 'No. He'll only annoy you later anyhow.' She nudged Caitlin as she sat down at the side of the bed. 'Best to let him think he's involved,' she said with a big grin on her face.

She was smiling, but Caitlin was experienced enough to know that Natalia was slightly worried. It could be that she wanted her brother around for reassurance, and Caitlin couldn't blame Natalia one bit. Her surgery would be serious. For all Caitlin's skill, there was no guarantee that everything would go perfectly. Every pa-

tient was different and, in surgery, Caitlin had learned
to expect the unexpected and never to take things for
granted.

It was time to make some compromises. She could
let Javier play a small part in his sister's care. If Natalia needed reassurance, that was fine.

Caitlin turned her electronic tablet to face Natalia.
'Let's have a look at your test results and what they
mean. Then I'm going to explain some other tests that
we need to do. I'll also explain the procedure to you.
I'm going to make a few minor adjustments, based on
some of the results I've seen today, but I'll go through
all that with you.'

She'd always known it would take up to two weeks to
do all the tests she needed. Some surgeons might proceed with the most basic of tests. But some surgeons
weren't Caitlin McKenzie. She was more than thorough.
She had no intention of going into Theatre and being
surprised by anything she hadn't thought of. Some patients found the process of tests exhausting, and Caitlin had made sure to space all of Natalia's tests out. It
would also give her time to explain all the results to
Natalia and let her process them.

She could sense Javier sitting straighter in his chair,
and she could practically read his mind with the number of questions he must want to ask.

Caitlin didn't have brothers or sisters, so she could
only imagine how he must feel right now. She turned
and gave him a smile of acknowledgement. 'Feel free
to ask any questions, Javier, as we go along.'

His face was tighter than normal. He was worried,
he was stressed. She could see the shadows under his

eyes and wondered if he'd slept at all after their disastrous breakfast in the café across the road.

He didn't say a word, just gave a nod, and for him that was strange.

Caitlin focused her attention on Natalia. She went through the blood tests, the chest X-rays, the cardiac echo and the MRI. Replacement valves were not normally a difficult procedure. But Natalia had some previous scar tissue and some cardiac damage from an infection years ago that had started her heart problems. Her heart was already working harder than it should. It was Caitlin's job to take a long-term approach here. Natalia was only twenty-nine. Quality of life was important. She also had to take into consideration that Natalia might want to have a family at some point. Most women didn't think about it—because they had no reason to—but pregnancy put the heart under considerable strain, as did labour. Caitlin had even taken the trouble to pick up the phone to Natalia's now retired paediatrician; he had first recognised the cardiac infection and Caitlin wanted to be sure she had the full picture before she even lifted a scalpel.

She kept her words factual but tried to be as supportive as possible in the news she was due to deliver.

Natalia took a deep breath as Caitlin told her the final part of the news. 'So I'll need both a mitral valve and an aortic valve?'

Javier was on his feet, pacing already.

Caitlin nodded. 'Neither of your valves are functioning well. It's putting extra strain on your heart. We'd initially only planned on surgery for the mitral valve. But it's clear we need to replace the aortic valve too.

Opening up your chest is a big procedure; the detailed studies we've done have picked things up at an earlier stage. Because of other risks, it's best if we do both surgeries together. I'm still going to run another few tests before I make a final decision.'

Natalia swallowed nervously, and Caitlin handed her the glass of water on the bedside table. 'It's a lot to take in. I'm here for any questions that you have.'

She tried not to look at Javier. His pacing was annoying her, but she knew exactly why he was doing it.

Natalia leaned forward and stared at the screen. She pointed at a few of her results and asked some questions. Caitlin smiled. This was a bright, intelligent woman who'd already considered aspects of her treatment. Being the sibling of a doctor wasn't without its benefits, and Javier and Natalia had clearly had multiple discussions about her care and treatment.

Caitlin did have regrets here. It was clear the news had thrown Natalia as well as Javier. Risks were higher here. The overall statistics on five-year survival for both surgeries were around fifty-five per cent. But age adjustment on those studies meant that someone of Natalia's age had much better odds.

'Sit down, Javier.' Natalia glanced up at her brother but her words were soft. She understood he was concerned. She smiled at Caitlin. 'If only he would spend so much energy on pressing grapes.'

Javier obediently sat and rolled his eyes good-naturedly at his sister. 'If only you would let me near them.'

Natalia laughed and shook her head at Caitlin. 'As if. Let's just say that Javier is much better at operating on people than he is at harvesting grapes.' She lifted her eyebrows. 'Let's just say that takes *real* skill.'

Caitlin laughed too. This was how she remembered them from her holidays at the estate so many years ago. Full of good-natured teasing. It was clear that the siblings loved each other, and she envied that a little. Someone who would always be there to have your back.

She'd never had that. In fact, her relationship with Javier had been one of her few experiences of having someone who had treated her as though she were a priority in their life. His constant niggling at her, competing against her and teasing her had never felt malicious. Sure, it had annoyed her on occasion. But Javier had felt like a steady presence in her student life.

Her mum and dad had both drifted from her life. First with drug and alcohol issues, then with multiple relationships, which inevitably never worked out. It wasn't that she didn't care about them. She did. In a kind of far-off way. Much like the way they obviously felt about her.

As a child and teenager, her neighbour next door had been more of a constant in her life, encouraging her to study, occasionally feeding her breakfast or dinner and helping her apply to university.

When Mary, her neighbour, had taken poorly a few years ago, it was Caitlin who had gone to see her, and looked after her before she'd died. Mary's diagnosis had been very late, but she'd been happy and her pain well controlled. 'I'm so proud of you,' she'd whispered as she'd stroked Caitlin's face. It was Caitlin who'd been holding her hand when she'd taken her last breath and she'd known it was absolutely the right place to be.

There was no one left in Caitlin's life that she had that kind of connection to. Of course she had friends. But nothing like the relationship she could see in front of her now, and it left her feeling a little empty inside.

Caitlin pulled up some other screens on her tablet and took Natalia through the operation, step by step. There were more questions, and she got the sense that Natalia needed some time to process.

She put her hand on Natalia's arm. 'This is a lot to take in, and I want you to take some time to think about everything. Like I told you earlier, I am always around if you have questions. Just tell one of the nursing staff to page me.'

Natalia gave a nod of her head. 'Thank you for this.'

Caitlin gave another nod, keeping her hand gently on Natalia's arm. 'The final decision on this rests with you. I can only give you my recommendation for surgery. I need to know that you understand all of this fully, before we continue.'

Natalia took a deep breath. 'I know you're the best at this. If this is what you think, then this is what we'll do. I'll let you know if I have questions.'

Caitlin stood up. Part of her felt relieved that Natalia clearly understood the procedures and the associated risks. But she recognised it was time to step away and give her time to think.

She gave Natalia a nod at the doorway, 'Let's talk later.'

She started to walk down the corridor but had made it only a few steps before she felt a hand on her arm. 'Cait—'

She spun around. Javier. The shadows under his eyes looked even darker out here.

'Can we talk?' The strain was evident in his voice and she felt a pang of sadness. She didn't like seeing him like this.

'Will you have a coffee with me?'

She'd said no before. But that had been about them. This was about his sister, his family member, who was about to undergo major surgery that came with associated risks. If this had been any other patient she wouldn't hesitate to sit down with their concerned relatives. How could she say no to him?

She gave the briefest nod. 'Let's find a quiet corner in the canteen,' she agreed.

Javier's thoughts were racing. He had a million questions. Not that he was disagreeing with the principles behind Caitlin's decision-making and her request for further testing. He knew they would be sound. But he needed to understand them himself. He wanted to know that, faced with the same set of facts, he would make the same decision about his sister.

Part of him wished she'd told him first. But they'd lost the familiarity they'd once had, and Caitlin would always put her patient first. He knew that too.

That was the thing about knowing someone as well as you knew yourself. He couldn't help but regret the fact that they'd lost that.

Before he even had a chance to think, Caitlin had bought two coffees and was gesturing with her head for him to follow her.

She walked to the back of the canteen, near a wall of windows that looked out over St Aelina's park.

Javier sat down opposite her and shook his head. 'This is getting to be a habit.'

'What is?'

'You footing the bill. It has to stop. You know it drives me crazy.'

'Maybe that's why I'm doing it.'

And with those words he felt his body sag. This was the way they used to talk together. 'Banter' Caitlin had always called it. And it was the first bit of normality he'd felt in so long. For the first time since he'd got here he finally felt relaxed.

'I know you're concerned.' Her voice was calm and steady. She turned her tablet back to face him. 'Here are the test results. Natalia said I can share them. Take your time.'

So he did. He read everything that she had. It didn't take him long to see exactly why she'd come to the decision she had.

He pushed the tablet back to her. 'Okay.'

Caitlin looked him in the eyes. Those green eyes were brighter than he could ever remember. Fascinating. Mesmerising.

He pulled his gaze away and looked out across the park. A few parents were there with strollers, pushing their children on the swings. In another corner with benches he could see some older residents putting the world to rights.

'I'm glad you did those other tests—and suggest the new ones. Without them we wouldn't have known what we do now, and I appreciate you taking time to confirm everything.'

They were relatively new tests and not every clinician used them. But one had shown the strain on the cardiac muscles. It had shown how even a tiny bit of regurgitation from one of Natalia's valves was having detrimental effects, and how quickly these would exacerbate.

'That's why you recommended me to look after your sister, Javier. That's why you know she's in good hands.'

He leaned forward and put his head in his hands for a second, running his fingers through his short hair. When he lifted his head he met her gaze. 'I just want to say that I understand the risks. I know that something can happen. And if it does I know it won't be down to you.'

Caitlin flinched and blinked. Her eyes looked watery, as if she were trying to keep tears back. She shook her head determinedly. 'It won't happen. Don't think like that.'

He wanted to reach across and touch her hand. But something stopped him. Every time their skin had come into contact since he'd got here it had been like a lightning bolt to his heart. It just took him back to that night together. The one imprinted on his brain.

The one he definitely wanted to repeat.

For a second their gazes clashed again, and tiny pink spots appeared on Caitlin's cheeks. She turned her head quickly to the park. Had she been reliving their night together, just like he had?

He swallowed. If he could turn back the clock he would. He'd been confused that morning when they'd woken wrapped in each other's arms. Caitlin had seemed to brush the whole thing off, and he'd known deep down that his life would eventually take him in a completely different direction. And that direction was about to hit home even more imminently now. He would have to step up. He would have to step away from his patients in Madrid. Things would be confusing. He'd never learned the business on the estate the way that his sister had, so the learning curve would be steep. But he had to be there. He had to make sure she made a good recovery from her surgery; he had to protect her in a way she'd never needed before. So, sitting here and thinking about a naked Caitlin, the feel of her skin next to his, the smell of fruit shampoo from her hair, or of the moisturiser she used on her skin that reminded him of sunshine, the touch of her soft lips on his, was all too much of a distraction right now.

He pushed those thoughts from his brain. That wouldn't help him now. He had to stop thinking about Caitlin the ex-lover, and think only of Caitlin the expert cardiothoracic surgeon.

There. He could do that. If he had the right mind frame just being in her company helped. She grounded him.

He'd watched her with his sister and admired how good she was with her patients, compassionate, factual and accessible. Everything that could be desired in a clinician.

It was as if she read his mind—or needed a distraction, just like him. She flicked something else up on her tablet. 'So, we're both night shift. One of the first things you mentioned to me was that you were here to help me get the waiting list down. How would you feel about fitting some surgeries in?'

He leaned forward, interested.

'I have a small waiting list. These are more complicated surgeries that I knew would need assistance from another experienced surgeon. My trainees are great, but they're not quite there. So, apart from any emergencies, how would you feel if we scheduled a few of these surgeries while you are here?'

He smiled, glad that she'd brought it up. 'How will your patients feel about an unconventional surgery time?'

'They will just be glad to have it scheduled. You, myself and my staff are all scheduled for night shifts. We won't be over-tired. We will be prepared. I'm sure we can make this work.'

Javier gave a nod. This was perfect. It would keep his mind on the job, instead of fretting over his sister constantly. The surgeries sounded challenging. He was happy to assist. In fact, he wanted to.

'Introduce me to your first patient then,' he said with renewed vigour.

Her smile broadened as she pulled up a patient history. 'Okay,' she started. 'Jean Bishop, fifty-six-year-old male with a history of previously undiagnosed Kawasaki disease...'

They bent their heads together and started discussing the case.

CHAPTER FOUR

IT WAS LATE in the evening. Javier was pounding the running track around the very impressive park next to St Aelina's. He hadn't really wanted to admit how good the park was to Caitlin, but it was certainly a big draw for the staff. The whole vibe of St Aelina's was around staff health and wellbeing. He noticed that whilst on duty staff spoke about the gym and the swimming pool. Most attended some of the affiliated classes—yoga, spin. There was even a book group that apparently was very well attended, with usually lots of discussion around their book choices.

He liked that about this place; he admired it. Whilst he loved his own hospital in Madrid, it did have a more traditional outlook. Several of the hospital staff were the sons or daughters of consultants or surgeons who had worked there before. Although no one had ever suggested it, he wondered if his status as a Count had helped with the job offer he'd received. He knew Caitlin hadn't applied to the Madrid training programme, but would a poor girl from Scotland have been offered a place—even if she was the most brilliant trainee? He

didn't even want to contemplate what the answer might
be, because he knew he wouldn't like it.

Being here was giving him a new outlook, a fresh
perspective. Had his life been so insular in Madrid that
he hadn't stopped to consider other things?

He heard running footsteps approaching rapidly from
behind. Two seconds later Caitlin jogged past. 'Do you
always run this slow?' she threw over her shoulder.

He laughed and quickened his pace to catch her. She
was wearing a set of dark grey running gear, her auburn hair in a ponytail on top of her head that bobbed
as she ran.

'Not everything has to be a race,' he said as he easily caught up with her. 'Some of us are in it for the
long haul.'

After a few moments she turned her head to look
at him as she kept running. 'But you're not any more,
are you?'

Her words came out of the blue and his footsteps
stumbled, slowing him down to a stop.

She stopped next to him, leaning over and breathing heavily.

He looked at her, his chest tight because he'd stopped
so suddenly. 'What makes you say that?'

She stood up and put her hands on her hips. 'I've
been thinking about it some more. 'I can't believe you're
even contemplating leaving.'

Neither could he. And it was the last thing in the
world he wanted to do. But it felt disloyal saying it.

'Family comes first.'

She blinked and pressed her lips together. He knew
her family circumstances had never been great, so

maybe it wasn't a fair thing to say. But it was the truth, and he had to lay it on the line. He would do anything to try and ensure his sister's health.

Caitlin sighed and looked off sideways towards the lit-up city. He couldn't take his eyes from the pale line of skin from her throat and neck, leading down to the scoop of her top. He'd good memories of that part of her skin.

'I get that,' she said, her voice a little throaty. 'But I don't like it.'

She was being blunt. Caitlin had spent most of her life teasing him, but this was different. She was blunt when she was annoyed, or verging on angry.

He bent over and put his hands on his knees. There was so much pressure on him right now. He hadn't had the time to talk things through with anyone. Because he had no choice in all of this. Javier Torres would always do the right thing.

His colleagues in Madrid had been dismayed when he'd had the initial conversation, as a starting point, to break the news that he might have to leave.

He'd started to be copied in to numerous emails about the family business and estate. It was overwhelming. He actually didn't know where to start, because he hadn't paid that much attention before. There was so much he didn't know—even though it had always been part of his life.

He knew the people, the generations of families that worked at Maravilla. At least that worked in his favour. Except it didn't. Because those families relied on the continued success of the business for their livelihood. What if Javier got there and made stupid decisions be-

cause he just didn't know better? What if he got something wrong about the grape harvest and wiped out a
year's worth of work?

There was so much at stake. Not just the picking of
the grapes and fruits at exactly the right time, but all
the processes that followed that too. Every one of them
had a crucial failure point. How could he even begin to
explain all this to Caitlin? She had such a different background from him. Would she even begin to understand?

'We don't always have the choices we would want,'
he replied, and she turned around, glaring at him with
hostile eyes.

'I think you haven't looked at other opportunities.
There must be something else you could do. Bring in
a new manager. An assistant. You don't have to do it
yourself.'

He reached over and put his hands on her arms. 'No
one else is the Conde de Maravilla. That's me, Caitlin.
It's my job. My inheritance. My responsibility.'

He sighed and looked up at the dark sky. 'I've been
living on borrowed time. I knew eventually my father
would expect me to return and take over. I probably
should have done it a few years ago, when he died. But
Natalia was very determined. She's worked on the estate
all her life. It's much more hers than mine. And when
she told me everything was under control, and I could
continue what I was doing, I was delighted.'

He was still touching her arms and she was staring
at him with those big green eyes. 'I shirked my responsibility then; I won't shirk it now.'

Caitlin tilted her head. 'There's no talking you out of

this, is there?' She lifted one of her hands and touched a finger to his cheek. It was a delicate movement.

'No,' he said, so quietly it was almost a whisper.

'So you'll be here the next few weeks, and then that's it?'

He nodded and their gazes locked. He could feel his heart sizzle in his chest. He wanted to stay right here, in this moment in time with Caitlin. When they were both surgeons in the same city together, and they might finally have a chance to reconnect.

Some people got a second chance in life. Might they?

Caitlin was still annoyed. She'd finished her run with Javier yesterday evening and they'd said goodnight, agreeing to meet this morning for breakfast at his hotel.

She wasn't quite sure why she'd agreed to meet here. She'd never eaten in a hotel like this before and as she walked through the lobby she felt strangely out of step.

The concierge greeted her and showed her to the elevator, taking her to the top floor, where the bar was situated. Javier was sitting at a table waiting for her. He smiled and stood up. 'I thought we might have breakfast in the sunshine and enjoy the views.' She nodded and sat down next to him.

She'd heard about this rooftop bar, and seen the occasional celebrity snap from up here, but it was the first time she'd been here herself. Its outlook across the city was incredible. Fourteen floors above the city gave a view of most of the surrounding area—even better than the view from the helipad on top of St Aelina's. The view of the Sagrada Família was impressive, even though it was far away. Looking the other way, she could see the cruise ships coming into Barcelona with their thousands of eager tourists and the sparkling blue ocean.

She settled back in her chair, giving the waiter her order and accepting some coffee and orange juice while they were waiting. She opened the folder she'd brought with her, with the list of patients.

'So, we have three already scheduled. But let's look at the others. I can get them in for their pre-op assessments in the next few days, so we can get up-to-date bloods and scans.'

'You haven't already done those? At my hospital we do those before we even discuss the patients.'

She was irked by the implied criticism. The words 'at my hospital' certainly didn't help.

She gave her best smile. 'At my hospital I don't start pre-operative assessments on patients I haven't completely decided to schedule for surgery. It creates a false expectation if you do that, don't you think? Imagine knowing you have a condition; you come in, get a complete pre-op assessment, bloods, scan, thinking that they're going to give you a date for surgery, and instead you get an "I'm sorry, you're not really suitable for surgery".' She raised her eyebrows. 'Imagine how devastating that is for your patients.'

'It would be,' said Javier smoothly, 'if it had ever happened. But at *my* hospital I know from first referral if someone will be suitable or not. If they're not, they simply don't proceed any further.'

Caitlin leaned back and folded her arms. 'That sounds like a very unthorough approach. Doesn't every patient deserve a full assessment?'

Javier could clearly sense she was baiting him. 'Only if they are suitable for surgery.'

'And you can tell by your X-ray vision and your clear ability to know someone's blood results just by looking at them?'

The waiter appeared and set down their breakfast plates, quickly retreating as he looked at the expressions on their faces.

Caitlin looked down at her perfectly cooked poached eggs on toast. She wanted to dive in. But she wanted to win this argument first. If he said the words *my hospital* again in that smooth, smug accent he might find himself wearing them.

He gave a soft laugh. 'Granted, I don't quite have space age technology yet. But let's be reasonable; do you really think it is that far off? I bet in the next few years we'll be able to get a full set of blood readings from a finger prick.'

'Maybe,' she agreed. 'But you still can't tell just by looking at a patient. No one is that good.'

The words were like a challenge across the table, and Javier gave her a smile. 'I guess we'll wait and see.'

'What about all the questions you've been asking my staff?'

He looked surprised. 'What do you mean?'

A few of her staff members had mentioned how friendly Javier had been, asking lots of questions about processes in the cardiothoracic unit and the rationale around some of the protocols that had been developed. It had started to make her wonder if he was actually checking up on her—checking up on them all—before Natalia's surgery.

'They told me you've been asking questions about lots of things.'

'Wouldn't you expect me to? I need to be up to speed about what's normal in your unit. I'd hate to find out that you routinely order a particular test and I've missed it, or that you use particular wound dressings or drugs. We all have our favourites. I'm just making sure I'm consistent with the approach you take at St Aelina's.'

'So why not just ask me?' It was a simple question. She would have happily talked Javier through everything he needed to know. She'd already left checklists of particular procedures that included all this information in the patient records she'd left for him to study.

'You're too busy. You have so much else going on. I'm trying to be a help, not a hindrance.'

'Feels like you're checking up on me.' The words came out automatically.

This time it was Javier who leaned back in his chair, his face serious. 'I don't need to check up on you. I brought my sister here because I thought you, and your staff, were the best. Should I doubt that?'

'Do you doubt that?' she countered. 'Is that the reason for all the questions?'

He gave a soft laugh and his dark brown eyes met hers. He was exasperated with her, obviously realising this was a fight that, no matter how he answered, he couldn't win. 'I'm satisfied with everything I've seen,' he said firmly.

She nodded. Nagging doubts still filled her. Along with a whole host of thoughts as to how she might be acting if this was a relative of hers, and their roles were reversed. Truth was, Caitlin might actually be a thousand times worse than Javier was being. The nurses had been flattered by his attention, and it irked her that it could be another reason why his questions had annoyed her.

Javier lifted her lists and looked over them critically, getting straight to the point. 'This patient, Luis Car-rero, wouldn't you just do a direct replacement valve?'

Caitlin picked up her knife and fork, determined to have at least one bite of her poached eggs before she launched them across the table towards him.

'Look at his cardiac scan in detail. There's minor heart muscle damage. There's something else going on with this man.'

Javier leaned over to take in more information as Caitlin took a sip of the surprisingly good coffee. 'Wow,' she said in appreciation.

'I had them mix it for you,' he said without look-ing up.

'You did what?'

'That coffee you used to like—I remembered the blend and asked for it this morning.'

She was quietly stunned. 'You remembered coffee from all those years ago?'

He gave a nonchalant shrug. 'Some things stick with you.'

Caitlin pressed her lips together. There had been an old French coffee shop down the road from the univer-sity that she'd loved. The coffee from that shop had been her wakeup call in the morning. 'I always thought that place had superpowers.' She smiled, remembering. 'As soon as I tasted that stuff it was like my brain switched on and everything fell into place.'

Javier gave a nod. 'I asked about the blend, years ago, and always remembered.' He lifted his cup. 'Is it close enough for you?'

'It's perfect,' she agreed, still shocked at his thoughtfulness. That was the thing about Javier. He'd always managed to surprise her. They could be fighting one minute during their studies, arguing over the best way to complete a procedure or the diagnosis of a potential case, then the next moment he would appear with food for them both, or chocolates, or sometimes just a crate of beer.

It seemed that even though a number of years had passed, they were still as connected as before. It was unnerving. And she wasn't quite sure she was ready for it.

She leaned back further in her chair, letting the early morning sun heat her skin, and closed the file on the table. These surgeries would be scheduled. She would do things her way, by assessing all patients completely and making the call on appropriate surgery when she was ready to. 'Let's leave this for now,' she said simply. 'After all, these are my patients. I'll tell you what I need you to do.'

She was drawing a line in the sand—just like she knew Javier would if their roles were reversed. He didn't object, just gave her a thoughtful look.

'What else has been going on in your life?' she asked, trying to change the subject.

Javier smiled. 'Apart from life, love, estates and surgery?'

She nodded. 'Have you visited any other hospitals?'

It was something she'd done regularly while working on the new tool for surgery and carrying out her heart valve research. Visiting other specialist hospitals was always useful for getting new ideas and seeing where others were in relation to procedures.

He nodded. 'I've been to Berlin and Los Angeles in the last year. What about you?' He didn't even need to tell her the names of the surgeons he'd met with; she already knew who worked in these hospitals.

'I spent some time in Zurich, and in Ottawa.'

'Canada?'

She nodded. 'I think I'm going to go back there. I met a really interesting surgeon who I'd like to try and poach.'

'You did?' He was clearly amused. Research hospitals were always trying to steal the best staff from each other.

She nodded and gave him a curious glance. 'So, what else has happened in your life?'

He gave another shrug. 'My mother tried to get me married off. It didn't work. I guess I'm just an eternal disappointment to her.'

'You were engaged?'

'You didn't hear?'

'I don't keep up-to-date with gossip magazines or popular news. It's not really my thing,' she admitted. 'Who were you engaged to?'

'Elisabeth—she's a German duchess. Charming lady. Perfect in a lot of ways.'

She should be annoyed right now, but something about the way he said the words struck her as odd. There was no deep, abounding affection in them, more like a fondness.

'And it didn't work out?'

He shook his head. 'Much to my parents' disappointment. They loved her.'

Caitlin's heart sank. A German duchess would be a very suitable wife for a Spanish count—unlike a girl from a council flat in Glasgow. Elisabeth and Javier sounded like a match made in heaven.

'And you didn't?'

He flinched, her words clearly striking a nerve. 'I… liked her very much. And I tried hard to make things work. But could I see myself growing old with her?' He shook his head. 'No, not really. And that matters. She tried too, but something held me back. I just didn't love her the way I was supposed to.'

'But your mother liked her?'

He gave a sad smile. 'My mother still holds out hope that one day we will reconcile. But it will never happen. For lots of reasons.'

He left things there. But Caitlin wanted to ask a dozen more questions.

She kept her mouth closed. It was inevitable there would be many things about Javier she didn't know, after twelve years of being out of touch. But what startled her was how out of sorts that made her feel.

She had no right to expect to know things about him; she'd actively avoided looking him up in any way. But now something was burrowing away at her, making her feel annoyed—as if she had a right to know about Javier's life.

What on earth was wrong with her?

She gave a signal to the waiter to top up her coffee. If Javier had gone to the trouble of finding her favourite from long ago, then the least she could do was drink it.

She gave him a smile. 'We don't always do what our parents expect of us. Doesn't make us bad people.'

He raised one eyebrow. 'Your parents have been in touch?'

She shrugged her shoulders. 'My mother wants me to buy her a flat somewhere. My father wants me to give him money to pay off gambling debts. I'm basically just a chequebook to them.'

She could see him hesitate before he spoke. 'And... have you done it?'

She shook her head, knowing she was unable to hide the sad expression on her face. 'Nothing has changed. They're still not interested in me. And I'm big enough not to allow myself to be used.'

Something crossed Javier's face, and the edges of his lips moved upwards in an approving, sympathetic smile. He raised his coffee cup towards her. 'And that's why we are friends.'

A warm feeling swept over her and she lifted her newly filled cup in response. 'Friends,' she agreed.

CHAPTER FIVE

THEIR WORKING ASSOCIATION continued so easily. The long discussions over complicated patients. The pre-operative assessments, and the scheduling at short notice of these patients.

The relief from the patients and their relatives was palpable. They were getting two expert surgeons to perform their operations.

Caitlin was surprised at how comfortable she felt around Javier again. She couldn't pretend that the attraction wasn't still there; she could still feel the underlying buzz. But she could also ignore it and let her brain focus entirely on her patients and their care.

There was still that tiny underlying feeling that he might be checking up on her. That he was watching her practice in order to make sure she was as good as he hoped she was.

But in some ways she could understand this. Natalia was his sister. He was worried. And she wasn't entirely sure she would be any different if she'd had a brother or sister in a similar position.

She'd ordered another few tests for Natalia, and was happy to let Javier feel involved in the treatment plan.

After all, once surgery was over, he would be the person who would be closest to his sister to monitor her ongoing condition.

She wondered how he would manage that—whether he would want Natalia transferred back to Madrid or transferred back to the family home. They hadn't discussed that yet, but they would. She wanted to oversee all of Natalia's care, including her recovery. She was sure that, at some point, Javier would want to discuss all that with her. Right now, his focus was on the surgery, and she got that. But soon they would need to go over the possibility that Natalia might require some time for rehabilitation.

She was already getting feedback on Javier. People liked him. There had been the inevitable comments about him being easy on the eye. But people were also talking about his amiable manner and his extensive knowledge. He'd been asked for a few consults, and colleagues had been complimentary about him taking his time, being thorough, looking at all contributing factors and giving recommendations.

She'd even had a few curious queries about whether he was attached or not. Those had made her bristle, which had surprised her. Twelve years was a long time. But she couldn't deny the way she felt when she was in the same room as him. It was as if every cell in her body remembered him. Remembered the electricity between them, and what his touch could do to her. It had been a long time since she'd been distracted at work with thoughts like those.

The night-time surgeries had so far proved a success. Two patients had been operated on, and both were still in hospital and recovering well. Her pager sounded, just as they were about to review files for the next patient.

Javier looked up from his screen. 'Want some help?'

She glanced at her pager. 'It's the ER. Another chest injury from an RTA.'

They headed for the stairwell and went down to the department. It wasn't quite as busy as the last time they'd been there, but Marco was on duty again.

'You might want to meet this one in the bay again,' he said. 'Isabella has radioed in that she thinks it's a flail chest with cardiac complications.'

They looked at each other. Normally a trauma surgeon would deal with a flail chest, but if there were cardiac complications both were happy to assist.

They ran out to the bay just as the ambulance pulled in and Isabella Rivas threw open the back doors. She jumped down, efficient as always. Caitlin started walking alongside the stretcher. 'Isabella Rivas, this is Javier Torres, a visiting surgeon.'

'Pleasure,' said Isabella quickly. 'Francesca Corien, thirty-seven. HGV collided with her car. I suspect a flail chest and cardiac complications.' She nodded at the monitor, where the heart rate was erratic.

'No problem,' said Caitlin automatically, 'we've got this.'

She trusted Isabella, a more than capable paramedic who was extremely efficient. She missed nothing, and often picked up on things that others might not have noticed. If Isabella suspected a cardiac complication, she would be right.

Their patient was visibly ill; a flail chest was a devastating injury, caused by direct impact on the chest wall and resulting in ribs fracturing and leading to other injuries.

'Pneumothorax,' said Javier as he listened to Francesca's chest and turned around to open a pack and insert a chest tube.

'Same this side,' said Caitlin as she also set up a pack. The radiographer wheeled in the machine for the portable X-ray and they pulled lead aprons over their heads for a few moments. Once it was completed, the X-ray was automatically sent to the screen at their side. There were no surprises; it was exactly what they'd expected. Isabella was still there; she always waited that extra few seconds to make sure her patients were settled and in good hands. The ER could be chaotic at times, and it wouldn't be the first time Caitlin had walked into the resus room to see Isabella calmly assisting.

She gave her a smile. 'Did you enjoy your last few days of good surf weather?'

Everyone knew that Isabella was a skilful surfer. She'd taught a few colleagues to ride the waves and normally talked about her hobby with complete passion. But today she was strangely quiet. She gave a small nod. 'Everything's good here. I'll leave it all with you.'

She lowered her head and walked out, making Caitlin curious as to what was wrong. But she didn't have time to think about it much as she continued to open packs.

The technician next to them did her best to try and get a heart tracing while they prepared. Marco administered some pain relief to their patient and made sure her airway was clear and oxygen in place. 'You go first,' said Caitlin, standing back for a few minutes to let Javier insert the tube to reinflate Francesca's left lung.

Javier did the procedure expertly. There was no hesitation, no hanging around. After some local anaesthetic was injected, it was a simple neat incision and the tube was in place and connected. Caitlin did hers next. It only took another few minutes. Once they had both listened to the lungs and were satisfied they were inflated, Caitlin took a transducer and pressed it lightly on Francesca's chest wall. She had to get a view of the heart. The monitor continued to show runs of dangerous extra beats.

'Tamponade?' asked Javier, already taking a needle from a nearby trolley.

Caitlin nodded as she watched the image on the screen. It was definite cardiac tamponade. The pericardium that surrounded the heart was filled with extra fluid—likely blood—that was stopping it beating properly. This was a life-threatening injury.

She moved around to the other side and bent her head next to Javier's, their faces brushing against each other as Javier carefully guided the needle into the pericardial sac to withdraw some of the fluid. She wasn't thinking about anything other than their patient.

But she couldn't ignore the feel of his stubble next to her cheek. As he steadily withdrew the fluid from the heart she couldn't help but turn her face slightly towards his. Last time they'd been this close they'd been kissing.

'Well done,' she whispered, aware that he might be thinking the same thing.

There was a twinkle deep within his dark eyes. So much emotion. So much depth. She turned her gaze back to the dark red fluid being withdrawn, saving Francesca's life.

Caitlin let out a deep breath as she straightened up, her eyes on the monitor. Almost immediately Francesca's heart rate started to steady. 'We need to make sure that doesn't happen again. Is there a bed available in Coronary Care?'

One of the ER nurses nodded. 'I've asked the ward sister to come down. I want to give her a complete handover and I'd like her to take the patient back up to the unit.'

Marie, the night sister, came down a few minutes later. She was completely unfazed by the two chest tubes, and the other lines and equipment which had been put in place to support Francesca. She took the handover easily and nodded to Caitlin and Javier. 'Another dream team job finished. You two better watch out. Everyone is saying how well you work together.'

They exchanged a glance, and there it was again. That shiver across her skin. As Marie headed down the corridor with their patient and one of the porters, Javier gave her a look that could have no other meaning.

'Let's tidy up,' he said through almost clenched teeth.

'Sure,' she said, clearing the clinical trolley and disposing of everything while her eyes never really left his.

It was like doing some strange kind of dance. They watched each other every step of the way, as they tidied the resus room, quickly resupplying what had been used, then disposing of their gloves, aprons and masks and washing their hands.

The clean-up must have taken a whole two minutes but it seemed like so much longer.

Side by side, they started to walk down the corridor, but finally it proved too much for Javier and he grabbed her by the elbow and pulled her into one of the large storage cupboards.

She laughed as he pressed her against the metal shelf rack, his arm at the side of her head. She didn't even get a chance to speak before he kissed her.

And there it was.

The sensation she'd relived a million times. The memories came flooding back. Instinctively, Caitlin wrapped her arms around his neck and kissed him passionately. It had been too long. One of his hands slid up her side, the palm slipping under the scrub top and coming into contact with her skin.

Caitlin sucked in a breath and Javier stopped, pulling his lips back from hers. It had been seconds, and she couldn't believe the wave of regret at that single movement.

'Okay?' he queried. 'Am I going too fast?'

'I want to say no,' she said, smiling and grabbing the edges of his scrub top and kissing him again. This time she made herself pull back. 'But I don't think we should do this in here.'

It was an odd sensation because they'd never officially been lovers, they'd never had stolen moments like this before. They'd laughed and joked about colleagues being caught in compromising positions. No matter how many sensations were overwhelming her right now, her reputation here was untarnished. Shouldn't she try to keep it that way?

She took his hand. 'Walk this way.'

She strode down the corridor with Javier at her side. If anyone noticed the hand-holding nothing was said. They didn't even attempt to wait for an elevator, just ran up the four flights of stairs and strode quickly to Caitlin's office. She turned the lock on the door as soon as they were inside.

This time it was her who pushed Javier back against the door. 'Where were we?'

He smiled and pulled his top over his head. 'Somewhere about here.'

Her body reacted to his every touch, her clothes disappearing like his, all while their lips remained connected, making her laugh at their movements. All she knew right now was that she didn't want their lips to part again.

They fumbled back towards her large sofa as his kisses moved down her neck. 'Not sure you're doing my heart rate any good,' she laughed.

'It's an assessment,' he murmured, his mouth barely leaving her skin.

'How am I doing?' she whispered as his mouth moved lower.

'Top marks,' came the response.

Two hours later they were in a familiar position, limbs entwined, with no clothing left. 'So, now we're talking again,' asked Javier in a lazy voice, 'can we talk?'

Caitlin looked at him, a small furrow across her brow. 'What do you want to talk about?'

He ran a finger along her side. She flinched and let out a giggle. 'Stop that.'

'I'm making up for lost time.' The words struck a chord with her and she gave a sad kind of smile, a far-off look on her face.

Javier ran his fingers through her hair, coming back

to stroke her cheek. 'Why did we take so long to get together? Six years of being rivals, one explosive night and then…'

Caitlin lifted her hand to cover his. 'Let's not talk about the past. There's no point.'

He shook his head. 'But there is. I want more than this, Caitlin, and so do you.'

She closed her eyes for a moment, willing a million things away. The fact that he was a Count, the fact that she came from a place that could never be part of his world. In here, tonight, they were equals. But that was the only place.

'We're too different, Javier. I'm never going to measure up as a Countess—and I'm not sure I want to. I can't forget about where I was brought up, or how hard I had to work to get away from there. It's made me who I am.'

'And I think you're perfect.'

'Perfect for now. Perfect for this moment. But not for the future. I'd never want to leave this job for a life on a country estate—no matter how spectacular it is.'

'And I would never ask you to,' he countered quickly.

There was a tiny twist deep inside. Did he also think she wouldn't measure up?

'Why won't you let your guard down with me, Caitlin? You know me. You know who I am. Why won't you just trust me with your feelings?'

She gave a sigh and opened her eyes again. This close, those deep brown eyes made her feel as if she could lose her very soul to him. 'Trust is hard,' she admitted. 'You know my mum and dad flitted in and out of my life. But my dad was controlling. He was a liar and a cheat. My mother had a miserable marriage, and eventually she broke free and started to act exactly the way that he had. It was like her own secret revenge. And I was the pawn in the middle. I can never let that happen. I've always sworn that would never happen to me—I'd never let a man control me like that.'

'And you think I would be like that?' His voice was incredulous.

She took a deep breath. And maybe it would have been better to be upright and fully clothed, but it was too late now. 'I know what your parents' wishes were, Javier. I know you feel as if you have a duty and responsibility to fill—especially now that Natalia is unwell, and I can't guarantee her outcome.' It was her turn to stroke his face. 'I'll never be the Countess.' She smiled as she said it, because she knew just how true those words were. 'And that's fine. Because I have most of the life that I want here. My career, my home. I'm not an ancestral estate kind of girl. I don't want to move in high society circles. I have no idea who the important people are in Europe, and I have no wish to learn. As for winemaking? I'm happy to occasionally drink the stuff, but I want to learn more about cardiac muscles, not vineyards.'

He gave a long slow nod of his head. She could tell that he knew everything she said was true, and she was glad he didn't try to make excuses or tell her she was wrong.

'So, what do we do?' he whispered.

Caitlin took a breath. This felt easier than she'd expected it to. She'd forgotten how grounded he made her. How safe he made her feel.

She ran her fingers over his short hair. For a few moments Javier Torres actually felt like hers. 'I vote that we make the most of the here and now. What have we got—another few weeks? Why don't we use them wisely?'

The tone of his voice changed, along with the glint in his eyes. He ran one tantalising finger down the length of her spine. 'I think you should show me how you want to proceed.'

She tipped back her head and revealed the pale skin of her neck to him again. 'I absolutely agree.'

CHAPTER SIX

THEY'D MADE A PLAN. It was just under a week until Natalia's surgery and both had a few days off.

Caitlin tipped her head back and rubbed her eyes as they walked out into the sunlight. 'I think I'm a vampire,' she groaned. 'The thing I hate most about nights is the transition back to days.'

'Well, you're the best-looking vampire I've ever seen,' joked Javier as he sat her wide-brimmed hat on her auburn hair. 'Are you ready to hit the beach?'

'Absolutely.' They walked along the Ramblas, stopping at some of the stalls as Caitlin warned him to keep a hold of his wallet, and eventually headed down to the strip of beach. He knew, as a pale-skinned Scot, sun wasn't really Caitlin's thing, but she'd insisted on taking a walk down to the beach instead of going to the more crowded tourist attractions across Barcelona.

And he hadn't been joking; she looked incredible. She was wearing denim shorts, a short-sleeved yellow shirt, knotted at her waist, her wide-brimmed hat and a pair of flat sandals. Caitlin was a runner—she'd already shown Javier the route she favoured throughout the nearby park and streets of Barcelona. She'd always been a runner and, with her height, her athletic body couldn't help but attract a few glances.

As they walked, she slathered her arms in sunblock, chatting sometimes in English and sometimes in Spanish. Her Spanish had improved greatly since living in Barcelona. She'd learned basic Spanish whilst being regularly in Javier's company, and from visiting his family home. But now she'd learned the things you could only learn when you lived in a place, the local dialect, the lilt to certain words. She was a natural.

He reached over and took her hand, but Caitlin moved closer and slipped an arm around his waist. 'I prefer this—' she gave him a quiet smile '—then I get to put my head on your shoulder when I'm tired.'

He put his arm around her too and let the warm feeling spread over him. It was as if the connection had never really left them, and he wanted to drink it in for as long as he could.

His mother had already phoned this morning, with a few estate issues. She'd been asking him to make decisions he didn't feel qualified or experienced enough to make, but he understood exactly why she didn't want to ask Natalia at this time.

'Can it wait?' he'd asked in exasperation, part of him wondering if his mother was trying to give him a taste of what was to come.

'I suppose so,' she'd pondered.

'Then it should wait,' he'd said firmly. 'You have to let me do what I do best right now, and that's be a surgeon. I need to focus on Natalia now, and I get to stay here by being a surgeon.'

His mother had relented and he was grateful. He

didn't want to think about vine orders or harvesting times and processes right now. He wanted to concentrate on Caitlin. The time here was precious. He'd waited twelve years for this and didn't want to waste a second.

They bought takeaway coffee and fruit and lay on the beach under a parasol for a few hours. Then they drifted back towards the heart of Barcelona and found a bar that served sangria and bar snacks.

Caitlin stretched her legs out as they waited for their food. 'I don't get to do this often enough,' she sighed.

'Too busy with work?'

She nodded and smiled. 'I know you get it. We become immersed in things, and even though I mean to take time to go to the cinema, or read books or go for more dinners, it always comes back to those little things that prey on your mind. You know what I mean?'

He laughed. 'Oh, the *I'll just check those test results*, or *I'll just read that research study*, or *I'll just email a colleague at another hospital about work they've done on something*?'

She pointed her finger at him in jest. 'You get it!'

The waiter set down their jug of sangria and poured it into glasses for them.

'Okay,' said Javier in a low voice, because he loved how she looked right now—totally relaxed, her auburn hair tumbling over her shoulders and a tiny bit of colour in her cheeks. 'If I could wave a magic wand and this whole day was your own—let's imagine you didn't have to entertain a visiting surgeon and could spend it on anything but work. What would you do?'

Caitlin closed her eyes as she took a sip of the sangria. 'Hmm, let's think. Anything at all…' She kept her eyes closed.

Javier tried his best not to concentrate on those long legs, but it was harder work than he was willing to commit to. 'Anything at all,' he murmured in return.

'In that case, I'll use your magic wand and fly to Trinity College in Dublin and spend the afternoon walking around the dreamy Library, then I'll fly to New York and go up the Empire State Building, then fly to London and go to that posh hotel for afternoon tea.' She opened her eyes and gave him a wink. 'Your magic wand will be working overtime.'

She was playing with him, and he liked it. 'Wow, busy day. Don't you ever… I don't know…just relax?' He couldn't help the teasing tone in his voice.

She leaned forward across the small table towards him. 'Relax? From the master of relaxation?' Now she was teasing him even more. 'Tell me, Javier, what do you do to relax? An eight-hour surgery? A ten-K run?'

He held up his hands. 'Okay, you got me. Guilty as charged.' He liked this. He liked the teasing, the familiarity. And, even though they were joking about relaxing, it was clear to him this was the most relaxed either of them had been in a long time.

She reached her fingers towards his, clasping his hand. 'Actually, this has been kind of nice.'

'It has?' His hand folded over hers. She was right. This was nice. It was making him think of things he might have missed out on. It was making him understand why his heart had never been able to commit fully to Elisabeth. It was making him wish these few days or weeks could stretch into months or maybe even years.

'Maybe I would settle for this,' she said simply. *Settle*. Something about the word unnerved him a little. Was she really enjoying herself? Or was he reading this situation wrongly?

But she was smiling at him through her long eyelashes, leaning just far enough forward that he could see a hint of her cleavage.

He was done for.

It was a lazy lunch and afternoon. Caitlin started to flag with the heat. She was used to spending most of her day in the air-conditioned hospital.

Javier watched her through his dark glasses. This was exactly where he wanted to be, and she was the person he wanted to be with. He picked up his phone and dialled the hotel, leaving a few instructions with the concierge. As they strolled back later through the busy streets he bent down and whispered in her ear. 'I have a surprise for you.'

She smiled but gave him a suspicious glance. 'What is it?'

'Come back to the hotel with me, and you'll find out.'

She started laughing as they kept strolling. 'I've already had that surprise.'

He stopped and turned to face her. 'Caitlin McKenzie, have we ever been on a proper date?'

For a few moments she looked lost for words, then finally, 'Well, no...' she wrinkled her nose '...not really.'

'What's the "not really"?' he asked curiously.

'Our graduation ball; we did go to that together.'

'Yes,' he agreed, 'but it wasn't a proper date.'

She shook her head in agreement. 'No, it wasn't.'

'So—' he waited a few moments as he studied her

face '—how about we make this evening our first proper date?'

There was a curious glint in her eye. 'Now that sounds interesting, but...'

'But what?'

She stepped forward and put both hands on his chest. 'I'm all for a date; I'd like that. But I want to spend as much time with you as possible. We both know that, even though we aren't on call, we could get called into the hospital at any moment.'

He could read her mind. 'So, I might get the impression that you want to cut to the chase.'

Her cheeks were showing definite signs of pink, but she laughed. 'That could be true.'

He moved position and took her hand again. 'Let me promise you that there will be no time-wasting. Although our date will be at the hotel, we won't leave it. We won't waste time going around Barcelona.' He whispered in her ear. 'Let me assure you that this will be a *very* private date.'

'I'm intrigued,' she admitted and squeezed his hand. 'And I'm all for private. Lead the way.'

Caitlin looked around the room. Except it wasn't a room; it was a suite. And she had no wish or desire to know what this kind of suite cost on a daily basis. The rooms were beautifully decorated. The bedroom was huge, there was a second bedroom, along with a sitting room, dressing room, a study and two bathrooms.

'I took the liberty of arranging some things for you—for our date,' he hastened to add.

'What do you mean?'

He gestured towards the open door of one of the bedrooms. Caitlin took a few steps inside and stopped. On the bed in front of her was an array of elegant dresses, carefully positioned. There were also open boxes of shoes in a variety of styles. She walked over and touched the first dress. It was red; not a colour that someone would think of for a woman with auburn hair, but Caitlin did wear red when she wanted to. There was another style in black, one in deep purple, another in green and the last in silver.

A smell drifted towards her and she walked over to the bathroom. Inside, there was a bath already prepared, rose petals on the surface, and the light scent of oranges and jasmine. She smiled. It seemed as if Javier had thought of everything. She walked back to the dresses, holding each one up against her and looking at the reflection in the mirror. She wasn't quite sure which one she wanted to wear, the truth being each one was just as beautiful as the next.

She slipped off her clothes and stepped into the bath. It was warm and soothing. Javier had clearly remembered that the scent of oranges was one of her favourites. She frequently favoured candles, shampoos and oils with the aroma of oranges. He'd joked that one day he'd need to give over some of the vineyard for orange trees just to keep her happy, and a tiny part of her heart had saved those words in a little pocket of her brain as a memory to treasure.

At the time they'd still essentially been sparring partners—and it had been a casual remark, half joking—but for Caitlin it was something to hold onto. When she hadn't been shown much affection or interest by either of her parents, someone saying something so personal and thoughtful was something she clung onto.

By the time she emerged from the bathroom, her hair wrapped in a towel, she found a tray of appetisers in the room, along with a cold glass of rosé wine—another of her favourites. She nibbled at the appetisers and sipped the wine, thinking of how perfect the day seemed.

She dried and styled her hair, half clipping it up, then applied the little make-up she had in her bag and went to pick a dress. It seemed that Javier had remembered another detail. Underwear was now next to the bed, all in a variety of shades to match each of the dresses.

She picked up one of the bras and looked at the label. He'd even got the right size. Caitlin let out a laugh. Maybe she should be offended. Maybe she should feel controlled. But Javier was never like that.

This was pure and utter thoughtfulness and generosity. She'd always said no in the past. But this was special. It was their first official date, and she would have been unprepared otherwise.

After a few moments' contemplation, Caitlin picked the red dress. She liked the colour and, no matter what others might think, it did complement her hair. The luxurious fabric slipped over her skin, clinging to all the right places. The back lowered in a dangerous dip, and the skirt reached the floor.

Caitlin took a final sip of her rosé wine and walked through to the main room. Javier was waiting, in a black tuxedo, with a single red rose in his hand.

She couldn't stop smiling as she walked towards him. His eyes didn't leave her for a second. 'Stunning,' was the only word he said as she moved effortlessly into his arms, his hand resting at the dip of fabric near the base of her spine.

He sucked in a deep breath. 'You picked the one I liked the best.'

She kissed him gently on the lips. 'I guess we both have exceedingly good taste—' her hands rested on the top of his arms '—thank you. They were all beautiful. And you know I'll make you send the rest back.'

He pulled her closer towards him. 'Oh, I know. But I wanted you to be happy with what you picked. This is our first date. I've tried to think of everything.'

She slid her arms up around his neck. 'Do we really need to leave the room?'

His grin was broad. 'Only for an hour or so. I think you'll like what comes next.'

He led her to the private elevator that took them down to the second floor. A waiter met them as soon as the doors slid open and showed them down a corridor to a large, dressed room, with one table set in the middle of it, candles flickering in place.

While the lights in the room were dim, one wall had glass doors leading out to a balcony that looked out over Barcelona. It was the same view she had from her office window, and it stretched over the city.

Caitlin looked around, surprised. 'We're the only ones here?'

The waiter gave a quick bow. 'Private dining, as requested. Are you ready for dinner to be served?'

'Yes,' they both said, and then laughed out loud.

Javier held out Caitlin's chair for her to sit, then took the seat opposite. The wine glasses were filled and he lifted his towards her. 'We've agreed to run with this for as long as we're able, so let's keep it simple—to us.'

She picked up her glass and clinked it against his. 'To us.'

His gaze was fixed on hers, and she was glad there were no other guests around them. She wanted privacy with Javier. She wanted to focus her attention only on him.

The rest of the room was virtually empty except for a large grand piano in one corner. 'Did we throw the band out?' she joked.

He glanced over his shoulder and shook his head. 'I asked for it specially.'

'You did?' Now she was surprised. She tried to think back to medical school. She couldn't remember Javier ever playing any instruments—they'd had far too much else to worry about. 'Do you play?'

'We can find out later,' he said with a grin.

The waiter appeared with steaming plates of food and set them down. Caitlin looked at her plate and smiled. 'Do you remember all my favourites?'

He raised his eyebrows. 'I remember them all. But I couldn't ask the chef to make them all.' He leaned forward. 'I think if I'd asked him to do a very British beans on toast he might have spontaneously combusted!'

Caitlin threw back her head and laughed. 'I'll have you know it's still a favourite, but this…' she took a first bite of her food '…is just perfect. Thank you.'

They ate and chatted easily. The first course disappeared quickly, and the main course was another favourite. The wine continued to be topped up, and the sun dipped in the sky outside. Background music played quietly, soft soul music.

'Can you leave the bottle with us, please?' Javier asked the waiter, who nodded and placed it in the silver bucket next to the table.

'Will there be anything else, *señor*?'

Javier shook his head, and the waiter gave another nod and walked the length of the room. As he left, Caitlin heard the click of a lock.

She could swear a million butterflies just flapped their wings across her skin. They were alone. They had absolute privacy now.

Javier's hand slid across the table and gently closed over Caitlin's. His thumb started circling under the palm of her hand. She closed her eyes for a few moments and let out a deep sigh.

'You're so beautiful,' he said in a low, husky voice.

Caitlin didn't want to wait any longer. She moved out of her chair. Javier stood and lifted their glasses from the table. 'Let's watch the sunset,' he said.

One hand rested comfortably on her hip as they walked over to the full-length doors and stepped out onto the balcony.

The warm evening air was comfortable. Caitlin leaned on the balcony and stared out at the sunset again. 'Well, this is a bit different from our first meeting,' she teased. 'At least my hair is a bit more under control.'

His hand raised automatically to stroke her hair. 'Your hair is always perfect.'

'Charmer,' she teased. 'I bet you say that to all the girls.'

A shadow flitted across his face and he shook his

head. 'Only you,' he said in a husky voice as he bent down and kissed her shoulder blade.

She told herself to ignore that look, and not ask herself any questions or wonder. They only had a few weeks together at most. Everything else didn't matter.

Part of her was struggling with this. It was all her daydreaming self had ever wanted, but the time limit seemed like a weight on her shoulders. She couldn't fully enjoy their time together for wondering about when it would end.

'Hey,' he said softly, 'what's wrong?' It was clear he could feel the tension in her body. He held out her arm and started kissing along it.

She sighed and looked out over the beautiful city, silhouetted against the oranges and reds of the sunset. She set down her glass and leaned back into him. 'What could be wrong?' she asked. 'A beautiful city, a perfect date and a wonderful man.'

But Javier could read her better than that. He'd been able to pick up on her stresses about exams, her conflict with her parents and her absolute determination to let nothing get in her way.

His arms slid along the silk of her dress, skirting over her curves. 'How about we try something else?'

'What?' She looked at him curiously as she stepped away. Her blood was already racing around her body, threatening to set her on fire. Last thing she wanted was to put on a display for the world on a balcony overlooking Barcelona. The warm air surrounding her seemed to inflame the heat inside even higher.

'Want to dance?' He stepped back inside the room and held out his arms.

'Last time we danced was at graduation,' she said, as the memory flooded her brain. It had been the build-up of their long-standing attraction. The full-length body contact had left them both in no doubt as to how the evening should end.

'Let's redo things,' he said, and she could hear the tinge of regret in his voice.

Before she had a chance to think more, he'd twirled her under his arm and they'd stepped back inside their private dining room. He took a few steps backwards and held out his arms towards her. Caitlin didn't need to think twice, and she let her body fall into position, putting one hand on his shoulder and the other hand into his. He sighed too as he pulled her body next to his until they were touching all the way down.

'Are we supposed to move?' she said softly into his ear. 'Because I don't want to be apart.' The memories were sparking in her brain again.

'How about we just sway?' came the low voice. And then he moved slowly; it was so easy for her hips to be in unison with his, to feel every part of his body next to hers.

This was all new. They'd never made deliberate moves like this before—last time around it had been much more ad hoc and clumsy—and it made her wonder why she'd wasted the last twelve years. He traced one finger down her spine like he had the other night and she groaned. 'You're killing me.'

'I hope not.'

He moved, turning her around so her back was up against him and his hands were on her stomach, his mouth at her neck. 'How about some other music for my lady?'

Her eyes opened. 'Do you play?' She was curious. But why else would he have asked for a piano?

He took one of her hands again and led her over to the grand piano. She sat down on the large seat next to him as he lifted the lid and stretched his fingers.

'I never told you this,' he said before touching the keys. 'But this is what I do to relax now.' He started to play, and the notes were slow and soothing.

She didn't recognise the tune. But it was soulful, like the music that had been playing around them, which had stopped when he'd started playing. Each note seemed to tell part of a story. He gave her a lazy smile and she wound her foot around his leg.

'Are you trying to distract me?' he asked in a husky voice as he kept playing.

'Absolutely,' came the reply. Her hand slid around his waist and her fingers quickly found a chance to wiggle under his shirt and touch his bare skin. She laughed as he gave a shudder. 'Is it working?'

He looked down and then back at her face. 'Definitely.'

They both laughed, and she stood up behind him and pressed her body against his as she massaged his shoulders. 'I had no idea you did this to relax. When did this start?'

'A few years ago,' he admitted. 'Everything kind of went up in the air. Things were happening back on the estate. My mother and father were putting pressure on me. The hospital wasn't happy because I was being followed by media photographers, so they thought I would be distracted from the job. I went home for a few days and sat down at my old piano. I hadn't played since I'd been a teenager, and I found I loved it again. It made me forget about other things. Made me feel relaxed.'

Her hands were still massaging his shoulders as he spoke. 'What was going on in your life?'

'Nothing important,' he said quickly. 'But I just need some kind of outlet. I wanted you to see it. To hear it.'

She stopped massaging his shoulders and moved back around towards him. She pushed him back a little in his seat so she could step between him and the piano, ignoring the plinks of the keys as she hit a few with her behind.

He looked up at her with those brown eyes. She laid one hand on his cheek. 'You wanted to share this with me?' It suddenly struck her how personal this was for him. How much it meant to him. They'd been out of each other's lives for twelve years. How much more had she missed?

But now he was sharing this with her because it was important to him and he wanted her to know. The similarities between them were like a cloud of hail raining down on her. Just over a week. That was how long they'd been in each other's company again.

She knew that on a personal level she'd lacked that real connection with anyone else over those twelve years—had it been the same for Javier? Was there more to the story about Elisabeth? She was the only woman that he'd mentioned.

Was this why he wanted to share with her now? To let her know something personal about him too?

Whilst they had been good companions and friendly

rivals, both had kept quiet about aspects of their own lives. They'd been young then. Now there were no excuses. They were grown-ups. Neither could shy away from their own duties and responsibilities.

He leaned into her hand. 'Who else would I share it with?' he asked.

And that was it. Those were the only words she needed to hear.

She shifted position and smiled as her behind knocked some of the keys in a very undignified way.

She gave a small laugh. 'I guess my derrière doesn't have the same quality as you.'

But Javier was watching her as if he was entranced. She lifted one hand to his cheek. 'I'm glad that you shared it with me. You have no idea how much I've missed you. How many times I've wanted to phone or text you. Sometimes just to talk about the way things ended that morning between us, and how it always felt so wrong. And other times about work stuff—there were a million occasions I could have discussed patients with you. I would have loved your opinion on—' she gave him a cheeky smile and then bent down and whispered in his ear '—you know, just so you could tell me that I was right.'

He leaned his head further into her hand. 'Let's not lose this again, Caitlin. Promise me we are always going to be friends. In future, we will always be able to pick up the phone to each other.'

Her stomach gave an uneasy lurch. She was thinking about Natalia's impending surgery. There was always a chance it might not be successful. There was also the risk that something unexpected could happen. All of sudden, she didn't want to do that surgery.

She didn't want to be the person who had to tell Javier something had gone wrong and break his heart. She breathed in deeply. She couldn't admit that. She couldn't say that out loud. And she didn't want to. She didn't want to spoil this moment or this connection.

She leaned forward and kissed him. 'You will always be the first person I want to phone, Javier.'

He stood up, putting his hands on the silk of her dress and lifting her up onto the piano. She didn't care about the sounds coming from the angry keys as body parts pushed against them. All she cared about was the man she was kissing.

She pushed his tuxedo jacket from his shoulders, letting it fall carelessly on the floor. Her hands went to the white shirt, and she undid the buttons like the expert surgeon she was.

His hands pushed her silk dress up past her thighs and pulled her closer. This room was private. They wouldn't be disturbed.

'You were right,' she agreed as his hand traced down the middle of her body, making her catch her breath. 'This has been the perfect date.'

His head lifted and he gave her a wicked grin. 'And it's not finished yet.'

CHAPTER SEVEN

'WHAT'S WRONG WITH the echo?'

Caitlin was standing with her arms crossed in the doorway, listening to Javier question one of their interns.

It didn't matter that it was the middle of the night. Every scan was a teaching opportunity, and Javier was a great teacher.

She stood back, watching someone else take on the role that usually fell to her. It was actually nice sharing the load. Their teaching styles were slightly different. Caitlin liked to question students, see what she could pull from the back of their brain and sometimes make them puzzle their way to the answer.

Javier started with basics. He then cut to the chase and explained everything they needed to know. But they shouldn't get complacent, because the next time a similar case appeared he would expect them to have learned, revised and remembered. The mixture of both techniques seemed to be working well with the junior doctors that they were training and mentoring.

This intern was promising, pointing out the slight inflammation showing on the scan and asking a few pertinent questions. This patient had endocarditis—inflammation of the heart muscle, in this case caused by a dental procedure. It was unusual, and she was glad they'd picked it up. The condition was entirely treatable and catching it quickly would likely stop the possibility of long-term damage.

When Javier had finished, he glanced in her direction as his page sounded. He gave a thoughtful nod. 'Want to join me in the ER?' he asked.

She nodded as they walked along the corridor. 'It's a teenage patient,' he said. 'They just want a review before deciding if they send him on to Madrid.'

Caitlin nodded. The hospital in Barcelona didn't have a paediatric cardiothoracic surgeon, and some of their patients were referred on.

'Teenagers are the most tricky,' she said as they reached the stairs. 'It really depends on their size, weight and cardiac history.'

'You are fine dealing with teenagers?'

She nodded. 'Mostly. I can always dial in Josef if I need a second opinion. He's a paediatric cardiothoracic surgeon in Madrid who has a consultation contract with St Aelina's. And he's great; day or night, if I give him a call, he always makes himself available.'

'What about the younger children?'

She shook her head as they descended the stairs. 'No, too small for my big hands,' she joked as she held them up. 'And I don't go near the neonates at all. Was it Santiago who paged you?'

Javier nodded.

'He's our most experienced paediatrician. What I like most about him is that he doesn't hesitate to ask another specialist for an opinion. Whether it's cardiac, oncology, urology, renal. I respect that. He knows that we're mainly adult doctors, but he seems to value having a conversation with a specialist in whatever area the child presents with.'

Javier held open the door at the bottom of the stairs. 'My living nightmare would be to be a generalist—as is expected of many of the paediatricians. You can't possibly hope to know everything about every condition.' He gave an appreciative nod. 'I like that he asks questions, even if it is the middle of the night.'

They glanced at the whiteboard to find which patient Santiago García was with. It was a fourteen-year-old boy. Caitlin found the cubicle easily and pulled back the curtains slightly. 'Santiago, hi—all right to come in?'

The dark-haired doctor gave a broad smile and a nod and Caitlin slipped behind the curtain. 'Santiago, this is Javier Torres. He holds the same role as I do, and normally works in Madrid. He's here for a few weeks helping out and he's on call tonight, so he got your page.'

Santiago didn't hesitate to hold out his hand and shake Javier's hand. 'Pleasure to meet you. Thanks for coming.' He turned to the teenager on the bed. 'Two for the price of one,' he said with a smile. 'These are the guys I told you would come and take a look at your chest X-ray for me and listen to your heart. Are you okay with that?'

The teenage boy nodded. He had sandy-coloured hair and blue eyes. 'Joel is fourteen and plays football. Tonight, at a game, he felt short of breath and had some chest pain as he was playing. His coach drove him here—his father has taken his younger sister to relatives for the night. He'll be back shortly.'

Caitlin and Javier both nodded. Javier picked up an ECG that had been taken earlier, and Caitlin pressed the button on the monitor to recheck the blood pressure, which was higher than it should be.

The tiny fleeting glance from Santiago told Caitlin all she needed to know. He was worried. As the on-call paediatrician, Santiago would see lots of kids in the ER overnight, and Caitlin was happy to help out a friend. When she'd first arrived in Barcelona he'd been welcoming and happy to help her get settled. They'd formed a lasting friendship that had also grown into professional respect as they'd worked together the last few years. Caitlin had no doubt. If she ever had kids, Santiago was the guy she would want to be their paediatrician.

Javier had walked around to the other side of the trolley. 'Joel, tell me what happened this evening.'

'I was playing football. We'd been playing for around thirty minutes and I was feeling a bit out of breath.'

'Has that happened before?'

Joel shifted uncomfortably on the hospital trolley. 'Maybe, well...more so in the last few months.'

'What do you do when you feel out of breath?' asked Caitlin, knowing what the answer would likely be.

Joel frowned. 'Well, it's football, you're supposed to be out of breath, so I just push through.'

She could tell that Santiago already had the same suspicions that she had—that was why he'd called them.

Javier continued, 'And what happened next?'

'My chest started to feel tight. As if something was

pressing on it. Then I felt like I'd been punched, so I had to stop.' The teenager looked embarrassed. 'Coach made a fuss, stopped the game and made me sit out for a bit. When I still had the heavy feeling in my chest he brought me here. But it's nothing, isn't it? Can I play football again tomorrow? We have a school game.'

Javier gave him a cautious smile. 'How is your chest pain now?'

Again, Joel shifted. 'It's still there,' he admitted, 'but just a bit.'

'Can I have a listen to your chest?' asked Javier.

Joel nodded and straightened up in the bed. Caitlin waited while Javier listened. When he sat Joel forward to listen to his back, he gave her a nod and she put her stethoscope to her ears and listened to Joel's chest too.

A technician appeared, wheeling in the cardiac echo machine. Caitlin gave Santiago a grateful smile. He'd known exactly what they would need.

'Are you happy for me to continue?' asked Javier.

Caitlin nodded, pleased by his acknowledgement. He didn't need to do that, but the fact that he had made her feel warm all over. Javier lifted the transducer and explained what he was doing to Joel. Caitlin watched the screen and saw exactly what she'd expected to.

Santiago's tablet gave a ping and he turned it towards her. 'Chest X-ray is ready.'

She took the tablet for a few minutes and gave a nod.

Javier was talking football to Joel. Within a few moments the two of them were conversing in rapid Spanish, arguing good-naturedly over the best team and the most skilful player. The Spanish was so fast that even though she'd lived here for a few years she still struggled to follow it.

Once he'd finished the echo, he wiped Joel's chest clean. 'I'm going to see if your *papá* has got back yet,' he said, giving Santiago and Caitlin a quick look. 'We'll be back in a few minutes.'

Joel lay back on the trolley and picked up his phone, instantly scrolling.

The three doctors walked a little further down the corridor to the nurses' station.

'What do you think?' asked Santiago.

'The same as you do,' said Javier. He turned to Caitlin. 'Agreed?'

She nodded. 'It looks like he's had Kawasaki disease in the past. I've checked his notes and there's no mention of it. But he did have an ER visit as a three-year-old with a high temperature and viral infection.'

The other two groaned. Javier had his hands on his hips and shook his head. 'So, because it's been missed and untreated, we're just about to break this teenager's heart about when he can play football again. The damage is extensive. One of his coronary arteries is partially blocked and I think we need further studies on his valves.'

'His blood pressure is too high.' Caitlin was shaking her head. 'Give me a buzz when his blood work is back. If it's good, let's get him started on an ACE inhibitor, and consider a calcium channel blocker too.'

Santiago gave a serious nod. He checked with one of the nursing staff. 'Is Joel's father back yet?'

She shook her head. 'There's a road traffic accident. He's stuck in traffic but will be here shortly.'

'I'll speak to him alongside you,' Caitlin said to Santiago. 'I'm happy to wait around until he gets here.'

Santiago turned to Javier. 'You and Joel seemed to hit it off. Do you mind keeping him company while we talk to his *papá*?'

'Absolutely. I'll prepare him a little for what is coming next.' He gave Caitlin a regretful glance then walked back down to the cubicle.

Santiago turned to face her. 'Want to fill me in?'

She started, surprised by the sudden turn in conversation. 'What do you mean?'

'We're friends, right?'

She could feel blood rushing to her cheeks and wished she had a way to stop it. 'Right,' she replied cautiously.

He gave her a knowing smile. 'So, I called Javier down for a consult and you came too. And not because you're supervising or don't trust him. The two of you are joined at the hip. Should I buy a hat?'

She batted his arm. 'Stop it. You're being ridiculous. We're…old friends.'

Santiago laughed. 'Is that what we're calling it now?' He stared down the now empty corridor. 'Well, I like him. He's switched on. Seems good at his job. He's from Madrid?'

Caitlin nodded, knowing she could trust Santiago with a few details. 'His sister is upstairs. I'm about to perform surgery on her and he's worried, so he came along. He's here for a few weeks.'

'Is that all? What a shame.'

Something washed over Caitlin. The reminder that time was short.

'There's something about him,' said Santiago, his brow creased. 'I feel as if I recognise him.'

'Do you?'

Santiago looked thoughtful. 'Maybe we were at the same medical school.'

Caitlin shook her head. 'He trained with me in London.'

Santiago's eyebrows shot up. 'So, you are old friends.'

She gave him a nod. 'Of course. I told you.' A nurse gave them a wave and she was glad of the interruption. 'Looks like Joel's *papá* is here. Shall we go and have a chat?'

Santiago's face was serious again, his mind straight back to the situation. 'Absolutely, let's go.'

Javier was surprised by how much he liked this place. Hospitals were hospitals. But every hospital had a vibe. And not all of them were good. But St Aelina's was a combination of all the things he liked. Busy, sometimes frantic, with committed, friendly staff. No wonder Caitlin had settled in so well here.

He liked the people too. He'd heard a few of the staff discussing Santiago. He was well respected. He'd heard the same about some of the other staff he was working with. It gave him confidence in the place his sister would be operated on.

Of course, the most important person in that equation was the surgeon. And he'd always had confidence in Caitlin. If he were lying on a trolley, it would be Caitlin he'd want to operate on him, so of course he'd recommended her for his sister.

Natalia was sleeping right now. Thank goodness. She

hadn't been sleeping well at night and it was important she was well rested for her surgery.

His mother had been on the phone earlier, asking about his sister, then telling him she'd email with a list of priorities that needed to be dealt with on the estate. He felt like the naughty schoolboy who hadn't done his homework. There was no point trying to tell his mother that he was doing a full-time job here, overseeing his sister's care, catching up on referrals or reviews for his own patients back in Madrid and spending every other waking moment thinking about Caitlin. The estate didn't feature in his thoughts. Not really. Except for hanging in the background like a dark thundercloud.

He hated that he felt that way about the childhood home that was full of such good memories, and the place and business he knew that the rest of the family adored.

Maybe it was just because he was the only son. The new Conde. The expectations had been there from birth. There had been no opportunity for Javier to decide what he wanted to do with his life. In a way he'd been lucky that his mother and father had allowed him his dream of going to medical school and training as a doctor. They could easily have refused—or made his life difficult.

But his father had been well. The old Conde had expected to live for much longer than he had. He'd thought there would be plenty of time to bring his son back into his role to fulfil his family responsibilities. Unfortunately, life had decided to go a different way.

Javier sat down in a comfortable chair in Natalia's darkened room, lifting his tablet and connecting to his emails. He tried to read them—he really did. But his brain just couldn't focus. He was thinking of the young man down in the ER, and the expression on his face when Javier had gently told him that things might be more serious and taken him through a brief biology lesson of the heart and blood vessels. He was thinking what the future might hold for that young man.

A hand appeared on his shoulder and he jumped. 'Hey,' said Caitlin softly. 'Thought I might find you here. How about some company?'

He stood up and she slipped her hand into his and they walked back along the corridor to her office.

Javier had learned quickly that it was really her second home. She had a whole wardrobe in there, a fold-down bed, a functioning bathroom and a secret stash of chocolate. It was so Caitlin.

She pulled out her ponytail band and shook out her hair. She pressed the button to make her sofa bed fold down, which Javier loved.

'Isn't technology amazing?'

'Yes,' she agreed, flopping down onto the bed. 'Especially when it does this for me.'

He laughed and moved next to her, stretching his legs out.

'We still have another four hours to work.'

She sighed and turned onto her side, wrapping one arm and one leg over him. 'Okay then, any objections if I do it like this?'

Heat swept over him, just like any time he was around Caitlin. Everything about this seemed so right. This—here—felt like a perfect moment for him.

If an asteroid hit the planet right now and this was

his last memory, this was exactly where he wanted to be, and who he wanted to be with.

He hated that this was temporary. He hated that he could never dream of asking Caitlin to give up her career and job and come with him back to the estate. It was his duty, not hers. And in his head he could already see that neither of them would be happy.

But he would never ask her to do that anyway. He would never ask Caitlin to give up her dreams for him. He wouldn't dare. The Glasgow girl would probably kill him mid-sentence, and that made him smile. She could be fierce when she wanted to be.

Caitlin hid things well. He knew the relationship with her parents wasn't good. She'd opened up a little more about that, and it was a first. He'd always known they weren't particularly interested in Caitlin, and that amazed him. They had a wonderful daughter, intelligent, compassionate, and they barely noticed. It made him angry. But he knew his anger wouldn't help Caitlin.

He also knew that he'd lived a privileged life. Deprivation had never touched the early part of Javier's life. But being a doctor had brought him a much better understanding that where you lived and having limited choices could all affect a person's health. Caitlin had spoken briefly about the area in Glasgow she'd grown up in. He knew she had worked really hard to get a scholarship to go to medical school in London. He'd also helped her hide the fact she'd needed a job in order to eat at medical school. She hadn't wanted or asked for his help—in fact, he'd seen the panic in her eyes when he'd walked into the bookshop and realised she was working there. It had taken all her angry strength to ask him to keep her job a secret, something he'd willingly agreed to. Of course, he'd had the means to offer her financial support instead of keeping her secret. But he'd known straight away that her pride wouldn't let her accept that from him, and he'd admired her for it. Even on their date, when he'd arranged to get some dresses for her, he'd been part worried she would turn them down. Sure enough, everything but the one she'd worn had been left with instructions for them to be returned, but at least she'd accepted the gift in the spirit it had been intended.

'Are you ready for Wednesday?' he asked.

She lifted her head and kissed him on the lips. Wednesday was Natalia's surgery. Tonight was their last night shift together. Caitlin was swapping back to days to perform Natalia's surgery in four days' time.

He trusted her. He trusted Caitlin implicitly. But that didn't stop the deep-seated worries that something could go wrong for his sister.

Her fingers ran through his hair. 'Of course I'm ready. Am I nervous? Of course I am. Because this is your sister. You love her. She's my friend. I want the best outcome in the world for her, and I hope I can make that happen. But we're surgeons, Javier. We have to expect the unexpected. But I promise you I will do my absolute best to make sure everything goes exactly the way it should.'

Her green eyes were staring straight at him, full of emotion and sincerity. It filled his heart with joy, and a tiny bit of dread. He knew about surgery. And if something went wrong would he feel differently about Caitlin? Probably. And that made him shallow.

If the roles were reversed and Caitlin had a brother he was about to operate on, how would he feel? Terrified would be the short answer. Terrified if things went wrong, how it would impact on the relationship with someone that he loved.

Loved. He'd always loved her, but in a different way. He was loyal to his friends. Always had been. But things had changed between them. Even after that night they'd spent together, when his mind had been a reckless jumble, he'd known deep down how he'd felt about her.

When she'd acted as if their night together had been nothing—just a build-up of sexual tension between them rather than something more deep-seated—he'd been devastated. But, as a typical man, he'd acted with bravado instead of asking her to sit down and talk.

He didn't doubt for a single second that Caitlin would do her absolute best for Natalia. That was why he'd brought Natalia here. He'd brought her to the best surgeon that he knew, and someone he trusted completely. So much was at risk.

He knew that every family member felt like this. Even for the most basic procedure in the world, every parent, every sibling or every child had that moment of absolute fear when a loved one disappeared through the theatre doors. It was normal. It was natural. And he'd had this conversation a hundred times with family members to let them know their feelings were entirely normal. They weren't irrational. They weren't overthinking things. They were human.

Javier's problem was that he was usually on the other side of the theatre doors. He was usually the one with the words of wisdom and reassurance rather than the person standing at the other side. He didn't like this position.

He hated feeling as if there were things he couldn't control. And now it seemed as if there was so much around him he couldn't control. The surgery for his sister. His future as a surgeon. His relationship with Caitlin. So much that could all change in a heartbeat. Javier had never had so much uncertainty in his life. It made him want to cling on all the harder.

Tonight, as he lay in his perfect place with Caitlin, he could almost hear the clock ticking down slowly, calling time on their relationship.

He wished he'd spent the last few years with her. Even if it would still have come to this eventual outcome, he would have had a few years' worth of memories to take him into the next stage of his life.

Reflecting now was easy. He'd tried hard to love Elisabeth, but now he could see it would never have worked. Not when he'd always feel this way about Caitlin. He would never have been able to throw his heart and soul into another relationship. Not when his heart belonged to another.

As guilt pricked at him, he wondered how they should leave things. He wanted her to be happy. He wanted Caitlin to be free to lead the life she should, to find love, to get married and have a family if she chose to. He didn't want her to feel like he currently did—that their connection would never leave him, and he could never really love someone else.

Carrying those feelings was a definite burden. It didn't matter to him what came next. His life would be at the family estate; their plans for the future would never be compatible. Maybe his mother would try and matchmake again? Maybe he would meet someone who, for reasons of their own, would be happy to settle and just live a comfortable, companionable life.

He shuddered. What a thought.

'What's wrong?' asked Caitlin. Her fingers traced down his forehead to the tip of his nose, her touch as light as a feather.

'Nothing,' he said, pushing everything else away. 'I just know that after all of this I will miss you.'

Sadness flooded her eyes. She gave a smile. 'But we'll have this,' she said. 'This time together, and these moments.' She took a deep breath. 'And I can't be sad about that. I can't be sad about this.'

'Me neither,' he agreed as he pulled her even closer, then he laughed. 'So, our memories will be of a fold-down bed in an office in St Aelina's. Instead of in a luxury hotel with Egyptian cotton and a four-poster bed.'

'Oh, we can still make memories there too,' she whispered.

She slid on top of him. 'And you know what they say, practice makes perfect.' And she sealed those words with another kiss.

CHAPTER EIGHT

THE PAEDIATRIC CARDIOTHORACIC surgeon on the teleconference gave a sincere smile. 'I absolutely agree this is the way to proceed. Thank you for agreeing to take on this case.'

Javier gave a nod. 'No problem. I'll come back to you once the procedure is complete.'

He cut the call and turned to Caitlin. 'Anything you want to raise?'

She shook her head. 'I'm fine with everything that was discussed. Joel is almost the size of a regular adult. I'm hopeful that the angioplasty will be straightforward.'

Javier nodded. It wasn't the first time he'd done the procedure on a teenager, and Joel seemed to have struck up a rapport with him and they all agreed that was beneficial for the person performing his procedure.

For Javier it was something he did on a regular basis. The anatomy and physiology would be the same, just the age of the patient would be different.

'Do you want to assist?' he asked Caitlin. He didn't have to worry about her being offended by him asking. She nodded straight away. She was supposed to be off today, to give herself a little rest before Natalia's surgery, but Caitlin was, like him, always ready to work when asked.

He felt a pang of dread. This had been his way of life for so long. What would happen when he couldn't do this any more? Could he really find life fulfilling at the estate? He hated how he felt inside right now.

Javier tried to push it all to one side. He had a teenage boy to concentrate on. Joel's life had already changed irrevocably. It was up to him to attempt to control the damage and minimise the impact on Joel's life.

He waited while Joel was moved into the pre-op room and went to stand alongside him, asking him and his *papá* if they had any questions before they started, and letting Bill, the anaesthetist, explain how he would make sure that Joel was comfortable and wouldn't feel anything untoward during the procedure. He gave Joel some mild sedation and they waited for it to take effect.

Caitlin scrubbed up alongside Javier and then stood to one side as Joel was wheeled into the theatre.

Everything was in place. The staff gave him nods that they were ready to start and Javier turned to Joel. 'We're ready to start. At any point if you have a question, just ask. If you don't feel well at any stage, tell us too. Any discomfort at all, let Bill know and we'll stop.' Javier paused. All Joel's initial nonchalance and bravado had clearly been left at the door. 'I know this is scary. But it won't take long, and I've done dozens of these procedures. If this works the way it should, the blood flow to your heart will improve and you shouldn't have some of the symptoms you've been experiencing.'

Joel gave a nod, but he looked as if he could burst into tears at any second.

Javier nodded to someone to push a stool in behind him and he sat down at the edge of the operating table. 'Okay, let's talk for a while. Let's dream team. Pick your first player.'

Caitlin was smiling under her mask. Javier didn't care about theatre times. He didn't care about being the most prolific surgeon. What he did care about was this four-teen-year-old on the operating table.

And what she loved most about her workplace was the fact that everyone got it. No one sighed…no one rolled their eyes. She could sense them all smiling behind their masks too. Fifteen minutes later, Javier and Joel were still arguing over their teams and players. It was actually beautiful to watch.

When Javier finally moved into position, Joel was clearly much more relaxed. When Javier inserted the thin flexible catheter into his femoral artery via a small incision in his groin, Joel only flinched for a second.

Caitlin watched the screen as the catheter was guided up Joel's artery. The narrowing was clearly evident as they reached the blockage. 'Now,' Javier instructed Caitlin and she injected the contrast dye through the catheter. The blockage was even more pronounced than they'd initially thought.

This boy had been running around a football park with almost blocked arteries. They knew exactly what might have happened.

'Okay?' checked Javier. Sometimes when the dye was inserted, patients could feel light-headed or nauseous. But Joel was lying with his eyes closed and just nodded his head.

'Fine,' he murmured.

Javier was skilful. Now the blockage was clearly identified, he threaded the guidewire inside the catheter across the narrowed area. Next, a long thin tube was inserted. It had an uninflated balloon at one end and was guided to the blocked area.

Once Javier was sure it was exactly in position, he inflated the balloon, flattening the plaque within the artery and inserting a stent into place to ensure the artery stayed open. He kept talking quietly and steadily to Joel the whole time.

It was clear he had no idea if the sedation had taken hold of Joel and the young man had actually fallen asleep, or if Joel was keeping his eyes closed to try and relax during the procedure. What Caitlin absolutely knew for sure was that Joel was central to every single thing that Javier was doing right now. He was the focus of his entire world.

Part of her crumbled inside at the irony of all this. Javier Torres was a spectacular doctor. He was so talented, and the thought of him giving all this up to run a vineyard and ancestral estate just seemed like such a waste.

She knew he was a Count. She didn't really understand the aristocracy side of all this because it had never been a world that she'd moved in. But surgery was a world that she did move in. And right now she wanted to shout on behalf of all cardiothoracic surgeons about how ridiculous this all was. How many students could he train? How many lives could he save? What on earth could he use skills like this for in a vineyard?

More importantly, how many situations like this would be lost? She already knew that this fourteen-year-old boy would never forget Javier Torres. He would remember this whole experience based on the relationship that Javier had established with him. The jokes, the trust, this whole thing would be etched in his brain.

And Caitlin wanted to sit in a corner and cry for all those people who wouldn't get the chance to meet this wonderful doctor doing the job he'd clearly been born to do.

Life just seemed so unfair right now, and that was without throwing herself into the equation. Anger bubbled up inside her. She was glad she still had a mask on and that her expression was hidden.

Javier was still working away diligently. He removed the catheter and applied a collagen plug to help seal the wound, his eyes flicking to the monitors at the end of the table which showed Joel's blood pressure and heart rate.

He put a wound pad over the insertion point and moved up to the top of the table. 'Joel, that's us finished. You did absolutely great. I'm going to send you back up to the ward to rest, then I'll come and speak to you later about what happens next.'

Joel's eyes flickered open for a few seconds and he nodded. Javier gave Joel's hand a tap. 'I'll go and speak to your *papá* now. All I need you to do is rest. And I don't want you to get up for a few hours. So do what the nursing staff tell you.'

Bill, the anaesthetist, gave Javier and Caitlin a nod

and walked alongside the trolley as it was wheeled out to the post-op room.

Javier pulled off his pale green surgical hat and then his gloves and gown, breathing a big sigh of relief.

He gave a few instructions to one of the nurses and Caitlin moved alongside him.

'You did great,' she said, unable to hide the admiration in her voice.

He looked sideways at her as he started washing his hands again. 'Thanks. It was a simple procedure. I just hope it will make the difference it needs to for Joel's life. We're just going to have to wait and see. That's the hardest part of this job.'

No. It wasn't. The hardest part of this job was watching a friend walk away from the job they should keep doing for ever.

Every cell in her body wanted to take him away from here, drag him to the diner—or his hotel—across the road, and sit him down and talk him out of all this.

But she also knew that she couldn't. She'd absolutely no right to do that at all. The horrible fact was that Caitlin McKenzie knew exactly the kind of person that Javier Torres had been for six years of her life. What little she knew of him now told her that in principle he hadn't really changed.

Javier Torres took responsibility seriously. She knew that ultimately he would do what he thought was best. And he'd already told her what that was. He would take over the estate, as his parents had expected him to do, and to relieve the pressure on his sister. To let his sister make a full recovery after her surgery and possibly help her prepare for a different future. He would take the place that was his birthright.

Count Javier. His title would have already changed to the Count of Maravilla. His mother's title at this stage was honorary. If Javier married, then his new wife would be the Countess.

Caitlin had looked up the word *maravilla*. It could mean two things. One was marigold; the other was wonder. The Count of Wonder. She smiled again. Her brain had conjured a hundred different ways that Javier could be a Count of Wonder. Every single one of them would be entirely censored.

'What's wrong?' he said, nudging her with his elbow before drying his hands.

She shook her head. She couldn't have this conversation with him. She stared into those big, sincere brown eyes. This was why she thought so much of him. Because he was entirely *this* man.

She couldn't ask him not to do what he considered his duty. Just like he would never ask her to give up what she loved.

That struck her heart. Did he feel as deeply as she did?

Maybe it just suited her to think so, but in her heart she felt that he did. She knew that he wouldn't ask her to join him at his side to run the estate. He would never ask her to give up the life she'd fought so hard for. And she was glad. Because she wouldn't want to make that decision. She wouldn't want to choose between the two big loves of her life. He would choose for her. He wouldn't put her in that position.

'You okay?' he asked. She'd still been staring at him. Lost in the thoughts in her head.

She slipped her arm into his. 'Once you've finished talking to Joel's *papá*, let's take an hour out. Let's get changed and go and get a coffee and some cake at a café somewhere.'

He gave her a curious stare then his handsome face broke into a smile. 'Absolutely.'

She wanted to get some space. Out of here. Away from everything. Away from their past, and away from their future. Because, for the here and now, Javier Torres was still hers. And, no matter what else was going on around them, she was going to hold onto that for as long as she possibly could.

CHAPTER NINE

IT WAS THE morning of surgery and Caitlin was eerily calm. She'd hoped to spend last night with Javier. But the night had turned into a disaster, with both of them being called to separate theatres in the early hours.

As much as she'd wanted to spend every second with him, they'd reluctantly parted at three a.m. They had to. They both knew that Caitlin needed to sleep if she were to perform Natalia's surgery in the morning.

As it was, she'd pushed the surgery back from eight a.m. to ten a.m., thanks to another colleague who was always happy to take an earlier slot. It meant in theory she should have had enough rest, but her sleep had been restless and she'd tossed and turned.

It actually wasn't the thought of the surgery that had her so concerned. She was confident in the procedures and her techniques. It was the 'what came next' that made her stomach churn over and over.

She did all her usual rituals. Her lucky surgical hat. Her favourite surgical scrubs. A pair of coloured flat theatre shoes.

She had a coffee and ate a slice of toast.

She greeted all her theatre staff the way she normally

did, then spent ten minutes rechecking all test results, plus the bloods from Natalia that had been taken that morning.

She was joined by the surgical staff who would be assisting—clearly Javier was not allowed in the theatre—then she went to meet Natalia in the pre-op room. The anaesthetist, Andreas, was already with her and chatting easily. 'Morning, Natalia, apologies about the late start.'

'It's fine; Javier explained. He slept in the chair in my room last night.'

Of course he had. She wouldn't have expected any different.

'Would you like me to go over things with you again this morning?'

Natalia shook her head. 'No, thanks. I just want to get this over with. I want to wake up later today, with you standing next to me saying everything went fine, and knowing that my brother will finally breathe again.'

Caitlin reached over and took Natalia's hand. 'We will talk later, and let's go with your prediction. Because that's what I want too.'

Natalia squeezed her hand and Caitlin could see the tears in her eyes. 'Thank you,' she whispered, her voice breaking. 'And if anything…'

Caitlin shook her own head and put a finger to her lips. 'Don't. I have a rule that none of my patients are allowed to talk like that.'

Natalia gave a weak smile. 'Well, I've always been a rule-breaker. Promise to look after my brother.'

It was like a vice gripping Caitlin's heart and squeezing tight. She couldn't even let her thoughts move into that space at all. There was no room for thoughts like those.

She pasted a smile on her face. 'Natalia, I'll see you later today. Just like we planned.' She gave her a smile before walking back through to the theatre and starting to scrub.

She concentrated on her hands, the most important part of her body right now. Staff spoke to her as they moved around her. She was conscious of the trolley being wheeled in and Natalia being moved over to the operating table. As she finished scrubbing and pulled on her gloves, one of the nurses came up and tied her mask into place for her.

She waited until Andreas gave her the nod that he and the patient were ready for her before she nodded to her team to approach the table. For the procedure today, Caitlin would have to do the most traditional of incisions. Natalia would also need to go on cardiopulmonary bypass to stop her heart beating and allow the replacement of the valves to be carried out. There were risks for every part of the procedure and Caitlin was focused. This was more than her A game.

There was a viewing gallery above this theatre. She wondered if any other doctors would be watching today. The gallery had floor-to-ceiling windows, and screens so that the meticulous detail of whatever operation was being performed could be captured by the cameras in the theatre. It was a wonderful way for other surgeons to learn. Numbers in the actual theatre had to be kept to a minimum and this way the learning was shared with everyone.

But Caitlin would not raise her head. She would not

look. She would tell herself that Javier was not there watching her. She didn't need that extra pressure and her whole focus had to be on Natalia. She sucked in a deep breath and steadied her nerves.

Her colleague next to her started the procedures for bypass. They were a meticulous practitioner and Caitlin was lucky to work alongside them. When things were ready for her part, she swabbed her area for incision and ensured that Natalia was draped appropriately. She made the large chest incision, spreading the ribcage, allowing the heart to be exposed, then inserted the cannula into the right atrium to remove blood, and into the ascending aorta to return the blood to Natalia's system.

As soon as the cardiopulmonary bypass started, a theatre auxiliary started the clock.

When things were stable, Caitlin began her part of the procedure, removing and replacing the two damaged heart valves. Both were worse than she'd feared and she absolutely knew that they'd made the right decision bringing Natalia in for surgery.

Time ticked past slowly. At one point a staff member brought her something to drink through a straw. She took a few minutes to sit down on a stool as the anaesthetist changed some of the drugs he was administering and wanted to monitor things closely.

Both of her surgical assistants were clearly nervous. They knew that this was Javier's sister and both were on the cardiothoracic training programme in Spain. It was inevitable that they might meet him at some stage. She'd already been told good-humouredly by another staff member that one had been heard being sick in the changing rooms.

The sense of humour of theatre staff was unique, to say the least, and Caitlin had only enquired if the staff member was fit enough to be on duty. Both were doing well and she would give them good write-ups after their debriefing later today.

She arched her back. The temperature in the theatre was carefully controlled—particularly during a bypass procedure. It was always slightly cool, and Caitlin could feel it through the thin theatre gown on her arms, which she was pretty sure were covered in goosebumps.

As she put the final stitch in place, every muscle and bone in her body ached. She wanted to cry. She wanted to cry with relief that the surgery had gone well. She wanted to cry for Javier that he would now be able to shake off the dark cloud hanging over his head.

She wanted to cry for herself because she knew what came next. But Caitlin was professional to the core. Always had been, and always would be.

She lifted her head to address the staff. 'And…we're done. Thank you everyone; your hard work and attention to detail is much appreciated.'

Andreas moved around. The immediate recovery from anaesthetic was his domain.

There was a noise above her, and Caitlin looked up. She'd refused to lift her head during the surgery, wondering if Javier would be in the viewing gallery. He was leaning against the glass, looking down at her with an expression she'd never seen before. Even from here she could see a tear rolling down one cheek.

He pressed both hands into a prayer position and mouthed the word *gracias* to her.

She knew he wouldn't have come into the viewing

gallery until surgery was underway, to preserve his sister's dignity. She knew he would have turned his head away as the final stitches to her chest wall were being inserted.

She gave him a nod and walked over to the waste bin to strip off her theatre garb. Once she'd washed up, she went through to post-op where Andreas and a range of other staff were overseeing the care. Natalia's vitals were steady.

She gave a few last-minute instructions and let the staff know she had her page if they needed her, before heading out of the door.

Javier was in the corridor outside the exit from Theatre. Caitlin thought for around ten seconds before opening the door to Recovery and letting him through.

The gratitude in his eyes was more than she required. The staff were familiar with him now, and moved aside to let him look at his sister, hold her hand, stroke her hair and kiss her forehead.

Caitlin stayed for the next six hours, knowing they were vital, wanting to be on hand if Natalia threw off newly formed clots, or started bleeding from any of her wound sites. The blood's ability to clot could be affected in many ways due to the surgery type, the by-pass or the anaesthesia, and these first few hours were crucial. Javier sat patiently on the other side of Natalia's bed, barely speaking. He didn't need to. His eyes were flitting between every syringe driver, every pump and the constant changes on the cardiac monitor, showing heart rhythm, blood pressure and oxygen saturation.

When she was eventually satisfied the most important hours had passed, she finally stood up and stretched out her back.

When he followed her back outside his relief was palpable. 'Thank you,' he said.

She couldn't help the wave of sadness washing over her. The surgery was done. Javier would be leaving.

She held out her hand to him, her voice cracking. 'Time to say goodbye,' she whispered as he took her hand in his.

It was ridiculous. He knew it was. But it felt as though the weight of a thousand elephants sitting on his chest was finally gone.

They walked through the hospital corridors, saying hello to a few colleagues as they passed. More than a few glanced at their clasped hands. He could see the way people were looking at Caitlin with renewed interest. He guessed she usually didn't give them much to gossip about. They'd been mainly on nights together, so it was likely their closeness had been missed by some. But now, walking down the corridors hand in hand, it was like a huge flag waving. Caitlin didn't seem the slightest bit worried.

His mind naturally went back to how different she'd been twelve years ago after they'd spent the night together. Then, she'd seemed unsure and full of regret, brushing off their night together as if it had meant nothing. Today, she seemed sure about what she was doing.

They reached his hotel room quickly. And while Javier might have wanted to strip his clothes off in seconds, this was goodbye and he wanted to take things slowly.

He cupped Caitlin's face in his hands and whispered,

'I'm never going to be sorry about this. I'm going to take the best memories of us with me. You're always going to have a piece of my heart, Cait.'

She blinked, her eyes filling with tears, and pulled him close to her so the full length of their bodies was touching. She held him there, letting them both feel the heat of each other through their thin scrubs. He would remember this too. Remember the way the curves of her body fitted against his. Like perfect pieces of a jigsaw puzzle.

They moved over to the bed and made love for a final time. His emotions were wrought.

As they lay in bed with the bright sun streaming through the chinks in the curtains, he ran one finger along the curve of her hip.

He wanted to make a million suggestions. That she should visit him. Holiday at the estate. Meet up every few months or so. But what would that do to Caitlin?

Whilst it might suit Javier, ultimately it wouldn't let Caitlin live the life she should. It would always come down to the question of her not being able to live full-time with him on the estate, and their life being a transient one.

It wouldn't help either of them. He knew this should be it. Their final goodbye. Yes, they could be friends. But from a distance. This woman had more of his heart than she really knew. And it wouldn't do any good to tell her that. She had to be free to move on and meet someone else. Someone who could be by her side as her career flourished.

For all he knew, she might intend to eventually go back to Scotland. He didn't doubt that other hospitals in other countries would approach her and try to poach her from her current post. Cardiothoracic surgery was such a specialist area. He was absolutely sure that his own hospital in Madrid would make her an offer once he handed in his notice.

'I will miss you,' he said softly. 'And I will always treasure our time together.'

Her auburn hair was spread out across the white sheets and he picked up a tress and wound it around his finger. 'Every little part of it.'

Caitlin closed her eyes for a second, then moved and kissed him on the forehead. 'I have to move. I have to get back. I have a very important patient to review.'

He nodded. He'd known this. And he was absolutely determined to make sure that this goodbye wasn't like the last.

He swung his legs around, ignoring the wrench in his stomach at breaking away from her warm skin. He walked into the bathroom and flicked on the shower. He could hear Caitlin moving around too. A few seconds later there was the sound of the shower in the other room.

They had to keep everything in check. It was no good being overemotional or making promises they would both eventually break.

This time it really was goodbye.

Caitlin blasted her hair with the dryer in the room to take the dampness out of it, then twisted it in a knot at the back of her neck and pulled on her scrubs.

She was finding it hard to keep things together. A few seconds ago she'd wanted to hand in her notice and move to the country. A minute before that she'd been trying to work out how she could commute to the estate.

It was hopeless. And they both knew it. But saying goodbye was harder than she'd ever imagined. Her heart was truly broken.

It had to be this way, but it didn't make things any easier.

Her phone buzzed and she picked it up, reading the text and swiping it away. Her eyes went automatically to her feed and she flicked through a few headlines. None meant much to her. She didn't really watch the news. But a photo caught her eye and she stopped dead.

Javier. A photo of Javier was in the news. Along with the name of her hospital.

There was even a slightly blurred picture, clearly taken in one of the hospital departments. It was Javier, in pale green scrubs. He was working, talking to another person who must have been cropped out of the picture.

But it was the Spanish words that really captured her attention. They were asking questions about why the Conde of Maravilla was at St Aelina's when he had his own post in Madrid. There was also another connecting story and a whole host of speculation.

Caitlin's mouth was instantly dry. There was another photo, of a woman with blonde hair, coiled perfectly, and dressed in a green designer dress. Elisabeth—the German Duchess, his long-standing fiancée, who was apparently broken-hearted over Javier's actions. Her heart stopped. How many years did the paper claim he'd been engaged? Twelve. Twelve?

No. That couldn't be right. She flicked again, this time finding a search engine and putting in Javier and

Elisabeth's names. Dozens of pictures appeared. In all of them they were side by side and looking entirely the part as two members of the aristocracy.

It still irked that Elisabeth was a Duchess, even though it was irrelevant. Javier had spoken about Elisabeth in the past tense. But this article didn't. It maintained that Javier and Elisabeth were still together. Her blood ran cold.

Had she just slept with some other woman's fiancé? It referred to a very long engagement. Had he also been engaged to Elisabeth the last time they'd slept together? Had he even been engaged to her when they were graduating from medical school?

Fury started somewhere around her toes and quickly bubbled up through her chest. This just couldn't be happening.

She strode back through to the bedroom, where Javier was standing with his scrub trousers on, rubbing his damp hair with a towel.

'What is this?' she asked, thrusting the phone towards him.

He was clearly stunned. 'What?' His brow creased in confusion and he reached out to take her phone.

She watched his eyes scanning the screen, his head shaking slowly. 'No,' he murmured. 'No, this isn't true.'

His eyes met hers. 'Tell me you don't believe a word of this.'

'What words?' she snapped. 'That you're still engaged? That she's broken-hearted. That you've been with her for years. Which words am I not to believe?'

He looked stung. 'Elisabeth and I are not together. And she's not broken-hearted,' he insisted. 'She's married to someone else now. And she's very happy—and I'm very happy for her.'

'How on earth can I believe that when the papers are printing things like this? They even have a photo of you somewhere in St Aelina's. What about the staff there— what about the patients and their privacy? All because the press want to follow you. And how long were you actually engaged for, Javier? Twelve years? That's what they say. Were you engaged the first time we slept together, or were you only engaged this time around?'

She couldn't think straight. The fury was consuming her.

'Stop it,' he snapped. 'I wasn't engaged to Elisabeth either time we slept together. I told you about her. I told you things didn't work out between us—even though I tried. She never loved me, and I never loved her. That's why we're not together any more. She's no more broken-hearted than I was. This is all nonsense!'

'How can I trust a single word you say, when the papers print these kinds of things about you?'

Javier was stunned. He wasn't even sure how to start this conversation. It all seemed so ridiculous to him. Of course Elisabeth's marriage had been a secret. The press had never got hold of that story, and he'd kept his promise to Elisabeth to allow her to have some privacy in her new life. But he could understand why Caitlin would find this hard to believe.

He hadn't known Elisabeth very well twelve years ago. Their parents had been friends, in the way that titled people from fellow countries are. The press seemed to have conveniently forgotten that.

But, more importantly, didn't Caitlin appreciate how much she meant to him? Surely he'd spent the last few weeks showing her how much this time had meant to him. How he wished they could have a different future.

Had he imagined their connection? Why on earth would Caitlin believe something printed in some local rag rather than what he told her?

Javier held up his hands and took a long, deep breath. 'Trust? You want to talk about trust? Yes, let's do that, Caitlin.'

'What's that supposed to mean?'

'You've never really confided in me. You've never really trusted me. Do you trust anyone?'

He watched as Caitlin visibly drew back. He knew he should stop. But he couldn't stop himself. This all seemed such a mess. He hated the press. Hated that he'd had to put on a face for them. To live up to his parents' expectations. Now, they were interfering with the final day he would have with Caitlin. He had one more surgery to do, and then he could leave. But he'd wanted them to part under the best circumstances.

'What kind of thing is that to say?' she snapped.

He should stop. But he couldn't. He was too impassioned about this. It was as if all his frustrations were bubbling up inside him. Maybe it was because he knew they couldn't be together. There wasn't a way to work this out. They both knew that.

Had they been hoping for an unrealistic future—hoping they could spend one last night together and walk away with no regrets? Maybe this was always going to happen.

'It's the truth,' he said with a sigh. 'I get it. You never really told me how tough things were for you growing up. I was right there, Caitlin. I wanted to help; I wanted to listen. I understand you find it tough trusting people. But you should trust me; I'm telling you the truth.'

She shook her head. 'How can I trust you? Did it slip your mind that Elisabeth had got married? No one else seems to know about it.'

'What does that have to do with anything?'

'It's just one of the truths you didn't share with me.'

He was getting nowhere. She was slipping away from him. And maybe this was for the best. Maybe they were meant to leave things like this. Maybe arguing made it easier to walk away.

He took a breath. 'You don't trust me. You know me, Caitlin. You know me better than anyone else, and yet you still can't believe what I tell you. If you don't trust me, what do we even have?' His thoughts were turning in circles. It was probably best that this was over. It would do no good for him to go back home and start fretting about Caitlin. It would be hard enough to walk away from his career and the job he loved. The truth was he was probably better off alone. He already knew he wouldn't get over Caitlin and at least this way he could walk away and try his best to concentrate on his new life.

'Caitlin, stop. There's no point fighting here. We know this can't work.' He put his hand on his heart. 'I want to be with you. I'm not interested in anyone else. But we both know I have to change my life, and there isn't a way to make this work. I want us to be friends.

I wish we could spend the rest of our lives the way we have spent the last two weeks.' He shook his head. 'But I just don't know how to make this work. And if you don't trust me, why should we even try?'

Caitlin's face was a picture of fury. It was so unlike her. 'How can I trust you when you can't tell me the truth? You deliberately kept the secrets about Elisabeth's marrying someone else from the whole world. Why didn't you announce your engagement was over? Did you want people to think you were cheating on her with me? How shallow does that make me look? Did you think about how that might ruin my reputation? Or did that never even figure in your thoughts? Did I just not figure in your thoughts? Because, let's face it, I'm never going to fit into your world. Elisabeth would. She's a duchess. But me? Is that why you let everyone think you were still engaged? Was it easier that way? Are you embarrassed by me? Don't you think I'm good enough for you? Is that what all this is really about? You probably have another member of the aristocracy out there, ready to fill the place as your new Countess. Someone who will give up their own life and hopes and dreams, just park it all, to go and spend their time at your side, looking after the estate. That's what you want, isn't it?'

He didn't recognise the woman in front of him. It was clear that, right now, it didn't matter what Javier said, Caitlin wouldn't be listening. He wanted to deny all that she'd just accused him of. He hated that she even had those thoughts. But everything just seemed too far gone.

Before he had a chance to say another word she turned on her heel and headed to the door. 'Enough,' she called over her shoulder. 'I'm going to check on your sister. Once I'm happy, she can go home. I'll send you any instructions by email. We don't need to talk again. Let's face it, we managed twelve years without talking, I'm sure we can manage another twelve!'

There were angry tears spilling down her face. He wanted to reach out and grab her. Tell her to take a breath, to think about this, to give them some time, to give them a chance to try and come out of all this as friends.

But Javier wouldn't do that. It would only inflame the situation and make things worse. And that was the last thing he needed to do right now.

He watched her walk away with a sick feeling in his stomach. He put his hands on the desk in his room and took a few breaths. He wished he didn't need to go back into the hospital but he had one last surgery.

He steadied his breathing. After a few moments, he reached for his scrub top and pulled it over his head. He winced as he caught the aroma of Caitlin's perfume. It brought with it a whole host of memories he couldn't possibly deal with.

He stared at the bed. It too would likely smell of her skin, her shampoo, her perfume. There was no way he could sleep in those sheets tonight.

He picked up his room key and walked quickly out of the room. One more surgery, a check on his sister and then he would be gone.

He could make arrangements for his sister's care to

be transferred closer to home. That way he wouldn't have to deal with Caitlin again.

And, painful as it was, he would have to get on with his life.

CHAPTER TEN

CAITLIN COULDN'T THINK STRAIGHT. She just knew she had to get away from Javier. Being in his presence hurt. He'd told her in part about Elisabeth, but not all about her. Not the parts that seemed important to Caitlin.

Tears flooded down her face as she strode through the hospital corridors, ignoring elevators and taking the steps to the fourth floor two at a time. She was hardly even breathless when she reached her own department. Being a runner meant that it took a lot to get her out of breath.

One of her nursing staff caught the expression on her face and put out her hand gently to halt her stride down the corridor. 'Caitlin,' she said quietly, 'what's wrong?'

She couldn't answer that question. She just shook her head.

She continued towards Natalia's room. No one had paged her so she had to assume that everything was fine.

When she arrived, Natalia was sitting up in bed, her colour good and the readings on her monitor exactly where Caitlin would want them to be.

It didn't matter how angry she was with Javier. Her patients were always her priority.

'How do you feel?'

Natalia raised her hand to her chest wall. 'Apart from the fact you prised me open, surprisingly good.' She shifted her shoulders. 'I'm sore, obviously. But sore in a different way from before. The tightness in my chest has changed. The kind of underlying heaviness isn't there now.'

Caitlin nodded, understanding. 'I'm glad—all your signs are good. From my perspective the procedure went very well. All being well, I expect you to make an excellent recovery.'

Natalia gave a huge sigh of relief. 'You don't know how happy that makes me. I was so worried before the surgery—you know, just silly stuff. But I know Javier was worried too. It's such a relief to have it all over with. I can't wait to get back to work.'

Caitlin froze. She wasn't quite sure what to say. 'Are you going back to the vineyard?'

'Of course.' Natalia's brow furrowed. 'Why would you ask that?'

Caitlin took a deep breath. 'Because I understood that Javier was going back to take over.'

Natalia's frown deepened. Then a look of exasperation filled her face. 'This is my mother, isn't it? She and Javier think I'm some fragile girl who needs protecting. But the estate is my job, my dream. Javier doesn't know a single thing about running the estate, or about looking after a vineyard. He would be absolutely crazy to give up his job.' She paused and then looked at Caitlin again. 'And to give up you.'

She must have read the shocked expression on Caitlin's face because she continued. 'I might just have had heart surgery, but I couldn't help but notice everything else that's been going on around me. I've never seen Javier so happy. I always wondered how long it would take you two to finally get together, and now it's happened it has to continue. Don't think I've missed a single thing.'

Caitlin couldn't quite find the words. She shook her head. 'Javier and I can't have a relationship. He has to go back and be the Count. He says it's his duty.'

Natalia threw up her hands. 'He can be the Count and still be a surgeon. He trained for years to do this job. He can't walk away.' She started to look annoyed. 'I'm perfectly capable of managing the estate, and I can do it much better than he ever could. Where is the sense in all this?'

Caitlin was very still. 'Has Javier not spoken to you about all this?'

Natalia shook her head. 'He'll be protecting me, of course. Sometimes I think my brother just doesn't get it. Surgery is his dream and the estate is mine. I'm not going to give up my dream for him. I just need a few weeks for a full recovery, then I'll be better than before.'

Caitlin could feel a whole host of sensations sweeping over her. 'Have you told Javier this is how you feel about everything?'

Natalia gave Caitlin a sorry smile. 'Javier needs to learn to stop feeling guilty over our father's death. He seems to blame himself—he thinks that he should have predicted it. But he's not a mind-reader or a miracle-worker; he's a person. He's a surgeon—and a very good one—but he can't prevent every death. He thinks that he disappointed our father by not marrying Elisabeth. But you can't marry someone you don't love—' she looked Caitlin in the eye '—can you?'

Caitlin's skin chilled. 'Javier has made headlines this morning,' she said numbly.

'Really?' Natalia reached for her phone and swiped it open; within a minute she was shaking her head scornfully. 'Well, the only thing that's truthful in this is that he's here at St Aelina's. Everything else is ridiculous.'

'All of it?'

'Of course.' The furrow in Natalia's brow returned. 'Don't tell me you believed any of this?'

But she had. She'd been consumed with rage and had only thought about herself. She'd had no idea that Javier had carried guilt over his father's death. Guilt that had likely played into his decision to go back home and take over.

Natalia spoke quietly. 'Elisabeth got married in secret a few months ago. Her husband has some health issues. She didn't want the press following them everywhere and snooping into every part of their lives. She wanted some privacy, some time to themselves.' Natalia swept a strand of hair from her face. 'I know that she planned to reveal her marriage in a few months' time.' She shook her head. 'This is just bad timing. Her husband is also having surgery this week. He, like me, will hopefully make a full recovery. Then they can release a statement and a photo of their wedding.'

Caitlin's mouth was horribly dry. If Natalia knew all this, then Javier did too. If only she'd asked more questions. If only she'd dug deeper, she might have discovered all this and had the chance to talk to him about it.

Elisabeth's husband was having surgery; of course

Javier would have the good grace to stay silent, in order to allow them the privacy they wished for. It was just the kind of person he was—and Caitlin knew that.

He'd told her earlier that she hadn't opened up to him; now she was seeing that he hadn't opened up to her either and she wished she'd worked harder to persuade him.

Pieces were falling into place in her head. She'd been so angry, so worked up, she hadn't really given him a chance to talk.

She glanced at the clock on the wall. Javier had one more surgery. That was where he would be. She had to talk to him.

She was back down the stairs in a flash, not caring who watched her running down the corridor. By the time she reached Theatre she already knew what was happening by the vibe of the people around her. It was professionally quiet. Surgery had started.

She found the theatre manager. 'What time did they go in?' she asked.

The theatre manager looked up from her desk. 'Who?'

'Javier Torres. Theatre Seven.'

The theatre manager turned to her board. 'Four p.m.'

Caitlin's brain raced. The surgery Javier was performing usually took a few hours. It was likely he would not be out until after six p.m.

Just at that moment her pager sounded. She looked down and flinched at the message.

High risk alert. All personnel to Theatre.

The theatre manager's page went off at the same time and she picked up her phone. The conversation she had with the ER took seconds. She slammed the phone down and ran around the desk. Staff were already emerging in response to the page. 'Theatre Four, everyone,' the manager shouted. 'Pregnant woman being resuscitated. They suspect a massive MI.'

There was no shouting, no panic. People moved seamlessly and without any other instruction. Caitlin was in Theatre Four in an instant. She would need to do an emergency angio. The clot blocking this woman's artery had to be removed. Caitlin knew she wouldn't be the first to assist. An obstetric surgeon ran into the theatre beside her, quickly followed by a neonatal nurse pushing a warming crib. Caitlin moved to the sinks, the surgeon right behind her, and both started scrubbing.

The doors burst open behind them. The ER doctor was on the top of the trolley performing cardiac massage. Another member of staff was standing on the runners, bagging the woman to try and keep the flow of oxygen around her body.

The anaesthetist appeared, took one look at the scene and moved into place. 'Report!' he shouted.

Caitlin and the obstetrician turned to don gowns and masks.

Caitlin helped assist in the move from the emergency trolley to the operating table. Once she'd helped pulled the woman over, she connected some electrodes to ensure they could pick up any heart activity and reconnected the electronic BP cuff.

It was all hands on deck. She was prepared to assist in any way in a situation like this. If she had to do the angio while cardiac massage was ongoing, she knew this poor woman's chances would be slim.

The obstetrician listened to the report from the ER doctor as he jumped down from the trolley and one of the theatre technicians took his place, continuing massage.

He exchanged a glance with the anaesthetist. 'We're going to get this baby out. Mum has been down seven minutes already.'

The anaesthetist agreed. The obstetrician turned to Caitlin. 'As soon as I've got the baby out you can start, as I stitch her up.'

'Do you need assistance?' asked the ER doc.

Caitlin looked around. Javier was busy. She had no idea where her other staff were. 'I do,' she said quickly.

'Time,' shouted the nurse in charge.

Everything in Theatre was precise, and this team moved in perfect synchronicity.

'Stop massage!' shouted the obstetrician and they all watched the monitor for a second to see if there would be any heart activity.

There was one blip, and then silence.

'Continue,' instructed the obstetrician and moved into position.

Santiago burst through the doors just as the obstetrician made the first cut. The baby was out in under a minute and into his waiting hands.

Caitlin couldn't bear to watch her friend, and wondered where he'd just come running from. She held her breath, waiting for any sound from the baby.

But Caitlin had a job to do. She'd come here to speak to Javier, full of regrets and wanting a chance to talk. But maybe this was fate.

Who knew where she might have been in the hospital when this page had sounded? She might even have been outside the hospital. Officially, she wasn't on call; her page had sounded because Javier was already in surgery.

She didn't have time to think about anything else. A woman's life was at stake. She moved to put on her gloves before she started her procedure.

The ER doctor was in position next to her, as her screens flickered on. She made a small incision at the groin as the obstetrician started stitching the womb. It would be difficult to see the blockage while the heart, chest and vessels would be moving. But this had to be done. It didn't matter how hard it was.

'Any history?' she asked the ER doc as she prepared to thread the catheter into place.

'Presented with chest pain. Thirty-four years old, para three, gestation thirty-seven weeks. Blood pressure crashed, short episode of ventricular tachycardia before she arrested.'

There was a cry from the newly delivered baby, followed by an audible gasp of relief from many of the staff in the room. Caitlin could feel her own heart thudding in her chest. The baby cried again, more of a whimper this time. But it was alive. She didn't even know if it was a boy or girl yet. But she had to keep her head in the game.

'Medical history?'

'Didn't get it, I'm afraid. We don't have medical notes for her at this hospital. Our medical records team are contacting other maternity units as an emergency.'

Caitlin nodded. She raised her voice. 'I'm going to

have to ask massage to stop in a few seconds.' The red-faced technician in position nodded.

A colleague spoke up. 'I'll take over.'

No one could keep up cardiac massage for long. It was best the role was rotated among other staff. Caitlin couldn't help but wish that Javier was in Theatre with her. He might have some other ideas.

'I need someone to time for me,' Caitlin continued.

'Done,' shouted the theatre manager.

She used her best judgement as to when the catheter would be in the optimum position. She nodded to the ER doc, who had clearly worked on angios before. He moved into position, ready to inject the dye.

Caitlin timed everything in her head. 'And…stop. Time.'

The massage stopped. 'Now,' she said to the ER doc, who injected the dye.

She watched the screen to see the blockage. It was huge. Her hands moved like lightning, threading up the balloon and inflating it to try and relieve the blockage. She was praying she would do everything correctly. She'd never wanted Javier beside her so badly in her entire life. She couldn't let them see how terrified she was.

'Thirty seconds,' came the call.

She held her breath. It seemed as if the blood was thinking about moving again. She really needed to insert a stent. But unblocking the vessel was the biggest priority. Depending on what happened next, she might have to insert a stent later.

There was a quiver…something. All eyes went to the monitor. A few beeps. Caitlin was praying these weren't just ectopic, irregular beats.

Then something else happened. It seemed like an age, but then there were more regular beats.

The obstetrician looked up from his stitching. 'We need to talk anticoagulant,' he said.

Caitlin nodded. This patient would routinely require some kind of anticoagulant to stop formation of another blood clot. But right now, after an emergency section, it was essential that the uterus contracted properly, and this woman would have surgical wounds too. The balance would be tricky.

'I'm going to stop here,' Caitlin announced. 'The blockage is cleared and I can time her stent around other treatment.'

She couldn't help but wonder about some kind of unknown clotting disorder. It seemed far too risky to proceed without more medical details. Right now, St Aelina's had a baby and mother who'd survived a situation that could easily have gone wrong. She wanted time to assess further.

As she withdrew the catheter and applied pressure to the incision site, the theatre manager put a hand on her shoulder. 'Let me just say, Caitlin, I've never been so pleased to see you.'

Caitlin gave a nervous laugh and shook her head. 'I actually can't believe it.'

She looked around the room. All of the staff had performed magnificently, but a few of them looked quite stunned.

'We'll need to do a debrief,' she said in a lower voice.

'Agreed,' said the theatre manager, clearly assessing the room the same way she had.

The anaesthetist moved into position, giving instructions and taking over. Caitlin was relieved. Santiago gave her a nod as he wheeled the crib out, obviously taking the new delivery to NICU.

Caitlin's eyes went to the clock on the wall in Theatre. It was after seven.

Her heart flipped. Javier. She had to get to Javier.

But she had to wait. She couldn't just turn and walk out. She moved over to the anaesthetist. 'Do you still need me?'

He looked at her and gave a brief nod. 'Not right now. But come to Recovery in an hour. I'm going to recheck her bloods and we can confer with the obstetrician over further treatment.'

An hour. She had an hour. She could make that work.

She pulled off her surgical gown and mask and stuffed them into the nearest waste bin.

She walked, telling herself not to run, as she exited the door and headed to Theatre Seven. But it was dark—it had been shut down.

Her heart started to beat faster. She moved quickly to the changing rooms. Empty. There were a few other people, who glanced at her then put their heads down and continued changing.

She moved again, through the theatre complex, along other hospital corridors and heading to the exit. Should she go back to her own floor—might he be with Natalia?

Something told her no.

She was now half running, half walking to the exit. His hotel was straight across the road. The traffic was busy—of course it was. She dodged through the cars and buses and made it to the entrance.

Thankfully, the doorman must have recognised her because he didn't stop the slightly red-faced woman in scrubs.

She moved over to the reception desk. She'd never spoken to the staff here before—she'd never had to. Javier had always taken her straight up to his room.

The woman behind the desk gave her a curious stare. 'I'm here to see Javier Torres,' she said, knowing there was a catch in her voice. The emotion was telling on her now. She'd had a terrible argument with the man she loved, then performed one of her most stressful surgeries. All she needed right now was to see Javier, to have a chance to speak to him.

Even now she was aware that she'd need to go back to Recovery soon to discuss the patient she'd barely had a chance to meet.

The woman behind the desk hadn't moved. She wore an immaculate suit and her hair was swept back in a neat bun. Her red lips were pristine. 'I'm sorry,' she said politely, 'but Señor Torres, the Conde de Maravilla, has already checked out. I believe his flight is leaving shortly.'

Caitlin's heart sank. Barcelona was a sprawling city; the airport was far from here. It would take nearly an hour to get there, and there was no way she would reach him in time. She didn't even need to guess that he wouldn't be flying commercial. It would be a private flight.

He was gone. She'd been too late. She'd missed the chance to speak to him, to tell him how she felt, and how sorry she was about everything.

Her legs started to sag as the day's events caught up with her.

'Miss, are you all right?'

The woman clicked her fingers and the doorman appeared behind her and helped her into a chair. Before she had a chance to say a word, a bottle of cold water was pressed into her hand.

She breathed. Once. Twice. Then pressed the water to her forehead.

'Can I get you anything else?' The woman from the reception desk was kneeling in front her. She had remarkably kind eyes.

Caitlin shook her head. 'No, thank you. It's my own fault. I've just missed the chance to make up with a friend.'

The woman gave her a sympathetic glance. 'Maybe you'll get another chance.'

Caitlin knew she was trying to be kind, and she pushed herself to her feet. 'By then I'll be too late,' she said as she headed to the door, keeping the bottle in her hand. 'My chance will be gone.' She looked down at her feet, knowing she only had herself to blame.

Two chances with Javier. Both of them had been ruined. There was no chance to go back in time in this life. She'd heard enough sad stories as a doctor to know this was true. It was time to get back to the only thing she could actually get right.

Being a surgeon.

CHAPTER ELEVEN

JAVIER WAS HEARTBROKEN. There was no other description of how he felt. The look in Caitlin's eyes when she'd been angry with him would stay in his head for a long time.

They'd both agreed to a short-term thing. Maybe it would be better if he wiped the final twenty-four hours from his head and just kept the rest of the memories.

He'd arrived back at the estate after stopping off at the hospital in Madrid and officially handing in his notice. The board of the hospital were shocked. They'd hoped to keep Javier Torres for the next twenty years— and he would gladly have stayed there.

There had been many offers made. Reduced hours, some remote working. More staff. But for Javier this seemed like the time to rip the sticking plaster off straight away, rather than edge it off slowly.

He couldn't do half a job at his hospital in Madrid and half a job on the family estate. That way mistakes would happen. And that wasn't how Javier functioned. No matter what he was doing, he wanted to be at the top of his game, whether that was being a cardiothoracic surgeon or the Conde de Maravilla.

So he'd arranged to work his notice over the next few months, hand over his patients and take some of his outstanding leave.

That meant he was now back at the family estate, wondering where on earth to start.

As he stood on the balcony, looking over the vineyards, his mother came to join him. She gave him an enthusiastic hug. 'I am so pleased about Natalia. I was so frightened for her surgery.'

Although he'd never felt this low before, he returned his mother's hug with genuine relief. 'I was worried too, even though I trusted her surgeon. I know that I've had a million similar conversations with patients' relatives before, but it's different when the patient is family.'

His mother leaned back, her arms still around him, and gave an understanding nod. She reached out and touched his cheek. 'What's wrong, Javier? You should be happy. Your sister will be well again. But all I see is sadness in your face. I don't see you often enough. Has something happened?'

He didn't really know where to start. He turned away and put his hands on the carved stone wall that made up the ornate balcony overlooking the estate. As he looked, he breathed deeply.

'It's just a lot to take in,' he said softly. 'I love this place, but I've never taken an interest in the business side of the estate before. And now I feel as if I've already let Papá down. I should have paid attention earlier. There will be so much to learn, and the vineyard has always done so well. People love the organic produce from Maravilla. I'm worried that I won't have the knowledge to continue the business the way it should.'

His mother touched his hand, concern filling her face. 'Why on earth do you think you've let your *papá* down?'

Javier dipped his head. 'Because I didn't want to be here. I didn't want to do this. Papá hoped I would marry Elisabeth but...' he breathed out through his nose '... I just couldn't do it. I didn't love her. Not the way she deserved to be loved. Not the way anyone deserves to be loved.'

He lifted his eyes and looked back out over the vineyards. They stretched for kilometres. He could see people tending them even now. The work here never finished. A truck was taking the road to the side of the driveway, heading down to pick up the organic fruit from one of their orchards.

But Javier had forgotten just how astute his mother was. She squeezed his hand. 'How does someone deserve to be loved?'

His answer came with no hesitation. 'Completely. With no secrets. With compromise, and with trust.' He gave a sad smile. 'As equal partners. Even though you will always put that other person first—no matter what they say.'

His mother was watching him carefully, affection in her eyes. 'First of all, your father loved you with his whole heart.' She put her hand on her chest. 'If he were still here, all he would want is for you and Natalia to be happy.' She shook her head. 'Yes, your father was disappointed when you broke off your engagement. He thought you and Elisabeth were perfect for each other. But only you could know that, Javier—not us.'

'But then he took ill and died, and I never got the

chance to talk to him again. I never got the chance to say sorry. I hadn't seen him; I might have been able to pick up what was wrong with him.' His voice broke. 'I might have had a chance to save him. To save Papá—if I hadn't been so proud and foolish.'

'No,' his mother cut in. 'Javier, you could never have saved him. None of us could have saved him. I was here. It was over in seconds. Your father never knew anything about it. He'd had no symptoms. You know what he was like; he used to tell people he was as healthy as an ox. And now—' she looked out over the estate '—I know it was the best way for your father to go. I was shocked at the time. Devastated.' She gave him a warm smile. 'And even though my son is a very special surgeon, I had no idea what an arteriovenous malformation was. I can still barely say it.' She waved her hand towards the lush gardens of the estate. The lawn was manicured, the paths carefully paved. A large three-tier water fountain was just beneath them in a circular bed. Across the lawn, there were various shaped topiary, accompanied by splashes of colour in further circular beds. 'Look at this. Can you imagine how your father would have been if he'd had something like a stroke and couldn't get out in his gardens or vineyards again? He would have been miserable, and unbearable.'

She took a deep breath. 'I lost the love of my life, Javier. But I didn't have the pain of watching him suffer.'

Javier was looking at the lawns too. Deep down he did love this place. He always had. It was home. It was family. And could he see himself growing old here? Yes, he probably could.

'I'll do this, Mamá; I'll make this work. I'll make

sure the business is every bit as successful as when Papá ran it.' He was determined. He couldn't let his family down.

His mother's voice had laughter in it as she put her hand on his arm again. 'Javier, you need to listen. You need to stop shutting the world out and being so single-minded when you feel pushed into a corner.'

She gave him an amused glance. 'Let's go for a walk.'

He was surprised. 'A walk?'

'Yes, I want to show you some things.'

Javier nodded and joined his mother as she led him outside; they walked down the intricately paved paths towards the long driveway, and then down one of the roads which led from it. He knew exactly where this went. They walked for around half a mile. It was a beautiful day. The sun was high in the sky, and the air was warm and dry.

As they neared the vineyards and orchards, many of the staff waved or gave him a nod. They were all hard at work. A few came up to ask after Natalia. Javier and his mother answered all their questions. The vintner, the sales manager and viticulturist were all busy.

They carried on past the entrance to the vineyards and on to the orchards. Javier's mother held out her hand. 'The shift to organic working was already in hand before your father died. Natalia has handled every part of it since. We didn't have too much work to do from the processes already in place, but the technicalities were crucial. Natalia was key to this.'

She turned to Javier with a wide smile on her face. 'This is your sister's dream, and she is flourishing. She is maintaining the traditions, whilst bringing in new ideas. It's the perfect combination.'

'But the stress it puts her under...'

'Should be managed by her physician. From what I understand, Natalia's operation was a success. I spoke to her surgeon this morning.' There was a gleam in his mother's eye.

'You did?'

'She phoned me, with Natalia's permission. She gave me the full rundown on the surgery, and how long the recovery process should take. She was confident that Natalia should be back to full health in a matter of weeks.'

Javier didn't speak, just started to compute things in his head. He gave a slow nod. 'And if she needs assistance in the future?'

'Then, as a family, we will discuss what works best. I've already employed two very capable assistants for the vineyards and orchards.'

His mother looked out across the orchards with pride. She wasn't looking at Javier right now. 'Do you want to tell me about her?'

He swallowed. His mother had always read him better than anyone. 'Tell you about who?'

'The person who made you realise what love is?'

His shoulders sagged. 'You've met her.'

'The brilliant, feisty Scottish fellow medical student who visited a few times in the holidays? The girl who was never scared to ask questions?' Her smile grew as she kept looking at the orchards. 'The girl who turned into a very capable surgeon who has just saved the life of my daughter?'

Javier nodded. 'You knew?'

'Your sister may have dropped a few hints.'

Javier held out his hands. 'But she doesn't want this, Mamá. How on earth can we have any kind of relationship?'

'But you don't want this either,' his mother said plainly.

Javier looked at his past, his present and his future lying in front of him. It stretched for miles. Happy memories, a wonderful childhood, good people who worked hard.

'At least not like this,' she added. 'Not as a business.'

Javier let the tension release from his shoulders. 'You're right,' he admitted. 'But I feel if I say that I am letting you down.'

His mother's voice was kind. 'The only way you let me down is if you don't follow your heart. I lost the love of my life. Don't lose yours. Don't try and fulfil a family obligation that makes you miserable and lose the joy from your life. You have a wonderful set of skills, Javier. I am so proud that my son can save lives on a daily basis. So was your father. We remain immensely proud of you. I want you to be happy. That is the most important thing for me, that *both* my children are happy.'

The relief flooding through his body was like a welcome balm, the words from his mother exactly what he wanted to hear.

'So, it's decided,' she continued. 'Once Natalia gets the all-clear she will officially take over again here. You will be free to pursue your wonderful work, and to marry the woman that you love.'

The expression on his mother's face was triumphant,

and Javier couldn't bear to reveal the part that made his heart heavy. That for him and Caitlin it was probably already too late.

Caitlin was sitting in St Aelina's park. She'd already run around the perimeter twice this morning. Usually running helped deal with any frustrations. But not today. The frustrations were etched into her very soul.

Javier had been right about so many things. She'd let her past impact upon her future. It didn't matter that she had friends here. It didn't matter that she had a job she loved. She'd never felt so empty, or alone.

She leaned back against the park bench and lifted her face to the early morning sun. At some point, this had to feel better.

She'd spent the last few days doing her job automatically. Thankfully, both mum and baby were doing well. The little girl, Rosa, was breathing and feeding well. After being ventilated for a day, mum had her sedation decreased and was breathing on her own and conscious, between bouts of sleeping. She was still very tired and would require further investigations. But she knew her baby was here and was safe. That was the most important thing.

Caitlin should be relieved and proud of what she'd achieved with a few minutes' notice. As a mentor, she would normally have taken copious notes to use the case as a teaching episode for future students. And she likely would. But right now she just couldn't face it.

She was thinking about other things. Like Javier, and the expression on his face when she'd told him she couldn't trust him. The word *wounded* wouldn't come close to how he'd looked, and her gut told her she'd ruined their friendship for ever.

She was telling herself it was for the best. She didn't want to be friends with Javier. She wanted much, much more than that. But it couldn't work between them. And even that thought brought fresh tears to her eyes.

How could it be that you could know who your perfect mate was, but the world conspired against you to stop you from being together? It seemed like some rotten kind of fairy tale.

It didn't help that the newspaper involved had printed a retraction. She didn't doubt that lawyers had been involved somewhere. Or that she suspected a conversation had taken place with Elisabeth. A picture had emerged of a beaming Elisabeth on her wedding day. The accompanying text was clear. The Duchess had married the man of her dreams and was entirely happy. Her husband had recently had a small procedure carried out, and both of them would be available to speak to the press shortly. She had certainly not been broken-hearted over the breakup of her engagement to Javier Torres, but she thought he was a fine surgeon and wished him well for the future.

Caitlin had never felt like such a fool. She wondered if she would end up one of those ancient old spinster ladies who told stories to young people, about her days of yelling at a Spanish Count, wrongly accusing him of being a lying cheat.

They would be right to shake their heads at her and tell her she was a fool.

She sighed and watched as a few mothers with buggies walked past; others were jogging around the perimeter of the park like she had, and someone was sitting under a tree, reading a book with a coffee next to them.

She had work to do. She had patients to see. Natalia would be leaving tomorrow. Her recovery had been excellent. Her last link to Javier would be gone.

But she wasn't tempted to try and delay Natalia's discharge. Caitlin would never do something like that. This was all for the best. Natalia should go home to complete her recovery, get back to normal and resume her life.

She stood up and walked back to the hospital, ready to shower and change in her office. As she strode along the corridor the hospital director came towards her, an electronic tablet in her hand.

'Ah, Ms McKenzie,' she said. 'Quick chat. You still have four weeks leave to take this year.'

Caitlin blinked. Holidays weren't something she thought about much, too busy arranging her next set of surgeries.

'I haven't planned yet when to take them.'

'How about next week?' The director smiled.

'Why next week?'

'Forgive me,' said the director, 'but there needs to be some work done in Theatre Six. It's where you perform most of your surgeries and should only take a few days. I'd like to schedule it as soon as possible, and it would seem fortuitous to have it coincide with your holiday. You've been working very hard; don't think I don't notice. I've got to have my surgeons well rested.'

She said the statement like a question. Caitlin had the distinct impression she was being told to take holiday rather than being asked.

'I suppose I could work that,' she replied. 'There are only a few procedures that would need rescheduling.'

'Perfect.' The director smiled, tapping something into her electronic tablet and walking back down the corridor, clearly off to find her next victim.

Caitlin gave a small smile and walked into her office. A holiday wouldn't be such a disaster. It might give her a change of scene. Just what she needed right now.

As she walked into the office and switched on the shower in the bathroom, she spotted a note on her desk.

She picked it up.

Can Natalia Torres have a quick chat with you?

It had been left by her secretary. Of course she could do that.

She showered and changed and walked back along to the rooms on the fourth floor.

Natalia was sitting by her bedside in yoga pants and a button-down top. She looked relaxed and happy. The only thing that revealed her surgery was the edge of a surgical dressing near the button of her top.

'Hi, Natalia. I heard you wanted to see me. Is everything okay? Are you feeling all right?'

Natalia nodded. 'Great, but I wondered if you could do me a favour, part as a friend and part as my doctor?'

Caitlin was curious. She sat down next to Natalia. 'Of course. What is it?'

Natalia swallowed, fixing her eyes on Caitlin's. 'I wondered if you would accompany me home…and monitor me for a few days.'

'Oh…' The request took Caitlin by surprise; it was the last thing she was expecting.

'Isn't Javier taking you home?'

Natalia shook her head. 'He's had to go back to work in Madrid. He will eventually be back at home and able to monitor me, but he has some responsibilities he has to take care of in Madrid. They'd already been so good to him and gave him a few weeks' leave to be here. And, between you and me, I've always been nervous about flights in the helicopter.'

Caitlin nodded. She understood just how busy cardiothoracic surgeons could be. In a way, by doing extra surgeries at night, he had helped her lower her own waiting list. It was part of the reason she could take a holiday now.

Although the request was unusual, it wasn't out of the question. 'Well…' she smiled '… I've just been given a week's leave myself. So I'm happy to accompany you home and ensure you get settled.' She touched Natalia's hand. She hadn't expected Natalia to be so concerned about her recovery. 'This is all going to go fine, honestly.'

Natalia breathed a sigh of relief and nodded. 'Thank you. I appreciate you doing this for me. And you'll get to see all the changes on the estate too. Wait until you see the orchards. It's not just apples and oranges now. I have lemons, apricots, pears and peaches.'

Her face was glowing. Caitlin could see it as plain as day; Natalia loved the estate and the job she did there.

Although her stomach twisted uncomfortably at the thought that all her memories of the estate were tied up with Javier, she could do this. She could. It would actually be nice to see the beautiful ancestral home again, the well-maintained gardens, and what had been done with the vineyards and orchards. Javier wouldn't be there, so she might also have a chance to see the Condesa again, and offer her condolences since she'd missed the news about Javier's father.

Her stomach started to unknot. She was a grown-up. She could do this. It might even help her move on and put things behind her. Maybe, just maybe, she could write a letter of apology and leave it for Javier somewhere.

Yes, that would be better than an email, text or phone call. She was more than a little worried that he wouldn't answer her at the moment. An old-fashioned handwritten letter seemed like a better way to deal with things.

She stood up and smiled at Natalia. 'When do you plan to leave? I'll need to pack a few things.'

'First thing in the morning?'

Caitlin nodded. 'Perfect. I'll meet you here first thing.'

Caitlin had remembered about helicopter hair and tied it back in a tight knot to keep it from flapping around her face. This time Natalia didn't require a trolley and monitors for transport. She could walk to the helicopter just like Caitlin, ducking their heads low as they climbed in and fastened their belts. One of Natalia's private staff carried their luggage and this time they had a female pilot.

She gave them a broad smile. 'Just waiting for clearance to take off. Our flight time should be around two hours. Give me a nod if there's anything you want to see on the way.'

They settled in for the flight and took off smoothly. Barcelona passed underneath them in a matter of minutes as they made their way down the Spanish coast.

With her ear defenders in place, the noise of the blades was muffled. Caitlin leaned back to enjoy the ride. She'd only ever flown in a helicopter on a transfer with an emergency patient—and at that time she couldn't look out of a window.

Today she got to enjoy how beautiful Spain was from the air, as they passed over miles and miles of countryside, coastline and some towns.

As they approached the estate, Natalia gave her a nudge to switch her transmitter on and started to point out parts of the estate to her. In the twelve years since she'd seen the place there had been multiple changes visible from the air. New roads, new fields and a few smaller new properties.

Natalia beamed as Caitlin noticed them. 'They are for the staff. We don't just have seasonal staff any more. We have full-time staff, so we needed somewhere for them to stay. We also have a large residence with single rooms for harvest time.'

'It looks magnificent,' Caitlin said with a sigh. She was remembering why she'd loved visiting this place so much. Yes, it was a huge ancestral estate that was somewhere she could never live in or buy in a lifetime, but it was also a family home. It didn't matter that it had forty bedrooms, sprawled throughout the various wings of the estate, it still had a feeling of home. Javier, Natalia and their parents might have had staff, but they'd also made food in their own kitchen, served themselves and curled up on a comfortable sofa at night to watch movies together. It had been in Javier's home that Caitlin had got her first true sense of what family was. They'd all clearly loved each other and cared about each other. She'd witnessed their good-natured teasing. Yes, they were of a different class than she was. But she'd never been made to feel different, or less in any way. They had always been welcoming to her.

The helicopter set down gently on a landing area marked away from the main house. Caitlin and Natalia jumped out as a few staff members from the estate came to greet them.

As Caitlin glanced up at the house she'd once found a little imposing, she was struck by how pleased she was to be here. Even from here, she could pick out the room she'd once stayed in, and her eyes ran along the windows, knowing exactly which room had been Javier's too. She smiled. That was where she would leave her letter, and hope they could at least part as friends.

Javier crossed the grounds. The helicopter had landed a few minutes before he'd expected it to. He'd offered to collect Natalia in Barcelona, but for some reason she'd asked if someone else could collect her. He could only imagine that Natalia hadn't wanted him to run into Caitlin again. And he was trying not to think about that. Could it be that Caitlin had told her she didn't want to see him again? He'd hoped the retraction in the newspaper might have caught her eye, but there was every chance that she hadn't seen it.

There were a few people standing outside the helicopter. Natalia walked towards him, with two of their staff carrying her luggage, giving him a cheeky wink and smile as she kissed him on the cheek. She didn't say a word, just kept walking towards the house, leaving one person behind.

Caitlin.

Her auburn hair was pulled back from her face. She was wearing a navy jacket and jeans and a white T-shirt. She'd never looked more beautiful.

For a moment all he could do was stare—just like when they'd been on the roof at St Aelina's. His heart was in his mouth.

Caitlin looked as shocked as he was. He realised that Natalia had tricked them both and planned this. He would thank his sister later.

But Javier knew he had to follow every instinct in his body. He ran towards Caitlin, just like she ran towards him. He'd never been so grateful for a hug in his entire life.

'I'm sorry,' she said breathlessly. 'I'm so sorry for everything I said. I didn't mean it. I came to find you, but you'd already left the hotel and I didn't know what to do.' It seemed as if she was going to continue talking, so Javier silenced her with a kiss.

Caitlin responded just the way he'd hoped. His hand went to the back of her head, quickly releasing the tight bun she had at the nape of her neck and letting her auburn hair escape to frame her face.

'I should never have let you go,' he whispered into her ear. 'You're all that I've ever wanted.'

'We can make this work, somehow,' she said, her green eyes sincere. 'I love you, Javier. The most important thing to me is that you're happy. We can stay here this week and find a way to make this work for us both.'

'You love me?' he asked, his hands cupping her cheeks.

She grinned at him. 'I've always loved you. I've just never been brave enough to tell you. And yes, I trust you. I just hated that I thought I might not be good enough for you—might not be enough for you at all.'

He shook his head as he continued to cradle her face. 'How could I give my heart to another when you already had it? You'll always be good enough for me, Caitlin.'

She couldn't stop smiling at him. His eyes were lost in hers. This was where he was supposed to be. Home would be wherever this woman was. And it seemed as if every part of his life was finally beginning to fit.

He gave her another smile. 'You are a magnificent surgeon. I'm reliably informed that Natalia should make a full recovery, and my mother has hired some extra staff to help her.'

'You've spoken to your mother?'

He nodded and pressed his forehead against hers. 'Yes, I've spoken to my mother. She doesn't want me here. She wants me to be a surgeon. She wants me to live the life I should be living with the person I want to live it with.'

'And that's me?'

He hated it that she still needed that reassurance. 'It has always been and will always be you.'

He could feel Caitlin shake a little in his arms. 'Hey,' he said, running his hands through her hair. 'You are the person who makes me feel like home. Not this place. Not anywhere. I will go wherever you go.'

Caitlin's eyes widened. 'But how can we?'

He held his arms wide. 'Say the word; my family know that I want to be with you. They will love you just as much as I do. We can go anywhere, live anywhere, work anywhere. You choose, Caitlin. I'm all yours.'

'Really?' She blinked back the tears that had formed in her eyes. She wrapped her arms around his neck. 'But Javier, I love your house, I love your family. We can find a way to make this work together. Most of all I love you. If I have you, I have everything.'

He pulled her close again. 'Okay, so how about we recreate our past?'

'Which part?' she asked, her nose wrinkled. It was the cutest she'd ever looked.

He whispered in her ear, 'The night we never forgot.' As he pulled back his eyebrows were raised.

Caitlin grinned at him. 'In that case, I think we have a number of rooms we can choose. Let's try them all.'

So he slipped his hand into hers and led her back towards the house, and recreated that night again and again and again.

EPILOGUE

One year later

'HEY, YOU,' JAVIER SAID, sliding his arms around his wife's waist.

'Hey, you.' She leaned back into him, enjoying the heat from his body. The roof of St Aelina's might be one of their favourite places to escape for private moments, but at times it could be chilly. Barcelona was spread out beneath them, yellow and white lights illuminating various structures within the city. They'd missed the sunset and were left with an inky black sky.

'Did you have a stressful afternoon?' he asked.

She shook her head. 'No, it was fine. Both procedures went well, and I've assessed all my patients for Theatre tomorrow.' She turned her face sideways to catch sight of her husband. 'How about you?'

'Helped Santiago with a cardiac case and saw fifteen patients at a clinic. At least four of them need surgery.'

She reached a hand up to her shoulder and he instantly put his there to join hers. 'Any we can do together?' she asked with a smile. It was her favourite part of her role these days, the surgeries she could do with her husband.

They'd reached a compromise—one which suited them both. They worked two days a week in Madrid and two days a week at St Aelina's in Barcelona, in a unique job-sharing role. It meant that both hospitals had eight sessions with cardiothoracic surgeons, with the only unusual part that they worked the same days together at each hospital.

The conscious decision to have one additional extra day off a week meant that they could choose to visit the family home, Maravilla, or they could choose to spend the day in bed.

'There are always surgeries we can do together,' Javier murmured in her ear, nuzzling her neck. 'I'm starting to like this,' he joked. 'Easier access to your neck.'

Caitlin had decided to cut her long hair to a more manageable length the day before. She was still getting used to the length, just hitting her shoulders, and had blinked a few times today as she'd passed a reflective surface and wondered who she was looking at.

'Just trying to save some time,' she said breezily. 'Who wants to spend so long drying their hair when we can find other things to do?'

He kissed the skin at the base of her neck and she started to giggle. 'Stop it, you'll put me off the gorgeous view of our city, and my memories of that night a year ago.'

Javier lifted his head. 'You thought I'd forget, didn't you?'

'Never,' she said, laughing.

'How could I forget the first night I saw you again after twelve years? Talk about making a guy wait.'

She turned in his arms so she was facing him instead of staring at the city. 'Some people might consider me worth the wait.'

'Your husband might agree with you.'

She put her hands around his neck, the large diamond glinting next to her plain gold band. As soon as she came out of surgery she always put her rings back on. She liked the feel of them on her hand. Loved the security and message that washed over her every time she slid them back onto her finger. Javier had proposed a few weeks after their reunion at his home, with their wedding hastily planned for a few months later in the chapel on the estate. Both of them had wanted to cement their union, with a wedding filled with their friends and colleagues.

'I brought us something to celebrate the moment,' he said.

'You did?'

He reached down and picked up a bottle of Caitlin's favourite organic wine from the vineyard at home, along with two glasses. Neither of them was a fan of champagne.

'How about we toast to the next year? We have holidays to plan. Staff to train. A new flat to buy, and lots to enjoy.'

Caitlin gave him a curious smile. They had agreed the one-bedroom flat she owned in Barcelona was a little small for them and had been viewing properties to find something more suitable.

They had also developed a new plan for those training to be cardiothoracic surgeons, to get them into Theatre earlier, learn all the techniques they needed and give them adequate mentoring and supervision. It was due to be rolled out across Barcelona, Madrid and Seville at the same time. They had been extremely busy.

Javier looked at her. 'Are you sure you're okay? You look tired. Is the travelling between two bases taking its toll?'

She knew how lucky they were. Javier piloted them between the cities in the space of just over a few hours, leaving the helipad on the roof of St Aelina's and landing in an airport a few kilometres southwest of Madrid. She could go from St Aelina's to a ward in the hospital in Madrid in around three hours. If anyone should be tired it should be him. But then again, he didn't have quite the same additional stresses on the body that she had.

He opened the wine, poured a little into each glass and handed one to her.

She held it up, looking at it, and smiled. 'Sorry.'

He frowned. 'What do you mean?'

'I want to celebrate the anniversary of our meeting again, but I'll have to sit this one out.'

He was still frowning. 'How come?'

Her smile grew wider. 'Doctor's orders.'

It took only a few seconds for him to catch on. 'Really?'

'Really.'

He took her glass, setting them both on the ledge overlooking the city, picked her up and swung her around, letting out a loud whoop.

She laughed, hitting his shoulder as he set her back down.

'When did you find out?'

'About an hour ago. You're right; I was tired and couldn't quite work out why. Then I checked the calendar and nipped along to Obstetrics to nab a test.'

He was shaking his head. 'You've spoken to someone?'

She rolled her eyes. 'Oh, I was caught by Martin Hernández. He said as soon as we want a scan, to go on down.'

Martin Hernández was the obstetrician she'd worked with on the pregnant woman. They'd become friends during the debrief of the incident and he'd attended their wedding.

Javier put his hand on his wife's stomach. 'We'll need to rethink some plans. We have a new Count or Countess on the way.'

Caitlin kissed her husband on the lips. 'And I can't wait to meet them.'

* * * * *

THEIR BARCELONA
BABY BOMBSHELL

TRACI DOUGLASS

MILLS & BOON

To my writing sprint group
for all the support and ideas and laughter.
Completing two books in four months is a LOT,
and I wouldn't be here and still sane without you all!

To my wonderful editor, Charlotte,
who always knows exactly what needs fixing
to make my books better and tells me in such a kind,
helpful, supportive way.

To my awesome agent, Jill,
who has talked me down from the ledge
more than once so far and who continues to have my back.

To my new writing "partner" Karley,
a fluffy, furry ball of love and energy
who never fails to make me smile. Love you, puppers!

And to everyone who picks up one of my books.
You are the reason I do what I do, and I feel so lucky
and blessed and grateful every single day to have
the opportunity to create stories you want to read.

Thank you!

PROLOGUE

April

EVENING GLASS-OFF had arrived.

Isabella Rivas dug her toes into the still-warm sand of Playa de Bogatell and stared at the gorgeous sunset, the horizon streaked with vivid oranges and pinks and purples. This was her favorite time of day—when the Barcelona tourists had cleared out and the wind and waves had died down. Water smooth enough to skate on. So quiet and peaceful and...

"Help!" a woman cried from down the beach. "Help! My husband!"

Dropping her surfboard to the sand, Isabella sprinted toward the woman. "*Señora, qué pasa?*"

The woman, white as a ghost and frantic, waved her hands at Isabella, saying in a British accent, "I don't speak Spanish. Please, you must help my husband. He's drowning out there!"

"Got it, ma'am," Isabella said, switching to English as she raced for the water. "I'll get him in. Let the life-guards know!"

She ran into the shallows, then dived into the deeper

water just beyond the sandbar, swimming hard in the direction the woman pointed. Black water surrounded her in the night, the neon red of the bobbing buoy ahead glowing like a beacon in the shadows. As her head surfaced between strokes, she spotted a vague white blob on the surface, and her adrenaline skyrocketed. In her periphery another person swam in the same direction. Too soon for the lifeguards on shore to catch up.

"Sir!" she yelled, treading water as she reached the man. "Sir! Can you hear me?"

No response.

His complexion was gray and lips bluish, and Isabella knew from her years as a paramedic that things were not good. Impossible to know exactly what had caused this, but one thing was clear—the man wasn't breathing.

"What can I do to help?" an accented male voice asked from beside her.

"Help me get him to shore, then he's going to need CPR." Isabella got on one side of the man, supporting his head while the other guy took the man's other side, and together they got the victim to dry land. The lifeguards met them there with a medical kit, and Isabella quickly told them who she was and what she needed while the Good Samaritan who'd joined her in the water began chest compressions. He seemed competent—more than competent—which was handy.

"My name's Isabella Rivas. I'm a licensed paramedic with Ambulancias Lázaro. We found this man unresponsive in the water by the buoy there, and he needed immediate medical attention." She turned to the man doing CPR. "Does he have a pulse? Respirations?"

"No," the man said, his focus on the patient. "Still nonresponsive."

"Do you have a portable defibrillator?" she asked the lifeguards in Catalan, the local dialect. "Call 061 now, please!"

One of the lifeguards pulled the machine out from their medical pack while the other went to comfort the frantic spouse and call emergency services. Isabella grabbed a nearby towel to dry the victim's chest before attaching the sticky defibrillator pads while the man across from her continued his compressions. Their eyes met briefly, his dark and chocolate brown, and she absently registered he was handsome, but now wasn't the time.

Once the pads were in place, she turned to the machine and pushed the button to cue it up. When the light came on and it beeped, she yelled, "Clear!"

The man across from her immediately lifted his hands away and scooted back, as if it was second nature. Isabella pushed the button, sending a jolt of current to the man's stopped heart. His body jerked but then returned to stillness.

"Any cardiac signs yet?" she asked as the other man pressed his fingers to the victim's carotid.

He shook his head. "No."

"Right." She readied the machine again and hit the button. The man's body jerked again, then flopped back onto the sand. His color turned grayer, and Isabella didn't like the look of it. In the distance, sirens wailed. Help was on the way, thank goodness. Whether the man had drowned or had a cardiac arrest, he needed to get to a hospital ASAP or he'd be dead. She cast the machine aside and took over compressions from the man to avoid tiring him out. He moved to the air bag the lifeguard had attached to a mask over the victim's nose and mouth to help him breathe. They got into a rhythm then, her with the compressions and him with the breaths, like they'd been working as a team for years. Nice to have someone she could depend on.

Eventually, the ambulance arrived, and Isabella turned the case over to her colleagues, giving them a rundown of how she'd found the man and what they'd done to assist him up to that point. The victim now had a faint pulse and breathed on his own and responded to calls, though mostly incoherently. Isabella guessed cardiac arrest, because of the still, smooth water. There were still rip currents, but none really to speak of where they'd found the man. For treatment they were taking him to St. Aelina's, the new, state-of-the-art training hospital nearby, so he was in good hands.

As she watched the ambulance pull away and the lifeguards return to their post tower, the mystery man beside her finally introduced himself.

"Carlos Martinez," he said. From his dark good looks, she'd say Spanish, but his accent wasn't local. "Good work on that victim."

"Same to you," she said, shaking his hand, doing her best not to glance down at his, tanned and toned almost-naked torso. "Isabella Rivas. Where are you from?"

His grin grew wider, his teeth white and straight in the gathering darkness. "Havana, Cuba. I just moved to Barcelona recently."

"Well, *benvingut a la meva Ciutat*," she said in Catalan, then chuckled at his slightly confused look. The local dialect wasn't much different from regular Spanish, but considering most people spoke Cubano, a form of the language, in his homeland, it made translation unnecessary, especially since they both had spoken English during the rescue. She laughed then smiled at him. "Welcome to my city."

He nodded, his widening smile doing all sorts of naughty things inside her.

Whoa.

Romance wasn't on her to-do list. She loved a good rom com with a happily-ever-after as much as the next person, but after spending years taking care of everyone else in her family, this time now was just for her.

Even with her off-the-charts attraction to this guy. And it wasn't just his gorgeousness that drew her to him. It was the cool, calm proficiency he'd shown during the rescue. She had a thing for men who knew what they were doing at work and at play, and this guy had *competency* written all over him.

"So, Isabella Rivas," Carlos said as they started walking back to where her surfboard still rested in the sand. "Would you like to get a drink? I know I could sure use one."

Taken aback a bit, she was glad to be bending over to pick up her surfboard so he couldn't see her face. Her cheeks were hot, and her heart slammed against her rib cage like she was a besotted teen instead of an independent thirty-four-year-old woman. She took her time getting the board, tossing her long, damp dark brown braid over her shoulder before straightening. Normally, she'd tell him she wasn't interested and be done with it. But she *was* interested. More than she should be.

One drink. What would it hurt? Besides, she could use a drink to ease her adrenaline buzz from earlier, otherwise she'd never get to sleep tonight, and she had a shift in the morning.

"Fine," she said, turning back to him, the chemistry crackling around them like fireworks. "There's a bar just up the way. Good food, reasonable prices. Want to go there?"

Carlos bowed slightly, giving her a view of the rippling muscles in his broad shoulders and upper back, and her mouth definitely didn't start watering. "Whatever you desire."

What she suddenly desired was to climb him like a tree, but that thought only unsettled her more.

Down, girl. Down.

She wasn't like this. She never flirted or threw herself at guys, but something about Carlos made her melt inside. She swallowed hard past the lump of rising lust in her throat and flashed him a wobbly smile. "Great. This way, then."

Isabella stowed her surfboard in one of the lockers nearby, then joined him again on the boardwalk.

"Do you come to Bogatell Beach often?" he asked. "You obviously like surfing."

"I do." She smiled, looking straight ahead and not at him, for fear she'd do something nuts—like kiss him or something. Seriously. She needed to get over this… whatever this was. Talking about surfing helped. Surfing always calmed her. Her go-to destressor. "I like it because it's quieter. Less tourists. The waves aren't great here usually, but every once in a while you can catch some good ones. And it's close to where I live."

"Interesting," he said, frowning slightly. "Some other locals I met in my uncle's bar talked about a place called Killers for surfing. They said it's kind of a secret."

She chuckled. "Yeah, I've gone there, too, several times, and the name suits it. Good action, but sometimes after work, I just want to relax and get away from people, you know?"

"I do." He grinned. "I hope I'm not intruding tonight."

"Not at all," she said, and surprisingly, she meant it. There was an ease about him that helped calm her. "You said your uncle owns a bar here? Which one?"

"Encanteri," he said. "Ever heard of it?"

"Absolutely. It's one of the hottest nightspots in town." She and some of her friends had been trying to get in there for months, but the lines were terrible. It would likely only get worse with summer on the way and the tourist rushing to the city. "Maybe I've got an in then, with you."

"Maybe you do." He met her gaze and held it a fraction longer than normal, and her pulse stuttered.

Oh, boy.

"Uh…" Isabella said, fumbling her words and her footsteps, getting her flip-flops tangled and nearly tripping. Thankfully, Carlos steadied her with a hand on her arm to keep her from face-planting on the boardwalk. Zings of fresh awareness stormed through her nervous system from their point of contact. "The, um, bar is just over there."

Isabella pointed to a glowing neon sign for El Chirinuito. Nothing fancy, but the food was good and the service excellent. They got an umbrella-covered table out on the deck overlooking the beach and the ocean beyond and placed their orders.

"So," Carlos said, once the server had brought their drinks—cava for her, sangria for him. "You said this beach is close to where you live?" She gave him a look, and he laughed. "Not trying to be a creeper. Honest. Just making chitchat. I want to know more about you, Isabella. You intrigue me."

She was intrigued, too. Way more than she should be. He was just so charming and nice, and low-key. In her job, she needed good radar for deceit and shady characters, and she got no weird vibes at all. Carlos seemed just what he said—a newly arrived expat from Cuba, looking to find his way in Barcelona. She found it completely endearing and disarming. Still, she wasn't an idiot. She wasn't giving some random stranger her address, no matter how hot.

"I live in El Poulenou," she said, taking a sip of her pink sparkling wine. The bubbles tickled her nose. "And you?"

"I'm actually living above my uncle's bar at the moment." Carlos watched her over the rim of his glass. "He's the one who convinced me to move to Spain in the first place. It's a nice flat, some might even say luxurious—at least by city standards."

"Nice." She smiled. "Is your uncle your only family here?"

Carlos's smile faded. He set his glass down on the table, his dark brows knit. "He's my only family period."

"Oh." She gulped more wine, the alcohol swirling nicely in her empty stomach, loosening her inhibitions slightly. "I'm sorry. Didn't mean to touch a sore spot." She sighed and sat back, letting her walls down a bit. "There were times when I wished my family would go away."

He gave a surprised snort. "That doesn't sound good."

She waved dismissively. "Oh, I don't really mean it. It's just hard, because I'm the oldest of six kids and ended up taking care of my younger siblings most of the time after my mom passed away when I was thirteen. My dad got sick shortly thereafter, too."

"Ouch. I'm sorry," he said, repeating her words from earlier. He leaned closer over the table, close enough for her to see the tiny flecks of gold in his brown eyes. Such nice, kind eyes. "Must've been really hard on you, taking on so much so young."

Rather than answer, she just nodded, grateful when their shared order of the bar's famous nachos arrived, smelling amazing. They each dished up a portion and ate.

"Anyway," she continued after devouring a mouthful of cheesy, spicy goodness, "one of the reasons I moved to Barcelona was to get away from my siblings once they were all grown and gone." She laughed. "Ironically, though, my younger brother Diego followed me here. In fact, he works at one of the local hospitals nearby, so I see him all the time now on my ambulance runs."

Carlos chuckled. "Funny how fate works out sometimes, huh?"

"Yeah," she said, looking up, their gazes tangling again. A tiny dot of cheese clung to the corner of his mouth, and Isabella licked her lips, imagining licking it off him instead. A wild, reckless sense of excitement had taken hold of her now, one she hadn't felt in a long time. Too long. From the twinkle in his dark eyes, Carlos felt the same.

It was ridiculous. Silly. And so on.

They had barely spoken a word about anything beyond dinner, but from the casual way his leg kept brushing against hers under the table, they'd be going to bed together. Nothing long-term, nothing more than a one-night stand. Light, fun, no strings attached. Just two lonely strangers enjoying a sudden connection and a moment together. Isabella couldn't wait to get him alone.

Beneath the table, she slipped her foot out of her flip-flop and slowly ran her toes up the inside of his bare ankle, loving the way he shivered beneath her light touch. Oh, yeah. This was happening. Her widening grin matched his own. "Yes. Funny how fate works sometimes."

CHAPTER ONE

June

"BP NINETY OVER sixty-eight. Low, but holding steady. O$_2$ sats normal," Isabella said, holding an oxygen mask to the face of a car accident victim as the ambulance rig rumbled toward Santa Aelina's University Hospital. The young kid, still just a teenager, really, at nineteen, blinked up at her, his face pale beneath his tan, fear making his dark eyes wide and frantic-looking. "It's okay. You're going to be okay, yeah?"

The kid swallowed hard, then winced, his chest contusions and broken ribs from the vehicle rollover obviously making any movement painful. Honestly, he was lucky to be alive, considering the state of the car they'd pulled him out of, but she wouldn't tell him that. Leave it to the police, who'd question him and take a report of the accident after the medical personnel patched the kid up and released him from the ER.

Isabella glanced out the window across from her at the sunny blue evening skies. Too bad the surf wasn't so good right now. She could've used some time in the water after the day she'd had. Nothing particularly bad had happened, but she just didn't feel great. Hadn't felt great for about a week or so now, truthfully. Probably the flu bug that had been going around.

She'd started a night shift, too. Her first in a month and…ugh.

Maybe when she got off work in the morning, if it was still this nice, she'd go for a swim anyway. Early, before all the tourists hit the beach. Not the same kind of high she got from riding the perfect wave, but it would help.

Her EMT colleague drove down the ramp to the ambulance bay at St. Aelina's, then jerked to a stop before the automatic doors. Mario got out and jogged around the back to open the doors, then he and Isabella lowered the patient's gurney down to the ground and wheeled him in through to where one of the ER docs waited for them, along with a couple of nurses and techs.

"*Resum per favor,*" the female doctor said from behind her mask. *Rundown, please.*

"*Si,*" Isabella said, wheeling the gurney down the brightly lit hall toward an open trauma bay along with Mario. She listed off the patient's vitals and the facts of the accident they had so far. Once they reached the trauma bay, she and Mario assisted the nurses to transfer the patient to the hospital bed. From across the bed, her eyes locked with one of the nurses', and they seemed…familiar somehow. Warm brown with flecks of gold and… Her pulse stumbled. Oh, God.

Carlos.

After their one passionate night together, they'd both gone their separate ways. She'd never thought she'd see him again, and yet here he was. Working in the same

ER where she did many runs. Where she'd see her one-night stand on pretty much a daily basis.

Perfect.

Her crap day notched lower into dumpster-fire territory. She already felt rough as hell. This wasn't improving anything. Not at all.

Never mind the traitorous fizz of unwanted excitement bubbling up inside her like uncorked champagne. Or maybe that was nausea. Hard to tell.

She quickly finished transferring the patient to the bed, then helped Mario wheel their empty gurney out to the hallway.

"I need to get a drink," Isabella said. "Meet you back at the ambulance."

"*Si.*" Mario took the gurney and headed out while Isabella made a beeline for the restrooms at the end of the hall, hot bile scalding her throat.

After she'd finished tossing her cookies, she splashed some cold water on her face, then stared at herself in the mirror. Man, she looked as rough as she felt. Dark circles under her eyes, cheeks a bit hollow from being unable to keep much down the past few days, her complexion tinged green. A far cry from the last time she'd seen Carlos on the beach.

That night seemed like a fantasy now. The dinner, the drinks, the conversation. After they'd finished at El Chiringuito, they'd strolled along the beach, laughing and talking and eventually holding hands. Then, under the stars, they'd kissed. The chemistry had been instant and hot as hell. She rarely let people close, rarely let herself be vulnerable and free and wild, but with Carlos, she had. Maybe it was the novelty of it, or the fact that they both knew it was just a one-off, an un-complicated night of sex and fun, that had made her so reckless. Whatever it was, she'd dived in headfirst and reveled in it.

They'd gone back to her flat, since it was closer, and basically fallen on each other the minute they'd gotten through the door. Clothes came off and inhibitions vanished. She'd been unable to get enough of him, touching him, kissing him, tasting him everywhere. He'd done the same to her, bringing her to orgasm over and over with his lips and tongue and fingers before finally entering her. It had been a long time. Too long, and he'd filled her completely. And when he'd moved... Well, it felt like her entire universe had shifted. They'd both been desperate for each other, straining, reaching and finally capturing that brief, bright pinnacle of pleasure, exploding into a thousand shards of brilliant light before floating softly down into the shadows and falling asleep wrapped in each other's arms.

When Isabella had woken up the next day, Carlos was gone. He'd left behind a rose on her pillow and a scribbled note, saying "thanks for the memory."

She'd kept his stupid note, for some reason, stuffed in her nightstand drawer, thinking it would be her one memento of that night. But now...

Gripping the edge of the vanity counter tight, Isabella rode out another wave of nausea, thankfully not dry heaving this time, then finally took a deep breath. In and out. In and out. She hated being sick to her stomach worse than anything in the world, and luckily she hardly ever became ill. Well, until recently, anyway.

Once she felt marginally better, she washed her

hands, then headed out. She could still use the drink she'd mentioned to Mario, so instead of heading toward the ambulance bay, she took the elevator down to the basement cafeteria instead. Time for a break about now anyway, and maybe tea and crackers would soothe her stomach.

"Blood pressure's up to one two six over eighty-two," Carlos said, checking the kid again in the trauma bay.

"All right," Dr. Gonçalo said in Spanish. "I'm going to take a look at your chest now, *si*?"

The kid groaned in pain but nodded.

The doctor did a quick but thorough exam, talking throughout. "Large, deep contusions over the pectoral area and sternum, consistent with a blunt impact from the steering wheel. Fifth and sixth ribs on the left fractured. Breath sounds are normal, but I want to make sure there's no bruising or injuries to the lungs from the accident. Please order an X-ray and CT."

Carlos nodded and typed the orders into his tablet as Dr. Gonçalo gave them, doing his best to stay in the moment and not dwell on his shock at seeing Isabella again. He'd known she was a paramedic, so the chance existed, he supposed, with him being an ER nurse. But Barcelona was a large city, and he'd figured the chances of them running into each other again were slim.

From the startled look in her eyes and the way she'd raced out of here like her butt was on fire after transferring the patient, she'd felt much the same way.

Carlos finished typing, then waited until Dr. Gonçalo finished her exam before following her out of the trauma bay. "I'll get right on those orders, Doc. And I'll get ahold of his next of kin."

"Thanks," Dr. Gonçalo said before rushing off to her next case.

The elevators dinged, and Carlos looked up in time to see Isabella get on, heading down to the basement, according to the green arrow above the doors.

Huh. His first instinct said go after her. But no. He had work to do. Besides, he wasn't here to get a girlfriend. He was here to work. Work and find out more about his father's family. The father who hadn't even cared enough about him to stick around after he'd gotten Carlos's mom pregnant.

Not that he was bitter or anything. Hell, he'd moved beyond bitter at ten years old.

Now, at thirty-four, he was more curious than anything.

Curious why a man would sire a child, with a woman he supposedly cared about deeply, then disappear without a trace. Granted, his father hadn't known about him at the time, but his mother and her parents had written to him repeatedly to tell him. Those letters had never been returned, so where did they go? The mystery persisted. What wasn't a mystery, however, was how Carlos had been treated, growing up a bastard in Cuba. Always on the lookout, always careful, knowing some kids would beat him up for his lineage, or lack thereof. Cuba might be a Communist country, but many people were old-school religious, and unwed girls and their babies were not exactly celebrated on their island. So, Carlos had developed a thick skin, learned to keep his emotions inside, to never show vulnerability to those who wanted to hurt him.

His old habit allowed him to keep things low-key now. Even in the high-pressure situations of the ER, Carlos never lost his cool. Getting angry or defensive only made things worse, in his opinion, so he strived to keep an even keel as much as possible.

But as he set up the CT scan and X-rays, his stubborn mind kept going back over his night with Isabella. The way she'd felt in his arms, the way she'd tasted of wine and wonderful abandon when he'd kissed her. The way she'd cried out his name like a prayer and a benediction all rolled into one when she'd come apart beneath him, around him…

"Here for the rib fractures," a tech said, stopping at the nurses' station, jarring Carlos out of his erotic thoughts.

He cleared his throat and frowned at his computer screen. "Trauma bay two."

Enough. Time to stop daydreaming about his one-night stand and start focusing on the patient under his care. He waited until the radiology techs wheeled the kid out of the ER and toward the elevators and the CT scanner, then made calls to the kid's family to let them know he was in the ER and okay. They were upset but thankful and said they'd be there shortly.

Done, he checked his watch, then stared down the hall toward the elevators. Time for his break, and it would be another hour or so before the CT and X-rays were done, given the busy radiology schedule. So, yeah. He'd grab a snack. And if he happened to run into Isabella, so be it. They should say something to each other, anyway, since they'd be working together. No sense making things more awkward than they already were, right? It would be fine. Great. Okay.

But as he boarded the elevator, his stomach fell for more reasons than just the ride.

That night had been special. A fantasy of sorts.

Am I ready to let the fantasy go and return to reality?

The night at the bar on the beach felt like a moment out of time. It had been so easy with her—talking, laughing. Easy to feel comfortable with her. For an expat from Cuba, still trying to get his bearings in a new city and a new country, it had been like balm to his soul. Made him feel less alone here, if only for a little while.

Not that he didn't have support. His uncle had been more than welcoming to him, even going so far as to rent the flat above his popular bar, Encanteri, to Carlos at a reduced rate. Cuba had much more affordable housing, so seeing a sixty-square-meter flat go for luxury prices had been a bit of a shock. His uncle Hugo had looked out for him, though. Said he felt responsible for Carlos after inviting him here to live, so, yeah. Plus, the place was clean and safe and fully furnished, so a guy couldn't argue, right?

He'd had many people over the years ask him why he chose nursing instead of continuing his education and becoming a doctor. He'd had the grades for it. But he hadn't wanted to spend more years in school. He'd wanted to get out and get to working with patients right away. And so he'd chosen nursing, because everyone who'd spent any time in a medical setting knew that the nurses had the real power, anyway. Doctors gave the orders, but the nurses were the ones on the front lines carrying them out.

The elevator dinged. The doors swished open and he stepped off, then held them for an elderly couple to board before heading down the hall for the cafeteria, the smells of baking cheese and fried food beckoning him. Unfortunately, though, he'd lost his appetite. Tension knotted his stomach, only getting worse when he spotted Isabella across the room, sitting in a secluded corner of the atrium.

He got himself an iced tea and paid at the register, flashing his employee badge for his discount. He shouldn't be nervous talking to her again. They were both adults. It would be fine. Besides, the night they'd met, they'd worked so well together on the heart attack victim. Been in sync from the first. No reason they couldn't continue now, eh? He thanked the cashier and picked up his tea to head to her table, and then she looked up and saw him, and nope.

Any hopes they could just pretend that night had never happened evaporated.

Something about the haunted, hunted look in her eyes made him pause.

Carlos took a deep breath, his chest aching, then slowly continued over to her table. The wariness in her expression only worsened the closer he got, and he wanted to tell her it would be okay. Wanted to tell her he wouldn't bring it up, it was already forgotten, even if it wasn't. Even if he'd never forget that night and the way she'd made him feel like more than an unwanted, abandoned kid whose father didn't care enough about him to make any contact at all. Who would never have a chance to talk to his father, to ask him why he'd run away, because his father had died ten years prior.

Shit.

Carlos shoved all that out of his mind. Until he'd come to Barcelona, he'd gotten on fine without thinking about his father. Of course, his mother's family never brought him up, either, which helped. For her part, his mother had been wonderful. Always loving and supportive and caring, as much a friend and confidante as a parent. They'd been as close as mother and son could be, because they only had each other. And while she'd never said anything specifically about how she'd felt being abandoned by the man she'd loved and lost, well…he could see it in her eyes, the permanent scars it had left on her soul. One more thing he didn't let past his barriers, that he kept hidden deep inside, because it hurt too much to bring it out into the light.

But then his mother had passed away last year, and he'd been devastated. As the last surviving member of their little family, it had fallen on Carlos to go through her things. Then he'd found the name of his uncle Hugo, the first relative on his father's side Carlos had discovered. And, being a believer in fate, he'd seen it as a call to his destiny. The same call he'd felt with his immediate and intense attraction to Isabella on the beach in April.

Before he could say anything, though, she blinked up at him, gaze inscrutable. "What do you want?"

"I…" he started, then stopped.

I want to start over. I want to get back to the happy, easy, connection we had. I want to thank you for that night.

He settled for, "We need to talk."

CHAPTER TWO

ISABELLA FROZE LIKE a deer in headlights the minute she saw Carlos heading her way. Too late now, though, so she sat there, first studying her phone, then looking up at him with as impassive a gaze as she could manage. "What do you want?"

Ouch.

Cold. Far colder than she'd wanted, and way colder than she felt inside. Honestly, she was burning up, and it had nothing to do with her nausea earlier and everything to do with man standing before her. She hid her wince, though barely.

If he took offense at her tone, he didn't show it, just watched her with those dark eyes of his. The emotions flickering through them were fascinating—desire, embarrassment, pleasure, pain. "I…"

Her heart stuttered, then slammed against her rib cage. What? What would he say? He regretted that night? It had been a mistake? Best forgotten? She'd certainly tried to put it out of her mind, but nope. Impossible. Those memories kept resurfacing. The two of them entwined in her sheets, entwined in each other, making love until the early morning hours, then parting ways.

"We need to talk," he said at last.

Yes. Talk. Good.

She swallowed hard, then glanced around. Too many other staff members were there. Too many nosy listeners. The gossip around St. Aelina's had just recently moved on from cardiothoracic surgeon Dr. Caitlin McKenzie falling for her temporary colleague, Dr. Javier Torres, after news got out he wasn't just a cardiothoracic surgeon like Cait, but an actual fabulously wealthy count. She'd met them a while ago when bringing in a patient with chest injuries from a car accident requiring their expertise. Isabella didn't want to be the next hot topic of conversation around here. So, she stood and gestured toward the exit. "Fine. But not here."

Carlos blinked at her a moment, then followed her out into the hall. There were several on-call rooms down here for the doctors to use to rest on long shifts, and Isabella found one empty for privacy. She flipped the sign and held the door for Carlos before closing it behind them.

"So…" she said, crossing her arms. Having a bed right there was more than a little awkward. They both glanced at it, then looked away fast. She cleared her throat and tried again, rushing ahead because maybe it would hurt less. Like ripping off a bandage. "Look, if this is about our…" Isabella made a vague gesture between them. "One night we had together, don't worry. I won't say anything. It's already forgotten."

Liar. No way she'd forget that night with him. Not possible.

His color drained a bit beneath his tan, and she felt bad again. She'd always been one to play her emotions close to her chest—less vulnerable that way—but he was nothing if not passionate. Both in and out of bed. Everything he felt was right there, just below the surface.

Sweat broke out on her forehead, and her stomach lurched. Oh, God. She was going to be sick again. Not here. Not now. Not in front of him. Too late. She turned to grab the counter but missed, stumbling forward and nearly falling on the floor. Feeling shaky and stupid, she allowed him to help her to sit on the edge of the bed. Carlos crouched beside her, taking her wrist to check her pulse.

"Hey, hey," he said, his voice soothing the roiling heat radiating off her cheeks. Through the haze of sudden dizziness, she held on to his hand like a lifeline, focusing on her breath. In, out. In, out. Until, finally, the nausea eased, and her vision cleared. Carlos still crouched beside her, holding her hand and stroking her hair back from her face. "You're okay. It's okay. Do you want to lie down?"

She shook her head, not trusting herself to speak yet.

"All right." He stood and dumped his tea in the sink, then rinsed the cup and filled it with water before returning to her side again. "Drink some of this if you can. It will help. When was the last time you ate?"

Isabella sipped, grateful for the coolness on her dry throat, washing away the sting of bile. "Uh, last night, I guess. I had a couple crackers this afternoon before work. I've had this stomach bug for a few days, so…"

"Okay." He took a deep breath, then straightened. "Well, it's probably not a bad idea for someone to take a look at you before you go back out on ambulance runs."

"Oh, no. I'm sure I'll be fine." She set the cup aside and tried to stand. Too fast, though, and her head spun again. She sank down on the bed and covered her face with her hands. Mario had to be wondering where she was by now. She needed to get back to work, but she just felt so icky.

Carlos snorted. "Fine people don't nearly collapse on the floor. Seriously. Let me help you upstairs to the ER. I'll have one of the doctors check you out. Maybe eat a cookie or two. I'm sure you'll be fine."

Isabella wanted to argue but couldn't. He was right. Maybe she should get checked out, get some meds or something and be done with it. She needed to be cleared anyway before going back out on runs with Mario. Standard policy.

"Okay." She got up again, this time with Carlos beside her, supporting her elbow. "Let's go, then." They started out, but she stopped with one foot into the hallway. "Are we okay with the other thing?"

Carlos's tanned cheeks flushed, and she found it far too endearing. "*Si.* We're okay."

"Good."

They rode the elevator back up to the first floor, and Carlos walked with her into the ER, then put her in an empty trauma bay. "Wait here," he said. "I'll grab one of the doctors. Be right back."

A few moments later, her friend Nina, a nurse, came in, smiling sympathetically. "Hi, Issy. What's wrong? Carlos said you're having some nausea, dizziness, too?"

"*Si.*" Isabella explained her symptoms and how long they'd been going on. "I'm pretty sure it's the flu or something. You know how those things go around."

"Yep. We've been seeing a lot of cases lately." Nina typed in some notes on the computer in the corner. "And when was your last period?"

"Oh…uh…" Isabella frowned. Come to think of it, it had been a while. But she'd never been exactly regular, and with all the stress she'd been under recently with work and all, not unusual for it to be late. She gave the last date to the nurse, then waited for her to complete her documentation.

"All right. Let me just run all this by the doctor and see what she wants to do," Nina said, smiling. "Hold tight."

Isabella waited a few more minutes for her friend to return, this time with a specimen cup in hand and a phlebotomist in tow. "Okay." Nina handed her the cup. "We need a urine sample, and we're going to take some blood for a CBC and to make sure your blood sugar isn't low."

"Where's Carlos?" Isabella asked as the phlebotomist got to work.

"He had other patients," Nina said. "Do you want me to get him?"

"No, no. It's fine."

The fact she kind of wished he was still there with her made her even more determined not to ask for him now. She didn't like to depend on other people.

The phlebotomist finished, and Isabella used the restroom to leave her sample, then more waiting. She managed to flag down Mario and let him know what was going on. Luckily it was a slower shift, emergencywise, and there was another unit on call as backup, so they weren't short-staffed. Mario even got her some juice and a granola bar from the vending machine down the way. She felt much better after eating.

Finally, the curtain around her trauma bay opened and a doctor stepped inside, sans Nina.

"Ms. Rivas?" the doctor said. It wasn't someone she recognized, so probably new. Maybe a resident. "I'm Dr. De Leon. We've got your test results back."

"Is it the flu?" she asked, ready put this whole embarrassing situation behind her.

"No. Not the flu." The doctor smiled. "I'm happy to tell you, Ms. Rivas, that you're pregnant. Congratulations."

Time seemed to slow. Isabella shook her head, sure she'd misheard. "I'm sorry?"

"Nausea is extremely normal, especially during the first trimester." The doctor scrolled through the file on a tablet in their hand. "Based on the date of your last period, I'd say you're about eight weeks along. I'll have Nina get you set up with prenatal vitamins and the name of an OB here in Barcelona, unless you already have someone."

Oddly numb, Isabella just shook her head. Pregnant? That couldn't be possible. She didn't sleep around and was always careful and used protection. The last time she'd been with anyone…

Oh, God.

No. No, no, no. This could not be happening. She could not be pregnant with Carlos's baby, the guy she'd just brushed off and nearly fainted in front of. No. Just nope.

The doctor left, and Nina came back in, cringing

slightly. "Oh, gosh, Issy. I'd say congratulations, but from the look on your face, I'm not sure if I should."

Dazed didn't begin to cover how Isabella felt about the news. But as the shock slowly wore off, cold fear set in. She couldn't be a mother. She'd already spent ten years raising her younger siblings after their mother died. Then their dad had fallen ill a few years later, and it had been her responsibility to care for him as well. Her siblings were now scattered all over Spain, leaving her behind to build a life for herself alone. Hell, the only one of her siblings she even spoke with on a regular basis was Diego, and only because he'd moved back here and worked at St. Aelina's.

Her stomach lurched again, but for very different reasons now.

"Oh, Issy," Nina said, walking over to rub her back. "I'm sorry. If there's anything I can do, any way I can help…"

"I'm fine." She slid off the table, her legs steady beneath her once more. Good thing, too, since the rest of her world had been totally rocked. "I'm a bit surprised. That's all." She opened the curtain to head out, not fine at all. The opposite, really, but she'd get through it like she always did—on her own. "I need to get back to work."

Work helped. Work would always help. Isabella hoped so, anyway.

A few hours later, Carlos waited by the ambulance bay doors for an incoming case. Seventeen-year-old male who'd gotten a deep wrist laceration while surfing.

They'd called down one of the ortho guys to consult, a Dr. Manuel Pérez.

He was glad for the distraction to get his mind off the disastrous meeting with Isabella earlier. God, could he have handled that any worse? Images of her gray face, her wary eyes, flashed in his head. And when she'd almost passed out on him, his stress levels had skyrocketed. He'd gone back to the trauma bay to check on her after he'd finished with a couple of other patients, but Nina had said she'd already left.

Our one night we had together, don't worry. I won't say anything. It's already forgotten...

Her words kept looping in his mind, cutting deep each time.

Because Carlos hadn't forgotten. Not at all. And though he'd never ask for more from her if she wasn't interested, casual hookups weren't his thing. That night, however brief, had meant something to him. It had made him feel less alone in a new city, for one. Had made him feel like he'd made a real connection with her, for two. The fact she hadn't felt the same hurt. Understandable, but it stung.

Then the automatic doors swooshed open, and reality snapped back fast. The EMTs wheeled in their patient, the guy moaning and writhing in pain, a blood-soaked beach towel clutched to his right wrist as they headed for the next open trauma bay. Of course, it was Isabella and her partner who'd brought him in. Carlos's heart jumped into his throat again as he took position alongside the gurney, guiding it down the hall.

Dr. Pérez followed along beside Carlos. "What have we got?"

Isabella frowned, staring straight ahead as she gave the rundown. "This is Felipé. He's seventeen, heavy bleeding from a deep laceration to his right wrist while surfing. Says he cut it on some sharp rocks near the Killers. I've been there myself and can attest those rocks are dangerous."

"I see." Dr. Pérez followed them into trauma bay one, waited until they'd transferred the patient from the gurney to the hospital bed, then proceeded to remove the towel from the patient's wrist to better examine it. Carlos stood by with gauze to stanch the bleeding in case an artery had been hit. "Sir," Dr. Pérez said to the patient, "can you tell me, when the accident occurred, did the blood squirt or ooze?"

"I don't know," the patient said, eyes glassy with pain. "I just grabbed a towel to put on it as soon as I saw the blood."

"It's down to the bone," Dr. Pérez said, peering at the wound. He performed a quick exam before glancing over at Carlos. "What's his blood pressure?"

"One two six over eighty-four," Carlos said, watching as Isabella and her partner left the trauma bay. Damn. He'd hoped to talk to her again.

"Okay. Sir? Can you open your fingers the whole way?" Dr. Pérez asked, drawing Carlos's attention back to the patient. The boy did as the doctor asked. "Nice. Okay. Patient has pretty good motor function. Good pulse here, too. Looks like a venous bleed that just went through the muscle to me. Tendons appear pretty much intact."

Carlos smiled at the patient. "That's good news."

The patient nodded then swallowed hard.

"Right." Dr. Pérez stepped back as another nurse applied pressure to the wound while Carlos checked the monitors hooked up to the patient. "From what I can see now, Felipé, the cut went through the muscle, but it appears your tendons are okay. The major stuff is intact, all right?"

Felipé nodded again, cringing in pain.

"I'm going to order some tests for you, make sure there's nothing more serious going on there I've missed." Dr. Pérez turned to Carlos again as other staff members flocked around the patient, attaching an IV and a O2 sat monitor to the guy's finger. "Let's get a stat MRI and X-rays of that wrist. Then book an OR suite upstairs so I can get that laceration repaired."

"*Si*, Doctor." Carlos followed him out of the room and back to the nurses' station. "I'll have them page you once the results are in."

They hadn't had a chance to even register the kid yet, but it didn't matter. St. Aelina's was a teaching hospital and took a lot of cases other facilities turned away. Part of the reason he'd taken the job here. He'd expected to be busy and hadn't been disappointed so far. Busy was good. Kept him from dwelling on the other reason he was in Barcelona—to find out more about the father who'd walked out on him and his mother before Carlos had even been born.

Once he'd gotten the patient scheduled for his MRI and the techs came to wheel the patient away, Carlos took a much-deserved break. He'd been on duty in the ER for hours already and had another seven hours ahead of him before his shift was done. Time outside would do him good. He left word with the charge nurse he was going on break, then headed toward the ambulance bay. He had his phone with him in case they had to call him back in sooner than the hour he'd clocked out for.

After stepping through the automatic doors, Carlos took a deep breath and stared up into the starry sky. Closer now to midnight than dusk. The quiet chirp of crickets filled the cool night air and helped release some of his stress.

"Hey." The soft greeting made him jump. He'd thought he was alone out here. Carlos looked over to see Isabella leaning against the wall, her ambulance parked and ready a short way away.

His pulse tripped and blood pounded. Just like that, he was back in that on-call room downstairs, feeling like a bumbling idiot with the woman he couldn't get out of his mind, even all this time later. She looked better now, her cheeks pink and her eyes sparkling. Still wary, but brighter.

She sighed and rested her head back against the cool stone of the building and looked at him. "Maybe we can have that talk now?"

"Uh, sure." He ran his palms down the front of his green scrub pants, then walked over to lean against the wall beside her, remembering her caution earlier. "Here, or…"

"Can we walk a bit?" she asked, then called down to her partner, "I'll be right back. Text me if another call comes in."

Mario waved back from inside the rig.

"How about the beach?" Isabella asked as they walked up the ramp to the street level. "It's not far from here. Just a block or so."

"Uh, sure." They strolled along, both quiet, until Carlos asked. "Are you feeling better?"

"Yes, thanks."

Right. She still hadn't really looked at him since they'd locked eyes over the bed back in the trauma bay. He wasn't sure exactly what would happen or what she would say after basically telling him she'd forgotten all about him and their night together, but his instincts said this was important, so he stayed and didn't try to push it or rush her. Whatever she had to say, she'd tell him in her own good time. Carlos had learned over the years to be patient.

They reached the boardwalk in front of Playa de Bogatell and walked for a while, the sound of the waves crashing onshore mixing with the conversations of tourists and the caws of seagulls. Scents of sand and food from the bars nearby drifted on the air, and a couple of cyclists whizzed past, making him move closer to Isabella, excusing himself.

Finally, they stopped near a deserted section of railing. A slight breeze ruffled their hair as they both looked out at the sea, blowing some stray strands from the low ponytail at the base of her neck against her cheeks. From somewhere, a low, sweet ballad played, suiting the oddly poignant feel of the moment.

Isabella inhaled deep, then mumbled something he didn't quite catch, still not looking at him.

"*Perdóneme?*" *Excuse me?* She couldn't have said what he thought she'd said, because that would mean…

She sighed, then turned to face him. "I'm pregnant."

Carlos blinked at her for a beat or two, thinking he must have misheard, but nope. She'd said it. *Pregnant.*

His brain swirled with a thousand different thoughts at once, short-circuiting his vocal cords. *A baby. She's having a baby. My baby. I'm having a baby.* Those ideas quickly ricocheted to the opposite extreme. *I'm not ready to be a father. How will I raise a child? We were careful that night. We used protection.* Except, now that he remembered back to that evening with Isabella, they'd both had a lot to drink, and things were a bit…murky once they'd hit her bedroom, so… Oh, God. His pulse raced and sweat prickled the back of his neck, making him shiver slightly in the cool night breeze off the ocean. *Say something. Anything.*

He managed to croak out, "*Qué?*" What?

Not helpful, dude.

"I'm pregnant," she repeated, not looking overjoyed about it. "And it's yours."

"Oh," he said, the words finally starting to sink in past his shock, a weird sense of pure joy and fierce protectiveness swarming his system all at once. They were having a baby. *My baby. My child.* And while he appreciated her clarifying for him, it wasn't necessary. He'd believed her the first time. *Father. I'm going to be a father. Please, God, let me do better than my own* padre *did for me.*

He vowed to himself then and there he would. Whatever it took.

Then her lack of enthusiasm landed hard, along with the fear in her eyes, though she tried to hide it. His heart sank. Perhaps she would not keep it. Carlos rested an elbow on the railing, knowing he needed to say something but also wanting to tread carefully. She needed reassurance. They both did. And the last thing he wanted was for this to go south again, like before. He cleared his throat around the lump of uncertainty there and hoped he sounded more sure than he felt at the moment. "Okay. Well, please know that I'll be there for you however you need me to be. Okay?"

CHAPTER THREE

AT FIRST, ISABELLA wasn't sure how to respond. She'd expected him to be shocked, surprised, maybe even a little defiant about the fact that she'd said the baby was his. After all, they really didn't know each other well. One night of sex didn't make a relationship, no matter how glorious.

The fact he'd just stepped right up and offered to help, though... Well, that knocked her back a step, frankly. Growing up the oldest of her siblings, she was used to people passing the buck of responsibility on to the next person. And the next person. And the next person. Until, usually, it ended up in Isabella's lap to deal with. She'd come to expect it, really, so having Carlos be right there with his offer of aid took a bit of getting used to. On the heels of that came another revelation—one that she wasn't sure made her as happy. If he'd offered to help, that meant he wasn't going anywhere.

While she tried to formulate her answer, he added, "How about we go have a drink and talk? My treat."

"Oh, uh..." She scrambled for an excuse. Not because she didn't want to spend more time with him, but because she did. And relying on people got into dangerous territory for her. "Don't you have to return to work?"

Carlos checked his smart watch. "Not for another twenty minutes. Come on," he said, gesturing for her to follow him back toward the hospital. "I know a place not far from here."

She hesitated, glancing over at El Chiringuito, the bar they'd gone to that first night. "What about there?"

He gave a dismissive wave. "Nah. I think you'll like this place better. Trust me." The tiredness and nausea from earlier still lurked around her edges, with the shocking news she'd received and, well, everything. Plus, she was thirsty again, so... "Fine."

They headed back toward the hospital, but instead of taking a left toward St. Aelina's, they went right, down a block and a half, then stopped before a gray stone building on the corner. The large blocks were rough-hewn, giving the place an old-world feel. Barcelona was known for its beautiful and artistic architecture, and this place fit right in. From the arched windows to the flower boxes overflowing with roses, it had a medieval feel to it. Fancy, too. An intricate, hand-painted sign above the door proclaimed the bar's name—Encanteri.

"Uh...maybe we should go somewhere else," Isabella said, balking at the entrance. She still wore her EMT uniform, and Carlos wore his scrubs. "I don't think I'm dressed for this place."

"Nonsense," he said, opening the door and holding it for her. His grin made her gut tingle for completely different reasons now. He was gorgeous. No doubt about it. He winked, and her heart fluttered. "This is my uncle's bar. Remember? I told you he owned it the first night. It's fine."

"Oh, I…" Isabella said as he put his hand at the small of her back. The heat of his touch penetrated the cotton of her shirt and made her far more aware of him than was wise. Although this place looked much fancier than what she'd expected, and she really wasn't dressed for this, he ushered her through the door anyway.

Inside, the bar lived up to its namesake of a magical spell or charm—two stories high, with lots of jars filled with what looked like bubbling potions and walls lined with glass canisters filled with brightly colored liquids. Near the center of the bar sat a contraption that appeared to come straight from a laboratory, with tubes and wires and fizzing concoctions flowing through it. The dark wood bar stretched along one side of the place, and small tables for two or four filled the other half. A balcony ran around the upper story where people stood and mingled, drinks in hand. She'd heard of this place before but had never been inside.

"You really know the owner?" she asked Carlos, voice barely above a whisper.

"I do." He gave her a side glance and another grin, then raised his hand in greeting to a stout older man behind the bar with short, thick gray hair. "That's my uncle Hugo, owner of Encanteri."

"Uh…okay. Wow." Isabella followed him up to the bar, where he introduced her. "Uncle Hugo, please meet Isabella Rivas. We're…" Carlos looked back at her then to his uncle again. "Friends."

"*Hola*, Isabella Rivas," the older man said, shaking her hand firmly. "Hugo Sanchez. Welcome to my bar."

"Thank you." She matched Hugo's friendly smile, noticing his accent—the same as Carlos's. "The place is lovely. Are you also from Cuba originally?"

"*Si.*" Hugo smiled and patted his nephew on the arm. "I've been in Barcelona for nearly forty years now, but Havana will always be home. Finally convinced this one to come see me, too."

Carlos chuckled. "*Si.* You did. Can we get a couple of sparkling waters, please, Uncle? We'll get a table in the corner there."

"Of course." Hugo waved to Isabella, then turned to get their drinks while they walked across the narrow room to a table for two in a secluded corner. Carlos held her chair for her and took a seat across the tiny table from her. Their knees kept brushing under the table, much the same as the first night they'd met, conjuring more memories for her.

"So," Isabella said, after the server who brought their drinks left. "You moved here to be closer to your uncle?"

"*Si.*" He flashed her a sad smile. "And to find out more about my biological father."

"Oh?" she said, glad for a topic to discuss that didn't involve her or the pregnancy she hadn't quite come to terms with yet. They would have to discuss it at some point, but maybe not tonight. "Was he from Barcelona?"

"No." Carlos's smile faded to a frown. "Well, honestly, I don't know much about him. He left my mother before she had me. After she passed away last year, I found Uncle Hugo's name in some of my mother's paperwork and decided to go exploring." He shrugged.

"Only after I moved here did I find out my father passed away ten years ago."

"I'm so sorry." Isabella reached for his hand without thinking, then pulled away fast.

"Thank you." He sipped his water. "Anyway, from what I've been able to piece together from Uncle Hugo, Alejandro—my father—was from Cuba originally, but his family traveled a lot back and forth from Havana to Barcelona. In fact, he and my mother met here in Barcelona over a holiday. They had a whirlwind romance, and she ended up pregnant with me. Unfortunately, she didn't realize it until she returned to Cuba again with her parents. They were very upset and tried to contact my father and his family but couldn't get ahold of them. They never heard from him again, actually."

"Yikes. That's awful."

"Hmm." He sat back in his chair, stretching out his long legs in front of him and causing those scrubs of his to stretch over his muscled body most enticingly. Not that she noticed. Nope. "Sounds silly, but I brought my mother's diary with me. Thought maybe I could retrace their steps here in Barcelona, visit some of the same romantic spots they did, to try and discover more about him and who they were together."

Intrigued despite herself, Isabella leaned closer, resting her arms atop the table. "That sound so cool. And interesting, too. I'd love to see that diary sometime."

"How about now?" Carlos asked, surprising her.

"Oh, uh…" Isabella sat back, unsure.

Some of her uncertainty must've shown on her face, because Carlos laughed and patted her arm. "I live above this place. It will take like two seconds for us to run up there, and I can show it to you." His smile faltered. "I mean, unless you don't feel comfortable doing that with me. I wouldn't want to pressure you into—"

"No. It's fine," she said quickly. Better than focusing on her and the pregnancy when she still had no idea what to do about that yet. She checked her watch. "I can give you five minutes, then I need to get back to Mario and the rig."

"Let's go!" Carlos stood and waved to his uncle, then led Isabella back outside and to a small set of wrought iron stairs behind the building. They led to a third-floor flat considered luxurious and premium by Barcelona standards. Two-bedrooms, one-bath, a full kitchen with laundry facilities, large living room–dining area, and even a small balcony in the back. "My uncle gives me a break on the rent here, otherwise I'd never be able to afford it on my nurse's salary. Have a seat and I'll get the diary."

She did as he asked, taking a spot on the end of the overstuffed white sofa. Her own place was about the same size, maybe a little bigger, with an extra small bedroom she used as a home office. The view here at Carlos's was much better, though. He could see the beach from his balcony, while hers beheld a sea of more rooftops.

He returned a moment later with the diary and handed it to her. "There's a bookmark there where the story of their holiday together begins."

Isabella opened to it and began to read. Most of the places mentioned she'd been to many times, having lived in the city her whole life. La Sagrada Familia. Park Güell. Casa Milà. The usual tourist spots. Places his mother, Ana, would've visited with her parents, most likely. But a few were more romantic—Passeig de Gracia at night, El Borne with its exclusive boutiques, the gorgeous roses at the Rosalada de Cervantes and the garden maze at El Labyrinth d'Horta. Those, she imagined, would be perfect getaways for a young couple in love. Before she could think better of it, she said, "I know these places well. I'd be happy to show you around if you like."

Why did I say that?

Her plan had been to tell him about the pregnancy, then back away slowly, get some space between them again until she figured out her end of things. Now, she'd basically committed herself to being his tour guide. That would involve lots of time together, which meant lots of talking, which meant opening up and sharing things, and—ugh.

Too late now, though, based on his radiant grin. "That would be wonderful! Thanks so much for offering. I'd really like that. A tour from a native. Plus, it will give us a chance to get to know more about each other."

Not if I can help it.

"Great." Isabella stood and pulled her phone out, staring at the blank screen. "Looks like another call has come in, per Mario. I need to get back."

"Sure, sure," he said, putting the diary on a shelf nearby then joining her at the door to follow her out, locking up behind them. "Me, too. I've still got the rest of my shift to finish." They went back down the stairs and headed toward St. Aelina's. Didn't say much until they were standing outside the ER again, and Carlos turned toward her. "Thank you again, Isabella. For offering to show me around. It means a lot. And I meant what I said earlier. Whatever you need, let me know and I'm there, okay? You're not alone in this, no matter what you decide."

She nodded and smiled, then waved before walking back to the rig.

You're not alone in this...

That's what scared her. Alone meant comfort. Alone meant security.

Alone never let you down or disappointed you.

Alone never left you behind.

CHAPTER FOUR

A WEEK LATER, Carlos stood in front of La Sagrada Familia—the large, unfinished minor Roman Catholic basilica in the Exiample district of the city—waiting for Isabella to show up to be his tour guide. According to his mother's diary, this was the first place she and his father had visited. After that night at his flat, he and Isabella had agreed to do their tour today, one of the few times they both had off work, and the weather was sunny and warm without being too hot. Perfect for walking, though he did worry about her overexerting herself with the pregnancy. Not that he'd tell her.

Things around the pregnancy were still a bit awkward. They'd talked more about it after that night, mainly in passing, when her team would bring in a patient for Carlos and the other ER staff to treat. They'd shared coffees in the cafeteria, or tea, in Isabella's case, and talked about tests she'd had done, due dates and so on, though Isabella still kept the situation a secret from everyone else. He wasn't sure why, exactly, except perhaps she was still deciding whether or not to keep the baby, or maybe because it was still early and things could go wrong. Either way, it left him on pins and needles, and he hadn't been sleeping well.

He took a seat on a shady bench nearby to wait, taking in the mishmash of languages around him. Back in Cuba, you mainly heard Cubano, with a smattering of Spanish and a bit of English. Here the main language with the locals was Catalan—just different enough for him to have difficulty picking it up at first, and he'd made many mistakes in talking with patients in the ER those first few weeks. But better that than not trying at all, because if there was one thing he'd noticed here, it was that the locals of Barcelona were fiercely loyal to their Catalan, with regular Spanish second and English third. Isabella had taken pity on him that first night, though, and they'd bonded over English and had stuck with it since. He appreciated that about her. Appreciated a lot of things.

Like how she'd given up her first free day in forever to show him around. He'd looked forward to it, probably far more than he should. But Carlos hoped that, being away from the hospital and their work, they could dive deeper, really get to know each other better and maybe—finally—he could discover where she stood on their baby.

Wasn't long before he spotted Isabella heading toward him across the crowded street. She wore a yellow sundress, which set off her tanned, toned body and long dark hair to perfection. She was gorgeous, no two ways about it, with her wide, friendly smile and legs for miles. Even now, if he closed his eyes, he could still remember the feel of those legs wrapped around him as he'd lost himself inside her, warm and wet and wonderful and…

"*Hola,*" Isabella said, putting a hand atop her floppy sun hat to prevent it flying off in a strong breeze that gusted by. "Are you ready to go?"

"*Si.*" Carlos stood and cleared his throat from the sudden constriction those steamy memories had caused. "Ready when you are."

As they stood in line to enter, Carlos looked up at the intricate carvings on the walls of the building, then farther up toward the three towers above them—the Jesus Christ tower, the Virgin Mary tower and the evangelist tower. Even with the cranes and scaffolding around them due to repairs and restorations, the place was magnificent. The Art Nouveau period had always been his favorite. He'd had several street artist friends back in Cuba who'd adopted that style in their work. So, to see the work of Antoni Gaudí, one of the masters of that type of architecture, up close and personal like this was amazing. He could see why his parents might have started to fall in love there.

Isabella must've noticed him staring upward, because she pointed to one of the towers. "Did you know that once the construction is completed, the Jesus Christ tower will be the tallest thing in Barcelona?"

"*Si.*" He grinned at her. "I did know that. I did my homework for today."

"Really?" She gave him an appraising look. "Well, then you know that the cathedral itself was never finished during Gaudí's lifetime."

"*Si,*" he said again. "But he did leave behind detailed drawings and blueprints, so they are able to continue work on the building now."

She looked impressed. "True. They're going to make

it so people can go all the way up to the top of the Jesus tower once it's done. You'll be able to look out over the entire city and feel closer to God, as Gaudí intended originally."

Finally, after a few more minutes, their group went inside. First past the gorgeous Nativity doors with their lush green leaves and tiny pink birds, and then into the interior of the building. There, a hush fell over the world. Even though there were about twenty people in their group, you could hear a pin drop. The temperature dropped about ten degrees as the bright sunshine outside dimmed. Cool white stone surrounded them as they passed through the narthex and then into what Carlos could only describe as heaven on earth. Soaring ceilings, gilded arches and a rainbow prism of colors streaming through the gorgeous stained-glass windows. Columns that split like tree branches above to support the weight of the ceiling. All the intricate swirling lines and nature-themed carvings showed the beauty of creation and took his breath away. Isabella must've felt the same, because she moved closer to him, their hands brushing as they took in the glory around them.

"This is one of my favorite places in the city," she whispered reverently. "Growing up, I'd come here sometimes, just to sit and wonder about everything. After my mother died and my father got sick, it was my sanctuary."

His gaze flicked from the architecture around them to her face, her expression full of rapt awe. She looked even more beautiful now, if that was possible, and his heart squeezed. "I'm sorry about your mother. And your father."

Isabella looked at him, blinking for a second like it took her that moment to register what he said. Then her cheeks flushed pink, and her gaze darted away again. "Thank you."

He wished she'd let him in, reveal more about herself, but they had the whole day in front of them.

"And here," their group's guide said, "we are now in the central nave. The light in this case is defined by the color of the stained glass. At the east side, when the sun rises, there are the green and blue colors, because it's the Nativity facade. And it's turning the colors to the red, orange, yellow and a little bit dark at the Passion facade at the west, when the sun sets, so the experience and atmosphere will be different, depending on the time you come inside."

They spent a few more moments being dazzled by the glorious cathedral, then went back outside to continue their tour. Carlos wasn't sure how anything could be better than that, but being with Isabella, he was willing to be surprised.

"Should we visit Casa Milà next, since that's spot number two on the list? It was also designed by Gaudí, so it is somewhat related architecturally, too," Isabella asked as they moved back into the sunshine, the heat welcome after the cooler church.

"Of course." Carlos smiled and gestured for her to lead the way, and they started walking toward their next destination. Lots of people were out and about now, and the city seemed alive and sparkling. After the intimate feel of the cathedral tour, he was eager to keep the lines of communication open. "We don't really have anything like La Sagrada Familia in Cuba, but we do have our

Museo de la Revolución." He raised his fist in the age-old sign of rebellion and defiance, then chuckled. "It's not nearly as grand as your cathedral, even though it's housed in the old presidential palace."

"Hmm." Isabella smiled, glancing sideways at him. "I've never been to Cuba. I've heard the beaches are good, though, even if it's illegal to surf there."

"True." Carlos chuckled. "There's actually a whole underground around it now. Young people who've watched a bunch of surf movies and thought they could do it, too. It's still a risk, though. For decades, all water activities were prohibited, including surfing, because they feared people were fleeing to America. Of course, people still went into the water and even did some surfing, but only in certain areas, and then the surfers had to make their own boards and things. It's quite a thing."

"Sounds like." They waited at a light to cross the street. "I wouldn't have done well there, growing up. Not sure what I would've done without my beach breaks. Surfing kept me sane during those years after losing my mom."

He waited until they were walking again to gently probe for more information, offering a bit more about himself, too. "My mother passed away last year, as I said. She had cancer. Ovarian. Stage four by the time they diagnosed it. Cuba has amazing medical facilities, but even they couldn't save her." He sighed, the old grief pinching his chest even now. "I still miss her. You?"

Isabella didn't answer right away, and he began to wonder if she would at all. But then, finally, she took a deep breath and said, "I miss my mother, too. She died of cancer, too, but brain. She had headaches and they got progressively worse. They discovered the tumor on a scan, and because of the type, fast-growing and inoperable, she died seven months later."

Her tone sounded so forlorn, he couldn't help reaching over and taking her hand in a show of support. She didn't pull away.

"We were all in shock. My youngest siblings were just babies then, too young to even know what happened. The older ones were sad and knew she died, but we had to keep going. As the oldest, I took over what I could, to help Papì. Then he got sick, too. Multiple sclerosis." She shrugged. "It's rarer in men, and from what I later found out, probably ran in his family, but yeah. By the time they diagnosed him, his symptoms were getting severe. The following year, he wasn't able to work anymore, and so I got a part-time job after school to help supplement the family's income."

"Oh, Isabella." He gave her fingers a reassuring squeeze. "I can't imagine how difficult that must've been for you."

She nodded, staring straight ahead, her eyes hidden now by large dark sunglasses, though he could feel the tension in her through their joined hands. "Hard, yes. But I survived it. It made me stronger, I think."

He'd always had a thing for strong women, having been raised by one himself. Which explained his ever-growing attraction to Isabella. Not just her beauty, but the person inside as he learned more about her. "Is that why you became a paramedic?" he asked. "Because of what happened to your mother and also your father's illness?"

"Maybe." Her expression turned thoughtful. "Probably the caretaker aspect, too. I'm used to taking care of other people, and I'm good at it."

Hmm. She was good at taking care of people, from what Carlos had seen so far, but he wanted to ask...

Who takes care of you?

Isabella had tried to keep the focus on the city that she loved that morning and not get too personal with him. A defense mechanism she used a lot, especially with her patients. Working with people during the worst times of their life, which health crises often were, tended to make patients feel closer to their caregivers than they normally would. They often told her things they never would otherwise. She once had a man rattle off his bank account numbers to her on the way to the hospital for a heart attack. He'd feared he wouldn't make it and wanted someone to know how to pay for his final expenses, if necessary. Other people told her secrets about their love lives or their children or their pasts. Emergencies bred intimacies. Or so it seemed.

But today wasn't an emergency. In fact, up until now, it had seemed relaxed and easy. Then he'd gone and asked about her family and those old wounds opened right back up again, stealing her oxygen.

Silly, really. She knew that. She was grown adult woman with a successful career and a life she loved. She shouldn't be hung up on the past anymore, shouldn't care about the sacrifices she'd made for her siblings so they could go off and leave her behind. Bitter bile burned hot in her throat before she swallowed it down. She didn't resent it. She didn't. She wasn't that kind of person.

Still difficult, though, remembering those years when she'd felt alone and exhausted and like everything was closing in on her.

She took a deep breath, raising her face to the bright sunshine, staring at the gorgeous pink pastel building in front of them. Man, she loved Barcelona. It was fun seeing it through new eyes with Carlos, too, even if she had no intention of telling him about her innermost feelings and hurts. Still, when she glanced over at him, those deep, dark eyes of his compelled her to share something with him, especially after he'd shared with her about his family.

Isabella sighed and went with the least painful thing she could find. "I became a paramedic because I wanted to help people, like you. But I also wanted the freedom of new experiences every day. New cases, new patients. I like not being tied down to the same place with the same people all the time."

"Hmm," he said as they stopped for another light, seemingly really considering her answer. Weighing it. She couldn't help noticing he still had a hold of her hand and hated to admit how nice it felt. She should've pulled away but couldn't bring herself to. Didn't want to think too hard about why. "Will you continue working after the baby's born?"

"I'll have to," she said, smiling at him before taking off across the street to the front of the Casa Milà once the light turned green, towing him along behind her. "Got to support myself, right?" He opened his mouth like he wanted to say more, but she didn't want to hear it. Couldn't hear it, in case he offered to take care of her and the baby. No. She had to keep her freedom. "Looks like the lines aren't too long to get inside. Let's get our tickets, eh?"

They headed off across the plaza toward the ticket booth, only to stop sharply at the sound of a woman screaming. "Help me! Help! My husband collapsed!"

Just like on the beach that first night, Isabella and Carlos switched immediately into medical mode. They sprinted over to where a middle-aged man in shorts and a Hawaiian shirt sprawled on the pavement, looking pale and lifeless.

"What happened?" Isabella asked, taking off her sun hat and setting it beneath her tote bag so it didn't blow away. "I'm a paramedic. Whatever you can tell me will be helpful."

"We're here from Texas. Out sightseeing. I told Henry to take it easy because it's so hot out, but he wouldn't listen. Just kept pressing on, saying we had to stay on schedule if we wanted to fit everything in this trip."

"Pulse and breathing are rapid," Carlos said, scowling as he met Isabella's eyes. "Skin hot and dry to the touch."

"Heatstroke," they said in unison.

"Right." Isabella looked up at the frantic woman again. "Ma'am, I need you to call 061. That's the emergency number here. They'll send help. Your husband needs to go to a hospital right away."

The woman turned away to do so while Isabella and Carlos focused on their patient.

"We need to get him into the shade," Carlos said, waving over a young guy nearby and speaking to him in rapid

Spanish. "Can you grab his feet while I lift his shoulders? We'll carry him to the shade by the door there."

Together they lifted the patient and moved him while Isabella ran alongside them. "I could've helped you."

"No," Carlos said, his gaze flicking from her eyes to her abdomen then back again. "You couldn't."

She'd forgotten about the baby. What if she forgot when it really mattered?

Oh, God. She'd be a horrible mother. What the hell ever made her think she could do this?

Then, just as quickly as she fell into her funk, she climbed out of it. Focusing on her work, her patient. She'd deal with the pregnancy like she dealt with everything else in her life, because she didn't have a choice.

"Get his shirt open," Isabella said as they waited for the ambulance crew to arrive. "See if we can get some water to help cool him down."

The man's eyes fluttered open, and he tried to talk, but his words were slurred and slow.

"Please, sir, lay still," Isabella said, taking the bottle of water Carlos handed her and opening it to pour on the man's chest. It would soak his shirt, but better that than the alternative. "You're suffering from heatstroke. Just stay calm. We've got help on the way."

Carlos stood and surveyed the area. "I can hear the sirens. They're getting closer."

"Good." Isabella smiled down at her patient. "They'll be here in no time, and then we'll get you and your wife to the hospital."

She continued to fan the man with a souvenir booklet someone had handed her while a small crowd gathered around them, people snapping photos and taking videos of the scene. Isabella ignored all that, focused on keeping her patient comfortable while Carlos performed crowd control, then took over fanning duties for her when her wrist got tired. Again, they worked great together, not even needing to talk sometimes— just a look or gesture communicated what they needed.

Finally, the EMTs arrived, a different crew than Isabella usually worked with, since they were in a different section of the city now, but still efficient. They took over care of the patient and got him and his wife loaded into the rig.

The woman reached out and took Isabella's and Carlos's hands before they closed the doors on her. "Thank you both for your help. Not sure what we would've done without you."

"You're welcome," Carlos said.

"They're taking you to St. Aelina's hospital. Newest and best in the city," Isabella said, squeezing the woman's hand. "You'll be fine."

"Thank you," the woman said again, then the EMTs closed the back doors to the ambulance and they were off.

For several seconds afterward, they both just stared after it, a bit stunned.

"Well, that was unexpected," Carlos said.

"Yeah." Isabella bent and picked up her tote and put her hat back on. "Seems we can't get away from work, even on our days off." She looked at the line, then back to Carlos. "Should we get our tickets now? Unless you'd rather not continue the tour."

"Are you kidding?" He laughed, a low, rich sound that made Isabella's knees wobble against her will.

"There's nothing I'd love more than to spend the rest of the day with you. You were amazing there, by the way."

"Same," she said, smiling, realizing that she did feel the same way. Which both amazed and terrified her. Somehow, without even trying, he'd found a way past her barriers. Now she couldn't imagine anyone she'd want to spend her time with more than Carlos. "Let's get our tickets, then."

For some reason, his compliment made her feel warmer inside, and that heat had nothing to do with the temperatures outside. When they got up to the ticket counter, the man there refused to sell them anything. On the house, he said, for what they'd done to help the tourist. Isabella thanked him, then walked over to get in line again with Carlos. Once again, they moved to the head of the line, the other waiting people applauding them and thanking them for helping. Isabella couldn't help but smile. Nice to have your hard work recognized, even if she wasn't used to it.

Once inside, they followed a tour guide, who explained the history and architecture of the place much better than Isabella ever could.

"Welcome to Casa Milà, also known as La Pedrera or the Quarry in English. This structure is regarded as Antoni Gaudí's most iconic work of civic architecture due to its constructional and functional innovations, as well as its ornamental and decorative solutions, which broke with the architectural styles of his era." The tour guide waited as her assistant translated that into French, Spanish and Japanese for the tourists before continuing. "For Gaudí, La Pedrera represented the most advanced approach to a building on a chamfered street corner in the Eixample district of Barcelona. It consists of two blocks of flats, each with its own entrance, structured around two large, interconnected courtyards with ramps down to the garage for vehicles."

As they learned about the building's facade and curtain wall, the ornate wrought iron gates, and the fact that Gaudí had designed with an eye for the future, with a parking garage in the basement—even if only for carriages and not cars—Isabella became more aware of Carlos beside her than she'd expected. His gentle warmth, the solid, supportive feel of his body next to hers, the fact that working with him and seeing how cool and confident and competent he was under pressure, made him sexy as hell. At least to her.

Stop it.

"Hey," Carlos said, leaning in to whisper in her ear and making her shiver. "How about we skip the rest of this tour and head straight to the roof? While this is lovely, I could use some fresh air."

She nodded, and they slowly made their way to the back of the group before following the signs up to the roof. The building really was spectacular, with its colorful murals and gorgeous inner courtyard. But nothing beat the views from the top. They emerged onto the roof amid a sea of statues and walkways. Other tourists milled about, but it wasn't nearly as crowded as below, and they found a spot near the railing overlooking the city with a nice breeze blowing around them.

"So, your parents got to know each other while touring Barcelona," Isabella said. "It's very romantic."

"It is." Carlos leaned his forearms on the railing beside her, his smiled relaxed as he looked her way. "Are you seeing anyone?"

A bit shocked, she shook her head. "Uh, no. I don't really have time for that right now. With work and everything. Besides, I'm young and enjoying my freedom."

"Hmm." Carlos tilted his head, his expression turning serious as his gaze flicked down to her abdomen, then back again. "That may change, though, yes?"

Frowning, she looked out at the cityscape again. Guilt squeezed her chest tight. She shouldn't worry about losing her freedom when the baby came. It was natural to have your life change after a birth. And she didn't feel guilty, really. More…scared.

A lump of pain lodged in her throat. She wouldn't be alone in this. Carlos had already pledged to help her in any way he could. He would be a good father, she could already tell. Generous, attentive, good-hearted. *But is being good enough?* The pinch in her heart grew stronger. Her own father had been such a good man. The best man, really. And still, he'd failed. Felled first by the loss of their mother and then later by a disease that no one saw coming. So, being good wasn't enough, but it would have to do. Because the only thing worse, in Isabella's opinion, than having a father not able to be there for their child, because of health or other reasons, would be for their baby to grow up with no father at all. As poor Carlos had done. And he still searched for the remnants of the man, even all these years later.

She didn't want that for her child. And while losing your parents was inevitable, no sense putting a child through that before their time. She should know.

Isabella felt Carlos's gaze on her and shrugged. "No. Not necessarily. Women raise children on their own and have careers all the time. Regardless, I will make it work. We will make it work."

"It's not easy, though."

"No. I imagine it's not." She sighed, resting her hip against the cool wrought iron. "Did your mother have a hard time raising you?"

He shrugged, turning away again. "She did okay. Her parents helped a lot, watching me while she worked and after school. Do you have people to help? You mentioned siblings."

"Sure," she said, though wasn't entirely convinced they'd run to her rescue. The youngest four—Eduardo, Frida, Luis and Paola—were scattered all over Spain now. Only Diego lived here, and he was busy with his new wife, Grace, so…

She and the baby would be fine on their own. Without thinking, she placed her hand over her abdomen. Until that moment, she hadn't realized she'd decided to keep it, but she had. She wanted this baby. More than she'd ever wanted anything else. With or without a partner to help raise it.

"That didn't sound too convincing," he said.

"No, I mean, I'll be fine. We'll be fine."

"You're keeping it, then?" he asked, the look on his face a mix of hope and hesitation that made her heart ache. "Our baby?"

"*Si*," she said, confirming it for herself and the world. "I'm keeping it."

Carlos grinned then, so brightly it rivaled the sun above, and it felt like a weight lifted off her chest. Before she could react, he leaned in and kissed her fast, then hugged her, enveloping her in his warmth and the scents of spices and soap and something indefinably Carlos. She remembered it from their one night together, and it brought back a rush of memories from that evening—the feel of his hands on her, his kisses, his moans of pleasure, his body wrapped around hers, inside her, making her feel cared for and precious and beautiful and treasured…

He pulled back, tiny splotches of crimson dotting his high cheekbones. "Sorry. Didn't mean to overstep there. I just…" He took a deep breath and looked up at her through his dark lashes, and even that was endearing, like basically everything else about him. "I'm very happy to hear that, Isabella. Thank you."

Okay. Awkward. Having a baby wasn't really something you thanked a person for, right? Though considering what she knew about him, she could see how he got there. "Um, you're welcome? I guess." Then, to get their day back on track, she said, "Are you ready to move on to the next spot on the list?"

"Why do you do that?" he asked, frowning.

"Do what?" A gust of wind blew, stronger this time, and she put a hand on her hat to keep it in place.

"Deflect."

"Deflect?" Now she scowled. "I'm not sure what you're talking about."

"I've told you a lot about my family, where I come from, what I'm here for, but each time I ask about you, I get nothing in return. You changed the subject fast. Don't you think that if we're going to be having a baby together, I should know more about you?"

"That's not true," she said, turning toward the view once more. "I told you about growing up the oldest kid, my mother passing away, then my dad getting sick and me having to take care of everyone. What more do you want to know?"

"Well, how about how all that made you feel?" He narrowed his gaze on her. "I want to know what makes you tick, Isabella Rivas. I want to know the inner you that you don't show to anyone else."

That all sounded very intimate and vulnerable and scared her half to death, frankly. Yes, they'd had sex, which some people might consider the most intimate thing two people could do together, but for Isabella that wasn't true. She'd spent the last twenty-one years learning to be self-reliant, learning to keep her emotions to herself to get done what she needed. To open up now, to Carlos, felt like jumping out of a plane with an iffy parachute. Maybe he'd catch her fall, maybe he wouldn't, but she couldn't find out without taking a leap of faith.

After a beat or two, she took a deep breath for courage, then nodded. "Fine. What do you want to know? And can we walk and talk at the same time? Because we've still got a lot of ground to cover today."

CHAPTER FIVE

By THAT EVENING, they'd been to three more spots on his parents' whirlwind romance tour, including the Park Güell, the gorgeous Palau de la Música Catalana and the Parc del Laberint d'Horta or Labyrinth Park, where his parents had shared their last kiss before saying good-bye forever.

Now, tired and feet sore, they were dining in a charming restaurant called Jardinet d'Aribau. It was unlike any place Carlos had ever eaten before—a blend of fairy tale and fantastical, with lots of bright pastel colors and plants and vines growing wild around them. Like dining in a wonderland. Then again, he'd kind of felt like he'd been in a dream all day. Touring the city with Isabella had been everything he'd hoped for and more. He'd expected they'd get to know each other better. What he hadn't expected was for their connection to grow even stronger. And though she didn't mention it, he could tell from the way Isabella watched him when she thought he wasn't looking that she felt it, too. More than just desire. Or the baby. No. This felt like some-thing deeper, stronger, richer. Something that might last if they allowed it to. Carlos wasn't sure how he felt about that yet.

"So," he asked, picking up his menu. "What's good here?"

"No idea." He raised a brow, and she laughed, the sound washing over him like fine music. "This is my first time here, too. But I've always wanted to try it."

"Ah." He smiled. "We are both new arrivals in this instance. Good."

When the server returned with their drinks—sangria for him, sparkling water for Isabella—they asked about the specials, then both decided on the blackened salmon with baby chard salad and a basket of Iberian ham and bread with tomato for an appetizer. Left alone once more, Carlos settled back in his seat, his feet brushing Isabella's beneath their cozy table for two in the corner.

"Thank you again for taking me out." He sipped his sangria, enjoying the cool, fruity taste. "It really helped make the pages of my mother's diary come alive for me. I can see why you love this city so much. It's beautiful."

"You're welcome." She smiled, seemingly much more open now than before. "Barcelona *is* beautiful. I wouldn't want to live anywhere else in the world."

"What was it like, growing up here?" he asked, skirting around the issue that had made her shut down earlier. He was still so interested in her and her past. He wanted to know more.

Isabella sighed then leaned forward, resting her elbow on the table, swirling her straw in her water. She looked tired but happy, and he hoped he hadn't worn her out too much. "Good. My family had a house in the Sarriá-Sant Gervasi district. Nothing fancy and far too small for all of us, but we were happy there. Lots of outdoor space to explore and safe neighborhoods. There were a lot of expat families living there, too, because it was close to the international schools. Our father was a handyman. He fixed electrical and plumbing, did construction, all of it. Made a good living doing it, too, at least until he got sick." She sighed and sat back, and for a moment Carlos feared she'd close him off again. But then she continued, and he gave an internal sigh of relief. Perhaps she'd come to trust him after all. He hoped so, anyway.

"I think my mother's passing hurt him very deeply. He would never talk about it much, always trying to be strong for the rest of us, but it ate away at him, inside. Perhaps that's why he got sick." She gave a little shrug, staring at her water glass instead of Carlos, still stirring, stirring, stirring. "They say a patient's mental state has as much to do with their disease process and recovery as the physical medicine."

Carlos nodded. "I believe that, too, with my mother's cancer."

She glanced up at him then, the vulnerability in her eyes making his chest ache for her. "*Si.* I think after my mother died, something in my father's spirit went with her. His symptoms from MS gradually worsened and worsened until he could barely get out of bed. He couldn't work anymore, hardly ate. Like he wanted to join her in death. We were all sad, but he was grief-stricken."

The server came with their appetizers and to refill their drinks.

They each took a plate and filled it with ham and

fresh-baked bread and ripe tomatoes from the basket, then began to eat.

"I won't lie," Isabella said after a few minutes. "At the time, being thirteen and all, I took it personally."

"What?" Carlos asked, frowning.

"His withdrawal from us." She shrugged, eating another bit of bread and tomato before continuing. "I mean, looking back, I can't imagine the pressure he was under, trying to deal with all us kids and his work and everything else on his plate. But at the time, it was hard for me, losing my mother at that age. Then, when he got sick and I had to take over running the household, things only got worse."

"Couldn't he have hired someone to come in and help?" Carlos sipped more sangria, watching her over the rim. She'd let him in now, and he couldn't get enough. Wanted to keep her sharing if possible. "Or wasn't that an option?"

"No. Not really. Without his handyman work to support us, money was very tight. Luckily, he'd built up enough of a nest egg in savings to pay for the basics until I was old enough to get an after-school job to help supplement things, but we had to watch every penny."

She sighed and pushed aside her empty appetizer plate. "And at that time, the youngest ones were still barely walking, so, yeah. Not much of a life for me outside of cooking and cleaning and caring for everyone else in the family outside of school."

"Wow." He shook his head and sat back as the server came to clear their plates and refill their drinks again. Once they were alone again, Carlos reached over and took Isabella's hand, and she let him. "Well, as I've said,

I'm sorry you went through that, but it explains why you're so strong and resilient."

"Hmm." She flashed a sad little smile. "Forged in fire, right?"

"Sometimes that's the only way."

Their dinners came then, and they stopped talking for a while—well, about anything other than the delicious food. The salmon was cooked to perfection and the chard salad its perfect cool, crispy complement. After they were full and happy, they paid the bill and walked back outside. The sun had set, and cooler air moved in off the ocean. Stars twinkled in the sky above, and people milled about, laughing and talking, out for a good time.

"Well, I guess it's back home, then," Carlos said, not wanting the evening to be over yet but not wanting to push his luck, either.

"Actually—" Isabella checked her smart watch. "There's one more spot I can show you tonight, if you're up for it."

"Always." He grinned, feeling that connection between them vibrate stronger, like a tuning fork, pulling him closer, keeping him in perfect resonance with her. "I'm yours."

Her dark eyes widened slightly at the innuendo of his words, then she grinned right back at him, taking his hand and tugging him alongside her down the cobblestoned street. Awareness zinged up his arm and straight down to his groin. Could've been the sangria. Could've been the woman leading him away to who knew where. Could've been the magnificent city around them. He felt free and fantastic and laser focused all at the same time. Mainly on Isabella and how her hips swayed so enticingly under her yellow sundress.

"Hurry," she said, looking back at him over her shoulder, her long dark hair swishing down her back, her sun hat long tucked away in the tote. "We'll miss the show."

"What show?" he asked just before they rounded another corner, and boom. The view took his breath away. Just ahead, past a sea of tourists, a huge fountain sat atop a slight hill, spraying high into the sky, multicolored from the lights inside, in time to music playing from speakers set around it. Dazzling. "That's…wow!"

"It's called the Magic Fountain of Montjuïc," she said. "It's in the diary, too."

They stood watching the show, pressed close together to avoid being separated by the other tourists around them, holding hands because…well, because it felt so good. Carlos spotted a rose vendor off to the side of the fountain and excused himself a moment. They were all over the city, eager to make a buck off people looking to be romantic. He paid the guy and pointed toward Isabella, easy to spot in her bright dress, then made his way back to her to watch more of the show.

A sweet rendition of "The Way You Look Tonight" started playing when the rose man came over. "*Per a la dama,*" he said, giving a deep bow while holding out a single red rose to her.

Isabella frowned. "Oh, that's not for me."

"*Si,*" the rose man insisted. "It's for you."

She looked at Carlos. "Did you buy this?"

"What? Me? No." He shook his head, praying the rose vendor would keep going along with the ruse he'd planned. He'd thought it might be the perfect ice breaker to get things moving in the right direction again, because damn. Carlos had been dying to kiss her all day, and more than just the little peck he'd given her earlier. Still, he didn't want to be obvious about it, especially if she wasn't feeling the same about him. And sure, they'd already slept together, and he thought she might be into him, too, but he wanted to be sure. When Isabella hesitated, he squeezed her hand gently. "Go ahead. Take it."

"Well…" Her gorgeous smile rivaled the beautiful fountains in front of them. "If you insist."

"I do." Carlos gave the vendor a sly wink, and he returned it, then moved on to the next customer, leaving them alone again. "A pretty flower for a pretty woman."

In the glow from the fountains, he could see her blush slightly as she sniffed the rose. "Thank you."

"I didn't…" he started, then shrugged. "You're welcome."

Through her lashes, she looked up at him. "I hope it's not too much, all the things I told you at dinner. I don't usually say all that to people, but…"

"No, no. I'm glad you told me." He turned slightly to face her, reaching up to cup her cheek without even thinking. She didn't pull away. Her skin felt like silk beneath his touch, same as he remembered. Warm and smooth and addictive. His pulse tripped and blood pounded in his ears, drowning out the music and the people around them and everything but her. "I want to know more about you. I want to know everything about you, Isabella. And not just because of the baby."

"Really?" she said, staring into his eyes, a mix of

hope and vulnerability there that made his chest ache. "I'm not very interesting."

"You're the most interesting thing in the world to me," he said, meaning it completely. And then time slowed as he bent toward her, close, closer, so close their breath mingled and he could smell the sweet fragrance of the rose in her hand and the scent of her shampoo. Then his lips brushed hers once, twice, before locking on. So good. Better than any kiss he'd ever had, even the night they'd slept together. Because now he knew her; now they were connected in a way they hadn't been before. Now, it meant something.

It meant everything.

Carlos slipped his arm around her waist and pulled her against him as he deepened the kiss. She opened to him, and he swept his tongue inside her mouth, tasting the spiciness of the salmon and the lemon from her water and something indefinably Isabella. She sighed and wrapped her arms around his neck, her soft curves pressing into his hard muscles, and the world felt perfect in that moment. Nowhere else he'd rather be than there with her that night. Perhaps his parents had been right. Perhaps Barcelona was the place to fall in love.

Isabella returned to work with Mario on the ambulance crew the next day, and the emergencies were coming fast and furious. In a way, she was glad. Not because people were getting hurt, but because it kept her from thinking too much about Carlos and their fabulous kiss.

After their one night together, she'd been firm in her decision to put it all behind her. Then she'd found out he worked at the hospital, and then that she was pregnant.

Even then, she'd still been wary to let him too much into her life. She treasured her hard-earned freedom and had been prepared to raise the baby on her own. Then...

There'd been something about touring her city with him, showing him things his parents had done, that made her feel safe with him. After all, he'd showed her the diary and told her about his past. He'd made himself vulnerable. And while vulnerability was probably the scariest thing in the world to her, she trusted him. They hadn't known each other long, but something about Carlos made him seem steadfast and trustworthy. It's what made him so good at his job and good with his patients. That calm, cool collectedness. Like whatever happened, it would be okay.

She and Mario raced to another accident scene— this time a cyclist who'd been knocked off his bike near the boardwalk at the beach by a slow-moving motorist. When they pulled up to the scene, pandemonium ensued, as usual. The police were trying to cordon off the area while tourists swarmed around, filming it all with their smartphone cameras.

A woman and a man were standing nearby, talking with a police officer. Isabella took the man, leaned over, holding his gut. Mario took the woman, who was shaking and crying.

"Sir?" Isabella set her medical pack near her feet. "Are you all right? Can you tell me where it hurts?"

"I... I don't know." He shook his head, the sun reflecting off his dark green bike helmet. "It all happened so fast. My chest is kind of sore." He frowned and rubbed the area over his sternum. "I think I hit the handlebars of my bike when I fell off."

Right. Isabella got out her stethoscope and helped the man lean back against the police car parked behind him, then listened to his breathing and took his pulse. Both were normal. "Did you hit your head? Lose consciousness? Any shortness of breath? Irregular heartbeats? History of high blood pressure?"

"No. I didn't hit my head or black out." The man winced. "I'm pretty healthy overall. I ride my bike down here all the time. This is the first time anything like this has ever happened to me."

"Oh, God!" The woman driver's Southern American accent stood out sharply among all the Spanish speakers on the beach. "I'm so, so sorry. I tried to get my stupid GPS to show the right location and I glanced down for just a second and…"

Isabella finished an initial exam of the man, then straightened. "I don't see any acute injuries, sir, but you should let us take you in and have a doctor check you out in the ER to be on the safe side." She inspected a cut on his forearm and a couple scrapes on his knee and leg where he'd landed on the ground. "If you get into the rig, I can bandage up those lacerations for you as well."

The man nodded, and Isabella led him around the back of the ambulance, then helped him inside. Soon Mario joined them, with the woman who'd hit the cyclist. She appeared close to hyperventilating now. He guided the woman into the other seat and helped her put her head between her legs to keep her from passing out.

"Ma'am," Mario said in English, "please calm down. Everything will be fine. I'm going to check your blood pressure now, okay? Are you on any medications?"

She shook her head, and he wrapped the cuff around

her arm, then inflated it before slowly releasing the air as he listened with his stethoscope. "One thirty-two over eighty-nine."

"Is that good or bad?" the woman asked.

"Good." Isabella concentrated on the wound she was treating on her patient's arm. Considering how bad things could have been on this run, everyone involved had been lucky. She talked to the man to distract him from the sting of the antiseptic she used. "Hydrogen peroxide doesn't really disinfect things, like many people think. Only cleans it out a bit." She finished with the gauze, then tossed it into the biohazard bin beside her before applying more clean gauze pads atop the cut and wrapping it all in an ACE bandage. "Okay. Sir, have you decided if you want us to take you in?"

The man frowned at his arm, then at the scratches on his legs before shaking his head. "No. I think I'm okay, really. Has anyone checked my bike?"

"I did," Mario said. "It's fine. Put it against the front of the rig to keep it out of the way."

"Then no." The man ran his hand through his dark hair, still a mess from being under his helmet and sweaty. "I don't need to go."

Isabella had him sign a waiver refusing transport to the hospital, then gave him a card with all the information for St. Aelina's in case he changed his mind or required treatment later. By then, Mario had gotten the lady calmed down as well, and she looked much better. They sent both patients on their way before heading back toward headquarters to await another call.

They didn't have to wait long. Mario had barely turned into the parking lot when the dispatcher's voice rang through their radio and they got called out on a three-year-old boy with difficulty breathing. Within minutes they pulled up to the scene and climbed the stairs to the second floor to find the little boy on the sofa and his anxious mother nearby.

"Hello," Isabella said, moving to crouch in front of the boy, her medical pack at her feet, while Mario talked with the mother. He was on the small side for his age, wearing an orange-and-black knit cap on his head and a red-and-white-striped shirt with jean shorts. His little feet were bare. She smiled at him. "My name's Isabella. What's yours?"

"Barto," his mother said from her position near the sofa.

"Hello, Barto." Isabella pulled out her stethoscope and hung it around her neck. "Can I listen to your lungs?"

The little boy eyed her warily, wheezing.

"It won't hurt, I promise." She held the end of the stethoscope. "I'll just put this against your chest and listen."

Barto seemed to think about that, then nodded.

"Okay. Good." She leaned in and to check his lungs as Mario questioned the mother.

"When did his symptoms start?"

"Last night," the mother said. "I tried a humidifier and menthol rub on his chest along with his asthma meds, but it's only gotten worse."

Isabella sat back and nodded. "Sounds like croup."

As if in confirmation, Barto gave a hacking, wet cough.

"Oh, no." The mother's voice quivered.

"It'll be okay, ma'am." Mario patted her on the arm. "We're here, and we'll make sure your son gets the care he needs."

"Are you the police?" Barto asked Isabella.

"No." She grinned, then attached a pulse oximeter to the little boy's finger. "Not the police. Why? Are you under arrest?"

"No," Barto said, shaking his head, wide-eyed.

So cute. Reminded her of her younger brother Luis when he'd been that age. Isabella got out her pediatric blood pressure cuff next and held it up. "Can I see your arm?" The little boy extended it, and she put the cuff on. "Have you ever had your blood pressure checked, Barto?" He shook his head. "No? Okay. Well, this cuff is going to squeeze your arm a little bit, but that's all. Good. Relax your arm for me. There you go." She inflated the cuff, then slipped her stethoscope beneath the edge, listening for his heart sounds. "There you go. Great. You're doing amazing, Barto!"

The pulse oximeter beeped, and Isabella exchanged glances with Mario. The kid would need oxygen to help him breathe. His lips were already turning a bit blue.

"All right, big man," Isabella said, taking off the blood pressure cuff and keeping her tone cheerful. "We're going to give you a mask to wear. It will help you breathe better, okay, Barto?"

The boy balked a bit as Mario approached him with the clear oxygen mask. Isabella took it from her partner and held it in front of the little boy. "Here, it goes over your nose and mouth like this." She held it to her own face to show him. "There's medicine in there, too, to help you feel better. Take a deep breath in. Can you do that for me?"

Barto stared at the mask, his expression curious, then he reached a tentative hand for it. Isabella helped him hold it in front of his face, her eyes locked on him the whole time. "There you go. Breathe it in. That's right. In and out. In and out. Can you hold it there by yourself?"

He nodded.

"Excellent." Isabella stood and stuffed her gear back into her medical kit. "Barto, are you ready to go to the hospital now?"

"No," the little boy said. Everyone laughed.

"Come on," Isabella said, straightening. "It'll be fun. You'll ride with us. Your mother will be with you the whole time, okay?" She glanced at the mother and smiled. "Barto, do you want your mother to carry you out to the ambulance?"

"Yes, please."

"Okay." Mario stepped in. "Barto, I'm going to secure the mask to you with this strap, so you don't have to hold it anymore, all right?"

The little boy nodded. "Will it hurt?"

"Not at all." Mario got him taken care of, then stepped back. "There you go. You look like a dragon now. Want to be a dragon?"

Barto nodded.

"Cool." He gave the little boy a high five. "You're a dragon now."

They walked outside and waited while the mother got her purse and Barto, then locked up her flat before she joined them downstairs on the sidewalk. Once they helped them inside the back of the rig, Isabella joined them in back while Mario drove them to St. Aelina's.

Isabella took the opportunity to fill in more questions about the boy's history. "You said he had a fever?"

"Yes. Last night. It started at one zero two but then went up to one zero four."

"And did you give him anything to bring it down?"

"Acetaminophen," the mother said.

"Good." Isabella made her notes on her tablet. Barto looked to be feeling better, but they were taking him in to the ER anyway to have him evaluated. Protocol with the boy's asthma. He'd calmed now and the medication they gave him through the oxygen mask had lessened his cough. Dr. Santiago Garcia was on call tonight, if Isabella remembered correctly, so Barto and his mother would be in good hands.

A small tingle went through her as she realized she'd get to see Carlos again, too. They hadn't seen each other much today, and she missed him. Isabella smiled to herself. He was a good man, and they had a lot in common. They clicked well, and not just that one night they'd had together. She liked talking with him, spending time with him. She wasn't ready to call it more than a good friendship yet, but maybe she could see them getting there. Maybe.

They pulled into the ambulance bay at the hospital a few minutes later and took Barto inside. Sure enough, Carlos and Dr. Garcia, pediatrician, met them at the doors.

"What have we got?" Dr. Garcia asked as they led the boy and his mother down a hallway to an open exam room.

"His name is Barto," Isabella said, giving him the rundown. "He's three years old, history of asthma. Started having a wet, hacking cough last night and fever of up to one hundred and four. His O2 sats were low, and we started him on oxygen and corticosteroids."

"Very good." Dr. Garcia waited until the mother sat on the exam table, little Barto on her lap, before wheeling a stool up in front of them and taking a seat. "Hello, Barto. My name is Dr. Garcia. I'm going to help take care of you now, all right?"

Barto nodded, his head against his mother's chest.

Other staff filtered in, including Carlos, and Isabella caught his eye from across the room. They shared a little private smile before Carlos got to work on setting up a room for the boy.

"Okay, Barto. We're going to get started here," Dr. Garcia said, focusing on his patient and the mother. "A lot of people are going to be in here, doing different things, but I just want you to keep on taking those big breaths in and out for me while I listen to your chest…"

Isabella and Mario left the room and wandered back to the ambulance bay. Mario climbed into the back of the rig to clean up and restock while Isabella headed back inside. "I'm going to get something to drink from the cafeteria. Want anything?"

"Nope. I'm good, thanks," Mario said. "I'll text you if another run comes in."

"Thanks. Be right back."

She went downstairs to the cafeteria and got a bottled water, went back to the lobby, then took a seat in the atrium, where she could see Mario and the ambulance through the window in case they got another run. She felt a bit odd. Not sick, really, just…nostalgic, maybe. Seeing little Barto earlier had stirred up things inside her. Old memories and new fears. She realized she'd have a little son or daughter of her own soon, and while she was happy about the pregnancy, she was also scared. Scared she might mess things up. Scared that she might not be a good mother. Scared being a mother might be all she'd ever be…

"Hey," Carlos said, taking the seat beside her. She'd been so lost in her thoughts she hadn't even heard him arrive. He looked good, as always. Even the green scrubs he wore seemed custom made to flatter him, the color making his tanned skin look more bronzed, his dark eyes sparkle more, his voice deeper, sexier.

Okay, maybe that last one was her, but still.

She straightened in her seat and gulped down some water, glad for the coolness on her parched throat. "Hey."

Then he reached over and took her hand, and wow. Her pulse sped and her knees tingled. She had it bad for this guy, and that wasn't good. She couldn't bolt, though. Not here, where people knew her. She didn't want to cause a scene, so she stayed put, enjoying the warm press of his hand on hers far more than she should.

"How are you?" he asked, his thumb stroking small circles on her palm, reminding her all over again of their kiss the other night.

"Good," she said, the word squeaking out. She coughed and drank more water, than tried again. "Good. Thanks. Just tired."

"You aren't working too hard, are you?" His dark

brows knit, his dimples disappearing beneath a frown. He leaned a bit closer to whisper, "You should rest more, with the baby."

His soft, minty breath tickled her cheek, and if she hadn't been sitting, Isabella believed she would've swooned. Which wasn't like her at all. If she'd been on the beach, she'd have taken her board and dived head-first into a whitecap to get away. Now, she had to endure this sweet torture.

Rather than give in to her urge to snuggle closer to him, she turned to irritation instead. She hated being babied. Tugged on her hand in his, but he didn't let go. "I'm fine."

"Hmm." He watched her curiously. "I didn't mean to upset you."

She harrumphed, feeling prickly and out of sorts.

Carlos, charming as ever, darn him, just chuckled, continuing to stroke her palm like she was a wild horse he was trying to tame. He stared down at their joined hands, his expression unreadable. "You take care of others but don't like them taking care of you." He glanced up and caught her gaze. "You've told me a bit about your past, but not all. Why is it you don't like to be taken care of?"

For a moment, she considered getting up and walking away. But something kept her there, in her seat. Something warm and wild and far too scary for her to want to think about just then. She tried to shake his question off with a nonanswer. "I don't know. I guess it's a carryover from my job."

"Hmm." He sat back, blinking at her. "Which one?"

She frowned. "What do you mean?"

"Well, it seems to me you have two jobs. The one you work now, as a paramedic. And the one you left behind when your siblings moved out."

Wow. She'd known he was very empathetic, but no one had ever gotten her so well, so quickly. Too stunned to deny it, she just nodded. "That's true."

Carlos nodded, then slowly brought her hand to his lips to kiss the back of it gently. Mesmerized, she didn't even care that the staff behind the desk across the way were probably staring at them. She never intended to talk about any of this, especially here at work, but no one else was around them, and even in the large atrium, things between her and Carlos felt very cozy and intimate.

"I'm the caretaker. I've always been the caretaker," she said, her tone hushed as memories flooded back. "Ever since our mom passed, as the eldest, I had to take over. I cared for my younger siblings and then also my father after he got sick. I had to stay strong for them. I did stay strong for them."

"You did," he murmured, tucking her hand against his chest, right over his heart. His scrub shirt had slipped down a little so her bare skin brushed his and, oh, Lord. All the oxygen disappeared from the room. She gulped in a breath, blood pounding in her ears. It was too much. It wasn't enough. "You were so strong, *hermosa*. You still are. Strong, independent, beautiful."

His pulse beat in time with hers beneath her touch, and their gazes locked. The world shifted beneath her, and in that moment, Isabella realized that no matter how things turned out with Carlos, her life would never be the same. "I must be careful," he said, and there were those dimples again, drawing her further under his spell. "You could steal my heart, *hermosa*. And we can't have that."

She watched him, eyes half-closed, unable to move, unable to breathe, unable to do anything except lean closer to him. Somewhere in the back of her mind, caution alarms went off, but she ignored them.

At least until her phone buzzed in her uniform pocket.

Carlos sat back and she fumbled for her phone, pulling it out to see a text from Mario saying they had another call to go out on. She didn't dare look out the window to where her EMT partner stood for fear of seeing the knowing look on his face.

Dammit.

She stood and finished her water before tossing the bottle in the nearby recycle bin, saying a silent prayer for small miracles. If she wasn't careful, Carlos wouldn't be the only one losing his heart here.

"I, uh, need to get back to work," she said, face hot and scalp tingling.

"What about dinner? Tomorrow night?" he asked, following her to the ambulance bay doors. "We can get a table at my uncle's place, near the back. Talk more, have some good food. Just relax."

Isabella knew she had a choice to make then, and her rational brain wanted to say no. Being around him made her forget everything else, and that was too seductive and dangerous. But the other part of her all but tumbled over itself to say yes before she could stop herself. "Fine. Text me the time. I'll meet you there."

Then she walked out the door as fast as her feet could carry her. Running to an emergency or away from another, she couldn't really say.

CHAPTER SIX

THE NEXT EVENING, Carlos stood on the sidewalk outside Encanteri, waiting for Isabella. Excitement and anticipation buzzed through his bloodstream, making him antsy. Several groups of tourists and locals stood nearby, chatting and laughing, but Carlos couldn't concentrate on anything but the woman he feared he'd fallen for too hard and too fast.

After all, they'd only spent a few hours together, touring the sights of the city, getting to know each other better. And yes, they'd slept together once already, but that had been a while ago, and now he started to wonder if it had all been a dream. Well, no. Not a dream, since Isabella was pregnant with his baby, but still.

What had happened to him with his father had left him shaken, and he was hesitant of relationships in general and didn't like to label things. Labels were bad, in his opinion. He'd dealt with enough of them in his life. But this thing with Isabella wasn't going away. In fact, their connection seemed stronger than ever, and the more he learned about her, the more he wanted to know. Unsettling, that.

And if her phone hadn't gone off the day before in the

lobby, he would've kissed her right there in his work-place, which wasn't like him. He never lost control of his emotions. He felt for his patients, yes, of course. But never did he let those feelings rule him or override his judgment. Only with Isabella. A problem indeed.

"Sorry I'm late," she said, rushing up to him at the curb, looking stunning in another sundress. This one light pink and purple, like the sunset above them. "An older neighbor caught me on the way out of my building and wanted to chat. I didn't want to be rude."

"I understand," he said, and he did. Many times, the older patients in the ER just wanted company, someone to talk to, and Carlos was happy to be that person for them. He considered the contact part of his job every bit as important as the medicine.

They went inside, and Carlos managed to flag down his uncle, who worked behind the bar, helping one of the bartenders with some complicated contraption for mixing drinks that looked like it came straight out of Dr. Frankenstein's lab. Lots of bubbling beakers and metal pipes and brightly colored test tubes.

"Wow. I'd forgotten how pretty this place was inside."

"It is, isn't it?" Carlos smiled, looking around. All the sparkling glass and carved woodwork, bottles and bits and bobs. A feast for the eyes as well as the palate. A low hum of conversation bounced off the rough-hewn stone walls, and streetlights glimmered through the arched stained-glass windows at the front. The mood felt casual and cool, and Carlos felt incredibly proud of his uncle's accomplishments here at the bar. Family meant everything to him after growing up without part of his. He never wanted his own child to experience that. Another reason to tread carefully with Isabella. He didn't want to mess up the coparenting thing with a messy romance, even if the prospect grew more tempting by the second.

His uncle wove through the crowded bar over to them, still smiling broadly. "Nephew," he said, kissing Carlos on both cheeks, then did the same to Isabella. Cubans were very warm people. "And Isabella. Don't you look lovely this evening."

She did, too. All long legs and smooth skin, and Carlos did his best not to notice. A failed effort. He couldn't not notice Isabella, it seemed. From the moment she was near, he knew it from the tingle in his skin, the thud of his pulse. Something primal and undeniable and, oh, boy. Not good. Not good at all.

"Did you save us a table, Uncle?" Carlos asked, hoping to move things along.

"Of course, nephew." He linked arms with Isabella, leading her away toward the back of the bar, leaving Carlos behind to trail after them. Through the din of talk around them, he made out his uncle telling her Carlos got impatient sometimes when nervous and she would have to see what she could do about that. Isabella laughed then, the sound musical and light, and he found himself becoming enchanted all over again. Ridiculous. Insane. Like drinking expensive, heady madeira straight from the bottle and he wasn't sure he'd ever get enough.

They finally stopped near a small table for two in the back corner near the windows. Candles flickered from the center of the table, and a bowl of red and pink roses completed the centerpiece. His uncle helped Isabella with her chair, then handed them each a menu. Isabella ordered sparkling water to drink, and Carlos got cava. "If I may suggest, nephew, let me pick your entrées tonight. The chef had made something very special just for you two."

"Oh." Carlos glanced at Isabella to find her wide-eyed and smiling. "I'm game if you are."

"Sure."

They turned in their menus to his uncle, who bowed slightly, a glint in his eyes. "Very good. I'll be back shortly with your appetizers and drinks."

Once they were alone, Isabella fiddled with her napkin while Carlos took an inordinate interest in the street outside. Finally, she said, "I didn't know your uncle Hugo waited tables, too."

"Oh, he doesn't. Usually. He just wants to keep an eye on us." Carlos grinned. "He's very nosy."

"He cares for you a lot." Isabella straightened her silverware next. "That's obvious."

"I care for him, too. He's the only family I have here."

Hugo brought their drinks, along with a basket of deviled crab croquettes and *bolitas de yuca.* "Enjoy," his uncle said before quickly departing, and now Carlos's suspicions rose. Both appetizers were distinctly Cuban in origin.

"Wow," Isabella said, putting one of each of the deep-fried, breaded balls onto her plate. "What are they?"

"These—" Carlos pointed to a croquette "—are deviled crab balls and should be eaten with the cocktail sauce there. And the other ones are *tostones.* Both

Cuban delicacies. And safe during pregnancy, as they've been cooked properly. In fact, the plantains in the *tostones* are an excellent source of folates. The sauce for those is avocado, lime and garlic. It's called *mojo verde*."

"Hmm." She dipped one of the round, smashed, fried green plantains in the bowl of green sauce beside it, then took a bite. "Wow! That's so good. I've never had Cuban food before."

"Well, I'm glad to be your first, then." He gave her a saucy little wink. "And yes, they are very good." He spooned out some sauce onto his own plate and put some more on hers as well. "The *mojo verde* really brings out all the flavors."

They both ate a few bites of each. For Carlos it felt like a bit of home, which he suspected was his uncle's whole plan. He might have mentioned how much he liked Isabella to his uncle and how much he wished he could show her his homeland. Knowing Uncle Hugo, this was an invitation to bring Cuba here, when Carlos couldn't just leave and go to Cuba.

"How is everything so far?" his uncle asked, returning to refill their drinks.

"Well, seeing as how it's all gone, I'd say it's going well." Carlos leaned in to whisper, "Thank you."

"Wait until you see what's next, *sobrino*." His uncle waggled his brows, then cleared away their empty plates. "Your dinner will be ready shortly."

Carlos waited until they were alone again, pleasantly full and relaxed a bit more now, thanks to the cava. He'd been wanting to pick up their conversation from the day before in the lobby but hadn't known how to start.

Maybe, if Isabella felt more comfortable, too, he could ease into it now. Deep down, instinct told him there was more in her past that kept her from moving forward.

"So." He smiled across the table at her, their legs tangling slightly beneath the table. Neither of them pulled back. A good sign in his book. "Tell me more about your family growing up."

Isabella shrugged, smoothing the tablecloth with her hand. She did that, he'd noticed, whenever she was uncomfortable. Cleaning things up, straightening them. Like trying to form order out of chaos. His heart tugged a little more toward her. If he wasn't careful, it would belong to her forever. He could blame his purple prose on the cava, but that would be a lie.

It wasn't all the drink.

"Not much to tell, really. Other than what I've already said."

"I don't believe you."

"I don't care." They stared at each other across the table, a standoff of sorts, and Carlos wished he hadn't blurted out those words like that, but dammit. His brain didn't seem to work when she was around. He was all feeling, all emotion. One big, raw, vulnerable nerve ending vibrating for her touch. He hoped she wouldn't get up and walk away. He prepared for the worst anyway. Her dark eyes sparkled with hurt and hesitation, like a fawn ready to race away at the slightest movement. Carlos stayed still, watching, waiting.

Then his uncle returned with a tray of delicious-smelling food, saving the evening. "Here we are, compliments of the chef."

As his uncle set out plate after plate of Cuban delicacies, Carlos's chest warmed even more. "*Tío*, what did you do?"

"I brought you a little bit of home," he said in Spanish. "I knew you were feeling a bit homesick lately and thought it would be a nice surprise for you and your lady friend."

Carlos stood to kiss his uncle on the cheek, then beamed over at Isabella, their earlier tension forgotten. "Tonight, you shall taste my homeland."

Her small smile grew, the wariness in her eyes disappearing beneath a sparkle of happiness. "I can't wait. I'm starving."

He almost made a comment about her eating for two but caught himself at the last minute. They'd agreed not to say anything yet until she'd told her family, and he didn't want to ruin things now that they were back on track.

Carlos waited until his uncle had laid everything out, then told her the name of each dish. "This is *ropa vieja*, Cuban-style shredded beef. Next, we have *fricasé de pollo*, or Cuban-style chicken stew, and finally there's *pernil asado con mojo*, marinated pork shoulder roast. Again, all cooked properly, so safe for you and the baby. On the side is rice and beans and more *tostones*. Plus, extra *mojo verde* to dip it all in."

"I…" She blinked at all the food, then back at him. "I'm not even sure where to start."

Carlos sighed and reached over for her hand. "How about over again? I'm sorry for my stupid question before. I didn't mean to put you on the defensive."

Isabella shook her head, staring down at her plate. "I'm sorry, too. I… My past is a touchy subject sometimes."

"I get that." He winked once more, then dished up food for them both. "Let's eat. We can talk later."

They dined and chatted, the tension easing away with good food and conversation, until, about halfway through the meal, Isabella sighed. "I wish I could be more open about growing up," she said, and he froze midbite, not wanting to move in case she stopped talking again. "But I don't know. I always get tangled up." She pushed a bite of rice around on her plate with her fork, not looking at him, brows drawn together. "I think maybe it's guilt."

"Guilt?" he said, too shocked to stay silent. "What would you have to feel guilty about?"

"I guess I always wonder if I could've done more to help my father. If I did enough for my siblings." She snorted softly. "Or maybe if I did too much and smothered them. Maybe that's why they all moved out and away as soon as they were able. Away from me."

"Oh, Isabella," he said, reaching across to take her hand. "I'm sure you did everything you could. You were just a child yourself. It's not your fault. None of that was your fault."

She shrugged, looking unconvinced. "Maybe. And I did do my best, but none of them had any idea how hard it was for me back then. They were all too small to understand. Then when they were older and left me behind to pursue their dreams, I was happy for them. But I was also hurt."

She shook her head. "Even Diego got married to Grace in the UK and didn't even invite his family." Isabella straightened and pushed her plate away, wiping her mouth with her napkin and still avoiding his gaze. "I mean, I know Father's death was inevitable, but I can't shake the feeling that I could have done more, should have done more to keep us all together after he passed. But then I also feel guilty for wanting escape myself sometimes. It's complicated."

She finally met his gaze, and he wanted nothing more than to hold her close and tell her everything would be all right. "I'm not sure why I told you all that. I feel like I've been running from those emotions for a long time. But somehow you make it okay for me to talk."

Carlos felt like his heart had swelled to fill his whole chest. He swallowed hard and squeezed her hand tighter. "I'm glad you can talk to me, *hermosa*. I want to be there for you, and not just because of the baby."

She smiled then, warm and sweet, tightening her hold on his hand. "Thank you. That means a lot to me." She lowered her head again, taking a deep breath. "I've stayed busy for years, using it as a distraction. It's probably why I like being a paramedic so much. The adrenaline rush, the fact that it's nomadic in a way. Always something new and different. Never the same thing twice. Never stuck in one spot. Not getting too attached."

"Oh, *hermosa*," he said, the words emerging gruff due to his constricted throat. "I'm sorry for—"

Isabella held up a hand, stopping him, her smile sad. "No, please. Don't feel sorry for me. That only makes it worse. I like my life. I'm happy. I never wanted to settle down after what happened to my parents." She shook her head. "Never thought a child would be on my agenda at all. Not after what felt like a lifetime of responsibility and my sense of failure after that." She took a deep breath, the beat stretching out between them, taut and tender. "But then I met you, and you changed things. Not just the baby, Carlos. When I'm not with you, I don't feel like a confident, independent woman. I feel alone."

He did get up then, couldn't help it, and pulled her into his arms. Except they were blocking an important aisle, so he pulled her out onto the dance floor instead. A small band had set up in the corner playing standards, and they'd begun a slow song. He held Isabella against him, letting her know without words that he supported her. He'd always be there for her, no matter what. As the music washed over them, she gradually relaxed against him and they swayed gently to the music, first one song, then another, then another, until Carlos lost track of time, of their location, of everything except the woman in his arms and the incredible things she made him feel.

Eventually, he looked over to find his uncle Hugo clearing their table, watching them dance with a fond smile. He gave Carlos a grin and a thumbs-up, and Carlos nodded back. His uncle had become a surrogate father, and he loved him for it. But right now, there were more important things on his mind. He wanted more time with Isabella—all night, if she'd let him.

He pulled away slightly, to meet her gaze, soft and sweet in the dim light. A simple question, but it felt like the most important one he'd ever asked. "Come upstairs with me, *hermosa*? We don't have to do anything. Just talk, if you like. But I don't want this night to end. Not yet." *Not ever.*

She watched him a long moment, then raised a hand

to trace her fingers down his cheek, making him shiver. An answering yearning lit her eyes, making his pulse notch higher and his blood sing. "I don't want it to end, either, Carlos."

They kissed, and his world rocked. He grabbed her hand and pulled her back to the table for a quick good-bye to his uncle. She grabbed her bag, then they were out the door and climbing the stairs to his flat. His fingers trembled and he damned near dropped the keys, but finally they were inside and Isabella was in his arms and kissing him, tasting of spices and sweet desire.

They made their way down the hall to his bedroom, not breaking the kiss, a trail of discarded clothes in their wake, until they fell onto his bed, naked and desperate. Different than the first night they'd been together. Then it had been all about exploring, getting to know what the other liked. Now, it was hot and intense, their feelings making every touch, every sigh more meaningful.

Carlos kissed his way down to her breasts, cupping them in his palms, then taking one taut nipple into his mouth. Isabella cried out, little mewls shooting like lightning straight to his groin. She pulled him closer, needing more. He gave her everything, putting all his want and need and love into his caresses. More than sex. Way more, at least for him. They were making love in every sense of the word.

Isabella thought she'd died and gone to heaven when Carlos kissed his way down her body to her abdomen, then lower still, tracing his tongue over her slick folds. While she wasn't a virgin by any means, being with

Carlos felt different from any lover she'd had before. Even their first time together. But before, it had felt heated and rushed and inquisitive. Now, she knew Carlos better, and it seemed to shed a new light on their lovemaking. His consideration and kindness extended to the bedroom this time as well, with him making sure she was comfortable and happy and satisfied before he took his own pleasure. He nuzzled and made love to her with his hands and mouth until she tumbled over the brink into orgasm, unable to keep from whispering his name over and over as the waves of ecstasy rocked her entire being.

At last, he kissed his way up her body again, stopping to nuzzle her breasts once more before propping himself up on one elbow while reaching into his nightstand drawer for a condom.

She stopped him. "We don't need that now, remember?"

Carlos froze, his eyes widening slightly as her words sank in. They could be together tonight with nothing between them.

Heat prickled her cheeks then, making her suddenly shy. "I haven't been with anyone since you."

"Me neither." He blinked down at her. "Are you sure, though, *hermosa*?"

Isabella nodded. She couldn't wait to feel him inside her with no barrier between them at all and reached up to smooth away the sudden lines of tension etched near the corners of his mouth and eyes. Then she trailed her hand lower, stopping once she'd encircled his hard length, stroking him until Carlos pulled her hand away and kissed her palm. "Too much of that, *hermosa*, and I won't last."

In answer, she drew him down for an openmouthed kiss while wrapping her legs around his waist and arching her hips into him. "Please, Carlos. I need you…"

He rose above her, holding his weight on his forearms, the tip of his hard length poised at her wet entrance. A beat passed, then two, before he finally entered her in one long stroke, then held still, allowing her body to adjust to his. When he did move at last, they both moaned deeply and began a rhythm that had them teetering on the brink in no time at all.

"Carlos, I…" Isabella cried out as she climaxed once more, her words lost as the universe exploded into a million iridescent shards around her. Maybe the pregnancy hormones made her more responsive. Maybe the magic of the night entranced her. Maybe they were so in sync, both in and out of bed, all her nerve endings twinkled like diamonds. Whatever it was, she felt like a live wire, sparking and shimmering with pleasure whenever he was near. He drove into her once, twice more, then his body tightened in her arms as he came hard inside her, his face buried in her neck and her name on his lips, murmuring sweet nothings against her skin.

Afterward, they lay in the darkness, listening to the crickets outside, his head resting in the valley between her breasts, over her heart, and her fingers in his hair, tracing lazy circles against his scalp. She felt sated and relaxed for the first time in a while, and she had Carlos to thank for that as well. Isabella opened her mouth to tell him so, but he raised up slightly to meet her gaze, speaking first as his frown returned, deepened.

"That…wow," he said, his voice quiet in the shadows. "I don't know what this is happening between us, *hermosa*, but I want it to continue. I want to explore it more."

She couldn't really see his face in the dark, but the vulnerability in his tone made her heart clench. Isabella wanted that, too, even if it scared her. He rolled over onto his back and pulled her into his side, her leg sprawling across his and her head on his chest as he pulled the covers up over them. Beneath her hand, his pulse was steady and true. "I'd like that," she whispered.

"Good." He gathered her closer. "You know, I came here to retrace my parents' last steps together, but it seems I've begun a journey of my own—with you. History is repeating itself." He sighed, hesitated. "I only ever wanted to belong somewhere. To know I had a place, roots. I had half in Cuba, but today I found the rest. Perhaps you could be my roots here, *hermosa*."

She nodded, his words bittersweet. Roots meant staying in one place, and that's the thing she'd fought against most of her adult life. But she didn't want to ruin this moment, this one perfect evening together, so she kept that to herself. They'd have plenty of time to talk about it tomorrow.

"Hmm. This is nice, too," he said, his words rumbling beneath her ear, warm and deep. "I hope you enjoyed tonight. My uncle felt proud to serve you that dinner." He nestled her head under his chin, and she snuggled closer into his heat, meaning every word. It was wonderful. The food, the company. Everything.

"Good night, *hermosa*," Carlos said, kissing the top of her head before drifting off to sleep, and Isabella soon followed him into slumber.

CHAPTER SEVEN

"SINCE THIS IS your first time, let's practice on the sand before we hit the waves." Isabella nodded to two surfboards a few feet away that they'd hauled down from her flat earlier. It had been a week since they'd slept together at his place and the first time their work schedules had coordinated, so they were spending time together, getting to know each other better still by sharing things they loved. Today was Isabella's choice, so of course, they were surfing. Isabella had checked the weather forecasts earlier this morning before they'd left her flat, and thanks to some storms brewing out in the Atlantic from off the coast of western Africa, thousands of miles away, the conditions were perfect at Bogatell. Well, perfect for an experienced surfer like her, anyway.

"Okay." Carlos took off his T-shirt and dropped it onto his beach towel next to his flip-flops and sunglasses. "Is that for me?" A black wet suit sat next to one of the boards.

"If you want it. The water's cold, but you get used to it quickly. Up to you."

"I'm good." He wanted to feel the salt water on his skin with as little barrier as possible, no matter how chilly it might be. With open-water swimming and surf-ing outlawed in his home country of Cuba for fear peo-ple would leave for good, it would be a relatively new experience. The only other time he'd been out in the water here was the first night he'd met Isabella, but with a man's life in their hands, his attention had obviously been elsewhere.

She smiled and led him to her board. "You've got sunscreen on, right?"

"*Si.*" He had a good base tan and he was olive skinned anyway, but still. One could never be too care-ful with the ultraviolet rays. Also, bringing along the stuff might give him a chance to get Isabella's hands on him again. "But…" He bent and picked up the bright yellow tube of sunscreen from his beach towel and held it out to her, not missing the way she checked him out. His skin tingled from more than the heat now.

"You didn't get your back," Isabella said, taking the stuff from him and squirting it out in her hand before walking around behind him. Beneath his striped board shorts, his body tightened at the first cool touch of her hand on him. "How's that?"

Carlos nearly moaned, his eyes slipping closed as she rubbed the cream into the knotted muscles between his shoulder blades. "Good, *hermosa*," he managed to get out, the words rough with suppressed need. They couldn't do anything here, not with all the tourists and kids around, but man. He wanted to. Boy, did he want to. "That feels so good."

Tingles exploded through his body, and it took all his willpower not to turn and scoop Isabella into his arms and haul her back to her flat, caveman-style, to have his wicked way with her. His breath hitched as she leaned in, her fingers tickling the hair at the nape of his neck. Isabella was tall for a woman and fit him so perfectly inside and out, he still had to pinch himself sometimes to make sure all this was real. But then he finally inhaled deep and smelled her scent over the sand and the sea and knew this was real. She smelled like fresh flowers and tropical fruit from her sunscreen and warm, sweet woman. And now he ached from this very normal, casual act and, oh, boy.

Bring on the cold water.

Isabella lifted her hands away from him not a moment too soon.

Thankfully, for the next several minutes, Isabella gave him a lesson on surfing on land, which required a lot of lying down on the board, so his front was hidden. Uncomfortable? Yes. Necessary? Also, yes. Carlos did his best to pay attention to what she taught him and forget about his traitorous body, copying Isabella's movements as best he could and hoping the learning process was long enough to commit the movements to his muscle memory. His analytical brain might be hard-wired better than most, but it was still hard to focus on the task at hand. Not when Isabella was there, too, and he could watch the strength and power in her supple, shapely arms and legs.

"I think you're ready," Isabella said at last, tucking her surfboard under her arm. "You good?"

Besides feeling like he'd just gone ten rounds with a prizefighter in the ring, yeah. Carlos gave her a thumbs-up. And prayed he wouldn't make a complete fool of himself out there.

The second the water reached his knees, his body shriveled in on itself and his breath caught in his chest, making it difficult to inhale. It wasn't that cold. Not really. It was June, after all, but the shock was still there. Exhales in rapid succession didn't help much, but Isabella's amiable voice did.

"Don't panic, *cariño*. You'll get used to it in a minute."

Maybe. But then the tide came at him with more force than he expected, and Carlos wavered.

Isabella moved the surfboard between them, obviously aware that he had issues keeping his balance on top of breathing normally. He knew how to swim. Had learned in his grandparents' pool in Havana. But the ocean was a whole different ball game. She pointed at the board, then him. "Hop on. I'll get us farther out."

Carlos maneuvered onto the board, getting into position on his stomach just like he'd been taught, and tried not to freak out. Probably watching Shark Week on streaming had been a mistake. Not to mention riptides. He heard about patients getting caught in those all the time in the ER. How deep did they have to go? His pulse revved.

A wave came at them, and Carlos squeezed his eyes shut as Isabella guided him over it. It splashed in his face, though, and he still managed to swallow a mouthful of the stuff before spitting it out.

"It helps to keep your mouth closed," Isabella said in a slightly snarky tone before winking at him.

So instead, he coughed and sputtered with his head tilted down, hoping not to draw too much attention to the fact he had no idea what he was doing. When they reached the strip of white water Isabella had mentioned during his beach training earlier, she spun his board around so that Carlos faced the shoreline.

From out here, the sand looked miles away. The gentle sway of the vast water made him hyperaware of his surroundings, and sudden fear plunged like a meteor deep into his gut. He understood now why the Cuban government warned people not to swim in the waters around the island. It would be too easy to be caught up and swept away. He grabbed Isabella's hand, ready to denounce all his machismo and say flat out he'd changed his mind.

But then he remembered the thrill of seeing the city with her, how she'd looked the first night standing on the shore, so wistful and wonderful. And all he'd been through before coming to Barcelona and after.

As if reading his thoughts, Isabella leaned in and kissed his cheek, then whispered, "You can do this, *cariño*. Remember what I taught you."

Then everything happened so fast, and Carlos had no more time to think at all.

"Now, ready…set…go." Isabella gave him a push.

He paddled like mad to catch the wave. Way too fast, the tide rolled over him and he forgot all the things Isabella had taught him. The surfboard bounced beneath him, and water curled above his head and Carlos squeezed his eyes shut and seriously considered vomiting.

You can do this, cariño.

Isabella's voice in his head forced his eyes open, and he pushed up to his feet on the board, arms out for balance, and for a split second he did it, riding on the water, powerful and free and…

He toppled sideways.

Next thing he knew, the riptide tossed him feet over head and pulled him under. Without thinking, he opened his mouth and immediately swallowed more salty water, and his eyes stung. All his swimming skills meant nothing here and the more he struggled against the current, the harder it became, arms flailing like mad, legs kicking but getting him nowhere. His lungs screamed for air.

Then, in his head, Isabella's training came back to him. *Don't fight it. Go with the current if you go under.* Even though it went against his every instinct, Carlos stopped fighting and relaxed, all his muscles going slack, praying silently that he'd reach the surface soon.

Ten, nine, eight…

In a few more seconds, he'd run out of air. Swim. He needed to swim. Diagonal to the shore, except he had no idea of the direction. Then, by some miracle, warm sunshine bathed his face, and he gulped for air.

He'd made it. Exhausted from head to toe, but alive. He caught enough breath to yell out a weak "Help" before slipping back under the water. Arms wrapped around him then and pulled him above the surface once more. He breathed, more deeply than he ever had before, eyes closed because it was hard to keep them open. He felt himself being dragged forward through the water. Voices echoed around him, muffled and incoherent. A cool, hard surface met his back, and the warmth around him faded away. "Carlos? *Cariño.* Can you hear me?"

"Ye-yes," he whispered.

"Open your eyes." Isabella's voice had switched into

professional paramedic mode now, though he knew her well enough to detect the edge of fear beneath.

It took a moment, but he finally managed to pry his eyes open and blink up into Isabella's face. A blurry crowd had gathered around them on the beach. Disoriented, Carlos pressed his palms into the wet sand and tried to sit up, blinking hard.

"Hey," Isabella said, putting her hand on his chest, forcing him back down to the sand. "You're okay. Just lie there a minute and breathe, okay? Just relax. You're safe now."

"Sorry," he croaked out, his throat sore from all the salt water he'd swallowed. "I did that wrong."

"*No te preocupis,*" she said in Catalan, smiling down at him, stroking the damp hair from his forehead. It felt good. Soothing. His breathing slowed along with his pulse. And maybe he'd been in Barcelona long enough now, or maybe he'd just been around Isabella enough, but he understood what she said much quicker than before. *No worries.* Sitting there with her, as she stroked his head, he had none.

A lifeguard pressed between two bystanders, asking in Spanish, "Everything all right here?"

"Fine," Isabella answered back. They started talking then, apparently knowing each other from her paramedic route. It all went over Carlos's head. His now-pounding head, but nothing a few pain relievers wouldn't banish. His muscles were sore now, too, from his struggle against the riptide.

Murmurs ran through the crowd around them, several different languages at once—Spanish, English, French, even some Japanese. Barcelona was a cosmopolitan city, after all. Carlos lay there, thinking how odd it was to be on the other side of things. Usually, he was the medical professional, handling the patient. Now the tables were turned. He was glad Isabella was there for him, even as he feared he might trigger her fears again. She'd spent so many years caring for others. He didn't want to be a burden. Like he'd been a burden to his mother and grandparents.

Okay. Maybe he was the one triggered now.

"Let's give him some space, please," Isabella said to the circle of people around them, authority in her tone. Seconds later, sunshine instead of shadows filled the airspace above her.

Carlos raised a hand to shield his eyes from the bright sun and squinted up at Isabella. "I'm okay."

This time when he started to sit up, she helped him, eventually taking his hand and helping him to his feet. His legs still felt a bit wobbly but held. He reached behind him to wipe the itchy sand off his board shorts.

"Want to try again?" Isabella asked.

"Uh…no. Thanks." Carlos snorted. "I think one humiliation is enough. But you go ahead and surf if you want. The waves still look good. Be careful, though. I don't want what happened to me to happen to you."

"Are you sure?" Isabella frowned, then glanced out at the water. He didn't miss the yearning in her expression. She loved this. Born for it. All those old fears surfaced again inside him before he tamped them down. Isabella bit her lip and met his gaze once more. "And I'll be fine. I've surfed much rougher conditions than this in my life. But we can go back if you prefer."

"No." Carlos shook his head and smiled. "Please,

hermosa. I want you to enjoy yourself. I know you've missed this."

She sighed, then gave him an answering grin. "Yeah, I really have. If you're sure…"

"I am."

The crowd slowly dispersed, the show over, and Carlos stood there watching the woman he loved grab her surfboard and run straight for the water that had nearly just killed him, trying to figure out how they could be so different yet still make this work. For themselves, and for their child.

Isabella tried to be in the present, to lose herself in the water as she loved to do, as she done through her most difficult teen years. Because of the storms far out to sea, the waves were good sized, pounding the beach in the bright sunshine. Her pulse raced from a mix of residual fear for what had happened to Carlos and from the surge of adrenaline being this near to the ocean always gave her. She paddled out and caught a wave. Stood on her board, feeling the air rush past and the spray of water, the power of the eight- to ten-foot wave carrying her forward harder, faster. Making her forget everything—all the stress and doubts and longings—until nothing existed but her and water. Carlos had been concerned about her going out again after what had happened to him, but she'd waved it off. A risk, yes, but she was very experienced and could handle it.

Cursing herself under her breath for what had happened to Carlos, she turned around and paddled back out again to catch another wave and ride it in. Then another. And another. Hoping maybe the exertion would burn away her guilt, along with her excess adrenaline. Because if he'd died, then…

No. She would not think about that. Unacceptable.

Carlos was fine. Still watching her from the beach. He wasn't going anywhere.

Is he?

Isabella paddled harder now, ripping it up every single time. In the zone at last, she savored the weightless, surreal, nothing-can-touch-me existence where everything wrong and scary and overwhelming disappeared and all that was left were the good feelings.

Like what she felt for Carlos.

Because regardless of the weird things coming up from her past or the uncertainty of the future, the baby and their relationship, Isabella wanted to suspend time and just enjoy the moments of pure joy and tenderness and comfort she found with him. The pleasure and the understanding, before they disappeared under the stress of daily life and the realities of the things they would have to face soon enough. Custody. Caretaking. Co-parenting.

She took one more long, bumpy, fast-as-hell drop of a wave and rode it all the way in to the shore, finally walking out of the water to the applause of several tourists nearby. She even stopped and posed with her board for them to snap some pictures before joining Carlos on their beach towels, jamming the end of her board into the sand nearby so it stood upright to dry. Her long, loose hair dripped wet, and she squeezed out some of the excess water before plopping down beside him on the towel.

"Did you have fun, *hermosa*?" he asked, his hand warm on her knee through the black wet suit.

"*Si.*"

They sat there in silence a moment or two, staring out at the crushing waves, several other surfers still out there in line. Even a young boy, seven, maybe eight, beside his father, heading out there, his boogie board Velcroed to his wrist with a band. Isabella had started surfing around the same age, going out with her father before her mother had died and Dad had gotten sick.

"You looked at home out there," Carlos said, his voice quiet now, his expression contemplative.

"I love it," she said, wrapping her arms around her knees. "When I'm on a wave, time ceases to exist, and I'm in this intense state of euphoria, peace and excitement." She took a deep breath. "And when I don't have to worry about patients or work or anyone or anything else but me, it's like bliss. I can mess around with my technique and put toes on the nose if I feel like it."

Carlos nodded, sighed. "Sounds magical."

"It is." Isabella shifted slightly to look at him over her shoulder. This morning had been amazing, in no small part due to the man beside her. The fact that she'd nearly lost him only made her want to be near him more. "Almost as good as being with you." She leaned in and kissed him, then rested her forehead against his, eyes closed as guilt choked her throat. "I'm sorry about what happened to you, *cariño*. I never meant for you to get hurt. I should've been more careful with your training. My fault and—"

"Shh." Carlos cupped the back of her head, keeping her close when she started to pull away. "It's okay.

I'm okay. Nothing that happened there was your fault. I got distracted and I didn't follow your instructions." He took a deep breath, then exhaled, stirring the hairs around her face, making her shiver. "You are very sexy in your wet suit."

Isabella sat back slightly to look at him, gaze narrowed. Not what she'd been expecting him to say. "What?"

He smiled brighter than the sun coming out from behind a cloud, lighting her world. Everything faded away but the warmth in his gaze. She didn't deserve his kindness, didn't deserve him, but in that moment, as every second they'd spent together so far flashed through her mind, Isabella knew that she didn't just like Carlos. She loved him. And that was probably the worst and most wonderful thing of all.

Confused and concerned, she sat back then, pulling away from him slightly. She needed to gather her thoughts, process all the stuff happening inside her. He let her go, as if sensing she needed space.

"I got really nervous watching you," he said after clearing his throat again. "Those waves are gigantic. Were you scared out there?"

"No. Not even a little." Her father's motto had always been *No fear or go home*. "Fear is dangerous out on the water," she said. "As you learned. I've been shaken a time or two, but I put it behind me quickly and keep going."

It's the same with you.

She kept that last part to herself, realizing it was true. Letting him in had made her feel much the same rush she did surfing—off-kilter, off balance, but connected.

"Well, that's good." Carlos seemed to consider that a moment. "I guess you've surfed even bigger waves?"

"*Si.*" She reached over to trace her finger down his cheek. "You've got a couple more freckles than you had before."

"Do I?" He scrubbed a hand over his jaw as his cheeks reddened slightly.

"*Si.* I think the Barcelona sunshine likes you."

"I like it, too."

She took his hand in hers, entwining their fingers. "The weather reports said we could get rain later."

"Is that very common?" He brought her hand to his mouth and kissed it. "Rain this time of year?"

Isabella's attention stayed fixed on his mouth, those generous lips, remembering where else he could kiss her, lick her, bring her to ecstasy over and over...

Just then, the little boy and his father came running out of the waves, laughing. They were both drenched but obviously so happy. Her heart pinched a little, remembering her own father in the last days, bedridden and unable to take care of himself. She'd resented him then. Loved him, mourned him and resented him. That old guilt threatened to rob her of breath now.

"Hey," Carlos said, leaning in to kiss her temple. "You okay?"

She nodded, not trusting her voice just then. She wasn't, really. But she would be. Had to be.

"You're amazing, *hermosa*. You know that? Amazing and all good."

"I'm not all good." She frowned, her chest squeezing tighter. "The longer you're around me, you'll find out. Like my siblings. They all couldn't get away from me fast enough."

"I don't believe that." He kissed down her cheek to her jaw, then lower to nuzzle her neck. "I want to stay beside you."

"*Hola,*" a female voice said just then from behind them.

Isabella looked over to see two bikini-clad young women flash their brightest smiles at Carlos, and an unexpected wave of possessiveness dug its claws into her chest, which only freaked her out more. She didn't get jealous. They weren't a couple. They were just two people having a good time together.

And a baby.

Oh, God.

Carlos, for his part, didn't bat an eye. Just shrugged a little, his gaze never leaving Isabella as he said in return, "Hey there."

His dark eyes held so much real, authentic emotion tangled up there, and Isabella had to look away. Too much. It would never be enough. She didn't want any of this, but it was all right there for her, and she didn't know what to do. Her hand trembled in his, and she leaned her head on his shoulder, taking a deep breath to hold it together. God. This wasn't her. Raw and vulnerable and flayed open. She'd been there before when her parents died and had sworn never to go there again. But being with Carlos terrified her.

As if calming a startled colt, he cupped her cheek and smoothed his thumb across her chin. "I only have eyes for you, *hermosa.*"

And even that made her afraid. Did she want to be

his one and only? Part of her said yes. The other part wasn't sure. Being exclusive, being committed, meant sticking it out no matter what, through sickness and health, till death.

Her heart lodged somewhere near her throat, and when exactly had the temperature risen so much?

Then Carlos threw back his head and laughed harder than she'd ever seen him do before, and suddenly the chains around her snapped. He always surprised her. He probably always would.

"What?" she asked, confused.

"If you could see your face right now, *hermosa*." He shook his head, then met her gaze once more, eyes bright with humor. "Don't worry. I'm not going to ask you to marry me. Not today, anyway."

She sputtered. Had she been that obvious? "I didn't think you would."

He squinted at her. "Yes, I think you did."

Carlos traced a finger down her neck and across her collarbone. Goose bumps popped up on her skin, but she still couldn't quite believe him. No one praised her awesomeness. People just took her for granted. Always had. Then he pulled her into his arms, and she relaxed against him despite her wishes. He made it so easy. Too easy. Her pulse thumped wildly in her chest.

"Let's do something," he said, whispering the words into her hair. "You gave me a peek into your life. Let me do the same for you."

She looked up at him, her brows knit. "Like what? We've been to your uncle's bar already and toured the entire city, visiting all the places in your mother's diary."

"I've got something special in mind," he said, smiling down at her. "A place from the diary I've not shown you yet."

"Really?" She turned slightly to face him, his arms still looped around her middle.

"Really." Carlos grinned now, wide and intoxicating. She totally got why women swooned over him wherever they went. "Tonight. Be ready at seven. Wear something you can move in."

"That's it? That's all you're giving me?" Isabella shook her head as he laughed. "You know I don't like surprises."

"I know, *hermosa*." He pulled her in and kissed her soundly, then stood, holding out a hand to her. "But for now, you're just going to have to trust me. You can't always be in control."

Isabella blinked up at him, then finally took his hand and allowed him to pull her up. It wasn't that she always had to be in control. She bent to pick up their towels and shake the sand out of them. Okay. Fine. Yes. She liked being in control. But that came from years of *having* to be in control. As for the trust thing… Well, she was working on it.

She rolled up the towels and tucked one under her arm, then handed the other to Carlos to do the same. Then they each grabbed a board to head back to her place. Isabella curled her toes in the warm sand. "Fine. Have it your way. I'll be ready at seven."

CHAPTER EIGHT

AT EIGHT FIFTEEN that night, Isabella and Carlos stood in front of a nondescript gray stone building on a side street in Sant Marti. The sounds of a busy street nearby echoed around them, and the air smelled of fried food from the street vendors and the rain from a couple hours before. Not exactly the lovely romantic fantasy she'd had in mind. She scrunched her nose and looked up at him. "This is it?"

"This is it." He winked at her, then opened the door, leading her up a narrow set of steps inside.

"And your parents came here?" she asked, staring at his back in front of her, her hand in his, tugging her forward.

"They did." Carlos looked back over his shoulder at her through the shadows. Dim sconces on the walls cast yellow light and shadows everywhere. He waggled his brows at her. "It's where my mother taught my father the dance of love."

Isabella gave him a suspicious look. "Where exactly did you bring me?" Even having lived in the city her whole life, she wasn't familiar with this address. "It's not illegal, is it?"

"No, *hermosa*. Not illegal." He snorted. "Just relax and enjoy. It will be fun."

Great. Isabella really wasn't a "just relax and enjoy" kind of person, but she'd go along with it since Carlos seemed so excited to show her this place.

They stopped at the top of the stairs, and she squinted at the wall where a line of black-and-white photos hung. Couples dressed in clothing from the '50s and '60s, dancing and laughing and embracing, all smiling and looking carefree. Huh. All the people were more formally dressed than the pink top and skirt she'd worn. Maybe she should've chosen something else. Her pulse quickened and her chest squeezed. Maybe this was a mistake after all.

"Hey." Carlos stood behind her, his hands on her hips, his warmth melting the thin line of ice traveling down her spine. "Do you trust me, *hermosa*?"

She nodded, swallowing hard. She tried. Really, really tried.

"*Buena,*" he said, and she studied his reflection in the glass of one of the photos. Gorgeous, as always. Tall, lean and powerful. His dark, curly hair was loose tonight, not tamed as it usually was for work. After all the sun earlier, he looked tanned and freer now, younger and more approachable. His long-sleeved gray shirt drew her gaze to the muscled lines of his chest and taut abs. Around his neck, in the hollow of his throat, dangled the small silver cross that he'd told her had belonged to his mother.

By the time she glanced back up at his face, his bemused expression slowly transformed into a smile. "Come. Let's go inside."

At the end of the hall, they stopped at a door. There were no numbers or signs to give her a hint of what she might see on the other side. Carlos winked at her once more, opened the door and flipped on the lights.

A high ceiling soared above them, covered in beautiful, warm oak, and mirrors surrounded them on three sides. The floor itself was bigger than her whole flat, and a small stage sat at one end, filled with stereo equipment. Isabella gaped at it all. She couldn't have been more stunned if he'd presented her with a live elephant. "What is this place?"

Carlos grinned and closed the door behind them. "A dance studio. It belongs to a friend of mine from Cuba. You like it?"

"*Si.* It's beautiful." She followed him down to the small stage, where he started turning on the stereo equipment. "But where is everyone?"

"The studio is closed tonight." He put on a slow, instrumental piece full of soaring, sweet melodies and a singer lamenting love and heartbreak in Spanish. "It's just for us."

"Oh," she said, letting that sink in. "Oh!"

"*Si.*" He began to move with the rhythm, stepping and rotating his hips and oh! He was good at that. He held out a hand to her, but she shied away. Isabella had never had time for dancing when she was growing up and figured it was probably too late to learn now. Carlos gave her a look, then smiled slow, those dimples of his beckoning her to him. "Come, *hermosa.* Don't worry. I'll teach you."

The music changed then, and the air filled with the quick, throbbing, syncopated beats of a samba, the kind of music the clubs down by the beach played. The clubs Isabella didn't usually have time to go to because of work. She'd always liked that kind of music, though, and found her toes tapping despite herself.

Carlos waggled his fingers at her. "Come on. I let you teach me surfing. Let me teach you dancing. I love it. It's been a part of me since I can remember. Dancing is like life in Cuba. Everyone does it everywhere." He did a little turn on his heels and ended facing her again with a grin. "Trust me?"

She wanted to. She really wanted to. Fingers trembling, she reached for him.

His fingers tightened around hers, and he led her to the middle of the huge floor, then took her into his arms, his hand on her lower back and their bodies close. As if sensing her wariness, he leaned down and whispered in her ear, "Don't be nervous, *hermosa*. It's just dancing. You can't drown here."

That made her gasp and smack him. "I told you I never meant for that to happen. I'm so sorry about—"

He laughed out loud then, placing a finger over her lips to silence her. "A joke, *hermosa*. But it worked. You are not so nervous now, eh?"

She opened her mouth to argue, but he was right. Then he stroked his fingers up and down her spine, and a new kind of tension build within her that had nothing to do with nerves and everything to do with wanting the man holding her. "I might not be any good at this, you know. Best watch your toes."

"I think you will be amazing at it. Watching you surf, I already know you have superb muscle memory and grace. You just need to learn the right steps. Those I can teach you."

His crooked grin and warm gaze eased her concerns and Isabella nodded, closing her eyes and allowing the musical rhythm pounding in her chest to take over her body. Carlos's strong, solid grip made her feel safe. She peeked one eye open and glanced up at him through her lashes and saw him smiling, a spark of amusement in his dark eyes. "Ready?"

"Yes."

"*Buena.*" He used his body to lead her back a step, then forward. They did that a few times until she loosened up and stopped hesitating over each move. Then he let his arm slip away from her back and raised the other, and she did a little spin without thinking about it.

Once her brain kicked in again, Isabella froze and gasped. "Was that right?"

"*Si.*" He put his hands on her shoulders and massaged them lightly. "There is no right or wrong here with us. Just do what you feel. It's all good."

They started again. Backward, forward, spin. Backward, forward, spin.

He chuckled. "Feels better, eh?"

"How did you know?"

"Dancing is in my blood," he said, then winked. "And your body is relaxed against mine."

The music switched again, this time to something faster and lighter. An older song she'd heard on the radio many times growing up and loved, by a popular Latina singer in America. Carlos grinned and spun her around again before taking her into his arms once more. "Let's get loud, eh?"

"*Si.* I love this song!"

As the music played on and they danced more, Isabella forgot all about her nerves. She forgot all about her cares and worries and the stresses of the past and her job and just lived in the moment with Carlos. If his parents had done this during their whirlwind romance, she could understand why Carlos's father had fallen under his mother's spell. Dancing like this felt magical, freeing, fantastic. She'd never thought she'd feel the same emotions she did when surfing anywhere else, but here she did, and she had Carlos to thank. He'd given her this, and she felt so grateful.

Then she stepped forward when she should have stepped back and crushed his toes.

"Oh, God!" She covered her mouth with her hands. "I'm so sorry. Are you okay?"

"I'm fine, *hermosa.*" He winced slightly and shook out his foot. "I've been stepped on much worse than that many times before. You should see the salsa clubs in Havana on a Saturday night. So packed you barely have any room to move in there. I've suffered broken toes and all. You just keep dancing."

He coaxed her back into his arms again, though she felt stiffer than ever now. First the riptide, and now she'd stomped on his foot. She was hopeless.

"Relax, *hermosa.*" He ducked slightly to catch her eye, then held her gaze. "Look at me, yes? Just keep looking at me. Feel me. Then we will be fine. You'll see."

She did, stumbling slightly again, but he never let her fall. Then she got distracted by his soft, full lips and the memory of how they felt on hers. The music changed to a slow, beautiful piece once more, this time with a bit of melancholy in the melody. Carlos pulled her closer, leading her so naturally, just as he did in life. Responsive, strong, never pushy or overbearing—and she finally let go again. Closed her eyes and was just there, with him in that moment, and the rest of the world fell away.

At least until Carlos whispered into her ear, "Do you love me?"

Isabella froze, blinking at him, her gums throbbing with her pulse. "What?"

"I asked if you love the rumba," he said, looking at her strangely. "It's my favorite dance. Why? What did you think I said?"

"Oh…um…" The music had stopped now, leaving only the sounds of their breathing and the echoes from the world outside. She shook her head and looked away, face hot. "I'm not sure. And yes, the rumba is very nice." Her throat felt dry and scratchy, and she suddenly needed air. Fresh air. She backed away slowly toward the door. "I'm going to step outside for a moment. Get something to drink."

Carlos stood there, watching her, his dark eyes unreadable for once, as she fled the dance studio like a coward. Because yes. She did love him. Against all her wishes and better judgment, and now she had no idea what to do about that.

Carlos waited for a while inside the studio, shutting off the music and leaving a note for his friend, thanking them for letting him use their place. He still wasn't quite sure exactly what he'd done to scare off Isabella like that, but she'd been spooked.

Each time he closed his eyes, he saw her pale face, her wide eyes, the way she'd shied away from him like a wounded animal. So very different from how soft and free and wonderful she'd been in his arms. She'd been a great dancer, just as he'd imagined, when she let herself relax.

He sighed and shut off the lights, then closed and locked the door. He shouldn't have mentioned love. That was the problem. In his experience, love always meant loss or pain. And while he tried to face life with an open heart, it was still hard, and he remained guarded about many things.

Not about Isabella, though. Try as he might to fight it, to not open his heart to her too soon, she'd managed to get in anyway. Sweet and funny and kind and smart and wonderful and beautiful. There was no way for him to resist her combination. Isabella was everything he'd ever wanted in a partner and more. So much more. She'd somehow broken down his carefully constructed walls without him even knowing, and now, suddenly, he couldn't imagine his life without her. Didn't want to. No matter what fears she might have, he knew deep down that he loved her.

The truth of it vibrated through his bones like a tuning fork, solidifying like steel, making him both stronger and more vulnerable at the same time. *I love Isabella Rivas.* And now that the words were out there—in his head and his heart, anyway—there was no going back. He wouldn't tell her yet, though, especially after what had just happened in the dance studio. He'd seen the wariness in her eyes, the fear. Had felt the same himself in the past. But now he knew. And he loved her all the same. Deep and strong and alive. Scary, too, such a new realization, but exciting. Like a tiny bird that would grow into a giant.

But for now, he would keep it to himself. Get used to the idea. Perhaps think of a way to tell Isabella that wouldn't spook her or make her feel like he was trying to put chains on her or control her. Only that he loved her and wanted to be with her and their baby, however she would let him.

Si. Keeping it inside for now would work better.

After checking the hallway and not seeing her there, he jogged downstairs and went outside once more. He found Isabella leaning against the side of the building, staring down at her toes, looking sad. His first instinct was to comfort her, to wrap his arms around her and hold her close until she smiled again. But her earlier wariness made him cautious. So, instead, he just walked over and leaned against the wall beside her, not saying a word.

After a minute or two, she finally looked over at him beneath the orangish glow of the streetlight nearby. "I'm sorry for ruining things upstairs."

"You didn't ruin anything, *hermosa.* I just wish you could talk to me about what's bothering you."

"I…" She huffed out a breath, then stared at the quiet street in front of them. "I don't know. I misheard you upstairs, and it just… I don't know."

"Ah," he said, hiding his wince. So, it had been the *L* word. His chest ached knowing that she wasn't in the same place as him, but hopefully with more time, she would get there. Isabella's walls were built high and mighty, but Carlos was not a man who gave up on what he wanted easily. Still, they had time. Eager to move on to something less heavy and get her comfortable and smiling again, he tried humor. "So, you hated my rumba, then?"

"What?" She gave him a surprised stare. "No. The dancing was amazing. Seriously. I had no idea you could move that way."

He grinned, leaning his head back against the cool gray stone to stare up at the stars. "Like I said, everyone dances in Havana. I learned when I was four, I think, from my grandfather. He used to take me with him to the square in our neighborhood for the evening fiestas. Everyone gathered there. A little party every night. Food and drinks and music, to help people unwind. We didn't have much, but we had each other. Once the band started to play, they'd clear the tables away and people would dance. By themselves, together, didn't matter. All good fun."

"Sounds like it," Isabella said, mirroring his position. Always a good sign. She sighed and closed her eyes, her beautiful face lifted skyward. "The most we ever did in my house was game night. We'd play checkers or board games or whatever, once my younger siblings were old enough to be on teams. Someone always got mad, though, because they didn't win, or because they thought someone else was cheating." She laughed. "My dad even played sometimes. At least until his MS got too bad and kept him in bed all the time."

Her smile fell then, and Carlos would've given his

whole world to bring it back. Impossible, he knew, but maybe they could try something else instead. "Gelato."

"I'm sorry?" Isabella looked over at him.

"I'm in the mood for gelato."

"For dinner?"

"*Sì.*" He straightened and held out his hand to her, living and dying in those few seconds until she took it, her skin warm and soft against him. "For dinner. Unless you have something else you prefer?"

She tucked herself into his side, holding on to his arm and resting her head against the side of his shoulder as they walked away from the dance studio. "No. Gelato sounds perfect to me."

Not exactly the ending to the evening he'd imagined, and there were still many things—important things— they needed to discuss, but they could wait. For now, things were back to normal, and he was glad.

CHAPTER NINE

THE NEXT COUPLE of days flew by in a haze for Isabella. She felt happier and freer than she had in a long time, maybe ever, and the last thing she wanted to do was trigger her old issues when things were going so well with Carlos.

She really, really liked him. Isabella wasn't ready to go beyond that yet, because…well. They were still getting to know each other, and things were good between them. Very, very good. And no one fell in love that quickly, right? No. That was silly. Besides, Isabella didn't do love. Love meant obligations and responsibilities, and this thing with Carlos was all about exploration and freedom and…

"Hey, you in there?" Mario said from the driver's seat.

Isabella blinked over at him, realizing that she'd zoned out again, lost in her head. It had been happening a lot lately, and she couldn't blame it all on the pregnancy hormones, either. Nope. One more reason not to get carried away with Carlos. Too distracting. Even if the sex blew her mind and shook her world and…

The two-way radio in the ambulance crackled to life

with a new call from the dispatcher. "Units respond to a motor vehicle accident in the tunnel on Plaça d'Espanya. Vehicle has rolled over onto the roof. Driver trapped inside. Fire department is on scene already, waiting for paramedic assist."

"On our way," Mario answered in Catalan, then signaled to change lanes and head in that direction.

Unfortunately, it wasn't the first rollover they'd had in that area. People tended to drive too fast through there, and accidents happened. The problem with rollovers was, you never knew how badly the people inside were hurt until you got them out of the vehicle.

While Mario navigated through the early-evening traffic, Isabella went into the back of the rig to get everything ready for them once they arrived—she checked and stocked the medical kits and got their hard hats and heavy gear ready in case they had to get into the wrecked vehicle to help stabilize a patient. Cases like this were tough anyway, and the fact that she was pregnant would make it even harder, but she still hadn't told anyone yet, other than Carlos, and Isabella wanted to keep it that way if possible.

A few minutes later, they pulled up to the scene and found two lanes of traffic cordoned off by police, who were rerouting cars around the accident site. The vehicle lay on its top, one side resting against the stone wall of the tunnel. Shattered glass from the windshield sparkled on the black asphalt beneath the yellow lights above. The air smelled of burned rubber and exhaust. Isabella climbed out of the rig and headed over to a firefighter standing nearby.

"How many people are trapped inside?" Isabella asked him.

"Just one, as far as we can tell," the burly man said. "We'll hold the car steady if you want to check on the driver."

Isabella nodded, then headed toward the shattered driver's side window to crouch next to it, glancing up at the firefighters holding the car in place. "Make sure this thing doesn't flip over on me, okay!"

The fire crew chuckled and nodded. Isabella grinned back, then focused on the driver, calling out to Mario, who stood nearby. She was smaller and therefore better able to maneuver in the close quarters of the damaged car, they'd agreed. "He's alive and conscious. Tangled up in his seat belt. Sir, can you move your legs?"

The victim shook his head. "Caught on something."

"Okay. Sir, sit very still while the fire department removes this door for you. It will be loud for a moment, but don't worry. We're right here and won't let anything happen to you."

He nodded, and Isabella moved back to allow another firefighter in with the jaws of life to cut off the car door, which had been badly damaged in the accident. Once the area was cleared again and they'd stabilized the car, Isabella got back down on the ground to crawl inside the vehicle to better examine the patient. Pulse good, blood pressure slightly elevated, but not concerning given the circumstances. And the man seemed to be conscious and alert. The one thing that struck her as odd, though, were golf clubs scattered everywhere.

"Are you a golfer, sir?"

"I am," he said in American English. "On vacation

with my wife. She's back at the hotel while I went out to shoot a round or two at Can Cuyàs. On my way back to our hotel when this happened. I love golf."

A strong smell of alcohol clung to the man's breath, and Isabella wondered exactly how much drinking had occurred with his golfing. She was about to ask when a loud screeching noise issued from the metal frame of the car and the whole thing tipped forward, onto the hood. The firefighters shouted and golf clubs went flying around the interior of the car. Isabella turned to shield the patient, still tangled in his seat belt, when something heavy struck the side of her head and her vision tunneled. The last thing she remembered was the shouts of the firefighters and Mario's voice, echoing from far, far away.

"Isabella! Isabella? Get them out of there now!"

"Isabella! Isabella?" Carlos stared down into her pale face, his throat constricted. When the call had come in that they were bringing in a rollover accident, Carlos had prepped to receive the incoming patient with the rest of the ER staff. But then they'd brought in not one, but two gurneys, and his stomach had dropped. Even more so when Mario rushed in beside the second gurney, shaken and gray.

Carlos had made a beeline straight for Isabella's partner, knowing he had to excuse himself from the case because he and Isabella were involved but wanting to be by her side anyway. His mind whirled as he listened to Mario tell the doctor what happened. "We were on scene," the paramedic said. "The fire department had a hold of the vehicle. Isabella crawled inside to check the victim, and the car slipped. Something struck her in the head, and she lost consciousness."

Dr. Gonçalo checked Isabella's eyes. "Pupils even and reactive."

Good. That was good. Carlos tried to keep focused on the work, on doing what he was trained to do, but he couldn't. This wasn't just another patient. This was Isabella. The woman carrying his child. The woman he...

"Martinez?" Dr. Gonçalo called to him, breaking Carlos out of his thought bubble. "You okay?"

"Uh..." He stared down at Isabella's still form, her pale face, the already darkening bruise on her forehead and the shallow cut above her eyebrow, blood bright red against her too-white skin. Slowly, Carlos stepped back, trembling hands held up before him, palms out. "I...uh. No. I'm sorry. I can't do this. I can't treat this case. Isabella and I... We're..." Another step back. This wasn't how he wanted the world to find out they were a couple, but it couldn't be helped. "We're seeing each other."

A hush fell over the team as every eye in the room turned toward him. Only the beep of the monitors and the distant bustle of the ER outside their trauma space echoed around him. Then, just as quickly as the silence had started, it ended, and reality snapped back into place.

"Fine. Nurse Ramirez, please get CT scans and skull X-rays," Dr. Gonçalo ordered. "Once we have the results, we'll go from there." She leaned over Isabella again and patted her cheek. "Ms. Rivas? Isabella? Can you hear me? Squeeze my fingers if you can hear me."

Nothing.

"Isabella?" Dr. Gonçalo called, a bit more forcefully this time. "Can you wake up for me? Isabella?"

She stirred a bit on the table then, scowling, her eyes darting behind closed lids as she mumbled something indecipherable, except for the last two words—"...the baby."

Dr. Gonçalo frowned and looked over at Mario again. "Was there a baby involved in the accident, too?"

"No." Mario shook his head. "Only the one man behind the wheel. He's in the next trauma room."

"Then what's she talking about?" Dr. Gonçalo asked, her attention transferring to Carlos.

Heat prickled up his neck from beneath the collar of his scrub shirt. He swallowed hard past the tension constricting his throat. *Tell them. They need to know.* He blurted out the truth in a nervous rush. "She's pregnant. Isabella's pregnant. It's mine. She's just over two months along."

"What the—?" another male voice said. Carlos whirled around to find Diego Rivas, a neonatal surgeon at St. Aelina's and Isabella's younger brother, behind him. Diego grabbed Carlos by the arm and hauled him into the hallway, crowding him up against the wall with his body, his expression hard as steel. "Explain to me what you just said."

This wasn't going well. Not at all.

Carlos took a deep breath through his nose, his hot back pressed to the cool wall behind him, sweat itching on the nape of his neck. Part of him wanted to shove past Dr. Rivas and get back in there with Isabella, but the other part of him knew he wasn't going anywhere until they had this out.

He exhaled slow then nodded. "Your sister and I have been seeing each other for a few weeks."

"A few weeks?" One of Diego's dark brows rose. "Two months is more than a few weeks."

Wow. Okay. His stomach dropped from where it was crowding his chest to somewhere near his toes. He'd known Isabella hadn't wanted to tell her coworkers about the pregnancy because she didn't want rumors started, but he'd assumed she'd at least told her family. The fact she hadn't gave him a sour taste in his mouth. He blinked back into a pair of dark eyes nearly identical to Isabella's and said, "We had a very brief affair back in April. We were careful then, but…"

"Not careful enough, apparently." Diego squared his shoulders and crossed his arms, easing away a few inches, but not enough to let Carlos escape. The man stood a good five inches taller than Isabella and looked like solid muscle. Carlos kept in shape, too, but he really didn't want to get into it with her brother, especially right now. He wanted to get back in there and make sure she was okay. He sidled out from where he stood, but Diego stopped him, jaw tight. "What's happened to my sister?"

"A concussion," Carlos said. "They were working at a vehicle accident scene, and she struck her head. That's all I know so far."

After a flat stare that seemed to last a small eternity, Diego stepped back, allowing Carlos to relax a bit. His shoulders stiffened and his chest tingled. Uncomfortable and filled with foreboding, he sidestepped back toward the trauma room, where the radiology techs had arrived to take Isabella for her tests. "I, uh, I should get back in there."

Diego watched him, his expression unreadable. "We'll talk more about this later."

Carlos had no doubt. But as he walked beside Isabella's gurney toward the elevators, holding her hand, he couldn't help thinking all this secrecy about the baby couldn't be good for their future together. Hell, he knew better than anyone what lies and hidden truths could do to a family, and he never wanted a child of his to suffer what he had. Isabella kept everyone at arm's length, including him and her family. And while he cared for her a great deal—more than a great deal, honestly—this would never work if they couldn't be truthful with each other and with everyone else about what was happening and what they meant to each other.

They rode up to the radiology department, and Carlos watched from nearby as they did the head X-rays and CT scan, taking extra precautions due to the pregnancy. It wasn't until they were finished, and Carlos stood by her side again, that Isabella regained consciousness. She blinked open her eyes, squinting up at the ceiling and the bright lights.

"Wh-what's happening?" Her voice sounded thready and weak, making his heart clench tight. "Wh-where am I?"

Carlos kissed her hand, then smiled down at her, pulling up a chair to her bedside. "You're at St. Aelina's, *hermosa*. You were hurt during the accident. Do you remember anything about that?"

She frowned. "I remember being in the vehicle with

the patient, examining him, then a loud noise, and everything tilted. My head hurts really bad."

"*Si.*" Carlos gave her a small smile, then kissed the back of her hand again, holding it close to his chest. "The firefighters lost their grip on the car. It slipped and Mario said a golf club smacked you in the head."

Isabella gave a tiny snort. "I knew there was a reason I never liked that sport." Then she sobered, her eyes widening. "The baby. Is the baby okay?"

"The baby's fine," Carlos reassured her. "Hopefully, these scans will be clear and you'll only have a nasty bump and a bruise for a while."

He tried to keep his rising sadness and distress over the situation with her family under wraps, but apparently not as well as he'd wanted, because she narrowed her gaze.

"What's wrong?" she asked.

"Nothing, *hermosa*. I'm worried about you, that's all."

"Are you sure?" She looked unconvinced, but then the radiology techs returned to wheel her back down to the ER. Carlos walked along beside her, forcing a smile.

"I'm sure." The fact Isabella didn't try to pull away only showed him how out of it she was. Because if she'd been lucid, she never would've held hands with him within the walls of St. Aelina's. Too many people could see, too many rumors could start. And that made him more confused and sadder than ever.

CHAPTER TEN

"How are you feeling?" Carlos asked Isabella for what felt like the millionth time. "Anything I can get you?"

She bit back a snarky reply as he leaned her forward to fluff the pillows behind her head, like she was an invalid. Considering that since she'd come to stay at his flat following her release from the ER two days prior—at his insistence—she kind of felt like one. She gave him a bland smile instead. "I'm fine, thanks. You know, I'm perfectly capable of getting up and doing things for myself."

"Nope. Not yet." Carlos sat on the edge of the bed and gave her a stern look. "Dr. Gonçalo said nothing strenuous until she's seen you for a recheck tomorrow."

Being on the receiving end of convalescence wasn't something she was used to, and it rubbed her the wrong way. And while she felt grateful for Carlos being there for her, she couldn't shake the feeling that he was hiding something from her. Something important. She'd gotten the same weird vibes from him in the ER, when he'd seemed unaccountably sad.

Isabella had tried several times to get him to talk to her about what was bothering him, but so far, he hadn't said anything. Well, if she was stuck here with him pampering her to death, she'd get it out of him one way or another. Being standoffish hadn't done it, so maybe some genuine honey would work.

"Hey." She reached over and took his hand. "Thank you for all you've done for me. I appreciate you taking care of me. I know I'm not always the best patient."

He snorted, and she frowned. "You are so not the best patient. That old saying is true, about medical workers making the most awful patients."

"I'm not that bad."

Carlos gave her a flat look.

Isabella huffed out a breath, her shoulders slumping. "Okay, fine. Maybe I am that bad." She sighed and clasped her hands in her lap, leaning back against the headboard, cushioned by her recently fluffed pillows. Her head still ached a bit. Nothing major, though. She had an egg-size lump and a purplish-green bruise near her right temple where the five iron had beaned her good, but otherwise she was fine.

Isabella shook her head, smiling as an old memory resurfaced. "I remember one time, when I was about sixteen, I'd nursed the rest of the family through a bout of flu and then finally came down with it myself. It was awful. And my poor brother Diego had to take care of me. Talk about worst patients ever."

Carlos's warm smile faltered at the mention of her brother.

Isabella, ever observant, picked up on it immediately, and her stomach tightened. Diego working at St. Aelina's was a never-ending source of ugh for her. One of the reasons why she was so careful to stay out of the gossip mill at the hospital, too, because once Diego caught scent of something, he never let it go. She narrowed her gaze on Carlos. "What's wrong?"

"Huh?" He glanced up at her from where he'd been staring at their joined hands as if lost in thought. Carlos gave a quick shake of his head. "Nothing. Why?"

"Because I know you're lying to me."

He scoffed and straightened. "I'm not lying. What in the world would I have to lie about?"

"No idea." She crossed her arms, realizing maybe Diego wasn't the only stubborn Rivas. "But I know there's something. I can tell. You were acting strangely when we were in radiology after my scans. And now again, after I brought up my brother Diego." Isabella pursed her lips. "You might as well tell me, because I won't stop asking until you do."

For a moment, Carlos looked like he'd argue with her about it, but then his stiff posture crumpled, and he exhaled slow. He stared down at their hands again instead of meeting her gaze, his dark brows drawn together. "Why haven't you told your family about the baby yet?"

That knocked her back a bit. "Oh, well. I don't know. At first, like I said, I wanted to make sure it would be a viable pregnancy. Then, later, I guess I just never got around to it. I wanted to find the right time, I suppose."

Carlos nodded, his frown deepening. "Diego knows."

"What?" Eyes wide, she sat forward, the pillows behind her scattering to either side. "How?"

Dots of crimson darkened along Carlos's high cheekbones. "He was there, in the ER, in the hallway when I told Dr. Gonçalo about the pregnancy."

"Wait." She swung her legs over the side of the bed

and started to get up, swallowing hard at the wave of dizziness that overtook her. Isabella waited a moment, willing the bile burning her throat to recede before finally pushing to her feet. Carlos didn't stop her this time, which was a good thing, because she wasn't in the mood to be coddled now. She was too pissed off. "So, you're telling me that you specifically went against my wishes and told my brother about us and the baby?"

"What choice did I have?" He stood as well, raking a hand through his hair before taking her arm to steady her when she wobbled. "Please, *hermosa*. Sit down and let's talk about this."

"No." She pulled away from him and stumbled back a step before catching herself with a hand on the wall. "I don't want to sit. I want you to tell me exactly what the hell happened in the ER."

Carlos took a deep breath, then another, his head dropping until he stared at his feet. "When they brought you in alongside the man who'd been trapped in the car, I was as shocked as anyone. I had to excuse myself from the case, of course, because we are together. And when Dr. Gonçalo ordered the X-rays and scans on you, I had to tell them about the baby so they could take proper precautions."

He cursed under his breath, then met her gaze. "Your brother Diego happened to hear about you being brought in and rushed down to the ER to check on you. He was standing behind me when I told all that to Dr. Gonçalo. By then it was too late to take it back, and he pulled me into the hall to ask me about it."

"And you told him."

Not a question.

Isabella backed into a chair in the corner and sank into it, covering her face with her hands. It wasn't that she didn't want her family to know about the baby. They'd find out eventually, obviously. But she'd just wanted a little more time to…adjust herself first. To wrap her head around the fact that in less than seven months, she'd have a baby of her own, a little boy or girl to take care of, to love and cherish forever. But also a child she'd have to care for, support, worry about every minute of every day. What if they were sick? What if they were born with a disability? What if she was a horrible mother? *Gah!* She'd just wanted more time to come to grips with all her fears and foibles before springing the shock on her family. And then, of course, because she knew her siblings so well, she knew they'd all want to fawn over her, take care of her. And the last thing she wanted or needed right now was more coddling.

"Look," Carlos said, crouching beside her chair but not touching her. "I'm sorry that things happened the way they did, but I'm not sorry people know, *hermosa*. After how I grew up, after what happened with my parents, there's one thing I know. Happiness is fleeting and you must grab it where you can. I've found happiness, here with you and the baby. I understand things with you and your family are complicated, after your mother's death and you having to grow up and be responsible for everyone so young. But this is our future we're talking about, Isabella. Our baby."

"My future," she said, defensiveness flaring hot inside her, burning through her common sense. She loved Carlos, but her old fears and pain clouded her vision, made her shrink away. "My baby."

He blinked at her, raw pain and confusion in his dark eyes. "*Hermosa?* What are you saying?"

"I'm saying that you're getting too far ahead of yourself here, Carlos." She shook her head, holding herself tighter around her middle, like a shield against the things that were too scary and too intense to feel with him—for him. She pushed to unsteady feet, glad for the chair behind her to catch her, but needing to get this out now, before she couldn't anymore. It felt like she was thirteen again and the walls were closing in around her, leaving only one path ahead for her to follow, suffocating her with rules and responsibilities and a single choice for the future. She couldn't breathe, couldn't move, couldn't do anything except fight back. "There is no us. Not yet. Maybe not ever. We made a baby together, that's it. It's not a lifetime commitment. For you. I can do this by myself if I have to."

"No!" He straightened, towering over her, becoming angry for the first time since she'd known him, eyes bright and cheeks flushed. "This is my baby, too. I will not let my child grow up the way I did. Not knowing who they are. Not knowing who they come from. I will not do it, Isabella!"

"And I won't ever allow myself to be caged in again, Carlos. Not by you. Not by anyone. I love you, but I can't do this. I'm not ready yet. Maybe someday I will be, but not now. Not yet. I'm sorry."

They stared at each other across the span of a few feet, Isabella's cheeks wet with tears and the color slowly draining from Carlos's tanned face. The air around them chilled, and Isabella shivered with the finality of it all. Her heart ached and her chest squeezed tight. She loved Carlos. She did. But she wasn't ready to settle down and make a life with him.

It was obvious from the way his lips tightened and his breath hitched that he was ready to move forward with her. Or had been. Until she'd thrown it all back in his face. Voice edged in ice, he turned away, heading for the door, only to stop on the threshold and look back at her to say. "I see, Isabella. My mistake. I thought we wanted the same things here, but apparently not. Excuse me."

Isabella stood there after he walked out of the room, feeling more alone and desolate than she ever had in her life. She missed him already, but she had to carry on—for herself and for her baby.

"What did I do wrong, *Tío*?" Carlos asked later that night. He'd gone downstairs to Encanteri after Isabella had moved back to her own flat earlier—against his wishes. Their last discussion had not ended well, but dammit. The fact that she'd kept the pregnancy a secret from everyone, even those closest to her, triggered all his old doubts and fears. Now, as he sat there, nursing a beer that had grown warm over the past hour or so, his skin felt too tight and all his joints too loose. Discombobulated. A word he'd read once, and it seemed to fit, even though he wasn't totally clear on its meaning.

Uncle Hugo raised a bushy gray brow at him, then sighed. "It's nothing you've done, *sobrino*." He shook his head and frowned down at the glass he polished. For once, things were slower at the bar that night, so they could talk and hear one another. Even the music on the overhead speakers sounded slow and melancholy. Figured. "Sometimes, the heart wants what it wants."

Carlos dropped his head into his hands and groaned, sudden anger surging inside him. "Bullshit."

"Excuse me?" Hugo put the glass down and narrowed his gaze on his nephew.

"The heart wants what it wants," Carlos scoffed, hands flying now as he spoke. Heat prickled the back of his neck as people nearby turned to stare at him, but he didn't care. His heart hurt, and he'd kept a cap on his emotions too long, trying to earn Isabella's trust and love. Now she'd thrown it all back in his face, then stomped on his love on top of it all. No. No more. He was done. "That's a lie, *Tío*. Because all I ever wanted was to be with Isabella, and she's gone and..."

He managed to cut himself off before mentioning the baby—barely. And it didn't matter that he hadn't told anyone yet, either—well, except for the entire ER at St. Aelina's—because he had just been trying to obey Isabella's wishes.

Hugo inhaled deep, then exhaled slowly through his nose, as summoning all his patience. "Your father."

Carlos waited for him to continue, staring down at the dark wood bar top. When he didn't, Carlos finally looked up at his uncle. The sore spot in his chest that had been there pretty much his entire life where his dad was concerned pinched harder. He was thirty-four. He shouldn't care about his father anymore. The man who hadn't loved him enough to even try to find him after Carlos was born. It shouldn't matter. It still did. With more bitterness than he'd intended, Carlos said, "What about him?"

"I've never told you about how he was after your mother left," Hugo said, watching him closely. "You remind me of him, *sobrino*. Same impulsiveness, recklessness, always leading with your heart and not your head."

"I am not reckless!" The few patrons in the bar went silent, and Carlos realized he'd said that way louder than he'd meant to. Dammit. He slumped down on his stool and tried to make himself smaller to avoid the unwanted attention. "I'm not reckless," he repeated, quieter this time. "Or impulsive. If anything, I've tried my hardest to never be that way. The last thing I want to end up as is my father."

Then he winced. Uncle Hugo was the sweetest man Carlos had ever known. Generous, kind, compassionate. In fact, there'd been times he'd wished that Hugo had been his father. But he'd always been cognizant of the fact that Hugo had been his father, Alejandro's, brother. He'd never been too harsh in his criticisms to avoid hurting Hugo. But tonight, all his defenses had been trampled, and he had nothing left. Still, he hated the stricken look on his uncle's face, no matter how fast he'd hidden it behind his usual easygoing smile. Carlos hung his head and squeezed his eyes shut. "I'm sorry, *Tío*. I didn't mean…"

"You did." Hugo cleared his throat and put the glass away behind him before leaning his hands on the edge of the bar, leaning closer to Carlos. "And you're right."

Carlos looked up again, confused. "About what?"

"About everything." Hugo sighed and came around the bar to take a seat on the stool beside Carlos's. "Look, I can't imagine what you and your mother must've gone through back in Cuba." When Carlos opened his mouth,

Hugo held up a hand to stop him. "I know. I know that we've talked about a lot of things, but I also know that you've held a lot back from me, trying to protect my feelings, because that's who you are, *sobrino*." He flashed a sad little smile. "Such a good man. Better than your father. Better than me, too."

"That's not true. You are a wonderful man," Carlos assured him, his head muddled from too much emotion and too little alcohol. He should've gotten fall-down drunk and fallen asleep upstairs. That would've avoided this embarrassing scene in the bar and the raw vulnerability he felt inside. Maybe he'd have slept it off and felt better in the morning. Given the ache in his chest, though, he doubted it. "I'm sorry. I'm upset about Isabella, and I shouldn't have taken it out on you."

"Stop it," his uncle said, in a far harsher tone than Carlos had ever heard him use before. "Stop explaining and denying and excusing what is inexcusable."

"I'm—"

"No. You stop talking and listen to me. I'm going to tell you some things about your father. Things that I have kept back from you as well."

Carlos blinked at Hugo, more than a bit stunned. After the hours and hours he and his uncle had spent talking about the past after Carlos had first arrived in Barcelona, he'd doubted there was anything he didn't know about his father. But apparently, he was wrong.

"The letter. The one your mother wrote to Alejandro telling him that she was pregnant with you," Hugo said, staring down at his hands in his lap, his fingers worrying the edge of the apron he wore. "Your father never received it."

"What?" Carlos frowned, not quite computing that information. "What do you mean?"

"I mean, the letter arrived, but our parents intercepted it before your father had a chance to see it. He never knew about you. Not until after they died."

Jesus. The earth tilted beneath Carlos's feet, and he gripped the bar tight. "I don't even know what to say about that."

Hugo winced. "I know. And I'm sorry. We had no idea, Alejandro and I, that you even existed until they passed away fifteen years ago and I found the letters your mother and her parents had sent." He shook his head. "Even then, I kept it from your father. He still didn't know. I didn't want him to dwell in the past anymore. He'd been stuck there for so long, miserable, with no relief, no end in sight. I just wanted him to find peace and happiness after all those years. I intended to tell him. I swear I did, but then he got sick, and he passed away, and it was too late. I'm so, so sorry, Carlos. About everything."

"But... I..." This was way too much for him to take in. Like everything he'd thought was true wasn't. Lies. All lies. All those years, all that heartache. All those nights lying awake wondering about his father, where he was, who he was, if he missed Carlos like Carlos missed him. None of that happened, because his father had never known he'd existed. The ball of dread inside him sank deeper into a black hole of despair. "Why would you do that, *Tío*? I trusted you. I came here, to you, to learn more about myself, about my past. And you lied to me."

Hugo blanched beneath his tan, the lines on his face

more pronounced. Gone was the gregarious bar owner, always cheerful and laughing. In his place was an old man who looked every one of his sixty years. "I never meant to, *sobrino*. I swear. I just…" He took a deep breath, his gray brows drawing together as his expression turned earnest. "I swear to you, *sobrino*, I wanted to tell you the whole truth so many times since you've been here, but it never seemed like the right moment." He reached out to take Carlos's arm, but Carlos pulled away. Hugo flinched, his hand falling back to his side. "I understand how upset you must be."

"Do you? I don't think so, Uncle." Betrayal seared inside him, hotter by the second. His hands and knees trembled and his throat dried, making his voice rough. "Because I trusted you. I trusted you, and you lied to me. I thought I had finally found something real here, something true, but no. Lies. All lies."

He stood and slapped money down on the bar top. He'd never paid in Encanteri before, but now it felt like a necessity. He refused to be beholden to his uncle anymore. First Isabella and now this. It was too much. "I need some air."

"Wait!" Hugo grabbed his wrist. "You don't know how much your father suffered after your mother left. He was distraught. He argued with our parents continuously. He loved your mother and wanted to go to Cuba to find her." His uncle took a breath. "But times were different then, and our parents had both our futures planned out for us. College, then a job at the law firm where our father worked. There was no room for a baby. No room for deviation from the plan."

A muscle ticked in Carlos's cheek as he gritted his

teeth. *Leave. Don't stay and listen. Don't let him defend the indefensible.* But in the end, Carlos stayed rooted to the spot, arms crossed and shields up. He needed to know the truth, once and for all. "Go on."

"He never dated, your father. Not in college, not after he graduated. Always pining away for your mother. He tried to contact to her, tried to find her in Cuba, but things with the government there were not good, and after what you told me about your mother's family, I don't think they would've let her talk to him anyway, so…"

"And that makes it okay?" Carlos wasn't feeling particularly charitable to any of them, least of all Hugo. The news was still too new and raw and painful. "He just gave up then?"

"No. He never gave up, *sobrino*." Hugo met his gaze direct. "Never. Even after years of nothing, even after he finally met someone else and got married at forty. Even then, he never forgot. He used to talk to me about her. He'd come in here to the bar and we'd sit for hours, reminiscing. He still loved your mother even then."

Those words pricked his emotions, letting all the air out of the balloon of Carlos's anger and resentment. He slumped back down on his stool again, deflated and defeated. "I don't understand."

"After our parents died," Hugo said quietly, frowning as he fiddled with a napkin on the bar, "Alejandro and I went through our parents' house to clear it out before selling it. That's when I found the letters. The ones from your mother." He sighed. "Part of me wishes I had said something to your father then, about you. But it had taken him so long to finally find some small happiness after your mother that I couldn't destroy it for him, so I hid the letters away again." Hugo swallowed hard, his bushy gray brows drawing tighter together. "If I'd known he would pass away, too, such a short time later, I would have told him, Carlos. I swear to you I would have told Alejandro."

Carlos let that confession hang there a moment, feeling oddly numb. "But you didn't."

"No. I didn't." Hugo's voice grew gruffer, each word dripping with emotion. "Your father was a good man, a decent man, who would have loved you with his whole heart, just as he loved your mother. How he felt things, his emotions, were too big for this world, I think. That's why they killed him so young. Too young." His breath caught, and despite the animosity of earlier, Carlos couldn't help comforting his uncle, reaching over and placing a hand on Hugo's forearm. "But I always remembered you, *sobrino*. When I received the first letter from you after your mother passed, it felt like *destino*. Fate."

Fate. Carlos snorted. He and fate weren't exactly on the best terms right now. Seemed every time something good came into his life, fate took it away again. The move here. The fresh start. The fling with Isabella. The baby. Hugo. Everything seemed so up in the air and out of reach now.

But he didn't want to give up. He wasn't a quitter by nature. Maybe Hugo had been right at the beginning. Maybe it just wasn't meant to be, and he should let it go. He felt torn and twisted in the worst way. Carlos exhaled slow, then stood again. This time, his uncle let him.

"Are we okay?" Hugo asked. "Can you forgive me?"

"I… I can," Carlos said at last. "Not yet. Not tonight. But soon. I need time to think all this over."

Then he walked out into the cool Barcelona evening, feeling more lost and alone than he ever had before, hoping to find a way to ground himself again and find a new path forward.

CHAPTER ELEVEN

TWO DAYS LATER, *stir-crazy* didn't begin to describe Isabella in her flat. She wasn't used to having this much time off, and it drove her a bit batty. She'd cleaned everything she could clean about a thousand times, drunk tea, read books, watched streaming shows she'd let pile up on TV. But nothing eased the emptiness inside her.

She felt bad about the way she'd left things with Carlos. And she didn't know how to fix it. But all this stewing it over in her head wasn't getting her anywhere close to a solution, so she took a walk on the beach. The water and waves called to her as they always did, the smells of sand and sea bright in her nose. Isabella sat on the shore, watching a group of young surfers catching waves she would've been all over a few months ago, but now things had changed. She'd changed. And not just because of the baby.

Because of Carlos, too. He'd changed her, without her even realizing it.

And that's what scared her the most.

Up until she'd met him, Isabella had been living her life, taking risks, enjoying her freedom. Then he'd come along and made her wish for closeness and companionship and…well, love. She shuddered despite the warm temperatures and wrapped her arms tighter around herself. God. After years of cloying, enforced closeness with her siblings, of looking out for and serving everyone else's needs, the last thing she'd ever expected to crave this late in life was someone to care for. Not just care for. Love.

Isabella sighed and stood, brushing sand off the back of her shorts as seagulls cawed overhead and the brightly colored kites high in the sky caught her eye.

She loved Carlos Martinez, and she had no idea what to do about that.

Distracted and deep in thought, Isabella began to walk, not toward her flat just a few blocks away, but instead in the opposite direction. She wasn't even aware of where she was going until she ended up in front of St. Aelina's. Isabella stared up at the place and sighed. Seemed even on her time off, she couldn't get away from the place. Oh, well. She needed to talk to her brother Diego, and he was working today, so… The conversation was bound to happen, since he knew about the baby, so she might as well get it over with, considering she was feeling depressed anyway.

After taking the elevator up the floor he was making rounds on, according to the front desk, Isabella waited until Diego emerged from a patient's room, then followed him down the hall to an empty conference room.

Am I ready to do this?

No, not really. But it was too late now, so she summoned her courage and took a seat at the table while he closed the door behind them.

Silly, right? I'm a grown woman making my own

choices. I don't need anyone's approval or opinions, yet I'm nervous as hell.

Diego answered right away, scowling. "Isabella? What's wrong?"

She bit her lip and looked away. "Nothing's wrong. I thought I'd stop by and say hello."

He sighed and stepped aside to let her in. The place looked like any other conference room she'd ever seen, beige and boring. A couple of windows let in some natural light, at least. She glanced around then back at him. "How's Grace?"

"Away," he said, waving her off when she raised a brow at him. "Visiting her aunt in Cornwall."

Hmm. Based on his gruff tone and dark expression, she sensed trouble in paradise but didn't dare ask. She wasn't the only Rivas who liked their privacy.

Diego took a seat beside Isabella and rested an elbow on the table, his expression concerned. "How's your head?"

"Still there," Isabella said, her attempt at humor falling flat in the face of her brother's serious look. "It's better. Thank you."

He nodded, then looked away. "I'm worried about you, sis."

Now she frowned. "What? Why?"

His sideways glance said everything.

"Right." She took a deep breath, staring down at her lap. "I was going to tell you about the baby. I just wanted to find the right time."

"Are you going to marry him?"

"What? No." She shook that off, along with the involuntary thrill that went through her at those words.

Do I want to marry Carlos? Even if she did, it wasn't like he'd asked. Probably wouldn't now, either, given how they'd left things. Her chest burned a little more. She covered the discomfort by deflecting back to Diego, keeping her voice as calm as possible to hide her growing turmoil inside. "Why would you think that?"

"Well, one, because I've noticed how happy and content you've seemed the past couple of weeks. Never occurred to me why until I confronted him in the hallway."

She bristled, even as she realized he was right. "About that. Don't gang up on Carlos. He's a good man."

"He'd better be, if he's going to marry my sister."

"Stop saying that!" She stood to pace the room, nervous energy scattering inside her like bocce balls. "We're not getting married." She took a deep breath. "Honestly, I'm not even sure if he even likes me anymore after the fight we had."

Diego watched her a moment, then cursed under his breath before raking a hand through his hair. "Look, I'm sorry for how I handled things with him. I was just shocked and scared for you, and then when he said that you were pregnant with his baby, I..." He shook his head and stared out the windows. "I lost it. And I'm sorry."

She walked over and sat down again. "I'm sorry, too. I should have told you about the baby sooner. You shouldn't have found out that way." Isabella let her head fall back to stare at the ceiling. "Have you told the others yet?"

"No. Not yet." He mirrored her position, the same way they used to when they were kids. Shoulder to shoulder, heart to heart. Man, she'd really missed her family since they'd all gone their separate ways, even though they drove her crazy sometimes, too. Diego snorted. "I figured that one's on you. Let you take the heat."

"Gee, thanks." Isabella chuckled. Keeping a secret in the Rivas family was tantamount to treason. She'd get more than an earful from her siblings when the news finally broke.

"You know," Diego said, rolling his head to look at her, "we all give you a hard time, but really we all just love you and want the best for you, Isabella. We adore our *germana gran*."

She had to pinch him for that one, dammit. Even though *germana gran* was Catalan for "older sister," it made her feel ancient, so of course Diego had called her that every chance he got growing up. Such a pain, but she loved him anyway. He laughed and slapped her hand away, and just like that, they were back to being teenagers again, all the cares and fears of adulthood falling away, if only briefly.

"Remember the night of Frida's high school graduation? I made a cake that didn't turn out well at all and you guys still ate it?" Isabella laughed until her sides shook. "Only to find out later that I'd switched the sugar for salt."

"Yes! God, that was awful." Diego shook his head, his eyes watering from laughter. "Still wary of cake because of it. Had a hell of a time picking one out for our wedding."

"I bet." She sighed, sobering as old pain and nostalgia overwhelmed her, making her eyes sting. "Those were good days. When we were still together, before you all moved on."

That must've come out far sadder than she'd intended, because Diego frowned at her once more. "What do you mean?"

She shrugged, trying to play it off, even as her chest squeezed with old sadness. "Nothing. Seriously. Forget I said it."

"No." He met her gaze. "What did you mean by that, Isabella?"

She hadn't meant to get into all this, but...well, everything else was messed up in her world at present, why not this, too? "I don't know. It just seemed like after all those years together, of my taking care of you guys, you all just moved on and left me behind."

The words tumbled out, messy and chaotic, mirroring her emotions.

"Oh, Issy. That's not true at all." He ducked his head to catch her eye, same as he used to do growing up, and her heart pinched a little harder. "Seriously. We all knew how much you worked and sacrificed for us, and we decided that we'd all try to move out as fast as we could to give you your life back. You deserved to live as much as we did, Issy. That's why we left. Not to leave you behind. Never that."

Isabella blinked up at him, stunned.

"And then once you got going, you did so well for yourself on your own that we figured you liked it that way, so we kept our distance." He glanced at the windows again, then back to her. "I even worried about taking the job here at St. Aelina's because I didn't want to cramp your style and make you mad at me."

Oh, God. She straightened fast, knocking Diego aside. "Is that true?"

"*Si.* Of course." He returned to scowling again. "Is that not what you felt?"

"No. Not at all!" She shook her head, scooting around the face him. "I thought you wanted to keep your distance from me, that you were all sick of spending time with me. Oh, God." She covered her face. "We've wasted so much time on silly misunderstandings."

He hugged her then, and they both just soaked in the moment.

When Isabella finally pulled back, she felt like a huge weight had been lifted off her. "Let's not do that again. The whole miscommunication thing, okay?"

"Agreed." He took a deep breath then stared down at his hands. "I wish all problems were solved so easily."

"Me, too." She couldn't stop thinking about Carlos. How she'd messed things up with him, how she wanted to apologize now, but wasn't sure how without making things worse.

"When are you due?" Diego asked, his dark brows knitting.

Isabella flinched a little. She'd been so wrapped up in her own problems, she hadn't even thought about how many times Diego and Grace had tried to conceive and how she'd miscarried three times already. They'd been married five years and still no children, even though both wanted them very much. She sighed and reached over to place her hand over her brother's. "January."

"Wow." Diego looked up then, his smile warm and genuine. "Guess I better learn how to be a great uncle by then, huh? First time and all."

"Yes." She leaned in and hugged him again, just because it felt so good to have her family back. "But you'll already be the best uncle ever. And don't tell Eduardo or Luis I said that. I'll never hear the end of it."

Diego laughed then kissed her cheek. "Promise."

She started to get up but stopped when her brother took her wrist gently.

"Wait," he said, pulling her back into her seat. "What about this man? The baby's father."

Isabella hung her head, smoothing a hand down the front of her shirt. She barely had a bump yet, but she couldn't help imagining what the child would look like. If it would have her eyes and Carlos's nose. Or his hair and her smile. Whatever way it came out, she'd love their child completely.

She shrugged. "What about him?"

"Does he want to marry you? Be with you and the child?" Diego asked, watching her closely.

Isabella sighed. "He does. At least, I think he does. He says he'll be there for us, whatever we need, but…"

"But what?"

"I don't know." She put her head back and covered her face, her throat burning. After a moment, she shook her head and dropped her hands. "I'm scared, Diego."

Her brother frowned and sat up. "Scared? Why? Has he hurt you? Because if he has, I'll—"

"No!" Isabella grabbed him by the shoulders, the same way she used to when they were kids and Diego got angry at one of the neighborhood bullies and threatened to beat them up. "No. God, no. Listen, Carlos is a good man. The best man. He's kind and smart and funny and sweet, and he'd never, ever hurt me like that. Ever. I trust him completely."

It wasn't until those words left her mouth that she

realized they were true. She did trust Carlos. The problem was trusting herself. "I just…" She looked away, searching for the words to explain the knot of tension inside her. "I'm scared of being trapped again."

"Trapped?" Diego tilted his head, his expression confused.

"Like when we were kids. Mom passed away, then Dad got sick, and I had no choice but to step up and take over, because otherwise they would have split up our family. I did what I had to do." Guilt squeezed her gut, making her wince. "Not that I resented helping out, but…"

"But it wasn't what you would've chosen for yourself." Diego nodded. "I understand, Isabella. You were just a child yourself. It's an awful burden to put on someone so young. Please don't feel guilty about that."

"I don't…" she started to say, but he raised a dark brow at her, and she snorted. Diego had always been a good reader of people. Probably why he made such a fantastic doctor now. "Okay. Yes. I've been carrying around some guilt about that. But it's like, over the years, it's become who I am. The guilt. The need for freedom. The independence." Isabella lifted a shoulder, fiddling with the hem of her shirt. "What if I'm with Carlos and I lose myself again? What if something happens and I must take charge? What if we get married and it doesn't work out?"

Diego waited a beat or two, then straightened, taking her hands again. "None of us knows what tomorrow will bring, Issy. That's the beauty and horror of life. All we can do is seize what's right in front of us, take the joy where we find it. The love. And cherish it with all our hearts." He met and held her gaze. "If this Carlos is half as wonderful as you think he is, my guess is he'll stand by you no matter what. Through thick and thin. That's what marriage is. Not a trap. Not even a cage. It's a framework of commitment and trust. One you build together to withstand the good times and bad. One that supports both of you when you need it most. If you can find that with Carlos, sister, then you should hold on tight and never let go."

"What if I'm too late?"

Her brother laughed. "Based on what I saw in the ER, he's so far gone over you, Issy, he's still reeling over all this. If you don't wait forever, I'm sure you can fix things."

Isabella hugged him tight, then pulled back, smiling. "When did you get so smart?"

"Well, if you ask Grace, I've still got a long way to go." He gave a sad little chuckle, then stood before she could ask him any more about it. "Now, let's talk about how exactly you're going to win this man of yours back."

CHAPTER TWELVE

THE NEXT MORNING, Carlos woke up determined. He'd barely slept the night before, tossing and turning, trying to find a resolution that would make everyone happy and failing miserably. Not to mention the things his uncle had told him about his father.

His whole life, Carlos had believed that his biological father didn't want him, but now he knew differently. He was unsure how to feel about that yet. Part of him felt happy, overjoyed, to know that there wasn't something wrong with him, some defect that made him unworthy and unlovable. But the other part of him felt fury. All the lies, the deception, the hidden secrets.

Bah! He'd had enough of those to last more than a lifetime.

Grumbling, he rolled out of bed and headed for the bathroom. After a brisk shower and shave, he pulled out a fresh pair of jeans and a T-shirt from his closet and put them on before padding barefoot to the kitchen to start a pot of coffee. More caffeine needed.

He was scheduled to work the night shift at the ER later but had the rest of the day free. For the best, since he had a lot of thinking to do. He checked his emails and waited for the coffee maker to ding, then fixed his mug and had a seat at the small dining room table, head full and heart aching.

Hard to keep his two problems separate, no matter how he tried to work out one issue at a time. The breakup with Isabella had been bad. Very bad. The way they'd left things felt undefined and raw, and he didn't like it. He still wanted more than anything to be there for her, to be with her, but she'd stated clearly that she didn't want him crowding into her life. Maybe he should just accept that and move on. Given the state of technology, there were many ways to stay connected to people you cared for without living with them. They could call or text or FaceTime. He could continue to be a part of their baby's life no matter how things ended up between him and Isabella.

Deep down, though, Carlos knew that wasn't enough for him. Would never be enough.

Which brought his own situation and those letters right back to the top of his mind. How could Hugo have hidden that from him? From his father? Worse, how could their parents not have told Alejandro and Hugo the truth before it was too late? Before Carlos had spent his whole life believing he was an unwanted bastard from Cuba? Even now, those words were a gut punch to him.

He drank more coffee and stared at the wall across from him as new realizations came to light. Honestly, Uncle Hugo hadn't been the only one who'd kept secrets. Carlos had never shared with him or anyone else the humiliating things he'd suffered growing up. Not even his mother. She'd been through enough because of his father. She didn't need to know that her son was getting attacked because of it, too. But Cuba was very different than Barcelona, and unwed mothers something to be pitied and looked down on there. But being called names, beaten up and bullied by the other kids in his neighborhood in Havana because of his parentage had taught him the benefit of being likable, of being easygoing and affable and kind. Other kids didn't punch you so hard if you were funny or did nice things for them. So, he'd learned to deal with things the best way he could.

God. So many years. So many wasted years.

He scrubbed a hand over his face, feeling bleary despite the caffeine. After a deep breath, he sat back. The walls seemed to be closing in on him now. Everywhere he looked in the flat, all he could picture was Isabella. The sofa where she'd sat the first night to look at his mother's old diaries. The table where they'd gone over pictures and places for their tour of the city. The bedroom where she'd stayed after he'd brought her home from the hospital, where they'd fought, where they'd ended things for good…

No. He needed to get out, get some fresh air, get some new ideas of how to fix this into his head.

Carlos dumped the rest of his coffee down the drain and rinsed out the cup before setting it in the holder beside the sink to dry. He shoved his feet into some shoes, then grabbed his keys and headed out for a walk. He wandered without really thinking about it, past buildings and tourists and vendors, ending up down by the beach again. Even here, he saw Isabella everywhere. The place where they'd saved that man with the heart attack. The restaurant where they'd shared their first meal. The spot where they'd decided to keep the night going and headed back to her place.

Chest tight and temples throbbing, he plunked down on a bench and stared at the horizon. He loved her. Plain and simple. He loved Isabella Rivas, and he loved their baby. But they didn't love him back. Not enough to want to be with him. So…what?

Let them go.

He flinched. No. He didn't want to give up. Didn't want to let go. That would only repeat the mistakes that had happened to him. He would never desert his own child. Never.

A sea breeze blew, ruffling his hair and cooling his heated skin. But he didn't want to force himself on Isabella, either. Didn't want to go against her wishes. That would be no better than the other idea.

He closed his eyes and hung his head again, allowing the conversation with his uncle the night before to replay in his head. Truthfully, he felt a bit guilty about how that conversation had ended. The way he'd spoken to his uncle. He'd been angry, yes, and rightfully so for the things that were kept from him. But the more he thought about it, the more Carlos could understand why his uncle had hidden the letter from his father. Hugo had cared for his younger brother and he'd wanted to protect him, no matter how misguided his actions might have been. So, no. Carlos didn't blame his uncle. Not really. If he wanted to be upset with someone, it should be the parents, his grandparents. On both sides. They were the real villains here. But they were all long dead, so that did him no good, either.

At his core, Carlos knew the healthiest thing to do

would be to let it go and start fresh. Easier said than done. He snorted. God, how many times had he talked to patients and given them that advice? He was lucky they hadn't told him where to get off, even if the advice came from a good place.

Difficult to listen to the tiny voice inside your soul, for sure.

He sat there awhile longer, going in circles in his head without really reaching a conclusion before finally heading back to his flat. Maybe he'd clean or take a nap or something to use up the time before his shift, because if he kept thinking in circles like this, it would drive him nuts. Then, about half a block from his place, it hit him. The thing to do to help him get out of this mess. His original reason for coming to Barcelona in the first place.

The diaries.

He went back up to the flat and grabbed his mother's book. Maybe if he retraced the steps of their final moments together one more time, it would help him gain clarity over the past and the present now. Maybe find some context in those final entries that would apply to his current situation. He walked out and jogged down the stairs with the book under his arm—only to nearly crash into Uncle Hugo on the sidewalk.

They both stood, warily eyeing the other, uncomfortable together for the first time.

Finally, Hugo cleared his throat and frowned down at the sidewalk. "*Mi sobrino.*"

"*Tío.*"

"I…uh…" his uncle started, then shook his head. "I

want you to know how sorry I am about everything, Carlos. I never meant to hurt you."

"I know," he said, and meant it. But he still felt torn up inside and wasn't ready to go back to normal just yet. He edged past his uncle and pointed vaguely in the direction he was headed, holding up his mother's diary. "I'm on my way to Parc del Laberint d'Horta. Figured I'd visit the last place where my parents saw each other. Seems fitting."

Hugo looked up at him and gave a curt nod, a moment passing between the two men. Not forgiveness, because Carlos had already forgiven his uncle, even if he hadn't forgotten the pain yet. More of an understanding. They knew each other now, on a deeper level, the good and the bad, and they were okay. Or they would be, soon. Once Carlos got his current knot of a problem straightened out. "I hope you find what you are looking for."

"Me, too, *Tío*. Me, too," Carlos said, giving his uncle a small, sad smile before turning and walking away.

Isabella stood on the doorstep of Carlos's flat two hours later and took a deep breath, running through the coaching session she'd had with her brother Diego the day before. *Tell the truth. Listen to what he has to say. Compromise. If you love him, you'll work it out. That's what love is. Not a trap but a framework to build on together.*

Her hand trembled slightly as she knocked on the door, then smoothed that same hand down the front of her yellow sundress. The same dress she'd worn when they'd toured the city together. Carlos had told her how much he liked that color on her, and it had significance for her because she'd also been wearing it that night when they'd shared their first kiss. Well, their first kiss after the fling—their first kiss when it really counted.

She waited. Waited some more. Nothing.

Huh. Isabella knocked again. She'd checked the roster at St. Aelina's earlier when she'd checked in with Mario about her first shift back after release, and Carlos wasn't scheduled to work until that night, so... Maybe he went grocery shopping. Or for a walk around the city.

Or for a date with someone else already.

No. She scowled. Given how busy they both were, time wasn't on their side when it came to a social life. Probably why lots of people in the medical profession ended up dating other medical people. Besides, Carlos didn't go from one relationship to another without a thought or care. He wasn't the type. He felt deeply. One of the things she loved most about him.

So, then. Where had he gone?

Isabella knocked once more time with no response before she headed downstairs to the bar. If Carlos was out, she'd leave a note with his uncle asking him to call her when he could. No pressure, just opening those lines of communication again between them after she'd severed them so brutally a few nights earlier. She managed not to cringe at that last regretful thought—barely.

Even at lunchtime, patrons filled Encanteri to capacity. She sidled past a group of tourists waiting for a table near the entrance and headed through the packed interior toward the bar. Carlos's uncle was helping mix drinks and deliver food, bustling around the place like a man half his age, chatting and laughing with customers.

At least until he saw Isabella and froze, his expression changing from happy to guarded in seconds. Nervous, she fidgeted near the bar while he finished with a table of guests before finally making his way back to her.

"*Hola,*" he said, his tone much cooler than their previous exchanges. "What can I get you?"

"I hoped to speak with Carlos," Isabella said past her tight vocal cords. "Will he be back soon?"

"I'm not sure." Hugo fiddled with some bottles and taps, not meeting her gaze. "Does he want to see you?"

Yikes. The bluntness of his question smacked her hard in the heart. And honestly, she wasn't sure. Her dismay must've shown on her face, though she tried to hide it, because Hugo cursed softly, then set a glass of sparkling water in front of her. "I know something is going on between you two. He didn't tell me specifics, just that you turned him away, Isabella. You hurt my nephew, badly. I don't like it when people I love are hurting."

"I know," she said, blinking hard against the sting in her eyes. She didn't want to cry now. She'd done enough of that already the past two days. And this was too important for tears. She had to get this right. "And I'm so very sorry for hurting Carlos. It was never my intention to do so. He's the most wonderful man I've ever known. But I'm scared."

"Of him?" Hugo gave her a confused look, his bushy gray brows knit.

"Of everything." She took a sip of her water, grateful for its coolness on her parched throat. "I'm not sure how much you and Carlos have talked about me."

"Some," he said, giving her a kind smile, so like his

nephew's. "I know that you had a hard time growing up. You are a strong woman. That strength is not forged from happiness."

"No, it's not." She laughed softly, shaking her head as she stared down into her glass. "This whole thing with Carlos—it all happened so fast, and I panicked and…" She sighed and glanced up at Hugo. "I'm afraid I didn't handle it very well at all. I'm not used to having other people to depend on during difficulties."

"I understand." Hugo patted her hand atop the bar. "I am an older sibling, too."

"Oh," she said, then when that sank in, she looked up at him. "Oh."

"*Si.*" Hugo sighed and came around the bar to sit on the stool beside hers. "My nephew and I, we had some issues, too, last night. I shared some things with him about his father that I should have told him long ago. It's hard, isn't it? Keeping secrets."

"*Si.* It is." She turned slightly to face him. "That's how misunderstandings occur. My younger brother and I had a similar talk, about things that happened that I had interpreted one way, but my siblings had meant in a totally different way." She gave a sad little snort. "Communication is hard."

"It is. Necessary, too." He narrowed his gaze on her. "How are you?"

She considered telling him about the baby, but no. Carlos should be the one to share that with his uncle. The sooner the better. Because the time for keeping silent about the pregnancy had long passed, and Isabella found she didn't want to stay quiet anymore. She wasn't scared now—at least not as much as she had been, anyway.

"Good. Sad and lonely, but good." She took a deep breath, frowning down at her hands in her lap. "I really am sorry about hurting Carlos. It was wrong of me to walk away. I regret that now, more than I can say. But I do love your nephew, more than I ever thought possible, and I want to make it up to him, if he'll let me."

Hugo's smile increased to a grin. "*Lloeu Jesús. L'amor jove guanya al final!*"

Praise Jesus. Young love wins in the end.

His voice boomed through the already boisterous bar, loud enough for table nearby to turn and look at them. Heat prickled Isabella's cheeks as Hugo pulled her off her stool and into a bear hug. Shock froze her in place for a moment before, finally, she laughed, too, and hugged him back.

All this openness, this vulnerability, felt amazing—if still a bit terrifying.

Maybe that's how true freedom was. The same rush of the waves, the same quickening of her heart she felt surfing a huge curl, only now her feet were firmly planted on the ground and without a beach in sight.

"Right." Hugo released her at last. "You must go to Carlos and tell him how you feel."

"Where is he?" Apprehension and anticipation sizzled through her veins in equal measure.

"Parc del Laberint d'Horta." Hugo winked. "Have you been there?"

"*Si.*" She clenched her fists, hoping to dispel some of the nervous energy fizzing inside her. "We went there together, with the diary." Everything came full circle now and she had to go, to go to Carlos to say her apologies and make him see how much she loved him and wanted to be with him, whatever that looked like for them. She saw her future, and it was Carlos. Carlos and their baby. After a quick kiss on Hugo's cheek, Isabella hurried toward the door. "Wish me luck, Hugo."

"*Molta sort, carinyo!*" he called after her, waving. "*Molta sort.*"

CHAPTER THIRTEEN

THE CLOCKS HAD struck noon by the time Carlos stepped off the Metro from Sant Marti and walked across the plaza to the Parc del Laberint d'Horta. Admission was free on Wednesdays, so even midweek, lots of people and tourists milled about. Bright sunshine lit the area, and the blue skies above reflected in the small pools he passed near the entrance before heading down a shady tree-lined gravel path, not seeking anywhere in particular.

Being outside, in nature, soothed him and helped calm his mind. As he wandered, Carlos opened the diary and read several pages of his mother's writing. About meeting his father for the first time while visiting La Sagrada Familia. Seeing someone across a crowded room and knowing they were the one.

Carlos took a deep breath and continued walking. Thinking back on that first evening on the beach with Isabella, he'd kind of felt the same. The same tug of recognition, the same pull of inevitability that this person would be important to him in his life. At the time, he'd tried to write it off as infatuation, as lust, since they'd made love for the first time that same night. But now, looking back, he could see that, no. It wasn't just a fling. It had been love. Even then. For that's the night they'd conceived their child together.

He walked down a flight of steps and continued past several stone buildings and statuary before coming to the large reflecting pool. Many tourists stopped here, sitting on the short walls surrounding the pool or cooing to their children in strollers. Carlos smiled. Perhaps someday, that would be him and Isabella with their child. The thought filled him with joy.

His heart still pinched, though, knowing they might not be a couple, but he needed to learn to be okay with whatever happened. Isabella wasn't his father. She wasn't leaving him, because they'd never actually been committed in the first place.

If he had to do it all over again, he would've asked her sooner to be his, he thought. Not marriage, just yet, because his Isabella was gun-shy there, and for good reason after what she'd been through growing up. But he would have pledged himself to her and made sure she knew that he would be there with her through it all, in whatever way worked for her. Maybe if he'd done that, they wouldn't be where they were now, but nothing for it now.

Continuing past the pool, Carlos stopped on a small footbridge overlooking a creek running through the park. Quieter here, the chatter of tourists drowned out by the rush of water beneath the bridge and birdsong above. Here, he thought of Uncle Hugo and their argument. He was ready to forget it now, as he hadn't been earlier. Hugo meant well, but he'd made a mistake. Water under the bridge. Literally.

He stared down into the channel below, diary in his hands, and said a silent prayer to his mother above for wisdom. Help to finally do the right thing with Isabella and break the cycle of the past, of the secrets and lies and hidden things and get it all out in the open at last.

Ahead were the stairs leading down to the maze. Surprisingly, not many people were there yet, and it seemed fitting to get lost in there awhile, to work his way through it as he worked through the tangle of problems and emotions inside him. Uncle Hugo had been right, Carlos realized. He was impulsive, and maybe even reckless in his own way—with his emotions, certainly. He always cared too much, too soon. Allowed his feelings and instincts to lead. Sometimes it turned out well. Other times not. But that was him, and he didn't want to change. Wasn't sure he could at that point.

Carlos liked being on the front lines, helping people, caring for people, making people's lives better. And if that made him impulsive and reckless, then so be it. He'd gladly wear those titles.

The one thing he didn't want, though, was to be reckless and impulsive where Isabella and the baby were concerned. He hesitated, stopping at a corner in the maze, looking this way and that, choosing which path to take. Voices of others, somewhere inside the puzzle, too, echoed around him, but no one else appeared. Only him and his instincts. Diary under his arm, he turned right and continued deeper into the maze, the smell of cedar trees and the crunch of gravel beneath his feet his only companions.

So, how to handle things with Isabella. She feared commitment, feared being trapped again. That's what she'd said. Deep down, he thought, she also feared making a mistake and not being able to change course. Carlos got that. For many years, he'd felt trapped in Cuba, locked into a past he had no control over and a hazy future, at best. Breaking out and coming to Barcelona had been one of the best decisions he'd ever made.

Carlos supposed he could just tell her how he felt and let her decide how to proceed. But part of him feared she might shut him out completely, given how she'd reacted the other night at his flat. Then again, the reckless part of him—the part he'd inherited from his father, according to Uncle Hugo—said he should take the chance, take the risk, because otherwise he'd regret it for the rest of his life.

And if his parents' tumultuous love affair had taught him anything, it was to live with no regrets.

Finally, after what felt like a small eternity, he made another turn and emerged into the center of the maze. Curved stone benches encircled a beautiful statue of Eros, the mischievous god of love. Alone, he took a seat near a towering cedar arch to rest his feet. Set the diary on the bench beside him and turned his face up to the sky, eyes closed and heart open, whispering a prayer for guidance, "*Madre, por favor ayúdame. Dame una señal. Dime que debo hacer.*"

Mother, please help me. Give me a sign. Tell me what I should do.

With tourist crowds, it took Isabella about a half hour to get to the park and through the entrance. The Horta complex itself was huge, though, and other than the visit with Carlos a few weeks earlier, where they'd stuck to the main path to the maze, she hadn't been there for years.

She followed the same path now, trying to put herself in Carlos's mind-set and think where he would go. The maze, obviously, at the center of the park, but there were many routes to get there, some longer than others. Perhaps the best thing she could do was head in that direction, then wait for him. He'd show up eventually, she felt certain.

Isabella started down a shady path to her left, enjoying the break from the heat of the sun beating down on her. She'd healed well from her concussion and really the only thing she noticed now, other than the bruise, was a slight twinge near her temple occasionally. But otherwise, her dizziness had gone, as had the fogginess in her brain. She felt clear again, finally, and wanted to take advantage of that today with Carlos.

Clear. Such a glorious word.

Truthfully, she hadn't realized how many misconceptions she'd held about herself, about her family, for so long. Diego had set her straight, thankfully, but how many years had she lost, years she could've spent with her family, being close to them, sharing their lives, if only she'd spoken up about how she really felt, and they'd done the same? The lesson wasn't lost on her. And she refused to move forward with the same mindset that had gotten her here. Time for new thinking, a fresh start. One that would include Carlos and their child, together, if things went well today.

After talking with her brother yesterday and then Hugo today, Isabella knew deep inside that Carlos was her person. She loved him, more than she'd ever thought possible, and she wanted to spend forever with him if he'd forgive her. She'd said and done some awful things, and it hurt remembering him walking away from her that night, but she needed to be strong now. She realized love wasn't a cage. Love wasn't a trap. Love truly set you free.

Giving yourself fully to another person and having them do the same to you.

Vulnerability was the only freedom, really.

Now, she just needed to find Carlos.

Isabella continued down the path and emerged into Lion Square. She remembered coming here with her parents when she'd been maybe three years old. One of her first memories. Her mother, pregnant with Eduardo at the time, had pushed baby Diego in a stroller. She'd been so happy, laughing and pointing out things to little Isabella. Her father holding her hand, buying her a bag of bread crumbs to feed the birds, getting her lemon gelato to eat as they walked through the park. Those had been such happy times, before it all went wrong.

Instead of feeling sad or burdened remembering, as she had in the past, she felt hopeful and grateful. Wishing one day to build such happy times with her own child and Carlos. Maybe they would bring the baby here, show them the gardens, feed the pigeons. She passed a small fountain and spotted a young mother doing much the same with her toddler. Yes, that would be very nice indeed. Isabella smiled at the woman and her child as she passed.

She stepped out of Lion Square, a warm breeze stirring her skirt around her legs, taking the long way around and stopping at the bosket and the Minotaur's

Grotto. So beautiful, so serene. She wished Carlos could be there to enjoy it with her. Maybe next time. *Please, God. Let there be a next time.* Isabella walked onward toward the romantic channel and took the small stone footbridge over it. Stopped to make another silent wish that things would work out for them well in the end, then continued over to the neo-classical pavilion and the large reflecting pool there in front of the fountain of nymph Egeria.

Isabella stopped and closed her eyes, letting the gentle gurgling sound of water surround her, calming her rapid pulse and easing away the last ripple of her nervousness. A sense of rightness filled her. She wanted to be with Carlos, make a life with him, a future with him. *Now's the time.*

After a deep breath for courage, she crossed back over the bridge and headed into the maze at last. So peaceful and quiet there, but she kept moving at a brisk pace. If Carlos had arrived here before her, she didn't want to miss him. As was usual, though, she got lost, turning corner after corner only to find another dead end or another path to follow. A story spread among the locals said once upon a time a newly married young couple had gotten lost in the maze with their young baby. When they finally found their way out again, their child was an adult. She hoped it wouldn't take her that long to find her happily-ever-after with the man she loved.

Time lost meaning in there among the green cedars and the short shadows cast by the sun as it passed overhead, the heat of it prickling her bare shoulders. Eventually she made a final turn and stopped cold.

Carlos sat on a stone bench in the innermost circle of the maze, head bowed and his mother's diary open on his lap as he read. His tousled dark hair gleamed almost midnight blue beneath the bright sunshine, and he looked so handsome her heart skipped a beat.

She hesitated, wanting to run and throw herself into his arms and wanting to hide all at the same time, but then he looked up and their gazes met, and it seemed all the oxygen in the world evaporated. She opened her mouth, closed it, then bit her lips as she put one foot in front of the other toward him, knowing this would be the most important journey she'd ever make in her life, stopping only when she stood in front of him.

He blinked up at her shielding his eyes with his hand. "Isabella."

"Carlos."

All the things she'd planned to say vanished from her head and she panicked, ending up taking a seat on the bench beside him, almost touching but not quite.

The air between them seemed electrified with possibilities.

"I went—" she started at the same time he said, "I talked—"

They both laughed, and a bit of the tension eased.

"Please, you go first," he said to her.

"No, no, you." Isabella swallowed hard, not knowing what to do with her hands, at last clasping them in her lap so he wouldn't see how much she shook. Not from fear, but from anticipation. This close she could see the hint of stubble already forming on his chiseled jaw, smell his spicy aftershave and the hint of soap and sweat mixed in, hear the catch in his breath, as if he felt nervous, too. They hadn't known each other that long, really, and yet it felt like they'd been a part of each other forever. Isabella never wanted to let him go again. "Please."

Carlos nodded, then cleared his throat, closing the diary and holding it on his lap, his gaze locked on the Eros statue before them as he swallowed hard, the sleek muscles in his tanned throat working. "I talked to my uncle Hugo after you left the other night. Found out some things about my parents I didn't know."

His dark brows twitched together in a brief frown, and he dropped his gaze to his toes. "The letters my mother sent to my father, telling him about me. He never received them, apparently. Uncle Hugo said their parents hid them from him, so he never knew he had a son. Hugo said my father spent years pining after my mother, trying to find her, but things with Cuba were not good then, and he never saw her again. Later, after their parents died, Hugo found the letters, but he decided not to show them to my father even then. Because he'd finally moved on, gotten married, found happiness, so he hid them again. Then my father got sick and died, never knowing about me."

"Oh, Carlos." Isabella reached over then, placing her hand over his, aching for him. "I'm so very sorry. That's terrible. But at least you know now that he loved your mother, that he didn't stop looking for her. That if he'd known about you, he would have loved you, too."

He nodded. A beat passed, then two, his skin warm under hers. Her eyes stinging with tears over all the time he'd lost, over the father he never got to meet.

She sighed. "I went to see my brother Diego the day

after I left your flat. We talked about growing up, about how I felt like they'd all left me behind and moved on without me after I'd done everything for them." She gave a sad little snort and shook her head. "Turns out I was wrong. My siblings didn't leave me behind at all. They talked and decided to get out of the house as soon as they could so I could finally have a life of my own. They did it for me." She sniffled, the tears falling anyway, despite her wishes. She looked up to the blue skies above, the sun slipping behind a puffy white cloud. "God, can you believe it? All that time, all those years, I thought they didn't care. I kept my distance, thinking I'd protected myself, my freedom, but it trapped me in misbelief."

"Oh, *hermosa*." Carlos shifted slightly, moving closer to slip his arm around her shoulders and pull her into his side. "We've both wasted so much time, kept so much hidden inside, waiting, watching." He took a breath, then kissed the top of her head, tucked under his chin. "I don't want to wait anymore."

"Me neither," she said, perfectly content tucked against him. "I've never been as happy as I have been with you. From that first night on the beach to now, you've shown me what a wonderful man you are. Kind, compassionate, caring. Everything I want in a man, a partner. After spending those years caring for my father and my siblings, I thought love was a trap. I closed in on myself for protection, pushing everyone away. But meeting you allowed me to be vulnerable, showed me that things could be different, if I dared to take a chance with you.

"I want to take that chance with you, Carlos. I want

a relationship with you. I want to rebuild connections
with my family. I want to tell everyone who'll listen
about our baby." She pulled away enough to look into
his gorgeous dark eyes and said what she needed to
say, no matter how scary. "I want a life with you, Carlos. I love you."

He smiled, and the sun broke though again above.
Then he kissed her, and warmth burst forth like fireworks inside her. Isabella wrapped her arms around his
neck and pulled him closer, opening to him as he deepened the kiss, sweeping his tongue into her mouth, his
arms going around her waist, holding her close, body
to body, heart to heart, as Eros looked down on them
and smiled.

When Carlos finally pulled back, they were both
breathless and grinning. He rested his forehead against
her, not letting her go. "*Hermosa*, I love you, too. I came
to Barcelona to trace my parents' story, experience what
they did, connect with them as best I could through this
place and through my uncle. But I never in a million
years expected to start a new story of my own with you,
Isabella. With our child." He moved one hand down to
rest on her small baby bump, cleverly concealed by her
yellow sundress. "I want to be with you, *hermosa*. We
can date. I can court you right. And when we're both
ready, we can live together, maybe even become engaged. Whatever you want, whenever you want. I just
want to be by your side, *cariña*. Now and forever. You
are my future. You and our baby."

They kissed again, slow and sweet this time, pulling back when a few more tourists entered the area and
began snapping pictures. Isabella picked up his moth-

er's diary and grinned. "Perhaps we should start a new diary of our own. That way when the baby gets older, we can read our stories to them, and they can keep them as they grow."

"*Si*. I think that's a perfect idea, *hermosa*." He kissed her quick, then stood and held out his hand. "Shall we go? Together?"

"*Si*." Isabella took his hand and pushed to her feet, his mother's diary clutched to her chest like a treasure. "I will go anywhere with you, *amor meu. Sempre amb tu*."

They headed out of the maze together, hand in hand, Carlos whispering in her ear, "*Sempre amb tu*."

Always with you.

EPILOGUE

Eighteen months later

Isabella stood outside the bar, her baby in her arms, and stared at the sign on the door that read *Cerrado para fiesta privada. Closed for a private party.* A big day. Little Ana Rosa's first birthday. They'd named her after both of their mothers. Hard to believe the time had gone so fast. Isabella felt excited and more than a little self-conscious, since she still carried some of her baby weight and her old clothes didn't quite fit yet.

"What do you think, baby girl, huh?" She kissed the top of her daughter's head, then smoothed a hand over her downy hair. Dark brown and curly like her father's and sticking up all over no matter what Isabella did. Little Ana Rosa was so easygoing, though, just like her *papá*, and Isabella couldn't love either one of them more. "Let's go inside and see him, eh?"

She pulled open the door and walked inside the sparkling-clean bar. Uncle Hugo had made sure the place gleamed from top to bottom for their big event. In fact, the air still smelled like lemon floor polish. Hugo came out of his office in the back and walked over to her, arms open. "*Mi sobrina!*" He kissed Isabella soundly on both cheeks, then took baby Ana Rosa from her. "And how's my *dulce niña* today?" He made a bunch of silly faces, trying to get the baby to laugh. Ana Rosa said something that was supposed to be "Hugo" but came out mainly gibberish. "You are such a good girl, yes, you are. *Tío* Hugo's good little girl."

The sight of the older man coddling their daughter melted Isabella's heart. Impossible not to smile, even though she had to warn him, "Don't jostle her around too much. I fed her before we came. She'll upchuck all over you."

"Well, that's okay, isn't it?" Hugo cooed, beaming down at his grandniece like she was the most wonderful thing in the world. Isabella felt the same way. There'd been a few odd moments when she'd been in labor where she'd worried about what might happen after the birth. It was her first baby, and while she and Carlos were committed to each other and their child, what if she did something wrong? What if the baby never bonded with her? What if she made a horrible mother?

But the moment she'd held tiny, red and squalling Ana Rosa in her arms and the baby had stared up at Isabella with pure wonder, every single one of her fears had fled. They'd formed an unbreakable bond in that moment, never to be severed. The most profound experience Isabella had ever had in her life. The second most profound? Falling in love with Carlos and trusting him. Really trusting him. Not just with words, but with her whole heart and soul. They had a healthy and strong and wonderful relationship, even if they hadn't made it official yet. Someday, it would come. Carlos respected her boundaries, he'd said. And she loved him for that, even if maybe those boundaries had changed and she wanted more.

"*Hermosa!*" Carlos called from the upper balcony and hurried downstairs to kiss her, then take his daughter from Hugo and put her over his shoulder—after another kiss, of course. "When did you get here?"

"Just now," she said, smiling. That seemed to be all she did these days, because she was just so happy. "Why?"

"No reason." Carlos leaned in and quickly kissed her again before leading her over to the bar, which had been decorated with streamers and balloons for the occasion. "The party starts in about an hour, and guests will arrive before that."

They'd invited their friends from work, of course, and Carlos's friends who owned the dance studio. Isabella's siblings, too, who were coming in from all over Spain to help them celebrate the happy day.

Ana Rosa talked animatedly to her father, gurgling and squeaking, happy as a clam. Hugo excused himself and went back into his office to finish up a few things, leaving the three of them alone in the bar.

"Hey," Carlos said to her over their daughter's head. "Before everyone else gets here, there's something I want to ask you."

He looked so serious all of a sudden that her heart skipped a beat.

"Okay," she said, her tone hesitant. "What is it?"

He hiked his chin to a small box on the counter, wrapped in silver paper, partially hidden behind all the decorations and other gifts for their daughter. "Open that one. It's for you, *hermosa*."

"Really?" She frowned and pulled the little box closer. "From whom?"

"From me."

Her fingers trembled slightly, and her pulse raced.

She looked up at him, then back at the box, blinking, tears welling as she opened it to find a sparkling diamond ring inside. "I don't— I didn't expect this at all, *cariño*."

"I know, *hermosa*," he said, smiling. "That's what makes it perfect." Carlos transferred their daughter to his other arm, then whispered, "Will you marry me?"

Isabella laughed, placing her shaking fingers over her mouth, unable to believe that everything she'd ever wanted stood right before her. "*Si*. Yes, of course I will marry you. I love you, Carlos. More than I ever thought possible."

He kissed her then. When they finally pulled apart, nothing could've removed the silly grin from her face. Ana Rosa squealed with delight. Isabella knew exactly how their daughter felt.

Carlos rested his forehead against hers, his dimples on full display. "Have I told you lately how much I love you?"

"You have, actually," she said, his words so heartfelt and so true and so real, Isabella ached inside, in the best possible way. "And I promise to love you with all my heart for as long as I live, Carlos."

"Same, *hermosa*," Carlos said, kissing her again. "Same."

Ana Rosa became enthralled with the balloons and

Isabella thanked her lucky stars for fate bringing Carlos to Barcelona and into her life. And as they laughed and played with their daughter, Isabella felt forever grateful for the transformative power of love and trust. True freedom. She knew that now. And it had made an amazing difference in her life.

* * * * *

COMING SOON!

We really hope you enjoyed reading this book.
If you're looking for more romance, be sure to
head to the shops when new books are
available on

Thursday 21st
July

To see which titles are coming soon, please visit
millsandboon.co.uk/nextmonth

MILLS & BOON

MILLS & BOON ®

Coming next month

FALLING FOR THE VILLAGE VET
Rachel Dove

'I've really enjoyed our date. I wanted to say that before we start talking about Portaloos.'

She burst into guffaws of laughter. He watched her with a very amused smile on his face. His hair was a little messed up, making him look more casual than usual. Ruffled.

'You're a goofball deep down, do you know that?'

'Yep. Just like you.' He looked her up and down slowly. 'Minus the colourful clothing.' He bit at his lip. 'I'm not all bad. I wish you'd known me before, when I was younger. I was different then.'

'Things change us in life,' she soothed.

'Nothing's changed you.'

She laughed again. 'Not now, no. It took me a while after my divorce to lick my wounds. I bought this place and just hid away at first.'

'Doesn't sound like you.'

He spoke as if he'd known her much longer than he had, but it sounded right to her too. They had seemingly been studying each other. Judged each other, yelled at each other, but yet here they were laughing, working on the charity drive together and enjoying the evening.

'It wasn't,' she breathed. 'I'm glad you came to live here. I'm not sure if anyone's actually said that to you yet.'

'It is nice to hear.' He was so close now. His eyes were taking her in, and she felt the stirrings of attraction sparking. 'Especially from you.'

'Your harshest critic,' she near whispered. They laughed again. 'What a battle-scarred pair we are.'

He laughed softly again, and something changed. It was so slight, so minuscule that she could easily have missed it, but he tore his gaze from hers, and poured them both a glass of wine.

'We'd better get on with the planning, then—I need to get back to Hendrix.' He wasn't rude, or surly. He was the man she'd come to know. The man who was so buttoned-up, she didn't think he'd ever get free. She hid her red face behind her wine glass, taking a good long pull. Trudy was coming to sort the dogs tomorrow, so she could sleep all day and then hide in work. Then she hid her disappointment at the date that wasn't a date. The non-date that had turned into a hot date and then back into a non-date. Just as she was starting to feel... Well, it wasn't anything, obviously. She sat up on her couch, pulled a pen from the pile on the table, and flipped open her notepad. Closing her heart at the same time.

Continue reading
FALLING FOR THE VILLAGE VET
Rachel Dove

Available next month
www.millsandboon.co.uk

Copyright © 2022 Rachel Dove

MILLS & BOON

THE HEART OF ROMANCE

A ROMANCE FOR EVERY READER

MODERN

Prepare to be swept off your feet by sophisticated, sexy and seductive heroes, in some of the world's most glamourous and romantic locations, where power and passion collide.

HISTORICAL

Escape with historical heroes from time gone by. Whether your passion is for wicked Regency Rakes, muscled Vikings or rugged Highlanders, awaken the romance of the past.

MEDICAL

Set your pulse racing with dedicated, delectable doctors in the high-pressure world of medicine, where emotions run high and passion, comfort and love are the best medicine.

True Love

Celebrate true love with tender stories of heartfelt romance, from the rush of falling in love to the joy a new baby can bring, and a focus on the emotional heart of a relationship.

Desire

Indulge in secrets and scandal, intense drama and plenty of sizzling hot action with powerful and passionate heroes who have it all: wealth, status, good looks…everything but the right woman.

HEROES

Experience all the excitement of a gripping thriller, with an intense romance at its heart. Resourceful, true-to-life women and strong, fearless men face danger and desire - a killer combination!

To see which titles are coming soon, please visit

millsandboon.co.uk/nextmonth

JOIN US ON SOCIAL MEDIA!

Stay up to date with our latest releases, author
news and gossip, special offers and discounts, and
all the behind-the-scenes action
from Mills & Boon...

 millsandboon

 millsandboonuk

 millsandboon

It might just be true love...

WANT EVEN MORE

ROMANCE?

SUBSCRIBE AND SAVE TODAY!

'Mills & Boon books, the perfect way to escape for an hour or so.'

MISS W. DYER

'Excellent service, promptly delivered and very good subscription choices.'

MISS A. PEARSON

'You get fantastic special offers and the chance to get books before they hit the shops.'

MRS V. HALL

Visit millsandboon.co.uk/Subscribe and save on brand new books.

JOIN THE
MILLS & BOON
BOOKCLUB

* **FREE** delivery direct to your door

* **EXCLUSIVE** offers every month

* **EXCITING** rewards programme

50% OFF
YOUR FIRST
PARCEL

Join today at
millsandboon.co.uk/subscribe

MILLS & BOON
True Love
Romance from the Heart

Celebrate true love with tender stories of heartfelt romance, from the rush of falling in love to the joy a new baby can bring, and a focus on the emotional heart of a relationship.

Four True Love stories published every month, find them all at:
millsandboon.co.uk/TrueLove